Breathe No More, My Lady
• • •
Shakedown For Murder
by Ed Lacy

Introduction by Cullen Gallagher

Stark House Press • Eureka California

BREATHE NO MORE, MY LADY / SHAKEDOWN FOR MURDER

Published by Stark House Press
1315 H Street
Eureka, CA 95501, USA
griffinskye3@sbcglobal.net
www.starkhousepress.com

BREATHE NO MORE, MY LADY
Originally published by Avon Books, New York, and copyright © 1958 by Ed Lacy.

SHAKEDOWN FOR MURDER
Originally published by Avon Books, New York, and copyright © 1958 by Ed Lacy.
Published in a condensed version by *Mercury Mystery Magazine*, August 1958, as "Listen to the Night;" and in hardback by Boardman Books, London, 1958, as *Devil for a Witch*.

All rights reserved under International and Pan-American Copyright Conventions.

"The Swing and the Follow Through" copyright © 2024 by Cullen Gallagher

ISBN: 979-8-88601-097-8

Cover and Book design Cover design by Jeff Vorzimmer, ¡caliente!design, Austin, Texas
Proofreading by Bill Kelly

PUBLISHER'S NOTE:
This is a work of fiction. Names, characters, places and incidents are either the products of the author's imagination or used fictionally, and any resemblance to actual persons, living or dead, events or locales, is entirely coincidental.

Without limiting the rights under copyright reserved above, no part of this publication may be reproduced, stored, or introduced into a retrieval system or transmitted in any form or by any means (electronic, mechanical, photocopying, recording or otherwise) without the prior written permission of both the copyright owner and the above publisher of the book.

First Stark House Press Edition: July 2024

BREATHE NO MORE, MY LADY

Norm Connor is the ad director for a New York publisher, and a man with a dilemma. One of their top-selling mystery authors, Matt Anthony, has been arrested for murdering his wife. The publisher wants to support Matt, but doesn't want the bad publicity that goes along with it. So Norm starts digging into the affair to determine himself whether he thinks Matt is guilty. What he discovers is a contradictory set of stories between Matt's friends who heard him threaten to kill his wife—but didn't take it seriously--and Matt's own confession, which he gave to the investigating cop. And the further Norm delves, the more he begins to wonder whether Matt the mystery writer is spinning a tale of his own.

SHAKEDOWN FOR MURDER

New York cop Matt Lund is on vacation, visiting his son's family in End Harbor. He'd rather be home with his cat. But he dutifully visits his two kids once a year. The last thing he wants is to get involved in the death of the local doctor. The town cops think it's an accident—his car was found smashed into a tree, and the doc was in the road, run over. But Matt can't help himself. He's got to show off in front of his grandson. He points out that it couldn't have been an accident—the door wasn't sprung. It looks like murder to him. Now Matt is deep into it, trying to make his daughter-in-law happy by proving that the man the cops have now arrested is as innocent as she claims he is.

ED LACY BIBLIOGRAPHY
(1911-1968)

Walk Hard—Talk Loud (1940 as by Len Zinberg)
What D'ya Know for Sure (1947 as by Len Zinberg; revised as *Strange Desires*, 1949)
Hold With the Hares (1948 as by Len Zinberg)
The Woman Aroused (1951)
Sin in Their Blood (1952; published in UK as *Death in Passing*, 1959)
Strip for Violence (1953)
Enter Without Desire (1954)
Go for the Body (1954)
Route 13 (1954; as by Steve April; Funk & Wagnalls)
The Best That Ever Did It (1955; reprinted in pb as *Visa to Death*, 1956)
The Men from the Boys (1956)
Lead with Your Left (1957)***
Room to Swing (1957)*
Breathe No More, My Lady (1958)
Shakedown for Murder (1958; UK as *Devil for the Witch,* 1958)
Be Careful How You Live (1958; reprinted in pb as *Dead End*, 1960)
Blonde Bait (1959)
The Big Fix (1960)
A Deadly Affair (1960)
Bugged for Murder (1961)
The Freeloaders (1961)
South Pacific Affair (1961)
The Sex Castle (1963; reprinted as *Shoot It Again*, 1969)
Two Hot to Handle (1963; two novellas: *The Coin of Adventure* and *Murder in Paradise*)
Moment of Untruth (1964)*
Harlem Underground (1965)**
Pity the Honest (1965)
The Hotel Dwellers (1966)
Double Trouble (1967)***
In Black & Whitey (1967)**
The Napalm Bugle (1968)
The Big Bust (1969)

*Toussaint M. Moore series
**Lee Hayes series
*** Dave Wintino series

As by Russell Turner
The Short Night (1957)

7
The Swing and the Follow Through
by Cullen Gallagher

15
Breathe No More,
My Lady

195
Shakedown
to Murder

The Swing and the Follow Through:
Ed Lacy's Breathe No More My Lady and The Big Shakedown
By Cullen Gallagher

1958 was a big year for Ed Lacy. *The year.* That was when he received the Mystery Writers of America's Edgar Award for Best Novel for *Room to Swing* (which had been published in 1957). That recognition guaranteed him a legacy that would live on long after the book for which he had won it went out of print. (Thankfully, as of 2022, the book is available from the Library of Congress/Poison Pen Press.) Despite being unavailable for decades, *Room to Swing* came to define Lacy's contribution to the mystery field: socially conscious crime novels that capture their particular moment, but also stand apart because of their humanity, political awareness, and daringness to depict marginalized communities that so often went ignored in many mystery novels at the time. "Ed Lacy was virtually the only American mystery writer consistently to espouse the causes of underdogs, and his opinions were generally those of the political left," Marvin Lachman wrote in his essay on Lacy in *Murder Off the Rack: Critical Studies of Ten Paperback Masters.* "His willingness to expand the boundaries of the mystery, by writing of people who had suffered discrimination, made Lacy one of the most interesting writers of paperback originals."

If you're reading this collection, you've probably already read *Room to Swing.* If not, it bears a brief synopsis, in order to better contextualize the books here. *Room to Swing* introduced readers to Toussaint Moore, a Black part-time mail carrier and aspiring shamus living in Harlem (the same neighborhood where Lacy was born and lived for much of his life). Moore's girlfriend wants him to take a full-time job with the post office so they can get married and settle down. Moore, however, wants to be a private detective. He's at a crossroads when Kay Robbens, a white TV producer, hires him to shadow a man soon to be arrested as part of a true-crime show. The job goes sour when Moore is accused of murder, and he takes off to a rural Southern Ohio town in hopes of uncovering the real killer. While he's there, Moore encounters the remnants of Jim Crow America he thought was in the past.

I'll say no more about *Room to Swing,* not only because I don't wish to spoil any surprises—but largely because that's not why you're here.

Breathe No More My Lady and *Shakedown for Murder* are

Lacy's two follow-ups to *Room to Swing*. Both originally published in 1958, *Breathe* has only been reprinted once (briefly by BlackMaskOnline), and *Shakedown* has never been reprinted since its initial appearance. These were both Avon paperback originals, as opposed to *Room*, which was in hardcover (from Harper). The binding distinction might suggest that publishers saw bigger potential sales in *Room* than the other two; more likely, however, it was a sign of the market and of the lengths to which a writer went in order to survive. "I'm a full time, working, freelance writer," Lacy explained in an autobiographical essay "I Dunit" in *P.S.* (August 1966), "and if you want to call me a hack, I won't be terribly upset. Every person who makes his pork chops from the sale of words is a hack, whether he realizes it or not. I also believe *all* fiction writers, including us honest hacks, are creative critters. You'd be astonished at the creative drive and skill needed to turn out formula stories."

Lacy's essay is of particular interest to *Breathe No More My Lady*, as it reveals the author's own journey through the wild (and not-too-well-paying) world of mystery writing in the 1950s, which formed the background for *Breathe*. A similar behind-the-scenes article, "Whodunit?—You?" ran in the February 1959 issue of *The Writer*, and here Lacy explicitly explains the parallels between his work and the novel.

> Frankly, I do not consider the mystery novel on any higher or lower literary level than any other commercial novel. And in my humble opinion no other kind of novel but the commercial novel has been published in the last 25 years. That goes for the books of Hemingway, Faith Baldwin, Faulkner, Spillane, Steinbeck, Jones, etc. (Should you be interested in more of my humble [or maybe pompous] opinions on pro writing and writers, gamble 35¢ for a paperback original of mine, *Breathe No More My Lady*. If it isn't on your newsstands, send 45¢ to Avon Publications, 575 Madison Avenue, N.Y.C. 22. This is a somewhat serious novel proving that writers take themselves far too seriously. It's also a kind of mixed-up mystery novel, but since it deals with writers and publishers, I managed to let off steam in all directions. End of plug.)

Breathe No More My Lady is as much a murder mystery as it is an exposé of what Lacy views as the morally depraved profit motive at the heart of the publishing world. The central dilemma is one that is not unthinkable in 2024: star author Matt Anthony is about to stand trial for the murder of his wife, Francine. His publisher is caught between severing ties—and losing money, which would look bad to the board. Or reprinting an old novel and capitalizing on the hubbub, at the risk of looking like they are profiteering off a woman's murder. Norm Connors, advertising manager, is tasked with finding out just *how* guilty Matt Anthony really is, and whether the company can get away with their profit scheme. Connors, meanwhile, is hoping to turn this success into a one-way ticket to a fancier job: "Matt Anthony was going to be my stepping stone to a lush Madison Avenue salary."

Connors resembles Sidney, the sleazy PR man in Ernest Lehman's short story "Tell Me About It Tomorrow!" (*Cosmopolitan*, April 1950), who was perfectly embodied on the big screen by Tony Curtis in *The Sweet Smell of Success* (1958). "It was one of those dirty, sweltering August afternoons when only two kinds of fools were in their hot city offices; those who had to be, and those who were on the verge of never having to be again, if they played their cards right," announces Lehman's protagonist: "I was tired of being one of those who had to be." As Lacy's novel progresses, it is clear that the most heartless person isn't the one who killed Francine, but Norm, whose sole interest is saving the face of his company, and propelling himself to a better office.

The second half of the book, the trial, certainly recalls Robert Traver's 1957 blockbuster hit *Anatomy of a Murder* (turned into a movie of the same name in 1959, directed by Otto Preminger and starring James Stewart). Both trials center around proving that the murder was committed in a state of temporary insanity. Anthony's defense, however, is more farcical than in Traver's book: in *Breathe*, the defense attorney argues that novelists are a special breed whose genius means they can't be judged by normal human standards. Clearly, Lacy is taking aim at writerly pretention, and it makes for better laughs than it does legal horse sense.

Lacy's most sympathetic character should come as no surprise to readers who know his own background. Professor Henry Brown, Anthony's former instructor, a former boxer who had recently lost his job due to his taking the Fifth when accused of political subversion. Lacy, real name Leonard Zinberg, was a Jewish Communist, and a one-time member of the Communist Party-sponsored League of American Writers.

Lacy knew firsthand the political minefield a writer faced, but he remained committed to his ideals and used them to inform the social eye that distinguishes his stories. Brown knows all too well the dangers of associating with him, and he doesn't want to cause any collateral damage to others. He's one of the few characters to take other people into consideration in the entire book.

Jackson Clair, Anthony's attorney, tries to reframe his client's books not as evidence of his criminal mind, but of America's twisted obsession with crime.

> I take it Mr. Wagner would have you believe that a man writing about crime must have a practical knowledge of crime. This is nonsense. How many writers of westerns can win a rodeo, as their fictional heroes do? In fact how many writers of cowboy stories have ever ridden anything but a library chair as they did their research? Millions upon millions of Americans read Matt Anthony's books for relaxation and enjoyment. Nobody forces them to, they do it out of free choice. Mr. Wagner would have us believe that America reflects Matt Anthony's books. In reality, it's the other way around, his books merely reflect America. We are a rather violent nation, quick to fight and anger.

Clair's defense brings to mind Lacy's own words from *P.S.*:

> Saying I'm a hack doesn't mean I'm a hack. The creative writer, with his deep curiosity about this fellow beings, must care about people, which is rapidly becoming a rare trait in our cynical world. I have never written anything I considered anti-human, jingoistic or bigoted. True, my stories often deal with violence and sex, but neither were invented by writers. (Although there are attempts to shoulder blame on us!) You'll find more real violence and brutality in the daily headlines than any fiction writer could dream up. We live in an age where the screams of a girl being stabbed to death around a dozen or so average citizens, sitting in their homes, and none one even bothered to call the police, where civil rights workers are murdered and the killers rarely brought to trial or found guilty. At best books can only reflect our way of life…

Lacy's social critiques didn't find favor with his usual defender, Anthony Boucher. Boucher critiqued in the *New York Times*, "I suspect that this of a mystery novelist on trial for wife-murder is intended to be something of A Serious Novel; but it is merely, in comparison with Lacy's less pretentious work, unduly long, terribly talky and clumsily constructed." It would be hubristic to suggest that Boucher missed the black humor, as well as the social critique, of *Breathe No More My Lady*—but since he's not around to knock me back to Earth, I'll go ahead and say it. Read the book yourself and see if you agree with Mr. Boucher. (And no hard feelings if you do—but I hope you don't.)

• • •

The second novel here, *Shakedown For Murder*, was much more appealing to Boucher. "I like [it] particularly... at once clever and credible," he wrote in his "Report on Criminals at Large" column. "It's a well above average puzzle, enlivened by honest and humorous observation." Curiously, Lacy's 1959 article "Whodunit?—You?" indicates his original title was *By Murder Possessed*—suggesting that it was written well before it hit the shelves, and that (no surprise here) the title was changed by the publishers.

Like *Room to Swing*, *Shakedown for Murder* is a critique of racial and class bigotry enshrouded in a murder investigation. Formally, Lacy experiments by opening with the murder of Doctor Edward Barnes on a rainy, Long Island road—but since it is told in the third-person, he withholds the identity of the killer. The rest of the story centers around Matt Lund, 58-year-old widower and NYPD cell block attendant, on vacation in the fictional "End Harbor" in the Hamptons, visiting his son Dan and his wife Bessie. Getting off the Long Island Railroad, Matt's cab driver is Jerry Sparelous, a Greek immigrant who is friends with Bessie (who is also Greek). Shortly after Matt's arrival, the town is thrown into a frenzy when Barnes's body is discovered. The doctor's last-known visit was to Sparelous. Blinded by prejudice, the local police arrest Jerry for the crime, but Matt easily finds evidence that the cabbie is innocent. Aiding Matt in his investigation is Jane Endin, a Native American painter gossipers assumed to be Doctor Barnes's lover—but who in fact was nothing more than a close friend.

Endin's character provides the opportunity for Lacy's

characteristic political scope to come into focus. The Endins (a fictional tribe invented for the story) are part of the Shinnecock Nation, and for whom End Harbor was named. Jane is the sole remaining member of the Endins left in End Harbor; the other Native Americans have relocated to a nearby reservation. The presence of both Jane and Jerry threaten the "whitewashed" image in which the town has tried to paint itself—Jane reminds of the town's true origins, while Jerry reminds of their own immigrant history. Even Matt is seen as a potential threat—the locals know that property value is on the rise, and Big City folk are coming for their land. Though *Shakedown for Murder* was written in 1958, like much of Lacy's work, these conflicts still (unfortunately) occur today.

One of the most interesting facets of *Shakedown for Murder*, which aligns it with *Breathe No More My Lady* (and even, to a certain extent, *Room to Swing*), is that the primary investigator is not a Hardboiled Superhero. Sure, Matt's a cop—but he's the first to admit he mainly guards the cells at his precinct and hasn't had any active duty in a long time. Norm in *Breathe* is an ad man. And even Toussaint Moore is more mailman than gumshoe. "Lacy's work benefits from his interest in the lives of everyday people," explains Mike E. Grost on his site *A Guide to Classic Mystery and Detection*.

> A book like *Shakedown for Murder* has no mobsters or underworld characters; instead it concentrates on the inhabitants of a small town, from the richest to the poorest. This means that Lacy completely avoids the conventional settings and characters of the hard-boiled novel. There is violence in this world, and tough guy encounters, but they are ordinary people, not mob types. So while the feel of Lacy's book is vaguely hard-boiled—it is definitely not cozy—the setting is much closer to everyday life.

• • •

"I have no idea what the fiction future holds, especially for the mystery novel. It hardly looks sunny," Lacy wrote in "I Dunnit." "I still pound my typewriter each day and I'm still selling, but it's rough. How I long for the 'old days' of a dozen or so years ago when you could earn about ten grand a year by leisurely turning out a mystery for the paperbacks every six months."

Breathe No More My Lady and *Shakedown For Murder* are the sort of two-a-year softcover originals of which Lacy reminisced. He may have been banging them out for "pork chops" (to recall his phrase), but they were damned good mysteries. I have the feeling that he'd be surprised as hell to learn these books are being reprinted some 76 years after their initial appearance—but I'm sure he'd be pleased.

—May 2024

Cullen Gallagher is a musician and writer living in Brooklyn, NY. He has written essays for many Stark House Press books, including volumes by W.R Burnett, Day Keene, Peter Rabe, Lionel White, and Harry Whittington. His non-fiction has appeared in the *Los Angeles Review of Books, Paris Review, Not Coming to a Theater Near You*, and the anthologies *Paperbacks at War: 20th Century Conflict from the Front Lines of Vintage Paperbacks, Pulps and Comics* (2021) edited by Justin Marriott, *Screen Slate: New York City Cinema 2011-2015* (2017) edited by Jon Dieringer, and *Cult Cinema: An Arrow Video Companion* (2016) edited by Anthony Nield. www.cullengallagher.com.

Breathe No More, My Lady

Ed Lacy

"Writing is like prostitution ... first you do it for the love of it, then you do it for a few friends, and finally you do it for money."
—Molière

PART I

Norm Connor

I rushed into my office at Longson Publishing at five to eleven. I was twenty-five minutes late and sweating a little, but it was neither my being late or the humid morning that made me sweat. As I nodded at Miss Park, she told me, "Mr. Long wants to see you at once. And Frank Kuhn asked you to phone him before noon. I was able to pick up some Turkish coffee last night and can't wait to try it iced. Mr. Long called twice."

"Oh, hell, what day is this? Sales conference on?"

Miss Park screwed up her face—as she always did when anything was out of whack. "Why Mr. Connor, the conference was on Monday, as usual. You know, if we try the Turkish iced, I think we should get some heavy cream, or even a can of whipped cream."

I nodded and walked into my office. I tossed the folded morning paper I'd been carrying under my arm on the desk, lit my pipe, and sat down and drummed on an ash tray with my fingers. I called the apartment. There wasn't any answer as I half expected. Drying my face with a tissue, I finally phoned the air terminal and had them check the Paris flights. The crisp, impersonal voice at the other end of the wire told me Michele had actually taken off at 6:15 A.M. I asked, "Are you positive? Mrs. Michele Connor? C-O-N-N-O-R. Are you positive?"

"Quite. A Mrs. Michele Connor, French passport, left on the 6:15 A.M. flight to Paris."

"Are you absolutely positive? At the last second she didn't cancel?" I realized my voice was a harsh shout, and I hung up.

I sat there, puffing hard on my pipe, feeling embarrassed and knowing I'd sounded like a fool. Michele had really taken the plane. Now what the devil was I to do? Run after her or ...?

My phone rang. William Long asked, "Norm?"

"Yes, Bill."

"I'm waiting to see you."

"On my way up." As I stood up I stared at my sloppy desk, trying to remember if I had anything to discuss with Bill. In a dizzy sort of way I was angry at the 'big boss' tone to his voice. I stood there, completely confused for a second, staring around my own office like a stranger. Suddenly the hollow ache I'd felt all night reached its peak. I felt terribly wrung-out and bushed.

Stopping at Miss Park's desk I asked, "Any aspirin?" She stared at my big hands and of course my eyes bounced over her remarkable breasts. Although I never asked, I had a hunch

Miss Park wouldn't abject if my hands and her superstructure got together.

"I'll go to the little gals' room. Should be some there."

"Never mind. I'm on my way up to see Mr. Long. Please order me a sandwich. I didn't have a chance to eat this morning. I overslept."

"Cheese, ham, egg, lettuce or?"

"Anything."

"It was an awful night, so muggy. And wasn't the news this morning amazing?"

As I walked out I mumbled, "It floored me." Riding the tiny self-service elevator to the seventh floor, I tried to think how a man gets his wife back. Or should I try? Would Michele ever come back? Maybe after a few weeks apart, she'll come around and realize how silly the whole thing has been. Or is she fed up with me? That's....

I couldn't think straight, my head hurt. Even smoking made me suddenly nauseous. When I stepped out of the private elevator I emptied my pipe into a huge, sand-filled, hideous elephant's foot. A highly polished brass plate breathlessly informed the world the beast had been shot by the first Mr. Long while on a safari in Africa. It was part of the air-conditioned mishmash of heavy wood-paneled walls, horrible old etchings and brightly colored modern furniture that made up the Longson offices. The carved wood panels, the etchings and elephant's foot to remind you that Longson had been publishing books for over seventy-five years.

Looking down into the ugly, sand-filled foot, I felt violently sick. If I'd had anything in my stomach I certainly would have made a mess. After a rough moment I was okay because I knew what it was, what had hit me the second I'd known Michele had actually taken the plane: I was already tasting the loneliness.

I put my hand to my mouth and smelled my breath, then opened the door. Bill Long merely glanced up from his desk. He was the great-grandson of the founder. William Long was a lean, stiff man in his fifties. He looked as if he had stepped out of a British whiskey ad, everything from his brushed moustache to polished shoes in its proper, immaculate place.

I sat down beside his desk and waited. After a few seconds Long asked, "What do you think about it, Norm?"

"About what?" I tried to get my brains to stop racing in circles.

Long touched the ends of his tiny waxed moustache, as if testing the sharp points. "Damn it, man, don't you read the papers, listen to the radio or TV?"

"No, sir." Our relationship was such I could "sir" him or call him Bill. At the moment I said "sir" to let him know I wasn't in the mood for any buddy-boss act. "I ... eh ... had a very bad night."

"Sorry. Have you seen a doctor?"

"Nothing for a doctor. What's up?" And that was another thing starting now—explaining where Michele was. How does a man say his wife has left him?

"Matt Anthony killed his wife." Long handed me the newspaper on his neat desk. "Read it through and we'll talk in ten minutes."

"Right, Bill."

I went back to my office, where I found a sandwich, coffee, and orange juice waiting. I almost forgot my own troubles as I read the headline:

MYSTERY WRITER KILLS WIFE

END HARBOR, L.I. Mrs. Francine Anthony, 44, wife of the well-known author, Matt Anthony, 51, died here while fishing today in her rowboat. Medical reports state death was due to a blow on the forehead. At first it was thought Mrs. Anthony's death was the result of an accidental fall, but late tonight Mr. Anthony is said to have confessed he struck her, causing his wife to hit her head against the gunwale of the boat.

At about 1 P.M. Mrs. Anthony had gone fishing on the bay in front of the Anthony house. Several hours later a maid, Miss May Fitzgerald, went to the dock to call out to the sportswoman that her guests were awaiting her return to go swimming. Miss Fitzgerald saw the body hanging over the side of the small boat. Mr. Anthony immediately phoned the police. At first it was thought Mrs. Anthony had fallen while casting, striking her head on the side of the rowboat. However, towards evening, while being questioned by Det. Walter Kolcicki, Mr. Anthony is said to have admitted he had been skin-diving and climbed aboard the boat when his air valve ceased functioning. In the course of an argument he is said to have punched his wife, knocking her face down against the gunwale. In an argument earlier in the afternoon, over a guest, Mr.

Anthony allegedly threatened his wife's life.

Mr. Anthony is said to have signed a confession and is now being held in the Riverside County jail.

Written by a "special correspondent," the piece had the ring of an amateur reporter. They used a picture of Anthony taken when he had sailed a thirty-foot sloop single-handedly across the Atlantic. It was a good shot: showing the dashing grin on his handsome face and the swimming trunks revealing the heavyweight body in all its muscular glory. I had used the same shot on the dust jacket of an Anthony book and in several ads.

The news item went on to list a few of Matt's novels, stated that several of them had been made into movies.

As I finished eating and reading I became wide awake. My headache vanished. I dialed Martin Kelly, my former boss. He headed the ad agency that handled all of Longson's books. When I had him on the phone I asked, "Marty? Norm Connor here. Listen, have you any fresh dope on this Anthony mess? I need some information in a big rush." He asked what we were going to do about it. Should he attempt to hush things up? "Stop it, Marty, how could we possibly put the lid on this? Look, do you know, or can you find me a reporter who's been out to the Anthony house? Swell, swell. That's a break. Have him phone me, fast. I need to be filled in on the facts within the next ten minutes. Now stop wasting time, Marty, and call that reporter. And thanks. Big thanks."

Eight minutes later, after a reporter had phoned me direct from Riverside, I went back up to Long's cool office. Dropping the newspaper on his desk, I lit my pipe and sat in a plywood bucket chair. I had a practiced way of casual sitting, as if slowly falling into the chair. I said, "Seems I skipped quite a mess in the papers."

"*How* messy is the first subject on the agenda," Long told me, pulling a thin dark cigar from a fancy tan teak humidor. He carefully nipped the end with an ancient, silver cigar-cutter, then ran his tongue around the cut end. Lighting the cigar, he puffed slowly and evenly for a few seconds, gazing at the ceiling. His cigar rituals fascinated me. I always had a feeling the anxious expression on Bill's thin face meant he expected the stinking rope to blow up at any moment.

The second his cigar was drawing smoothly, Bill placed it on an ash tray and said, "Norm, we must consider how this affects us: business-wise. Anthony has been on our lists for a number of years. I believe we have issued over a dozen of his novels. While we most certainly are not the type of house to capitalize on notoriety, the fact remains that Anthony is in the headlines and will continue to remain there for some time. And all during the trial. Much as we may dislike them, one still can't ignore facts."

"I've just talked with a reporter out in Riverside," I said cautiously, not getting the drift. Matt Anthony wasn't that important a writer to the house—he was merely a mystery writer. "Notoriety may be an understatement. For one thing the D.A. is seeking a first-degree murder indictment which—"

"Murder? That's bloody bull."

I nodded, combing my hair with my left hand. "Perhaps, but the D.A. is calling it murder. Secondly, it seems our Matt deliberately tried to cover up the killing, pass it off as an accident. He had some kind of alibi set up ... until a county detective got a confession from him hours later. I don't know, as of now, exactly what he's confessed to, but all of this doesn't put Matt in a good light."

"I suppose the papers will get this?"

"Of course. I didn't make any attempt to hush it up. Be impossible anyway—we don't advertise in the tabloids and this is a juicy item. And it could ruin us if such an attempt ever became known. There's another bad angle: earlier in the afternoon Matt and his wife had a drag-em-down fight over a guest—a Prof. Henry Brown. He was recently dismissed from his college chair for taking the Fifth Amendment in one of these investigations. True, Matt was—is—one of our writers, but in no way can Longson be considered responsible for the antics of a wild joker like Anthony. My advice is for us to say nothing, keep hands off."

Long took his time relighting his cigar before he said, "Norm, you have an admirable grasp of the situation, but unfortunately it isn't as simple as you paint it. One of our main stockholders is a frightful biddy, a nosey old ass who has a hobby of raising stupid questions over every minor expense item. I don't have to tell you, what with TV, the trade books business hasn't shown any zooming profits. While we're not losing money, still ... eh ... you know how it is with neurotic women with too much time on their hands. At our last meeting she made an issue of unrealized advances to our authors; a relatively small sum, under $17,000. However she picked on Matt Anthony. Claimed she'd never heard of him and he's into us for about $4,000 on a war book he never wrote."

Long stared at his desk, as if he'd just made a deep point. I nodded, as though I knew what Bill was talking about. Putting his cigar back in the ash tray, Long said, "Norm, it occurred to me that with all this bloody publicity we might reissue one of Matt's old novels. Since we already have the plates, production costs would be low. An edition of about 20,000 copies. Naturally the success of this would depend upon the advertising campaign you work up. If it comes off, things will be considerably easier for me at the January stockholders' meeting. You see, I'm asking for a new building, Norm, a really large outlay, and I wouldn't want the project side-tracked by minor squabbles. There's also this: I happen to know Matt is busted. While I'm not trying to sound mucky or altruistic he will be desperate for money now and I have the old-fashioned idea a publishing house should stand by its writers. I'm positive my father would have seen it that way."

"Very commendable, sir," I said, thinking, why is he giving me a lot of old-fashioned slop? Even if we sold out the 20,000 copies Matt's royalties wouldn't cover more than the four grand advance. "It will require a tightly planned ad campaign. If it looks as if we are capitalizing in any way on the ... the notoriety, it might affect our textbook sales. Bill, you realize that the moment we advertise, Longson is standing side by side with Anthony."

"Now we're at the core of the problem. It will be up to you to decide if we *should* advertise, and the type ads. As advertising manager the entire project will be your responsibility. In short, I want you to very thoroughly consider the consequences of the wrong kind of advertising—if wrong is the correct word. Now, it may very well turn out you decide we should forget the matter, that we should not reissue the book. In that case, I shall completely respect your judgment. Norm, I'm sure you know how much I hate pressuring people. Although the trial probably won't start for months, I've checked with our printers. They'll have an open press run on the 19th ... giving you ten days to decide whether we do the Anthony book or not. And by God, if we ever get this new building we're going to have our own presses in the basement!"

I stood up as I told him, "I understand, sir."

Long puffed on his cigar nervously. "I know it's a gamble. As you said, if it hits the public wrong, or seems done in poor taste—the consequences can be extremely rough. Against that we must weigh the matter of appeasing our stockholders, and our new building ... plus the integrity of the house in standing by an author in distress." Bill walked around the desk and placed an arm on my shoulder. "I fully realize I'm confronting you with a hell of a decision. As I said, I want you to feel perfectly free to turn it down if you think it's too risky. However, should you decide to go through with it, you must accept full responsibility. Do we understand each other, Norm?"

"Yes, sir. Since advertising is the key, it should be my decision." I almost added, "and I sincerely welcome the challenge," but I knew it would sound as phony as it was. And what was the old gag about beware a boss putting his arms on your shoulders—he's only placing you in position?

Walking me toward the door, Bill asked, "Have you ever met Matt Anthony?"

"Not really. I recall a story he did years ago in one of these literary anthologies; a charming bit about a Mexican kid who wants to be a football player. Quite different from his tough mystery novels."

"He's a holdover from the post World War I school of writers. Last of the big, blustering, hero type. Mad Matt Anthony he's sometimes called. These days ever since the decadent school has been in vogue, most writers seem to be precocious fags." Long laughed. "Don't quote me on that. All generalizations are fuzzy. But ... well, if you ever meet Matt, you'll know what I mean."

I said, "I lunched with him, years ago. I was working on one of those shoestring imitations of *Esquire*. The editor decided to bankrupt himself by paying $800 for Anthony's byline on a long adventure piece. Some horrible tripe about Matt's alleged visit to a Central American tribe of witch doctors. It was so bad no other mag would touch it. Anyway, Anthony wanted a thousand dollars, so we took him to lunch at the Algonquin—we were being very literary. Matt made the grand entrance, a salt-stained trench coat wrapped tightly around his big body. He was sporting a pointed beard and when he removed the coat he was wearing a faded sailor's striped Basque shirt and dungarees. I think he was between wives then and getting ready to sail the Atlantic. He talked loudly, drank a great deal, and of course we were the center of all eyes. The fact is, the editor became so high he finally agreed to pay the thousand. When we staggered back to the office I remember saying the article wasn't worth the money. The editor said, 'Sure, the sonofabitch can't write anymore, but ... by damn, doesn't he *look like a writer!*'"

Long clapped his thin hands together, one loud clap. "Norm, what a delicious story. '... but doesn't he look like a writer.' I must remember that, a perfect description of Matt Anthony. Well, enough of this. Let me know what decision you reach.

Take your time. Confer with Kelly, if you wish."

"No, this is my baby. I'll buzz you the second I get any clever ideas." And what made me say, *my baby?* Oh Michele.

"Responsible ideas, Norm, rather than clever. And don't be afraid to say thumbs down, if you feel that way."

Riding the elevator I thought, The bastard is giving me the horns. He wants to reissue the book but hasn't the guts. Norm, the whipping boy. Oh, hell, I'd do the same thing if I were in his position, I suppose.

As I walked into the office, Miss Park said, "I'm about to try the Turkish ..."

I shook my head and closed the door. Taking out my blending kit, I mixed enough tobacco to last the day, glanced at my work sheet. There wasn't a thing that couldn't be put off for a day or two. Or that Miss Park couldn't handle, although I didn't want her to get into the habit of handling too much of my work. When I got my pipe working I rang for her, said, "I don't want to be disturbed for the balance of the day. Not even a phone call, unless it's urgent."

"Certainly, Mr. Connor." She gave me a wise look that annoyed me. "Anything happen ... upstairs?"

"No. That is, I don't know—yet."

Turning to leave, she stopped at the door. "Do you want the new coffee iced or ...?"

"Goddamn the coffee! I don't want any!" She jumped and I grinned quickly, added, "Sorry I barked, Miss Park. Last night left my nerves on edge. Thank you, but I really don't want any coffee now. Perhaps later in the afternoon."

When she shut the door I opened my collar and sprawled in the leather desk chair. My mind was galloping in vast circles. Michele, Bill Long, Michele, the Anthony killing ... and then for no reason I thought of Miss Park, the way she had pressed her bosom against the door. "If I want an affair, this is the time," I told myself. "I'm a grass widower, or whatever the dandy title is. Crazy, all these years and I never called her anything but Miss Park. What's with me; that would be all I'd need, an office affair! But how did Michele cash a check so early in the morning? Or did she have the cash ready? Was the flight prearranged? Had she been wanting to leave me all ...? That was impossible, we had it made. But what do I do now? Forget last night.... think of *now*, the future. A great big fat day for decisions; Michele and now Anthony."

I was too restless to sit. I began pacing the office and felt ridiculous; the office was far too small for pacing. "I wish

Michele were here, I really need her on this Anthony thing. She has such a level head. We could talk out all the angles and ... here I am, wishing like a kid! I have to snap out of it, forget my personal problems until I rack up the right move on this or Long will throw me to the stockholders. Being jobless would be a new complication. But how can I forget Michele for a second? And how can I possibly know what the public's reaction will be to an Anthony book? Hell!"

And I was quite aware that I'd never had to make any real decisions before. I had lived a very happy and mild twenty-nine years. Everything had worked for me—until last night.

Last night.

Exactly what had happened last night? I'd been over it a hundred times since, trying to understand what had gone wrong. All I could come up with was: either I was dense or something had been cooking in Michele's head for a long time.

It had been a hot day, so muggy even the air conditioner couldn't do much with it. Perhaps the humidity had made our nerves ragged. But not *that* ragged. After a light supper at home, we'd been sitting around in our pajamas watching TV. The damp heat, the food and the dull TV show had left me sleepy. Through half-shut eyes I'd watched Michele's long face, the body under the sheer shortie nightgown. Her auburn hair was cut in an Italian bob and strangely enough the slight boyish look seemed to heighten the sensuous quality of her face. A swarthy face with crowded, delicate features. The eyebrows and lashes so jet black it was hard to believe she didn't use mascara. The lips heavy under a faint moustache. I loved to lie in the darkness and feel those demanding lips cover me with tiny hot kisses. I loved her moustache, and the three long hairs that grew from a little mole in the cleft of her breasts.

Often when I awoke first in the morning and didn't feel like getting up, I would analyze her body. Michele's face could belong to any nationality: it could be Semitic or Latin or North African. Here in New York I'd often been asked if she was Spanish or Italian. But from the neck down her body was strictly all-American. In fact I once had a slightly drunken argument with Michele about it. She claiming I was being a jingoist. She had the strong clean shoulders of a female athlete (although her only exercise was some mild swimming) and then her body V'd down past small breasts to a narrow waist and neat, solid hips, then the long, almost powerful dancer's legs. It was neither a slim nor a delicate body, but a very healthy one.

Completing the inventory I happily decided Michele had a

far better figure than any stage beauty's—but if she only had larger breasts. I grinned as I told myself to stop thinking like an ass. The bra ads were getting to me.

Glancing at me, Michele asked with her warm accent, "Are you amused by this dull nonsense on the TV?"

"What? Honey, I wasn't even watching it."

"And I only tolerated it for your sake," she said, crossing the room to switch off the set. She moved with a fast, sultry grace. I thought, Lord, I'm a lucky man. I have a girl out of a European movie living with me.

Pushing a foot stool toward my chair, Michele sat at my feet, like a good Continental wife. She said, "It has been such a sweaty day."

"New York's claim to summer fame. Perhaps we'll try Jones Beach this weekend."

"And roast again on the bumper-to-bumper ride back? Norm-man (she always said my full name when she had something important to tell me), one of the teachers at school, Edith—you remember seeing her, the plump one—well, she has recently inherited a small house in Connecticut. A quite wonderful old stone house with enough land. Also but a short ride from the ocean, the Sound."

"Honey," I asked, playing with her fingers, "who wants to move in the Westport social swindle? At least, who wants to now? That's big money."

"This is near Stamford and only a small ride, even by train, from New York City. Edith has no use for the house and will sell it for a modest price, to us. $6000, with $1000 down. Perhaps it will cost another thousand to fix it up, although it is not badly in need of repairs."

"Look, all these ancient handy man specials are falling apart and need—"

"Not this house. I have seen it."

I opened my eyes wide. "When? You never told me."

"Edith drove me up there this afternoon. It is a charming place with its own trees and dirt road. Very private. She could get much more from a real estate man, but being a friend, she is glad to let us have it for the ... how you say ... the assessed value. Norm-man, I seriously think we should buy it. We take $2000 from our bank, and for the rest we will need to pay only $50 a month."

"Honey, it will cost us a lot more than that. Furniture alone is at least another grand. What would we do with a house?"

"Live there in the summer, maybe all the time if it turns out well. After this year I do not plan to teach summer school. Darling, we would have cool air, our own orchards. We would swim every afternoon when you came home. And even in the mornings, too. We would buy a little boat. I love to fish. If we decide to live up there all year, we can give up this apartment and be saving money. Norm-man, I think we should buy it, really."

"Well ..." I sat up. "Hey, you didn't put a deposit down?"

"Of course no, not without consulting you. However, I said we would drive up to see it Saturday."

"Look, I want a country house, too, but not now. For the same reason we didn't buy a new car. Another few—"

"I didn't want a new car. Our auto works fine."

"Okay, but I did. Another year or so and I'll be ready to make my move. By then Frank Kuhn may be a vice president, grease the way for me. You know our plans, why I can't be bogged down."

She walked across the room to light a cigarette, although I had my lighter on the floor beside me. "Those are *your* plans. You have a respectable job, the pay is sufficient. It is secure. Jay was there for thirty-two years."

"Would you want me to stay at Longson's for thirty-two years?"

"You could do worse."

"Sweet, it isn't a question of doing worse but of hitting the upper brackets. I'm lucky. I have a chance at the big money if I play it smart. But I have to be ready to take the jump when the opportunity is ripe. And 'ready' means as few responsibilities, money worries, as possible. Especially with a recession in the wind. I've told you that and—"

"Yes, you have told me, over and over. We have been married seven years but you keep putting off having a baby, a family."

"Oh, now, it's far too hot a night to start *that*."

"If I cannot talk with my husband about a family who should I speak to?"

"For—hell, don't be corny," I said, getting up.

Moving backwards she said quickly, "Just stay where you are and talk. Norm, I want this settled tonight, but not with kisses and big talk."

"I suggest we discuss it on a cooler night."

"No."

"Okay, but don't start crying."

"I am not near tears."

"Honey, we're still young. And the way you talk somebody

would think we were having a rugged time, starving in a slum. If you want to give up your job, that's fine with me. All I ask is that you wait a—"

"There is no 'somebody' here, only myself and my husband. We are living very comfortably. I like very much to keep living like this, but with our children."

"I want kids, too. That's why I want to give them all the advantages of—"

"Ninety percent of the world's children would be more than happy with what we can give a child now. Norm-man, seven years! For seven years I have been wanting your children."

"How about letting me finish a sentence, if you don't mind," I said sharply. "And stop taking the children bit so big. You're not twenty-five yet, we've plenty of time. Look, Michele, this isn't Europe or France. This is America. To you I may seem a howling success but in the advertising world my salary is peanuts. I work for a publisher, not an agency. I'm not a pusher, a success chaser, but it happens I do face an opportunity, that I have some connections and I am the youngest ad manager in the business. I'd be stupid not to capitalize on this. You want me to stand still because you don't realize—"

"Stand still? I only want to further our happiness!"

"How? Listen, by comparison to what you were brought up on we may seem to be riding in the lap of plenty. But over here it's—"

"*Merde!*" Michele said, fighting back tears.

"What?" I mumbled, slightly shocked.

"*Merde!*"

"Isn't this dandy! If tears don't work, then change the act and start chattering in French!" I said sarcastically.

"It sounds better in your English? Dung! Crap!" she screamed.

"Aw, honey—"

"Or you rather that other expression I hear over here all the time, bull *merde*! Translation—"

"Damn it, Michele, take it easy. What the devil are you screaming about? A lousy old house isn't worth all this. Relax, damn it, relax!"

"Norm-man, you say take it easy," she wailed as the tears came. "Does anyone know how to relax here in America? We can't have a baby until you are a rich man. We can't enjoy the country, can't do this and that! Oh, yes, yes, people live very well here, indeed. We have many shoes and clothing here, we have hot water, cars, refrigerators, TV and clock that awaken us with radio music. We live very ... what you call ... high. Oh, very high. So what will you do with more income, buy *two* TV sets, a larger ice machine? Is that what our children must wait for?"

"Hon, what is this? Now you're being silly," I said gently, worried because I'd never seen her this upset before.

"Silly? You laugh at me because I say my prayers every night. And that is why I say them in French. Do you know, or care, what I thank God for each night? I thank Him that my husband makes a good living without strain at work he likes. The big words you mouth, ambition, opportunity, upper brackets; you are the silly one! You don't realize the ... the ... how you say ... the good deal you have at Longson. No, you are the fool wanting the rush and tension of Frank's job. Look at him and his big blonde, are they happy? All they are is nervous, and their faces full of worry and fear lines."

"Oh, you're talking like a European!"

"Indeed I am! Sure this is an exciting country but ... for all your marvelous plumbing and fancy cars, you live without dignity, must vacation on a psychiatrist's couch. The great American small talk: how many times has one been through analysis! My father makes few francs as a school head. In his house there is not any new furniture, nor even an ice box, nor a TV set, and most times no hot water. Yet my parents live. Norm-man, can't you understand what it means for two people to find warmth and dignity in each other, in their lives? To have a flat that is not merely a cocktail lounge or a place to sleep, but a *home?* To—to—" She suddenly held her face and lapsed into gushing, hysterical French.

Feeling hysterical myself, I raced across the room and held her tightly. "Michele, my darling Michele, the heat takes it out of all of us. Guess it was a mistake for you to teach summer school. Now get a hold of yourself. After all, in two weeks you'll be in Paris, then in the south of France with your folks. Things will look different. When you come back, we'll talk this through." My hands stroked the small of her back.

She pushed me away, her body actually shaking with sobs.

It was the first time she had ever pushed me from her and meant it. I said coldly, "Don't feel so damn sorry for yourself. Who am I ambitious for? Myself? It's for us, for you! Can't you get that through your head?"

She raised her wet face, and the tears seemed to make her more lovely than ever. "And can't you get it that I love you so much it is a torture not having children? I married you, not a ...

a ... medicine chest."

"All right, honey, I'm with you, remember? Cut the tears and ... I never knew it meant so much to you. Tell me, suppose it turns out we can't have kids? I mean, if we try for real. Then what? Are we finished?"

"If that is nature's wish then.... Oh, Norm-man, Norm-man, it is not only the matter of children. It is ... sometimes I think we live like man and mistress instead of husband and wife."

"Lord! Isn't that a peachy little thing to say!"

She turned away, muttering something in weary French as she closed the bedroom door. I understand French fairly well, when she speaks slowly. At least I can get the drift. I heard myself yelling after her, "What was that? What did you say?"

Through the closed door she whispered, "It does not matter. You can only understand what you want to see."

"Yeah? And what the devil do you see except your own nose?"

There wasn't any answer. I waited a few seconds, then went back to the table and jammed some tobacco into my pipe. I was sweating like a pig. I took a can of beer and drank it slowly, standing in the kitchen doorway that led to the garden. I stared at the lighted windows all around us, most of them open, and wondered how many people had heard us. I'd never seen Michele like this before, but the more I thought about things, the more indignant I became. I mean, what the hell! Where did she come off giving me that? Anybody listening would think I was giving her a hard time! That I was a penny pincher or a bottle-head! That I ran around with bimbos! Here she practically blew a fuse, and over what? Exactly *what?* That I didn't jump through the loop when she mentioned a house or a kid! It was positively an uncalled for—

I heard the bedroom door open. Stepping back into the apartment I told myself to cut it out; sometimes women get cranky and have no control over.... She was slipping on her gloves. Michele was not only dressed, but she had a suitcase beside her. "Where do you think you're going?"

"To the airport. I phoned—there is the possibility of a cancellation on a Paris flight. Please do not try to stop me."

"What the devil makes you think I want to stop you!"

Michele stared at me for a moment, her eyes sad and troubled. I thought she was going to bawl again. All she did was to say softly, "*Au revoir*, Norm-man," and walk out of the apartment.

The closing of the door hit me like a kick in the stomach. Then I laughed out loud, a shrill nervous laugh, as I thought:

She's only bluffing. Hell, European women never take the initiative, walk out on a marriage. Oh, that's a bunch of nonsense. Michele has to be bluffing, we've had it too good for it to be otherwise. A bluff. My God, of all the melodramatic corn—and she had the gall to complain about the TV show! Maybe I should have stood up to her more? But this caught me completely unprepared. Anyway, I couldn't be hard with Michele. I suppose I'll have to drive up with her and see this stone outhouse Saturday. Summer is half-over, I can stall until next Spring. When she comes back I'll tell her I want to see the house. She'll return by midnight. Taking a suitcase!

But a few minutes after twelve when I turned off the commercial-ridden old movie on the TV screen, I wondered what I should do. "I suppose I should get crocked," I said aloud. The words made such a lonely ring in the quiet of the apartment the very sound frightened me. And there was only a half a bottle of vermouth around, and some cooking sherry. Neither of us drank very much.

I stretched out on the bed, telling myself, "She's checked the bag and is walking around, acting like a kid. No point in my being childish too. Let her come home and find me asleep, as if nothing happened. She's gone to a movie. Or maybe visiting this Edith, or that UN couple she likes so well. I can phone and.... But how would that look? Damn, damn, we never had a spat anything like this before."

At 3 A.M. I could no longer endure the waiting or the hot silence of the apartment. I dressed and went out. It was too late to get drunk now, even if I wanted to. I walked across town and up a deserted Broadway, which further depressed me. At 72nd Street I decided I couldn't take it, that I would phone the house and agree to anything Michele wanted. While I still didn't understand what had come over her, still, she always was a level-headed kid, so maybe I was the jerk.

I phoned and there wasn't any answer. I tried to tell myself she was spending the night with Edith, but I was frightened and jittery. I started walking back downtown and suddenly went into a Turkish bath. I sat in the hot room for a while. I was alone and trying to think—and all I could think of was I must be in Hell. At 5 A.M. I went up to my room and fell into an uneasy, exhausted sleep. When I opened my eyes it was 9:45.

Miss Park opened the office door. "Mr. Connor, Mr. Kuhn is on the phone. Do you want to speak to him?"

"Damn, the last thing I need is a game of handball! Tell him

I'm tied up in a sales ... no. I'll talk to him." I waited until Miss Park left, then picked up the phone, trying to choose the right words. For a new thought had entered my head—Francine Anthony's death could very well be the solution to my own problems.

"Frank? Norm Connor here. Sorry as all hell I didn't get a chance to phone you back but I'm jammed up to my ass with work. Guess you've read about the Matt Anthony mess? Well, there's all sorts of complications here and I've been busier than a whore on a battleship." I threw in a few more cuss words, trying to make it all sound like "man" talk, and inwardly a trifle ashamed of the phony act I was putting on. The trouble was I hadn't decided what my play should be; impress Frank with the fact this had to be my own decision, or should I play the young squirt asking the seasoned older executive for advice?

Frank said he was busy as a bastard himself and needed a workout to shake up his brains. It would do me good, too. He finished with, "I've reserved a court at the Midtown for 1 P.M. Can you make it?"

"I think I can make time for it. You're right, be the change of pace I need. But only one game."

"Fine. Then we'll lunch at the Ad Club. By the by, I'd like to read the Moorepark novel you have scheduled for September. Judging by the catalog blurb, it will be a shocker. Can I get a copy of the galleys?"

"I'll see if I can sneak out a copy. But I'll have to have it back within a week." A deadline always seemed to heighten Frank's enjoyment of a book.

"Of course. One sharp, Normboy."

Hanging up I phoned the sales department for a copy of the galley proofs, told them, "And give me one that's marked up, if you can." The higher up you went the more obvious was the childish side of big money men. Or was it that I didn't expect to find any defects in the big shots? I never could figure who Frank impressed by reading galley proofs, unless it was himself.

Now that I had a plan in mind, I felt much better. Leaving my office I told Miss Park to see if the afternoon papers were out, and stopped at a vending machine in the hallway. I ate two chocolate bars for energy. I dropped in to see Maggie Gordon, who handles our mystery books. Maggie is a large woman with a plump face and a clear, perfect complexion, who goes in for tweedy skirts and long cigarette holders. She still speaks with a soft southern drawl, although she left Alabama more than a quarter of a century ago.

"Mag, has Bill mentioned the possibility of reissuing one of the Matt Anthony books?"

"Aha. I've checked with the paperback house that publishes Matt—naturally they're planning to cash in on the notoriety, too. They're going to put out a novel called—"

"We don't intend to cash in on any notoriety, Mag."

She gave me a fat wink. "Come, come, Norm, you talk your way and I'll talk mine." Mag held up a slim book with a mild pink dust jacket. The cover was a kind of surrealistic picture of a big-eyed, solemn-faced young girl leaning against a yellow mud adobe hut. She was gazing at a desert sun, very red and hot. A lean girl in smartly styled jeans and a chic blouse, she looked like a fashion model—except for a small gun in a jeweled hip holster. The girl and the clothes were in sharp contrast to the deadly gun, the plain hut. The title, *The Last Supper*, was printed in small, old-fashioned type. "This is one of his better books, Norm, in fact the best he ever did for us. Unfortunately it came out a few days before the Korean war and was lost in the shuffle. I like the jacket and the plot has a beautiful gimmick."

I thumbed through the novel. "This was before my time here. What's it about? Not wife killing, I hope."

"Naw. A gal who is a religious fanatic kills a young professor who is about to prove one of the Disciples intended to poison Christ during the Last Supper. Wonderful snapper: she kills the guy with a diamond bullet."

Mag looked up at me as if expecting a shout of joy. "She killed him with … a what?" I asked.

"A diamond slug. Being harder than the steel of the gun, the diamond completely changed the ballistics of the murder weapon, throwing the cops into a tizzy. Far-fetched, but it reads fast and well. Do you know Matt made a thorough study of the Bible for this book?"

"Can you spare this copy?"

"Along with 3489 unbound copies in the warehouse. Is all this definite, Norm?"

"No. Far from it. It's an advertising thing. Of course I'll let you know the moment it is decided."

As I reached the door, Maggie said, "Knew I had something to see you about. I have a French suspense novel that didn't do well on the other side, but my scouts swear it's a damn good yarn. Would Michele have time to read it for me?"

"Too bad you didn't tell me yesterday, she's in Paris now—or will be in a few hours. Her parents aren't feeling too well. I had to take her to Idlewild at five this morning." And my God, how the words dragged in my mouth like rotten cotton!

"Lazy-me, the lousy book has been on my desk for a week. Well, it can wait until she returns. Wish I could pick up my fat-self and put it down in Paris. Or Rome. I like Rome even better."

"Michele may be gone the balance of the summer," I said, leaving her office. The balance of the summer or the rest of my damn life?

I stopped at the promotion office to pick up a background file on Matt and when I returned to my office, Marty Kelly was waiting on the phone. He said, "I hear we're going to do pages of advertising around Matt Anthony. When do we start? Like to talk it over at lunch?"

"The goddamn office grapevine," I said, making with a mock groan. "Not true, Marty. We *may* do something. Right now everything is up in the air. And keep it quiet. I mean that."

"I get the message. How about having chow with your old boss anyway?"

"Remember that another day, I'm tied up for lunch," I said, wondering if I should tell him I was eating with Frank.

"I'll drop in to see you in a few days. I have some layouts on that prize book campaign I want you to okay. And listen, we can really go to town on Anthony, he's made to order for publicity."

"I'll let you know, Marty."

I got a pipe working, opened my shoe laces, leaned back in my leather chair ... and started reading the Matt Anthony file.

The son of a rural mailman and farmer, Matt had been born in a small upstate town near the Canadian border fifty-one years ago. He studied at Cornell on a state agriculture scholarship but dropped out after two years to go to sea. He entered NYU fifteen months later, working as a longshoreman to pay his tuition. He married a waitress for six months. When he was twenty-seven he became an English instructor at Brooks University, a small but heavily endowed Midwestern school. It was about this time that Matt started publishing in several literary quarterlies and soon gave up teaching to become a full-time writer. Anthony was very prolific, selling over a million words to the pulps within two years, along with a sale to *Collier's*. (I stopped to figure a million words at about a cent a word was ... ten thousand, or about five thousand a year. Not bad for those days—or these days, I guess.)

He worked on WPA for a few months (with that income?) and went to sea again during the tail end of the Depression. His first mystery novel had for its background the teenage hobos crisscrossing America in search of jobs. The book received only two reviews—mysteries were rarely reviewed then—both of them excellent. In 1937 he started making "headlines." He married a minor starlet in Mexico and was deported several days later for sending three policemen to the hospital during a drunken brawl. Matt himself spent several weeks in an El Paso hospital suffering from a concussion. That same year he placed in the Albany-New York outboard race, sold two books to Hollywood, and authored a radio serial called "Private Gun."

By an odd coincidence, he next made headlines the same week one of his books was published by punching a British police official in Africa, who was supposed to have been flogging a native. There was a one-day fuss until the State Department secured Matt's release. Some months later, he made the papers again when a bank was looted in a small California town. Matt Anthony the detective story writer was passing through and was "asked" to give the local police a hand. There wasn't any mention in the file as to whether the bank robbers were ever captured.

Francine had been married to a little known and alcoholic novelist. Matt's name was in the columns now and then, squiring some pretty actress around, so it was a mild shock (to whomever was interested) when he married the not-so-glamorous Francine three weeks before Pearl Harbor. Months later they were both in England, Matt an accredited war correspondent for a small feature syndicate. He went to Africa, to Italy—where he was hospitalized after too much drinking hardened his liver. He made headlines again when he was attached to the famed 442nd Combat Team in Northern Italy. He had been in a machine gun nest when a direct mortar hit had killed the soldiers and slightly wounded Matt. According to one news dispatch, Matt had gone "fighting mad" and like a movie hero had picked up a tommy gun and charged. There was some doubt as to whether he had killed two Nazi soldiers, but he had wounded and captured a German officer and had to be restrained from killing him with his bare hands.

Since correspondents are not supposed to be shooting, Matt was returned to the States and for a time lectured on the war bond circuit. His books sold well, sales being limited only by the paper shortage. He was supposed to be writing a war book, but never finished (or started) it. After the war, except for sailing the Atlantic alone and a brawl in a Boston bar, Matt kept out of the papers. Two years ago he had packaged the television rights to five of his books for "an undisclosed sum."

So that was Matt Anthony. I put the file down. He must have been married to Francine the time I saw him, just before he sailed the ocean.

I glanced at the two afternoon editions of the newspapers Miss Park had left on my desk. The killing was front page with a picture of a grinning Matt being escorted out of a bar by two cops (taken in 1948) and a studio photo of him in his correspondent's uniform which seemed to be strained by the broad shoulders and heavy neck. On the inside pages there was a snap of a gray, bushy-haired little man shielding his face from the cameras: Prof. Brown leaving a subversive investigation. There was another picture of a rowboat with a new outboard and a large arrow bluntly pointing to a slight dent next to an oar lock.

Keeping an eye on the time, I raced through the stories. There wasn't anything I didn't already know, except that Joel Hunter and his wife Wilma, the other house guests, were quoted as saying that Matt had threatened to kill Francine in a "family fight' over whether Prof. Brown should remain in the house or not.

At 12:30 I took the galley proofs and left for the gym, first telling Miss Park, "Phone Marty Kelly and ask him to get me the home addresses of the Hunters, this Prof. Brown, the maid, the detective who secured Anthony's confession, and the D.A. And I want to know who Anthony's lawyer is, if he has one yet. And ask Mag for the name and phone number of Matt's agent."

"After lunch be all right, Mr. Connor?"

"Of course. I'll be back at about three," I said, my eyes making their usual run below her neck.

I bought a later edition of a paper as I hailed a cab. The only new item was a picture of Mrs. Joel Hunter in a bathing suit. She not only had a good figure, but there was a certain boldness to her face, the way she posed, that impressed me.

Lighting my pipe, I relaxed in the taxi seat and wondered if I should let Frank win today. Being older and a little flabby but a much better player, Frank could usually loaf in the center of the court and count upon his wicked hop serve, or his accurate ceiling and wall shots to win. But if I made him move around, which meant I had to run around twice as fast myself, I could tire Frank out and win—when I wanted to.

(Up until last night I'd really been Norman Connor, the lad who always came up with a rose in each hand. To get a little exercise I'd started playing handball at a midtown gym twice weekly. My game was energetic if not skillful, and by chance I lucked up on a steady partner—Frank Kuhn. Frank is a former football star and a $25,000-a-year account executive in one of Madison Avenue's—even if his offices are located on Park—more aggressive agencies. We made a good team, usually winning when we played for a few bucks a man. Frank and I were interested in each other outside of handball, too. For some unknown reason he had a passion for reading galley-proofs of forthcoming books. The more penciled-in changes, the more he enjoyed the book. I was interested in Frank because he kept telling me he could double my salary if I wanted to change jobs. The truth is, he gave me a mild case of ambition.

(Frank and his high-powered blonde Texan wife lived in a penthouse, were members of several swank clubs, and entertained lavishly. They both thought Michele's accent was "too cute," and we could have easily become their closest friends. But Michele found them boring and I was careful not to wear out my welcome. I knew Frank was big league and I wasn't ready for that yet. Up until now I had been vaguely waiting for a "break." Now Matt Anthony was going to be my stepping stone to a lush Madison Avenue salary.)

The locker room attendant told me Frank was waiting on the court. I undressed and dressed quickly, spraying my arm pits with a deodorant. Up in the gym I found Frank already in a sweat hitting the little black ball against the four walls. (The silly black handball had given me a taste of ambition—had it also been the wedge between Michele and me?)

Putting on my gloves I told him, "No need for you to warm up, I'll be a pushover. Michele had a cable from her folks last night. They aren't feeling up to par, high blood pressure. So she put her vacation ahead a few weeks. I was up all night helping her pack, seeing her off at Idlewild at daybreak. I'm bushed, Frank." Mouthing the lies gave me a sudden queasy feeling, but I had to get it over with.

"Have to have you over for supper more often, Norm, when Liz learns you're a summer bachelor. We didn't get much sleep either last night. It got so damn muggy we drove up to City Island and spent the night on the boat. Here, I have a new ball—try it."

"Never mind. I've been on the go all morning. Play for serve."

We had our usual tight game and I made a few lucky killers to win 21-17. I didn't say a word about Matt Anthony although I sensed Frank was waiting for me to talk about the mess.

Over lunch at the Ad Club, when I gave him the galleys, he finally asked, "What about this Anthony thing you mentioned on the phone?"

In an off-hand manner I told him about Bill Long's pitch, what the deal was. I ended with, "So there it is, a minor matter blown all out of proportion by this biddy stockholder, and dumped square in my lap."

Frank toyed with a cigarette and shook his silver-white crewcut head. "I'd forget it. Difficult to gauge the public reaction to such an ad campaign. The biddy will find something else to make a stink about anyway, so no sense in hanging yourself."

"No, I'm going ahead with the campaign," I said softly. "What the hell, Bill Long practically ordered me to. He hinted at some big plans he wants to carry at the next stockholders meeting, so if we can lick this ... well, it is important. And I want to do it. Keep my mind off Michele. (I put in the proper, light chuckle.) Seriously, Frank, I have about a week's leeway and I'm going to interview everybody connected with the killing. I have to determine in my own mind if Matt is guilty."

"I'm not reading you, son. The man has admitted it."

"What I mean is, was it one of those things or real murder?" I said, taking a small breath and plunging in. "I know I hardly have to tell you of all people, Frank, that advertising has a creative, intrinsic quality. A fellow has to believe in what he's selling to do a job. Sure, one can peddle anything, and it will be a routine campaign. Well, this *can't* be routine. I can't afford a mistake or I ruin Longson. So I have to first believe in my product. Even though the D.A. is calling this murder, I have to make up my own mind, be damn certain—without any reservations—that it was ... well, an accident. In a moment of rage any of us might punch somebody, even a ... a ... wife. And if she bangs her head in falling, to me and the public that's not murder but a tough break. No matter what any D.A. claims. After all, even though you and I may know differently, part of the pitch has to be that we're helping Matt raise money for his defense. Therefore, I have to make the public feel that by buying his book they are also helping a worthy cause, so to speak. To do that, and I'm certainly not judging the man, I first have to be certain he *has* a defense. In short, if it really was murder, I wouldn't blow my nose to help him."

I was stirring and playing with my coffee as I talked, but out of the corner of my eye I saw Frank nodding in agreement. Frank said, "I like your feeling of loyalty to Longson, Norm, and your slant about advertising integrity. Certainly a man has to sell himself first. I once saw Anthony in action at some yacht club dance. A hell of a big bruiser, and what's more, he looked like a mean customer. I wouldn't want to tangle with him."

"What sort of 'action' was he in?"

"Nothing much actually happened. He drank a few too many and pushed somebody around. Now that I think of it, Francine Anthony was there too. I'd give odds he's taken a fist to her before."

"A bitch?"

Frank nodded. "I hate that word. I also hate to go by first impressions, but she struck me as *the* Bitch." He motioned for the check.

I finished my coffee quickly, added, "Of course all I've told you is off the record, Frank."

"I know. Look, we're going away for the weekend, but Liz will phone you early in the week for supper. And maybe we'll get in a few games before that. I'm anxious to know what you learn about Anthony. I'll finish the galleys over the weekend, send them to your office." Frank added this last sentence with a touch of self-importance that made me hide my smile with my napkin.

Riding back to the office I felt pretty good—for the first time since last night. I'd played things exactly right. Frank would tell a few people, the right ones—probably as part of some intimate bar conversation—and Madison Avenue would be watching my campaign. Do me good to get out of the office, and there won't be any trouble with Bill. Hell, he gave me a week to decide and things are slow in the office. God, the way the unexpected can shake up your life: if I pull this off, it will be exactly what I've been waiting for—the bang to land me in a big agency. And it fits. By the time Michele returns I'll already be established, prove how right I was. Then we'll start right in having a kid.... *By the time Michele returns* ... it hasn't worn thin, she will return, oh Lord, she has to come back ... please make her return.

I cabled Michele a dozen roses, then spent the balance of the afternoon cleaning up my desk. When I talked to Bill Long he was not only in favor of my idea of interviewing the people involved, but I knew he was impressed by it.

At five as Miss Park was leaving, I fooled with the idea of asking her to eat with me. I had this immediate dread of dining alone. My wife is out of town so let's go ...! But could I explain about not wanting to eat alone ...? I said goodnight to her and remained at my desk until six, cleaning up my pipes and doing other such important work. When I left at seven the night elevator operator said something about my working overtime. It was another warm evening and I had a light bite in a cafeteria. I took in a movie but my restlessness made the theater seat feel like a straitjacket. Also the picture was one of the so-called "adult Westerns," which bore me worse than the shoot-'em-up variety. I walked out in the middle of it, wandering around aimlessly. The good feeling of the afternoon had worn away.

I dropped into a quiet Second Avenue bar that seemed cool, and started to get tight. It seemed like something to do. I sat on a bar stool, along with a few other people, and watched the TV perched high in one corner. There was a half-finished drink and a pack of cigarettes on the bar next to me. I didn't notice them until a tall woman with an over-blonde ponytail walked out of a room cleverly marked HERS and sat on the stool beside me. She took a butt out of the open pack. I moved a little to give her room, said, "Excuse me." She was wearing a smart and slightly clinging odd print dress, the colors light and gay. Her face could be considered pretty, and I decided she could be thirty or even forty. I was going to light her cigarette, but she said "Thank you," and lit her cigarette—all in one motion—as she turned to watch TV. From the profile view I knew she was wearing a powerful girdle, but the upstairs didn't seem the work of any bra contraption and reminded me greatly of Miss Park.

As I sipped my drink a thought which I realized had been rattling about in the rear of my mind all day came into sharp focus: now was my chance for an affair. It had such a corny melodramatic connotation I smiled at myself in the clean bar mirror. Of course I knew the idea hadn't been born just today. But for the life of me I couldn't figure *why* I wanted an affair. Michele and I were not only able and willing bed partners, but we often reached heights of exhausting passion. Yet in the last—oh—year, especially whenever the papers played up a new call girl scandal, I had found myself thinking of having another woman. A hundred dollar a night call girl. Or Miss Park. Whenever I gave it any serious thought, I was frankly puzzled by this want and wondered if it came to all men after a half-a-dozen years of marriage. I was positive that no other woman could be as pleasing as Michele, yet ... I couldn't deny I had these thoughts. With Michele away, why if she ever found out, she certainly couldn't blame me ... now.

Whether it was the drink warming my insides or/and the slightly perfumed presence of the blonde beside me, I began to feel as excited as a schoolboy. When blondie groaned at an ancient joke the TV comedian pulled, I jabbed with, "He hasn't talent, merely courage." Which was as old as his gag.

She nodded. "I swear, all I can take on TV are the fights. I simply can't stand it when they try so hard to be funny, or clever—any of that intellectual jazz."

"I know what you mean—the high-water mark of mediocrity; that's TV." I motioned for the bartender. "Would it upset you terribly if I buy you a refill and act like a brash joker?"

She turned and gave me a coy, studied glance, then smiled. If her teeth said she was far nearer forty, her face was also prettier than I'd thought. She said, "Yes, I think a refill will be fine. And I like your frank approach. When it comes to drinks I don't stand on convention or any of that silly old jam ..."

Mrs. Wilma Hunter

The day started wrong. In fact it started in the afternoon. I awoke at 2 P.M. feeling wretched and lost with a terrible hangover. It was another muggy day and I sat on the edge of the bed for a long time, full of sweat and stale odors: the empty apartment making me want Michele so much I was afraid. I simply had this sense of fear, of foreboding.

I sat there in a haze, a whole slew of thoughts circling in my throbbing mind. Things like: Is any binge worth the hangover? How can people in love make each other so miserable? The constant thought—exactly *what* had I done to make Michele blow sky high? There was also the slightly sobering thought that I'd already wasted a half a day, ought to get on my horse.

The bedroom spooked me because it was so neat. I missed Michele's sloppy habit of leaving her underthings hanging on the backs of chairs and on the dresser. There was only one bright spot, I was so glad I hadn't tried to take the blonde in the bar to bed. I wasn't even sure she would have been willing, but the tenth time she said, "... all that *jazz*," I'd lost interest.

Sitting on the bed I realized I was listening intently. I didn't know for what, unless it was the sound of Michele washing up, or her footsteps in the kitchen. I told myself to cut it out. A cold shower and food left me with only a faint headache. After I shaved and dressed I went to "work." I took out the list of people connected with Francine Anthony's death, in one way or another. Prof. Henry Brown lived in a hotel on West 99th Street, the Hunters lived a dozen blocks from me. I phoned them and didn't get any answer. Next I phoned Brown's hotel. A man answered who couldn't speak English. I kept shouting,

"Prof. Henry Brown?" and he kept repeating, "Non," or something that sounded like that. Next I phoned Matt's agent and his secretary told me he was gone for the day.

I sat by my phone, smoking a pipe, feeling a bit helpless. I walked over to the garage and drove up to 99th Street. I worked up a fine sweat squeezing into a parking space that seemed to be the length of my car to the inch.

The "hotel" was a converted apartment house full of Puerto Rican men, women and children; mostly children. Actually it seemed more like a large pension than a cheap hotel—except for the faint stink of insecticide. The desk clerk was a stooped refugee, a plump man in a loud sports shirt, his bald head almost polished. This was obviously my pal on the phone, for when I asked for Prof. Brown he shook his head and tried to tell me something in God-knows-what-language. When I shook my head he smiled and tried saying it again in Spanish. I shrugged to let him know I didn't understand, and he shrugged back, pointed to the door and let it go. I was getting rattled by this run-a-round and the heat and the insecticide weren't doing my head any good.

When I asked if he spoke French the clerk's face lit up as he rattled back in fast French which I vaguely understood to mean he was delighted to meet anybody who could speak French. I asked in my best slow French for Prof. Brown and merely talking French made me want to cry. The clerk pointed to a wall clock and rattled on. I finally got the idea: Prof. Brown always left the hotel at about ten-thirty in the morning.

I asked if I could have some stationery and he looked embarrassed, as if I'd asked a stupid question. There wasn't any stationery. I told him I wanted to leave a note for Brown and any paper would do. The clerk started a wild search for paper, hunting through a kind of receipt book for a blank piece. I finally told him to tell Prof. Brown I'd be back in the morning, or rather told him as best I could.

There was a phone booth in the lobby and I tried calling the Hunters again. Still no answer. There was a tiny fan in the booth and I sat there for a moment, enjoying the breeze. The other people on my list were either in Riverside or End Harbor, and it was much too late to drive out there. Matt's agent was out—and actually I didn't know what I wanted to see him about. He wasn't at the house when Francine was killed. So what to do? I phoned the office and asked Miss Park if she had found out who Matt's lawyer would be. She hadn't: it seemed his regular lawyer was trying to hire a good trial man, and had promised to let us know that afternoon. I told her to call or wire me at home as soon as she knew. Miss Park started telling me about some ad in a Chicago paper that had come out badly smudged and I cut her off by telling her to take it up with Marty Kelly. When I hung up I had another bright idea. I phoned in a wire to the Hunters asking them to call me at home as soon as possible.

The desk clerk and I said good day to each other in French and I went out and got in my car. It was almost three and I didn't know what to do with myself.

I started driving down the Westside Highway, considered taking a swim, but any decent beach seemed too far away. It was fairly cool driving and I crossed the Battery Tunnel and drove along the Narrows. When I reached Coney Island I turned off and parked. I had a couple of good hot dogs and a root beer at Nathan's and felt much, much better. I bought the evening papers, strolled the boardwalk, remembering how Michele loved Coney Island. I finally found a seat out on the new fishing pier, took off my coat.

The papers had a rehash of the case on the inside pages. It was an open and shut deal, what could be new? One of them had already started the REAL MATT ANTHONY STORY. I felt sorry for the hack frantically digging through back issues, banging his brains out to keep a day ahead of a deadline. The *Post* said Matt would be defended by the "famous criminal attorney, Jackson Clair."

I watched the old people fishing. Their endless patience reminded me of the Seine fisherman; they never seemed to catch anything, either. Michele and I used to watch them.... I put my head back against the railing to get some sun, shut my eyes. I slept for a half hour and made a frantic inspection of my pockets when I came to. To my surprise I hadn't been rolled.

Sleeping like that frightened me. I started walking and had more hot dogs, clams, root beer, fried potatoes, pizza, and custard—all of it senseless, nervous eating. I still didn't know what to do with myself. Jackson Clair was in the phone book, and after making a note of his number, a trifle astonished there was such a name, I drove home. Undressing to my shorts, for no reason I dusted the apartment thoroughly, and hosed the garden. There was a letter from my mother, the usual small writing: something about she hoped Michele and I would come to California on my vacation. Vacation? Not this year. When I finished Matt's ads I'd be starting a new job on Madison Avenue.

Stretching out on the couch I got in about twenty winks when the phone rang. I answered it eagerly only to hang up on a wrong number. Like in a bad comedy, the second I fell asleep again the doorbell rang: A wire from Miss Park with Jackson Clair's office address and phone.

I got my pipe working and was watching a not bad Western on TV when the phone rang again. A throaty voice asked, "Mr. Connor?"

"Yes."

"This is Wilma Hunter. I just found your wire."

"I'm the advertising manager of Longson, Mr. Anthony's publisher. I'd like to talk to you and Mr. Hunter."

"Joel has gone away—for a few days."

"Can I see you tomorrow? Say for lunch?"

"Be rather hard, I work from noon on. I'm free tonight. As I told you, Joel's away."

"I'm a grass bachelor myself, if that's the correct term. If I'm outside your house in ... about a half hour, could we go to a quiet café and mix a little talk with drinks?"

"Indeed we can. It's eight-twenty now. I'll expect you at nine."

"Fine."

"Oh ... the hall bell hasn't worked in years. No point in you climbing stairs. Will you be in a cab?"

"Yes."

"Have the driver honk his horn a few times. I'll be down."

We didn't have to sound the horn. The Hunters lived in a narrow tenement facing the approach to the Queens Tunnel and the East River—an old building sandwiched between a truck garage and a swank corner apartment house. As soon as the cab pulled up a young woman in a yellow dress stepped out of the doorway, crossed the sidewalk toward us.

For an odd second I thought she was wearing shoe boxes—her legs were slim and she was in these wide form-fitting shoes. She seemed to walk with a slight flat-footed waddle. But when she bent forward and asked, "Mr. Connor?" I forgot all about her walk.

Wilma Hunter had a most attractive face. Not pretty—unless the face of any woman under twenty-five has a certain youthful beauty. Rather, it was a forceful, intense face, with bold eyes and features, and a warm, heavy mouth. Her bright, kinky red hair was drawn back into a severe bun, accentuating the bony intenseness of her face. She looked exciting.

If her legs were too thin, the rest of the body was solid. Of course, as she bent over, looking into the cab window, her dress top fell away a little and my eyes had to take in the rise of her breasts.

I said "Mrs. Hunter?" like an idiot as I opened the door. She slid in beside me. There was a slight odor of perfume, sweat and the smell of rye on her lips: adding up to a fascinating musky smell. She didn't look tight, merely high. "Have you had supper, Mrs. Hunter?" I asked, still full of bright talk, as the cabbie ran his eyes over her in the windshield mirror.

"Oh, yes. Oh, not really. It's too damn sticky-hot to eat." She turned and looked me over—very openly.

"Any special bar you like?"

"Tonight I like them all." The husky voice was probably practiced, I decided.

I gave the driver the address of a quiet place on 69th Street and she leaned back in the seat, said, "I hope this isn't one of those backyard joints. They're always hot and it seems crazy, sitting out there as if people weren't looking down from the surrounding apartment houses."

"This is a simple, air-conditioned spot, Mrs. Hunter."

"That's good. Also, I would appreciate your not calling me *Mrs.* Hunter. I'm not up to that tonight. Wilma will do. What do they call you?"

"Norm."

For a while we didn't talk; I sat there, staring at her. I offered her a cigarette, lit it, then took out my pipe. She asked, "What the hell are you, one of those gentlemen things? Oh, well, I suppose it is nice of you to caddy a pack of butts around. Joel is never that considerate. Not that I'm sure I'd want him to be."

"Sorry he's out of town, I want to talk to him. Expect him back soon?"

"Who said he was out of town?"

"You told me he'd gone away for a few days."

"The little sonofabitch is home, humoring his whims. If anything, he's out of this world at the moment, gone ... real gone." She suddenly laughed, a warm live sound that filled the car, made the cabbie grin. "Don't look so startled. A writer often has to get away from it all—and there's a devastating little phrase. Tell you, phone the house in two days, he'll be there. When you come up to the apartment you'll see this purple monstrosity he calls a den. Joel's too poor to hop a plane for Paris or Mexico, so when the routine gets him, or something upsets him—like this Anthony stuff—why he locks himself in his den with a bottle, some food and a stack of his favorite records, gets stewed on music and rye. Music really sends that boy. I hate it, but I can see his point: no radio, TV, newspaper, typewriter or people. He even has his own bathroom. After a day or two he comes out all rested up and rather proud of himself for 'losing time'—as he cleverly terms it. That's the way it is with writers, you have to put up with anything and everything with them. Suppose you can tell I hate the idea. I told you that already. And I know I'm talking too much. Sure, I'm a bit liquored up myself. But don't worry, I rarely get plastered."

"All sounds like a novel idea, at least," I said, not knowing what to say.

"It works for him. It would drive me nuts," Wilma said as the cabbie pulled up to the curb.

As we were getting out and Wilma was stooped over, I could see the outline of her bra and pants under the dress: rousing lines. I had this feeling I could sleep with her if I played it right; and I don't care how trite that sounds—I *had* the feeling. I was also pretty sure I was going to play it "right."

The bar had enough people in it to be comfortable. We got a table in the corner. She said, "I'm on gin, stay with it. Gin and tonic, please."

After I told the waiter to make it two, I told her, "You had me fooled. Would have sworn rye."

She gave me a long look, then nodded as she said, "I think you're okay, Norm. Although that could be called a snotty crack. But I don't think so. What was it we're to talk about?"

"Matt Anthony. I'm thinking of advertising one of his books and, the point is, I have to know more about what happened before we go ahead. In short, I'm doing research on Mr. Matt Anthony."

"That stuffed crud. I suppose I'm talking like an ingrate—we've freeloaded upon him often enough. But then he needs an audience. I'll bet he's looking forward to taking the stand at the trial."

"Do you think he murdered his wife?"

"Is there any doubt? He's said so."

"There's a difference between murder and manslaughter," I said as the waiter put our drinks on the table.

"Not to the victim. But I see what you mean. I read about the murder charge—that's ridiculous. He got steamed and clipped Fran, and it must have been a belt he'd been saving up for years. She was mostly drip—not that Matt was any dilly to live with."

"You sound like you know him very well."

"Anything in skirts gets to know Matt. His second sentence to any gal is, let's tumble in the hay. Actually, he was far more talk than action."

I hesitated for a moment, then had a hunch she wouldn't be angry, so I asked, "Strictly as a matter of curiosity and not minding my own business: did you sleep with him?"

"No. And I expected you to ask, the way I'm shooting off my gums. But I almost did. Joel and I were in Florida when we first met them ... and believe me the first dose of Matt Anthony is damn strong. He's got this great muscular body, the worldly chatter and you think this is *the* man. The truth is he was a doubly strong potion for me because Joel and I weren't hitting it off at the moment. I hadn't learned what it means to be a writer's wife yet and Joel—he's a front runner and things were breaking all wrong for him. Nothing went right. We'd just been married and I had this feeling that somehow I was to blame, that I was wrong for him too." She washed this down with most of her drink.

"Although I've been in publishing a number of years, I don't get what you mean by being a writer's wife. What's so special about that?" My eyes were taking inventory of her as if it was already agreed we would go to bed.

"It isn't anything special, merely different. You must get used to a lot of things. As a for instance: Joel doesn't have any set working hours, he's around the house all day and ... well ... being together twenty-four hours a day calls for a kind of adjustment. And there's the money uncertainty. I remember when we were first married and a couple of small checks came in. Why, I looked upon them as found money, rather than wages. Me, I come from a hardworking, and of course, poor family, and the writing dollar frightened me. Guess it still does. Too many ups and downs, nothing you can count on. Matt once told us how he was driving to New York from California, absolutely broke. Not even a dime for food or gas. In St. Louis he had to sell his old car and practically hitch hike to New York. When he finally got his mail he found over $3000 waiting for him, money he didn't expect. To quote Matt, 'I racked up a good score.' He bought a new car and headed back to the Coast. My nerves like to know what's coming in each week."

"Did Fran like being a writer's wife?" I nodded at the waiter.

"No. Although she sure had plenty of experience—her first husband was a typewriter slob too. First off, Matt is a joker who can really blow his money, live big. But it wasn't only the money part; she never learned that writers can't live in a rut—even an expensive one—or it dulls their work. They need shaking up, so to speak, but it has to be a shaking of *their* own choosing. Or it throws them off completely. What I'm trying to say is: A wife shouldn't try to dominate a writer. I suppose we shouldn't dominate any man, but especially a writer. Took me a long time to learn that. Take this mental jolting—you ever notice how writers are traveling all the time? Sinclair Lewis, for instance, was always on the go. Of course there were other complications with Matt, he never really cared for Fran. Told me that down in Florida. He married her after their first night together. I don't think Matt can really care for any woman because he doesn't know what sex is all about."

"What's that mean?" I asked, sipping my second drink slowly, warning myself not to get high.

"Usual male arrogance. Matt thinks he has a king's scepter dispensing divine favors. Any time he had a woman who wasn't a professional whore, and I'll bet that wasn't often, Matt was overcome with the tremendous 'sacrifice' he thought the female had made, and the wonderful 'favor' he had conferred upon her. Actually, he's a horrible prude. I think that's why he writes about sex so much and so badly. He simply can't believe there is joint enjoyment, in the equality of the sexes. Happily, I never let him bestow the 'favor' on me. Although we damn near landed in bed. Know what made me see the light? A fish. Really. As I told you, Joel was in a hell of a funk. He couldn't even get a drink of water without spilling it. When the four of us went fishing for a few days, my poor Joel couldn't get a bite. Then, on our last day, the very last hour of fishing, wham! Joel hooked and boated this great marlin all by himself. Biggest fish you ever saw. It was one of those things; gave us both new confidence. That's when I told Matt I quite literally wanted no part of him."

"And he gave up that easily?"

She laughed. "I'm trying to tell you he's a phony about sex. Every time I saw him, all last week, he'd get me aside and whisper like a hammy actor, 'Let me show you something out in the pines.' Or, 'Honey, isn't it time we see what sort of spring music we can make?' Real kid slobbering. I got so used to it I didn't bother answering. Bet if I had said yes he would have run. It was merely another muscle Matt liked to flex. Fran as much as told me—several times—he wasn't anything in bed. Nice wifey talk. You know he has a bad heart, showing his muscles will kill him one of these days if the State doesn't kill him first."

She dug in her bag for a pack of cigarettes, shook her head as I reached for mine. Lighting her cigarette, I said, "You don't seem to be exactly fond of the Anthonys."

"They bored me. But End Harbor is comfortable and I thought Matt was good for Joel."

"What's that 'good' mean?" I asked, motioning for the waiter again, but holding on to my glass.

"He's an old hand. I suppose I hoped some of his success would rub off on Joel. Oh, that's unfair—I think Joel is a better writer than Matt, even commercially. But Joel's afraid to take chances and writing is a gamble. I don't mind working, giving him time to make it. I even like getting out of the house every day. I want him to try TV or ... here, he has a wonderful idea for a modern fantasy novel. A woman like—Hatti Carnegie, Arden, one of these female Diors who set the fashions—she gets angry at the cosmetic industry, due to a petty, minor matter ... and, for Christsakes, don't blab or steal this idea."

"I'm safe as Fort Knox."

She blew a cloud of smoke at me. "I believe you are. Anyway, this woman deliberately changes the fashions to long, straight hair and no makeup. This knocks out all the cosmetic concerns, kills TV advertising, ruins magazines, in fact the entire country is on the brink of a depression as a result. In the end the President has to invite her to the White House, beg her for the sake of the country's economy to tell women to start using lotions and cosmetics again. It would be a wonderful satire, would make Joel. But he piddles around with the adventures of some bastard pussy cat, insists he wants to knock off enough children's books to feel secure first." She shrugged—and so many things danced. "Maybe he's right. Sometimes I get a chill; seems such a long chance, to base your rent and food bills on a mere idea. There's no kick to it anymore."

"Kick to writing?"

She nodded. "Joel has done some good stuff, really sensitive. He has a flair for that. When I first knew him it gave me a thrill to see his stuff in print. Now everything comes down to, 'Will it sell?' Tell me, would Joel gain anything by switching to Longson?"

"I don't know. We haven't much of a juvenile list."

"You're pushing Matt's books. There must be some way Joel can cash in on this publicity. He's so damn afraid it will ruin him. I keep urging him to capitalize on it but.... That's what I mean about the writing business, there aren't any rules, you don't know what to do. Norm, can we talk about something else except shop? Do you dance?"

"A little."

"I'm sort of keyed up. I'm out for a hell of a time. This place is too quiet."

"Finish your drink and we'll go. Did Matt really threaten his wife that afternoon?"

"Yes. But I thought it was only talk. And talking about that nightmare gives me the creeps. Have you a car?"

"Yes."

"Let's drive and cool off. And forget all writers, including Matt," she said, getting up.

We taxied to the garage and then drove out to Long Island, stopping at a dismal place where we danced and she had a few more drinks. I didn't even finish my first. For no reason I found myself telling her about Michele. Not all of it, I mean not all about last night. I merely said we had a spat. But I told her other things, like how I met Michele when I was a Press Officer in Paris, fresh out of college, and she was working as a typist in SHAAF while waiting for a teaching appointment. How we had acted like a couple of jerks, afraid to touch each other, not even a kiss. Michele hadn't wanted to act the sexy French gal of fiction and the dirty jokes. And I had to prove my French wasn't limited to *Voulez vous coucher avec moi ce soir?* I even told Wilma about that afternoon, it was our fifth or sixth date, when we were alone in Michele's house and rushed each other to bed. What a tremendous afternoon! And I told Wilma about my winning $739 in a crap game which let us honeymoon in the finest hotels on the Côte d'Azur.

I knew I was talking too much, but it all made me feel slightly better. Although Wilma was hardly my idea of a confessor. But she was a fine listener.

She said, "In her case running home to mama is some hop, skip and jump. If—"

"You should have seen how proud her folks were—he's the head of a school there—to have an American officer for a son-in-law."

"... if Joel ever hits it, we'll live in Europe. While I'm not on a baby kick myself, things are so unsettled for us, but if Joel had a regular job like yours.... I can see her point *maybe*."

Wilma decided the bar was too lonely and we drove on. It seemed to me as if we'd been together for a long time, but it wasn't quite midnight. We stopped in Long Beach for more drinks and I said she must have something to eat. In the middle of a seafood meal Wilma announced she wanted fresh air—in a hurry. I drove down a deserted road that ran along a bay until she moaned, "Stop. I'm getting sick."

Pulling off the road, I hit a soft shoulder or maybe it was some swampy sand. The car lurched, seemed about to turn over. There was a bad moment as I battled the wheel, stepped on the gas. We seemed to hang in air, then the car leaped back on the road. Ahead I saw a tiny dirt lane leading to the water. I turned into it a ways and stopped.

Holding one hand over her mouth, Wilma ran out of the car and into some tall swamp grass and gave up. I wasn't drunk, and I suppose it was the near accident and her being so messy—but I was suddenly very sober and tired. This would have been such a stupid way to die. And why was I being so childish about an affair when I had a wife like Michele?

Wilma came near the car, said, "Wasn't that a charming sight? Told you not to feed me." She shook her hand violently, looked around. "I know I smell like two other girls and I feel the same way. Seems to be a beach down there. Swimming, anybody?"

"Okay."

She undressed so quickly it seemed I glanced down to turn off the ignition and looked up to see her nude in the dim moonlight. The nipples of her breasts were as red as her hair. She ran toward the water, running gracefully, and dived in. A minute later she was running back, stuck her wet head in the window. "Well, Tarzan?"

The door window framed her breasts and shoulders. She arched her chest out, as though that was necessary, and said, "You see, they are real. Your eyes have been like a bra all night."

There was something so pat about it all, I became sore. I told her coldly, "That's me, very bosom conscious. Here's another book idea for your husband; no part of the human body, including the brain, has changed the world's history as much as a firm pair. In fact, at the moment, breast shots are the mainstay of a high percentage of our magazines; they're the new literary movement."

"Odd time for a lecture, isn't it?" Her big eyes were mocking me.

I slid along the seat and stepped out of the car on the other side, undressed. Wilma ran into the water and I followed her. The water was wonderfully salty and cool. Wilma was a good swimmer and we went out about a hundred yards before turning back. It was a fine beach, very few rocks or mud on the bottom. We walked up and down the beach, shivering a bit. She kicked up the sand with her toes and stared at me, her face more intense than ever. "You strip big, Norm. You really have good shoulders, and those hands.... so strong."

I looked down at the sand, kicked some on her feet. She seemed to have perfectly formed feet. "Why do you wear those funny looking shoes?"

"Find they relax me. The old gag about taking a cold shower—the swim did it for us, didn't it?"

"Did what? We wanted to take a swim, and we did. Let's go back to dry ourselves."

As we headed back toward the car Wilma took my hand. We walked along like a couple of kids. She said, "You have such hard rough palms, like a laborer's. What do you do at Longson's, use your hands for a paper press?"

"I play a lot of handball," I said, knowing I must sound like an idiot.

She suddenly placed my hand on her breast. And then we were thrashing around on the sand. It was all over before I could even think about it. Lying beside her I didn't feel a thing but confused. Then I wondered if I had let her down.

I glanced at Wilma and in the pale light she seemed to be smiling up at the stars. She was still breathing heavily. She turned, smiling at me, and said, "Talk to your juvenile editor about Joel. I think a change in publishers might be good for him. You see how I have to look after Joel, wear his pants. But I don't mind."

The words bounced off my face and I looked away, wondering if she was stark crazy. Then I realized it hadn't meant a damn thing to her ... or to me. It seemed so downright childish. Why had we done it, then? Instead of being full of sand and probably catching at least a cold as I lay beside this nutty broad, I should be with my wonderful Michele. The exciting, sensuous strength to her arms around my back. How embarrassed I'd been at first, the way she would embrace for hours afterward in sleepy satisfaction. I would finally awake in the middle of the night, my arms cramped and distant, but so aware of her soft beauty. I would be proud of her and ...

Now, all I wanted was to be rid of Wilma and this dirty sand. I stood up. "Shall we wash up with a swim?"

I pulled Wilma to her feet—and she still had this kind of patronizing smile on her face. She held up her face and we kissed with absolutely no feeling. She giggled as we walked slowly into the water and swam around. Then I jogged back to the car for our clothes. I tossed her my T-shirt for a towel, while I tried to dry myself with my shorts.

I tossed the shorts into the grass. Wilma threw the T-shirt into the back of the car. Being dressed again seemed to be an act of sanity. I drove back to New York, her head resting on my shoulder. She happily didn't talk until we crossed the 59th Street Bridge when Wilma sat up to ask, "What time is it?"

"Nearly three. Would you care for something to eat?"

"No, I feel fine. Norm, when you get straightened out with your wife, come over and visit. I think we can all be wonderful friends. Joel is very amusing, usually."

"Sure."

When I parked in front of her door Wilma held up her face and we kissed lightly. She said, "Don't forget," waved and walked into the house.

My teeth were chattering. I drove to the first coffee pot and had two cups of hot coffee. I still felt completely confused. The coffee warmed me and I thought, Okay, so now I'm a man, and all that slop. I've had my affair, got it out of my system.

Oddly enough, I did feel very much a man. And I also had the same childish feeling as when Frank and I would dress in old slacks and a sweatshirt some Sunday mornings, drive to the handball courts on the lower Drive. With stupid delight we would play a sloppy one wall game until we were "suckered" into playing for two bits a man with some of the other players. We'd tighten up, win. Between us we made nearly forty grand a year, yet winning a half a dollar gave us pure delight.

When I reached the apartment I sat in a hot bath for a while, then fell into bed, wondering if the coffee would keep me up. It didn't; I slept the sleep of the just.

I awoke at nine and felt so good I winked at myself in the mirror while shaving ... like a happy jerk.

Prof. Henry Brown

As I was closing the windows of my car in front of Prof. Brown's "hotel," I saw my crumpled T-shirt on the back seat. I stared at it for a second, almost with pride. Last night had been lousy but it had done something to my malehood, childish as that may sound, to know that these sexy-looking babes were not very good at it, as I always expected. True, I was basing this pearl of wisdom only on Wilma, but she was a fair sampling, I decided.

The heat and insecticide perfume hit me as I stepped into the lobby. The clerk waved as if I was an old buddy, then slapped his face and ran around the desk, rushed me to the door. I couldn't get his rapid French, but he kept gesturing madly at the back of the little man walking up toward Broadway. When I asked if that was Prof. Brown, the clerk nodded and waved his arm even more violently.

Thanking him, I walked and ran up the street, reaching Broadway in a blaze of sweat. Brown was making for the subway and I sprinted after him. He seemed to be in his late fifties, a slightly built little man, wiry and lean, walking with a neat stride. He was wearing an old tropical suit. As I caught up with him his face surprised me. It was a thin face, the skin tight, a sort of owlish expression under a great deal of brushed gray hair. Only owls don't have broken noses and the Professor's nose had been broken sharply, probably a lot of years ago.

I touched his shoulder and he jumped as I said, "Professor Brown? I'd like to talk to you. I'm—"

"I've nothing to say." He didn't stop walking.

"But Professor, I only want to ask you ..."

"I told you, I have nothing to say!"

"I'm Norm—" I never finished the sentence for he actually dashed down the subway stairs.

Wiping my sweaty face I felt angry and bewildered. But I hadn't run a block on a hot day for any brush-off. I raced down the steps and caught him at the change window.

He said, "Will you stop annoying me? I told you I—"

"Professor, I'm Norman Connor from Matt Anthony's publishing house. I only want to ask you some questions about Matt, and I can't understand your rude—"

"I'm sorry," he said quickly. "I ... eh ... assumed you were somebody else. I was rude and I apologize."

"Perhaps it was my fault, grabbing your shoulder. I was up to your hotel yesterday. Didn't the clerk tell you?"

"He merely said a man had been asking for me."

We stood there beside the subway change booth, awkwardly silent for a moment. Then I asked, "Shall we go into a bar for beers and talk?"

"No. We can go back to my room. I have beer there."

We walked up Broadway and over to the hotel without

saying a word. The clerk waved merrily at us as we rode a dirty self-service elevator to the sixth floor. The Professor unlocked a door and took off his coat. What they had done with the "hotel" was to take an old apartment house and make each room into a kind of unit. This one must have been the maid's room in the "old days." It was just wide enough to walk by the narrow bed. There was a small window, an improvised closet, a chair, and in one corner water was running slowly on something covered by a rag in the tiny sink.

Brown grinned at me as he said, "I imagine you must be puzzled by my performance on Broadway. I thought you were an FBI man. I've been stopped and harassed by them, and local agents, so often I've found the best policy is not to talk to them at all. In fact, I'd be more at ease this second if you showed me some identification, Mr.—eh—"

"Norm Conner," I said, pulling out a thick envelope the efficient Miss Park had sent in the morning mail—a number of synopses of fall books. Brown glanced at these, as he motioned for me to take the chair. He sat on the unmade bed. When he handed them back he said, "I apologize, if you feel one is needed, Mr. Connor. Take off your coat. Beastly hot. I'm trying to rent a fan. What can I do for you?"

"I trust I'm not putting you out, Professor—"

"No point in calling me 'professor,' I haven't been one in months. You're not putting me out at all: Saturday is not a day for job hunting. Are you Matt's editor?"

"Oh, no. I'm the advertising manager of Longson and—"

"Hmmm. I'm not sure there is any real need for advertising in the world. Sets up false standards. But we won't argue the matter."

I wiped my face, wishing he'd let me finish a sentence. "Mr. Brown, I'm going around interviewing everybody connected with the case. Longson feels they would like to help Mr. Anthony. We know he needs money and we're considering reissuing one of his old books. This would hinge on advertising. I feel I need a clear picture of what happened to work up the proper ad campaign."

"Why? And take off your coat."

"The 'why' is the reputation of the firm," I said, hanging my jacket on the back of the chair. "I suppose you know the D.A. is asking for murder in the first degree?"

"I've followed the papers."

"Then you must see our position. We publish a large list, including many textbooks. We can't jeopardize our textbooks by

"... well ... bluntly by being too closely associated with a murderer—if he is one."

"Young man, do you realize the nonsense you're spouting? Another form of guilt by association. Hell, you're merely trying to sell books. In this case, some of Matt's."

"Perhaps my choice of words was wrong. The point is, everything depends upon the type of ad campaign we wage. We would like to make some money for Matt but—"

"And for Longson."

"Professor ... Mr. Brown, take it easy. I'd like to know from you exactly what happened out there, your opinion as to whether it was murder or manslaughter."

"My opinion is that Matt didn't kill his wife."

"You think it was a pure accident?"

"I don't think he killed her."

"But he's confessed it. There's no doubt about his—"

"No matter what Matt signed or said, I don't think he killed his wife. I've known Matt for a long time. For an intelligent man to kill takes a certain amount of courage. Matt's a coward. Even if I didn't know him, I could tell that from his writing, his preoccupation with violence."

"But why would he sign a confession? Do you think he was third-degreed into signing it?"

"I don't know why he signed. I don't think he was given the third-degree—he's too well known to be subjected to that. It's allegedly against the law to rubber hose a prisoner. Yet it isn't against the law to lie to him, tell him, for example, his wife has informed upon him, that he might as well talk. To believe that your wife or friends have turned you in, is that any less torture than the lash of a hose?"

I felt I was drifting in a lot of talk, tried to pull myself together. "Wait a minute, Mr. Brown; you think he's a coward. From what I know of him, his sailing the ocean, his war record, his brawls—that's hardly the portrait of a coward."

He laughed, showing old yellow teeth. "I have a theory—a man who talks a good fight is rarely a fighter. Take his bar fights—I've seen him in a few. A bar brawl is usually a one punch affair, it's quickly stopped. A man as big as Matt rarely has to fight, he merely threatens and his size wins for him. Have you ever noticed that most writers who deal in virility—which to their musclebound brains can mean only violence—are generally big men? They almost look the part of their heroes. I believe this is a form of sublimation—they are afraid to be matadors, boxers, private detectives, so they do their shooting and punching via the typewriter. It is always the coward who glorifies courage, *per se*. You'll find it in any field, the person with the shallowest talent talks the loudest."

It seemed to me Brown himself was quite preoccupied with violence. But he was turning out to be an interesting little man. I said, "That's a strange idea. I take it you don't consider Matt much of a writer?"

"Matt and I almost got into an argument about this the other day. Let me put it this way: I think Matt had the capabilities of being a good writer. But we are a literate nation, everybody can write. With a little practice one can get the required skill of putting words together. It's *what* you write, based upon your insight and understanding, that makes for good writing. Lord, I'm wandering. You want to know what happened out there. Frankly, I can be of little help. I'd spent the night with a former student of mine in Hampton. I'm looking for a job and this man.... Anyway, I was out there and ran into Matt as I was walking toward the railway station. It was the first time we'd seen each other in ... oh ... at least ten years. He insisted I return with him to his home. I imagine he wanted to show off his wealth. I had a few hours before the next train, so I drove back with him. When his wife found out about my ... eh ... past, naturally she was upset. I'm a kind of modern leper, being seen with me can mean loss of job or career. It's not improbable that someone will come knocking on *your* door after you leave here."

He patted his pockets, looking for a cigarette, then said, "I was uncomfortable in Matt's house, refused to spend the night. Matter of fact, I had an appointment in town, about a job that—all this new publicity ruined that. All told, I suppose I spent a half hour out there before Matt drove me to the train. I was to phone him this weekend ... he wanted me to spend a few days at his place, talking over 'old times.' I told him I'd let him know—my wife is in Chicago, waiting to hear if I land a job here before she joins me. Otherwise, I shall return to Chicago where she has a job. As for the rest," Brown spread his hands on his legs, "all I know is what I've read in the papers."

"You don't think he could have punched his wife, hit her harder than he meant to?"

Brown gave me his yellow smile again, "Are you married, Connor?"

I nodded, almost said, "After a fashion."

"Have you ever slapped, much less punched, your wife?"

"No."

"Neither have I ever hit my wife. Neither would Matt."

"But Francine Anthony is dead. If Matt didn't kill her, who did?"

He shrugged. "I don't know. You asked my opinion—I refuse to believe Matt killed her."

"This is a big new can of peas," I said, trying to think of something else to ask. "What sort of a woman would you say Francine Anthony was?"

"I only saw her for a few seconds. I liked her ... in a negative way she was a realist. You see, she understood exactly what it means to be publicly tagged a 'radical' these days. But, Matt, he was a lot of well-meant blustering and bragging about how he wasn't afraid to help me. Of course he was afraid. He said he'd try to get something for me at Longson's—did he?"

"I wouldn't know. And he hardly had time to do anything."

Brown nodded, "That's true." He jumped to his feet, a very agile motion for a man his age. "Like some beer?"

"Beer would be fine."

He shut off the water in the sink, removed the cloth covering two cans of beer. They foamed as he opened them. He handed me one and sat on the bed again.

The beer was pathetically warm. Brown said, "If you subscribe to the rather dubious notion that the English like their beer warm, then we are being quite British at the moment."

"It tastes fine," I lied, suddenly liking the old boy very much. "Tell me, if you don't mind, what sort of trouble are you in, Prof.—Mr. Brown?"

"Be simpler if you call me Hank. I wouldn't say I was in trouble, rather that I'm caught up in the hysteria of the times. I suppose if I had to be classified I would be considered a retired liberal. In my time I've been a number of things, ranging from a member of the I.W.W. to a New Dealer. Brooks University is so well endowed it can afford to be liberal, to a point. However, because of that it has always been a target for the reactionary ward heelers who pose as educators. I called myself a retired liberal because I've been quiet the last few years. Maybe a desire to protect my old age, without my entirely realizing it. In my time I've signed any number of petitions, some of them quite radical I suppose. However, last winter I signed a petition put out by some antivivisection group against the brutal manner in which certain slaughter houses killed livestock. Evidently it offended somebody in power and with my progressive background ... well, I found myself before a state subversive committee. Naturally I took the Fifth as a matter of principle.

So you see the situation: The University being under attack on other fronts, backed down. Thus two years before I am due to retire I find myself unemployed. It would all be a comical tempest in a tea cup if I wasn't so strapped for money."

"Any job offers?" I asked, forcing myself to finish the beer.

"I can't get anything in teaching. I had an offer to ghost a series of general mathematics textbooks, but now that's out. At my age I can't get anything but a job as a messenger and—"

"That's ridiculous."

He shook his head as he wiped beer foam from his mouth. "I may not even get that until this new publicity dies down. It pays about $45 and my wife can get a clerk job, so we'll be comfortable. In two years I'll start drawing my pension from Brooks."

"There must be something a man of your intellectual background can do. Let me speak to Bill Long, my boss, and see—"

Brown smiled as he shook his head again. "If Longson is afraid of an ad backfiring, they'll never consider me. I doubt if I would either, if the positions were reversed. Of course, I'm willing to do ghosting, but even that makes hiring me a risk." He got off the bed to drop his empty beer can in a wastebasket. "Well, Mr. Connor, have I been of any help to you, re: Matt Anthony?"

"I don't know, your picture of him is an entirely new one."

"Take pity on Matt Anthony, he's a lost soul; an intellectual four-flusher—like so many others these days. But he's no killer."

"If he's a phony, why were you two friends?"

"Friends is a meaningless word. In the last dozen years we saw each other maybe two times—for a few minutes. Oh, Matt has a lively sense of humor and ... a kind of charm. Even his blustering is interesting. Of course when I first met him, as an instructor at Brooks, he was a rather earnest young man. I even liked a few of his earlier stories. There was one about a young Mexican kid who can dropkick a milk carton, a remarkable feat—although no one can understand how remarkable except the kid who—"

"I read that. It's the boy's sole claim to being somebody. It was a terrific story."

"No, it wasn't. It was veneer stuff but a good beginning. In those days I saw a great deal of Matt. We not only taught in the same school but Matt spent much time in our house. He became, well, interested in me when he learned I'd once been a professional fighter." Brown tapped his broken nose with a long finger. "The badge of the trade."

"You really were a pro pug?"

"Really," he said, faint sarcasm in his voice. "You sound like Matt."

"Come on, now, Hank, you must admit a professor who's been a leather-pusher is unusual."

"Unusual as what? Fighting is only a job, and a bad one at that. I had about a dozen bouts when I was nineteen—which was a very long time ago. I wasn't working my way through college or anything like that. I enjoyed boxing, hit hard for a bantamweight. You've never heard of Al Nelson but he became a contender, went on to fight Lynch and Herman, the other top man. I kayoed Nelson in two rounds. I suppose I had dreams of being a champion myself. My manager was a very wise and worldly man named Danny Bond. He died a number of years ago. He was broke and I buried him. A sentimental gesture. Danny wouldn't let a boy go on if he didn't have true ability. I didn't have it—I was never hungry enough."

"What's that mean?" I got up to throw the beer can away and sat down quickly—there wasn't enough room for the two of us to move about.

"You have good shoulders—are you a fight buff, Mr. Connor?"

"Norm is the name. No, I'm a handball player, of sorts."

"Perhaps I should tell you what I mean, it might help you understand what writers like Matt never understood—that pro boxing is an act of desperation. In my case I simply wasn't desperate enough. After I knocked out Al Nelson, I fought him again some three months later. I was a bug on physical culture. Al entered the ring completely out of shape. It wasn't any secret he had done most of his conditioning in a bar. I had him groggy at the end of the first round. The next thing I knew, I was on the dressing room table and Danny was stroking my battered face with an ice bag."

"You were flattened?"

"Aha, but in the fifth round. As Danny tried to tell me, I stopped a right cross and was out on my feet for four rounds. So was Al. Yet fat and puffing Al Nelson, his blood full of whiskey, was staggering around the ring in the fifth, while with all my better conditioning, I was flat on my face. I couldn't understand that until Danny said sadly, 'He was hungrier than you, Henry, that gave him more of a fighting heart. You got some book learning, there's other things you can do beside box. But, rummy Al, even if his noggin was fogged, he knew he *had* to win to get another fight. And if he doesn't fight he just won't eat.' Odd what sticks in a mind: I never forgot those words. And I never boxed again—as a pro. That's why Matt, London, Hemingway, even old G. B. Shaw, they can't catch the true picture of the ring because they fail to understand it isn't glory that makes men fight, but hunger. You can't pretty up the brutal."

"Then you think only former pugs can write about the ring?"

"No, no. But a writer can't write about anything—that is, real writing, unless he understands his subject. Most of those who write about the ring, the bull fighters, about war, they get sidetracked in the obvious violence. They try to put their own personal desire to escape from life into their boxers, and that's false because a boxer hasn't time to think of escape, he can only worry about eating. My, I'm off on a lecture."

"Please continue. I think this is what I'm after."

"I don't mind, although literature isn't my dish. But I've been giving much thought to the Matt Anthonys. We live in a highly disillusioned world of greed and violence and we try to escape the banality of life through narcotics, TV quiz programs, abstract study, drinking, speeding, advertising (a mock bow in my direction), making money for money's sake, travel. The longing for death, for suicide, of course is the strongest drug of all. In fact, for the intellectual—and I use the word loosely—the desire for self-destruction becomes a stabilizing personal philosophy. In short, nothing matters, he believes in nothing. They feel secure only when they are involved in romantic and daring action, with the basic motive being a secret hope that this time it will end in death. At the same time they lack the nerve to flaunt conventions. A drunk speeds at 100 miles an hour, a Matt Anthony sails the ocean alone, charges with a machine gun—all conventional ways of dying."

"Wait up, you can't place them all on the same level. A drunken brawl is one thing, a war correspondent taking a gun is a form of bravery."

Brown flashed his old teeth in a quick smile. "Courage, bravery have become confused words without much meaning. Take Matt Anthony rushing the Nazis with a machine gun during the war—was that an act of heroism or cowardice? I think it was merely a subconscious attempt to take his own life. You see it in his writing, even in his hack junk, in all such writing."

"I never saw anything like that."

"Those writers who are preoccupied with courage and violence, it is but a thin veil for their own personal escape. Not even that, for even the most confused must admit there isn't any escape from death. And if one wishes to find death, it is always waiting." Brown hesitated, walked over to the small window and stared out. "Perhaps I am not making myself too clear. Look: we call hunting and bull fighting, for example, sports. We find them exciting because death is concerned. But the reality of the situation is that this is all a cowardly fallacy. With modern rifles there is little danger to the hunter. Even in the bull ring the matador first, and with great care, tires the bull, teaches him to follow his cape before he attempts the kill."

"But matadors are gored to death and hunters killed," I cut in.

"Accidents. There's an element of danger in everything—many people die from slipping in the bath tub, too. The point is this: the matador, the fighter, they at least are doing it out of sheer need, although even for them it can also become an escape from reality. But what is there to be said for the idiots they call fans, including writers, who glorify such things with hoarse yells and words? What is there to be said except that in their hearts they are cowards? They cannot fight the bull, but they dream they want to. The truth is they do not even dare fight for the bread and security that would change their drab lives. That they are even afraid to dream about it! The writer who cannot face the reality of our world, who lacks the courage to write honestly about what he sees, his out is to become intoxicated with the cruel tragedy of the bull, of the bloody boxer. It is an easy task for he can see the violence, sincerely feel sorry for the bull, without seeing the whole stupid picture. His books become bloody bar ads, and in time his own words lose all meaning. For him the 'moment of truth' is another shot of rye; sex is rape; violence becomes a way of life—and all of it is but the trimmings of his own desperate desire to die, to escape from a life that bewilders and frightens him."

"And that's Matt Anthony?"

"In my opinion, to a T. I said most writers of violence are big men. They write about the bull ring, the boxing racket, about murder, best when they reach middle age. For then they are 'safe,' in the sense they are no longer physically capable, hence do not have to carry the secret shame they felt when they were young and physically able, at least, to do the things they write about so smoothly. Now do you understand what I mean by being cowardly?"

"Yes and no. Let's say you've given me a lot to think about."

"What are you going to do about Matt's books?"

"I'm not sure yet. As I said before, it isn't so much what we're going to do as *how* to do it."

"Do you want me to show you the can?"

"What?"

"Beer makes me run," Brown said with his aged smile. "Sign of old age, your kidneys weaken. I see it doesn't bother you. I'll be right back."

I had about seventy dollars on me and when he left the room, I had a wild idea of leaving the money in his drawer, or in his bags. But I knew that would be a wrong move.

I was putting on my coat when he returned. "Prof ... Hank ... it's almost noon. Can you have lunch with me?"

"Thanks, but I'm supposed to see an old friend. Job hunting is such a bore."

"We'll get together again, soon."

"I see you don't value your job."

"I'll chance that."

He put on a jacket and we went downstairs. He was going east and I told him to get in the car. As we drove toward the park I asked, "If you think Matt is entirely innocent, do you think he signed the confession to protect somebody else?"

"I don't know. No, I don't think Matt would do that. I have no ideas on why he signed that confession. Maybe they tricked him, beat him, or it can even be some sort of 'heroic' gesture on his part. Or he may feel certain, as I do, that the trial will prove his innocence. Knowing Matt, this could all be a big practical joke. I said *could* be. I doubt it, though."

He asked me to drop him at 93rd and Lexington. As he got out and we shook hands, I told him, "Thank you for your time, Hank."

"An old saw goes, I'm wealthy with time at the moment. But I am glad we met, Norm."

"Tell me—and I hope it doesn't sound like a stupid question, but I keep thinking about your career as a fighter—if you were younger, are you desperate enough now, to use your own words, to be a good fighter?"

"Oh, my, no. I still have a number of alternatives before me. I can beg from friends, I can also turn informer and be a 'professor' again. A true fighter must be one without any choice. Good day, Norm, I have to run."

I watched him walk down Lexington Avenue. In the middle

of the block he turned, saw me watching him, and I thought he frowned. He ducked into a drugstore. I wondered if he suspected me of following him?

Driving back to the apartment—for no reason—I thought about Professor Brown. For one thing, I got the impression he was quite a radical, maybe even a fanatic. And he sure had some odd theories—including the one that Matt had nothing to do with his wife's death. If that was true, it opened up a whole batch of new ideas. Who did kill Francine Anthony? Wilma might have done it. I laughed at myself in the rearview mirror over the windshield.

That was a fantastic idea. Still, a babe like Wilma with her intense drive could do something like that. Suppose she was giving me hot air last night about not going for Matt, knocked off Francine and Matt took the fall for her?

That was absurd: I was thinking like a character in Matt's books. The big deal was—what was I going to do with myself over the weekend?

I went upstairs and made myself a mild drink, considered latching on to Frank and Liz, but let it drop. If Joel was still up on his do-it-yourself cloud, I could try Wilma again. No sex, but to be with. Only I couldn't figure if being with Wilma was any better than the heat and silence of the apartment. The damn living room looked so orderly and impersonal—as though Michele had never lived here.

The outside bell buzzed and I jumped a foot. For a frantic moment all I could think of was Brown's remark about they might come "knocking on my door." Buzzing back, I wondered just what I'd do if it was the FBI.

I stood by the open door to greet a sweaty mailman holding out a card. He said, "Special Delivery for Norman Connor. You?"

We exchanged a dime tip for the card. It was an air mail from Paris. On one side a picture of an Alsatian restaurant in Pigalle where we'd often gone for their cheesecake. On the other side Michele thanked me for the flowers.

The card was a shot in the arm. I was amazed at the speed of things. I'd only wired the flowers yesterday ... or was it the day before?

Okay. The score was: Michele was thinking of me and it was still a hell of a hot Saturday and ... I suddenly knew what I was going to do. Mix business with pleasure, as the trite but so true phrase went. By driving out to End Harbor, seeing the maid, have a look-see at Matt Anthony's house.

I could easily kill the weekend and get in some swimming too.

Miss May Fitzgerald

It was a 110-mile drive to End Harbor, the traffic was light, and I made it in less than three hours. The farther out I went the more I saw of beaches and boats and I kept thinking of a lot of things: The house Michele wanted me to buy, a sudden longing to be on the beach at Nice with her now ... and what a queer one Prof. Brown was. Suppose he was right about Matt having nothing to do with his wife's death? And we ran ads hinting at that and then the court finds him innocent ... I'd be the whitest of white-haired golden boys! That would really be playing a long shot. But all Brown had was a hunch, nothing to back it up.

I watched the fishing boats and thought about whether I could risk trying to get my broken-nosed professor a job at Longson's.... And I didn't think too much about Michele and how she loved driving in the country, swimming.

End Harbor was a fairly neat village, a couple of supermarkets and a summer theater surrounded by some very old houses and a number of expensive summer homes. I stopped a big cop in a snappy blue uniform to ask for Matt's house.

"Take the next turn, that's Bay Road. Follow it for about a mile, then you'll see his roadway on the left. Can't miss it. You another reporter?"

"No"

"Had stacks of reporters snooping out here day after it happened. The Harbor don't go for that sort of publicity."

"Did you know Mr. Anthony?"

He nodded. "A great guy. Tops. Many a time I been on Matt's boat chumming for blues. Real regular."

"Think he'll beat the rap?"

Caution raced across his big face. "Hey, thought you said you wasn't a reporter? Now, listen, he may have been a great guy but that don't cut no ice when it comes to doing my duty. Sure Matt was a real sport, for a big shot, but let me tell you he had a hell of a temper too. Maybe his wife was a nag. Okay, my wife has a sharp tongue but I don't go killing her."

It was odd, and expected, the way he was already talking about Matt in the past tense. I asked, "Do you go along with the D.A. on this first-degree murder bit?"

"Convictions are the D.A.'s wagon. What I think or don't think isn't important. Bay Road is the turn at the traffic light,

Mac."

Bay Road passed a yacht club that wasn't as big as the rowboat house in Central Park but there must have been a couple of million dollars in cruisers anchored off the dock. The road turned away from the bay and then there was this well-kept, narrow, oiled dirt lane leading into the pines. An oversized hacksaw hung from a post with Anthony in white metal letters welded to the saw part. It took me a moment to get it—all such pure corn—Matt Anthony, the hack.

The papers had mentioned a "luxurious estate." I don't know what I expected. The lane took me into a clearing and there was this squat, hideous green house built of rough cinder block. It was a two-story affair with a narrow lawn and beyond that some rough piles of dirt, as though they had forgotten to finish the lawn. The whole scene was one of not belonging, including the big yellow umbrella shading some white iron outdoor furniture. There was a garage behind the house—this too looked unfinished—and a path that went into a line of fairly tall pine trees. Although I could smell the salt in the air, there wasn't any sight of the bay. The walk from the driveway to the house was lined with clam shells. I rang the polished brass ship's bell on the door and waited. When I rang again I heard a dog whine. Finally a woman's voice with a faint English accent announced, "I am not seeing any more newspapermen. So you can take your leave."

She seemed to be pressed against the other side of the door. I asked, "Are you Miss May Fitzgerald?"

"Indeed I be. But I will not see any—"

"My name is Norman Connor. I'm from Mr. Anthony's publishers, Longson's."

The door opened and I saw a dark-skinned young Negro woman in dungarees and a thin white turtle neck sweater. She was stooped over, holding on to something behind the door. Although her jaw was a bit too heavy, she was very pretty; hair piled high in a braid, her figure tall and slim. A large green jade pin was fastened on her sweater, between the sharp outlines of small breasts, and her full lips were painted a faint pink. She had a mild, spicy perfume that didn't distract from the exotic—yet wholesome—picture. I doubted if she was twenty-one. I said, "I'd appreciate it if you can spare me a few minutes, Miss Fitzgerald. I'd like to talk to you."

"Talk to me? How do I know you're not a blooming reporter?"

Between her and Brown this was identify-yourself-week. I pulled out the office letters, let her see my name on the envelopes. She nodded as she said, "Excuse me. But I have been bothered with so many darn newsmen. Are you afraid of dogs?"

"I don't think so."

"Clichy will jump at you, but only in play." She straightened up. She must have been holding the dog behind the door, for suddenly this smartly clipped, large black French poodle came at me.

I suppose I held my hands up before my face. The dog had other aims: he landed on my left leg, got a good grip, and began jumping up and down like a puppet lover. I gave May an embarrassed smile as the damn dog worked away.

Her dark face sad, she said, "Don't blame the poor beast. Mr. Anthony taught him this disgusting habit. Matt thought it was quite a joke. That's enough, Clichy." She pulled the poodle by his jeweled pink collar off my leg. I glanced down at my pants, expecting to see a spot or something. "Do come in, please, Mr. Connor."

She showed me into a large living room filled with colorful modern bamboo furniture. It was all rather shockingly gaudy; the rough cinderblock walls painted a terrible red. I sat on a yellow chair with bright red cushions. May let go of the poodle who stretched out on the polished floor, still panting, watching my leg with hot little eyes. As she sat on a couch, curling slim legs under her cut basketball-bottom, I glanced around the room. It was expensive, with a number of oils on the walls like in a gallery. The rear wall was completely glass and looked out on a wide veranda that seemed to circle the back of the house. I told her about Longson reissuing one of Matt's books and the rest of my pitch.

May lit a cigarette. I shook my head, got my pipe working. "Yes, he needs money," she said, with that odd slight clipped accent. On what wild adventure in the West Indies had Matt found her? "Matter of fact, I don't know what to do here. Whether I should close the house or not. There are daily bills, too, of course."

"Hasn't his lawyer been in touch with you?"

"No one has been to see me except the bloody newspaper people. Tramped all over the place without as much as a by-your-leave. And I can only stay here a few more weeks. I'm returning to college in September. There's back wages due me, too."

"I plan to see Mr. Anthony's lawyer in a day or so. I'll have him contact you. I'd like some general background information. Did you meet Mr. Anthony in the West Indies?"

Her face registered astonishment. "Oh no. An agency sent me out here from New York. You can save money on a sleep-in job. Oh, I see—my accent." She smiled. "I was born in Atlantic City but did most of my growing up with my grandmother down in Trinidad."

"Miss Fitzgerald, I want you to talk freely, and in strict confidence, so I'll be able to get the background material I need."

"I'm one for talking. What is it you wish to know?"

"I don't know myself, exactly. Let's take the day of Mrs. Anthony's death. What happened—from the start of the day?"

"Well, the Hunters had been down for about a week. Always a lot of guests here and a lot of work for me. Mrs. Anthony was a penny-pincher, really should have at least two in help here. Let me see, that day. After breakfast they all went swimming. Of course breakfast wasn't until ten. The Hunters and Francine stayed around the house, reading and drinking. They were hungover from the night before. Mr. Anthony drove off without saying where he was going. Francine was worried he'd gone to get a drink. His heart isn't strong, and the doctor had ordered him off liquor and exercise. I had finished the dishes and was—"

"Was Matt drinking the night before? You said they were all hungover?"

"They had been doing a lot of talking and nibbling but Matt had stayed with a mild concoction he liked, cider and a dash of vermouth; simply vile. I had finished the breakfast dishes and was cleaning up downstairs. As I said, Francine was certain Matt had dashed off for a toot and she was upset. Around noon Mr. Anthony returned with this friend he'd met in Hampton, a little old man with a strange face, Prof. Brown. Nobody wanted lunch so I went upstairs to make the beds. In a little while I saw Mr. Anthony drive off with this Professor, then return in about half an hour. I suppose he took him to the railroad station. I went on with my work. About three-thirty I was in the kitchen starting supper—you can never rest around here but to give Fran her due, the pay is very good. Well, Matt rang and they were out on the lawn, getting the sun. He told me to tell Mrs. Anthony to come in, that they were waiting to go swimming. Soon as I reached the dock, and saw her out there hanging over the side of the boat, I screamed. It was an awful sight. They all came on the run. Matt swam out and started to pull up anchor, but he left the boat and her out there, told me to phone the police. He said she'd been in an accident, not to touch things."

"Did he say Mrs.... Francine was dead?"

The maid stared at me over a perfect smoke ring. "You ask questions like a detective, Mr. Connor."

"An amateur one. How could he be positive she was dead?"

"My goodness, we all were. A person only had to glance at her to know she was dead. Seemed like I had hardly put the phone down when the End Harbor police were here. Then a doctor drove up. They had us stay off the beach while they pulled the boat in. They said Fran had stood up to cast when her shoe lace caught on the duckboards, causing her to fall. She had hit her temple on the side of the boat. The doctor tested to see if there was water in her lungs: did some other things. After they asked us many questions, they took Fran's body into the Harbor with them. The Hunters started to get drunk. They were very upset."

"Wasn't Matt?"

She nodded. "He cried a little—that was being upset for him."

"Miss Fitzgerald, were the Anthonys happy?"

"I think yes, but I never understood their relationship. It was like ... they were always testing each other, proving something. Francine was one of these very efficient women, she reminded me of an airline hostess. Matt, he—"

"She reminded you of what?"

I got a smile through another smoke ring. She was proud of those rings. "Hostess on an airplane. You know, nothing upsets them, they're always able to manage. That was Mrs. Anthony. Now, Matt, he was the opposite, always seemed to be playing, showing off. He'd think nothing of bringing five or six strangers he'd met fishing back for dinner, or going to the store for a newspaper and coming back with a new boat or an outboard. I know he makes big money but, believe you me, he can spend it faster than he makes it. Much faster. Sometimes our liquor bill was five or six hundred dollars a month. Well, let me finish with that dreadful day. About six, after the police had left, and the Hunters were watching TV and drinking steadily, Matt went to his den to work. I'll have to say this for him, no matter how many guests we had or what was going on, he'd take off for his room every day, including Sundays, and dictate for a few hours. Once or twice I've seen him go to work pretty drunk, but he never missed a day. Once a week he would mail the recording tape to a secretary in New York. She'd type it up and when he got it back, he'd go over the pages again, mail it back for a final typing."

"And Mr. Anthony worked the same day his wife died?"

"I told you, he worked every day, even Sundays. I think it relaxed him. I've seen him come in from tuna fishing, dirty and tired, all smelly. While everybody else was washing up or having cocktails, he'd be locked in his room, working. Still, it's only an hour or two a day, which is a sweet work day, and think of the money he was making."

"Have you read his books?"

"One—in manuscript form. He wanted my opinion—you know, as an average person. The book was ... entertaining. It's amazing how many odd little things he knows about. Of course, he's constantly reading up on crimes to get ideas. But he also has an entire row of books devoted to locks, technical books on various aspects of the body, poisons, guns, and a slew of—" She coughed and crushed her cigarette. "I've been smoking too much. And talking too much is giving me a frog. I'm going for beer—can you use one?"

I said yes. When she jumped to her feet—a boyish movement—and went into the kitchen, the poodle whined. I walked over to study the paintings. There was a seascape that could have been an original Winslow Homer, a print of Bellows' famous fight scene, a bamboo-framed Gauguin I'd never seen before, a confusion of vivid colors which might be a Miro, and several crude nudes in oil—the work of an amateur.

The crazy poodle suddenly charged across the room and hugged my leg. When I reached for his collar he growled, so I had to stand there while he jumped up and down on his shaved paws, looking for all the world like a tiny man in baggy pants. I called out, "Miss Fitzgerald, lover-poodle is at work again. Are you certain he won't bite?"

She came in with two simply huge glasses of frothy black beer and a plate of cheese on a plastic tray. Putting the tray down, she grabbed the dog, shook him. "Now stop it, you bloody pest. Here." She threw a hunk of cheese up in the air. The dog caught it expertly, sat around waiting for more. "That's all you get, Clichy."

"How do you spell the mutt's name?" I asked, taking a beer. It was thick as syrup and very rich tasting.

"C-l-i-c-h-y. After the street in Paris where they purchased him."

I was a bit relieved, for some reason, Matt hadn't been obvious and named him Cliché, "Very unusual beer. Imported?"

"From Austria. I love it. I'm hoping it will add a few pounds on me. But it hasn't to date, and I've been really hitting it. I figure I might as well use it up; don't know what's going to happen to the house and no sense in leaving such fine food around. Try the cheese, it's from Norway."

I took a piece and sat down. It tasted like pure smoke. The poodle came over, his mind on food this time, and I tossed the rest of the cheese to him.

Miss Fitzgerald asked, "Have I been helpful, Mr. Connor?"

"What happened after Matt went to his den?"

"Oh my, thought I'd finished with that dreadful day. Now where was I? I was making supper when the bell rang. I opened the door and there was a local cop with a detective from Riverside—that's the county seat. Had a Polish name I still can't even say. Looked like a detective too, you know, burly and ... well ... evil looking. I mean, a man without any feelings. I called Matt and they went into the den and I went back to my work. I kept waiting for Matt to tell me to serve supper and then the Hunters, I think it was Mrs. Hunter, she's a very nice person, she came in crying something awful and said Matt had confessed he had killed Fran. I couldn't believe it. I saw him as this detective was taking him away. Matt looked dazed, kind of sickly. The police came and questioned us all over again. Then, in the middle of the night, mind you, reporters started coming. The Hunters left about midnight. No trains then, I don't know how they got back to New York."

"Did you hear Matt threaten his wife?"

"No. Like I told the police, I was upstairs when all that happened."

"Do you think Matt murdered his wife?"

She shrugged and ate another piece of cheese. "Murder is a strong word. I think he might have lost his temper and hit Fran. As he confessed. I know they had an argument before over his wanting to skin-dive. Fran said it would be bad for his heart. Of course, they argued all the time, but I never saw him strike her, or even slap her. I think all this arguing was a form of ... well, kind of fun for them. They enjoyed it."

I took another sip of the thick beer. "Argued about what?"

"Anything. It was part of their testing each other. I've read someplace there's a thin line between hate and love—they were on that line most of the time. Well, like this: Matt was always putting on this big sexy act. I've seen him—" She hesitated, stared at me.

I stared back at her. "What's the matter?"

"Well, I'm a little confused. You see I never talked—I suppose dirty is the word, until I started working here. I know it's childish to call it dirty, and while I want to sound worldly and all that, if I say what I want ... don't get the wrong impression of me. That's not exactly what I mean but ..."

I smiled at her. "Please tell me—"

"Don't smile! You make me feel like a child."

"Miss Fitzgerald, talk anyway you wish. I promise not to get any wrong impressions."

"Then I shall talk boldly—as I really want to. What I mean, about the Anthonys, Matt's big act ... I've seen Fran bending over, you know, doing something, and he would come up and slip his hand under her skirt, pinch her behind. When she'd object Matt would say, 'You want me to find another can to play with? Be easy enough.' Shocked me at first, but I got used to them acting like blasted children. I shouldn't even call it sexy, he did it merely to annoy her. Like once I heard him get Fran hysterical during a bridge game by insisting she was frigid. Of course, she got back at him."

"How?"

"Matt has a great sense of humor. He was always telling dirty jokes ... some of them very funny. But she would tell him all he could do was joke about it. Her favorite gag was that Matt had joined the ... eh ... once-a-month-club. I've heard her say this in front of company. She would also goad him about being a show-off or make fun of his writing. Oh, Fran had a sharp tongue. So has Matt."

I said, "A charming couple."

"But I never thought they meant any of this. In their own way, they enjoyed baiting each other, and they were happy. Of course, it wouldn't be my idea of a happy marriage, but for them ... it worked. They enjoyed fishing together and he was proud of the way Fran could handle a boat. If she was after him for spending too much money, a good deal of what he spent was on her. Early in June he had to go to New York to see his agent. Fran gave him a list of things for the house: screen for the fire place, brandy glasses, lawn seed—things like that. Buy them cheaper in New York than out here. I remember she figured they would save eleven dollars. When he returned he had brought the things she wanted, along with a stunning mink stole. Matt said one of the department stores had been running a 'mink sale.' Fran bawled him out, even returned the mink ... still, it was a nice gesture on Matt's part. Despite his hard talk he wasn't a tough man. Maybe you'd best call him an overgrown child."

"Did he ever make a pass at you?"

"Why do you ask that?" She didn't sound angry or coy.

"Part of the background picture I'm trying to get of Matt Anthony," I said, and wondered if it was true or was I enjoying myself as a gossip?

"I guess I'm about the only female out here he didn't try to make. He thinks of himself as a great lover, but I believe that's an act with him. He never asked me because, I suppose, I don't count, being colored."

I had a mouthful of beer and almost choked as I asked, "Don't tell me Matt was prejudiced?"

"I don't want you to get the wrong impression," she said, lighting another cigarette. "I mean, I was never interested in Matt—you know, as a man. As for prejudice, it was the kind he didn't realize he had. Let's say he was patronizing—which in the long run is the same bloody thing. I told you at the start, or meant to, that I don't understand Matt Anthony. He would do funny things. Sometimes on a rainy day he would drive me to town to shop. I guess he was bored hanging around the house. We might go to Hampton, Riverside—wherever he felt like driving. He would always make a point of stopping at some swank bar or café, and we'd go in for lunch or a drink. Naturally, we would cause plenty of open mouths and stares. If for no other reason because we might be wearing shorts, or he'd be sporting a dirty sweat shirt. There never was any incident, but he'd walk in as if ready to slug anybody who said a word. That was his way of testing civil rights, I suppose. Or his insisting I call him Matt."

"That doesn't make him prejudiced."

"He means well, but you see he never asked me if *I wanted* to go into those places. He acted as if I was a pet dog he was showing off. In fact, he never asked if I wanted lunch, he simply took me into a café. Around the house, he and Fran did things in front of me because to them I wasn't a person, merely something in the kitchen. My God, he was always talking race relations to me and all that, but remember I was his *maid*." She was silent for a moment, blowing smoke rings. Then she smiled, added, "I don't want to sound too hard on him, I suppose in his own way he was trying to ... well, help."

I couldn't think of anything else to ask. I stood up, asked, "May I see the dock?"

"Sure."

I followed her out on the veranda. She pointed to a worn path that entered the pine trees. "Follow that. It isn't far. I don't like to leave the house—some of those blasted reporters might break in. Be careful in the woods, there's a lot of rocks. Matt was always going to take them up but never got around to it."

Glancing through the glass wall of the living room I pointed to the poodle with his front paws up on the table, eating the rest of the cheese.

May Fitzgerald sighed. "He's a sly thief. I hope the cheese doesn't give him the runs, the pest."

I said I'd be back soon and followed the path. The "woods" weren't more than a dozen yards thick and in the late afternoon sun, dark and delightfully cool. Stepping out of the trees I found myself on a white sandy beach with a magnificent view. This was a corner of the bay, and most of it except the beach, densely wooded. I saw POSTED signs all around the bend in the bay. If all the land was Matt's, it was like owning a private ocean, although of course one side opened upon the rest of the bay, or maybe it was the Sound. This was indeed real luxury.

A plain, square, white, wooden house, decorated with old anchors and fishing nets was at the beach end of a neat dock. Tied to the other end of the dock was this sleek, powerful black and red fishing boat with tall outriggers, swivel chairs and a day cabin. It looked about thirty feet long and like a dream. But the boat that attracted my attention was a plain rowboat sitting high on the beach, its canvas covered outboard raised. I walked across the sand to stare at the small dent on one side, where Francine had broken her head. I don't know what I expected, it wasn't much of a dent. But I was surprised the police had left the boat here.

Then I sat on the dock and smoked my pipe, staring at the clear water, the tiny waves as the tide came in. The place was so completely private I was tempted to take a nude swim. If Matt ever had to sell this, Frank Kuhn would be mad about it—clamming, fishing, swimming, your boat and dock, all in your own backyard. Although Frank wouldn't have this kind of money, or would he? At least $50,000. If I had that type of dough I'd buy it—it was a ghoulish thought.

Finishing my pipe, I looked into the bathing house. There was a shower, dressing stalls, lockers, and a small bar and kitchen. The walls were covered with garish paintings, originals of Matt's many book jackets, although *The Last Supper* painting wasn't among them. I saw towels and trunks hanging in an open locker. I quickly stripped and took a fast swim. It was quite out of this world, the bottom smooth and sandy, the water very salty and cool.

Toweling myself dry, I wondered who had last worn these trunks. Too small to be Matt's. I dressed and started back toward the house, feeling very good. I nearly sprawled on my face in the pines when I stumbled over a damn rock. My pipe flew out of my hand and it took me a lot of minutes to find it in the dark shade, with scores of little bugs clouding about me. I felt dirty and sweaty all over again.

I found May on the veranda, working on another glass of beer and reading some sort of textbook. I told her I'd taken a swim, asked about the land surrounding the bay: It all belonged to Matt, as I thought. She also told me the police had spent hours photographing and examining the rowboat. I thanked her for her time and Matt's beer. The mutt was stretching out on the floor, watching me with bored eyes, wagging his stubby tail slightly. May walked me to my car and as I drove off she called out, "Mr. Connor, don't forget, when you see Mr. Anthony's lawyer, ask what I'm supposed to do ... about the, house and money."

I waved, said I wouldn't forget. It was a few minutes before six as I headed for Montauk. In the rearview mirror I saw my T-shirt where I'd flung it on the back seat, or had Wilma tossed it there? I winked at it like a jerk and finally stopped the car, was about to throw it away, then in a moment of thrift, I stuffed it into the glove compartment. I took a room at a motel high over the ocean, drove on to have a good lobster supper, and like a hick, mailed cards to Frank and Liz, and one to Bill Long.

The lobster was a small mistake. Michele was crazy for lobster, and for a dreadful moment I wondered what the hell I was doing way out here by myself. About this time on Saturday night I'd be helping her with the dishes. Then we'd listen to the news on TV and try to decide if we should stay home, or maybe see a foreign movie—with Michele whispering the fine points the English titles missed—or we might be playing bridge, or sitting around with some UN friends and arguing.

But that was only a lonely moment. The rest of the meal was okay. I still had a little of that now-I'm-a-man feeling left from being with Wilma; and Michele's card made me feel it was just a temporary split—as Wilma said, she ran home to mama ... who unfortunately happened to be thousands of miles away. As I smoked my pipe I even felt a bit smug. l had a clear idea for the ads buzzing in the back of my head. If I carried it off, with any luck in a year or three I could afford to give Michele (and myself) a place like Matt's.

After driving around aimlessly I returned to the motel,

showered and stretched out on the bed. I felt quite nicely tired, sort of a good-day's-work-well-done stuff. I read through the book condensations Miss Park had sent me. Each synopsis ran about two pages. I like to play a game with them, stopping about half way through and trying to figure out the ending, see if I can outsmart the writer. Since in the synopsis form the plot is bare, it isn't too hard a game and very good for my ego.

I read through the batch, batting about .500 on the endings, made notes for possible ad ideas to send on to Marty Kelly. Turning off the light I fell into a light, lazy sleep. And suddenly I was sitting up wide awake, fear tightening and turning my stomach. I had this hunch ... and even though I kept telling myself it was silly, illogical, it was such a hard, strong hunch I *knew* it had to come true. I don't know whether I had a dream, or what, but it seemed as if I'd looked at a synopsis of my immediate life and had guessed the ending ... I'd impregnated Wilma Hunter! And that would be an ending, all right!

I sat on the edge of the bed, sweating in the cool night, positive it would turn out that way, *that it had to*. Perhaps it was a secret sense of guilt, but whatever the reason, I *simply* knew it would work out like this: I hadn't taken any precautions with Wilma. Michele and I had split about wanting a kid—how better could fate goose me than by having Wilma pregnant? And what would I do?

Would she agree to an abortion? Or would she raise hell and insist upon having the baby? Or want me to marry her? Wilma didn't look like the kind you could argue with—about anything. How could I ever possibly explain it to Michele? What was there to say? Some men cat around every night and never get caught. Wasn't it almost a cliché that once-in-a-lifetimers make that one time count? The new poker player always wins the first jackpot.

I walked the room, telling myself I was being stupid. I tried to be rational, even calm. I told myself I was believing in "fate" and dreams and hunches like an illiterate. Why, the odds were 100 to 1 against it, maybe greater. For all I knew, perhaps Wilma couldn't have children. Or I couldn't. My God, I'd be hanging around Gypsy tea rooms next.

I tried to be sensible, logical. But no matter what I told myself there wasn't any doubt in my whirling mind: Under everything I had this terribly *definite* feeling it *had* happened—that I had oh so damn correctly guessed another ending. I couldn't shake the feeling of doom, and after a while I didn't even try any longer.

It had to be so.

Detective Walter Kolcicki

I spent a restless night, having nightmares when I did sleep. In the morning I was up early, bought swim trunks and went out to The Hither Hills State Park beach. It was a clear warm day and the beach was fairly crowded with campers and soldiers, but nothing like the way Jones Beach gets crowded.

I stayed on the beach all day, full of crazy thoughts. I could deny the kid was mine. I considered running away, going to Michele in Paris and staying there—and God knows how we'd eat. Between times I told myself I was acting like an ass, there wasn't any kid. Yet when I went in for a swim I wondered if drowning was painful.

Hell, for all I knew Wilma would be glad to see a doctor. Or maybe she wanted the kid, pass it off as Joel's. But it was my kid and I wasn't sure I wanted that. I wasn't sure of a damn thing, except I was in a mess. The thought of losing Michele, of being married to Wilma—if it ever came to that—was sickening. I argued and pleaded with myself like a loon, but I couldn't shake this hunch I *had* made Wilma pregnant. I even had such silly ideas that if I could make big money I could keep Wilma and the kid on a back street basis ... although being a big apple on Madison Avenue seemed the very least of my ambitions now.

The horrible thing was, how could I ever possibly explain this to Michele? Oh, there was the SOP explanation: you left me and I got drunk and took a romp in the hay. But that was slop. If I told her the truth, that I'd been happy with her, delightfully happy in bed with her, but for some unknown reason I'd wanted an affair ... it would sound like I was ready for the couch. Maybe I was.

But all that didn't change the one factor banging at my skull like a club: What was I going to do about the kid? It would be *my* kid and I couldn't give him the short end—I was even sure it would be a him. Nor could I bear to think of losing Michele.

By noon I had a splitting headache and drove over to a bar, had a couple of hardboiled eggs and a few hookers for lunch. I returned to the beach and stretched out on the hot sand. I dozed off for an hour and awoke feeling deathly sick and very drunk. I walked way down the beach where a few people were surf casting, gave up and felt a little better. A swim helped my head and I watched a man catch a couple of sea robins and feel pretty excited about it.

Now all I could think of was how happy and simple life had been a few days ago, before Michele and I had our fight. One thing I knew I was going to do in the morning—buy that damn house in Connecticut, send her the deed. I decided no matter what came up, I wasn't going to lose Michele—if I could help it.

In the middle of the afternoon I went back to the motel, feeling completely knocked out. I climbed into bed and slept until six in the morning. A cold shower and a big breakfast made me feel pretty good. I was now on a Fate kick: What was going to happen was going to happen and there wasn't a thing for me to do but wait and see how the cake baked or if there was one in the oven.

It was the start of another hot day. I washed the car and took a swim. At nine I drove to Riverside, bought a fresh shirt and underwear, tried to see the District Attorney. After being politely bucked from one busy and/or bored official to another—and getting the impression Riverside was looking forward to the Matt Anthony trial as if it were the county fair, both with a sense of excitement and an eye on the business the crowds would bring—I was finally told A) the D.A. wasn't in Riverside that day, and, B) even if he was, he couldn't see reporters or discuss the trial. I explained once or twice about not being a reporter, but the moment I said I was from a publishing house ... evidently I had to be a reporter.

However, I had no trouble seeing Detective Walter Kolcicki, an experience which took my mind off my own troubles. He was a caricature of a detective, about forty-five, everything about him short and tubby. His round, emotionless pig face held hard, beady eyes, and his 250 or more pounds didn't add up to a few inches over five feet. A sweat stained brown polo shirt showed off fat arms, clusters of long hair on a barrel chest. The bull neck sat on ridges of thick skin and his teats would have made a stripper proud. There was sparse, dirty-gray hair on a perfectly round skull highly salted with dandruff. He was the comic picture of a lump. Sitting behind his desk, chewing on a cold cigar stub, I wasn't sure if he'd stood up or not.

Kolcicki wasn't used to talking but it was obvious he had recently acquired a sort of pat glibness. I merely said I was from Longson, publishers, didn't bother to explain I wasn't a reporter.

He was proud and pleased with himself as he assured me in a dull, flat voice the case would be the biggest thing to hit

Riverside. When I asked how he had obtained Matt's confession, he worked the cigar around his fat mouth for a moment until I thought he might spit in my face. He asked coldly, "Mister, you saying I third degreed him?"

"No." Matt Anthony could have torn this tub of lard apart with one hand. "What I mean is, the D.A. is asking for murder, yet Mr. Anthony's confession could easily be called manslaughter. I want your views on that."

"Hell, mister," Kolcicki grunted, "my job is to make an investigation, to interrogate a guy. I get the facts. The D.A. uses them the way he wants. Hardly expect a guy to sign himself into the chair. Trouble with reporters is you don't see being a dick is a business, operated about the same as you'd run a grocery store. Of course, some lousy bastards like Anthony think they can get away with anything because they're loaded. Maybe they can with some cops, but with me it's business."

"You mean he offered to bribe you?"

"Naw. I never gave him a chance to. I pinned him one-two-three. Bastards like him operate like amateurs, think they can fool a professional investigator."

"What does that mean?" He mouthed "investigator" as if it was a piece of cake he was tasting.

All that fat settled back in the chair. "What I was telling you about it being a business. The guy that's been doing it for years knows the ropes; the newcomer don't know his ass from his elbow. See, I been a cop for a lot of years, most of them a big city cop. Sonofabitch like Anthony, all this police crap he's been writing, guess he figured himself for a sharp cop. But it boils down to being a business. Like this: you got a store and the store across the street runs a sale on coffee. Well, what the hell, it's like a rule, then you got to run a sale, too. Ain't no doubt about it. They got rules in my business, too. When a guy threatens to kill somebody, in this case his wife, and a couple hours later she's dead—and I don't care if they say a friggin' flying saucer dropped out of the sky on her—I know damn well this guy killed his wife! That's what I told Anthony, told him this wasn't no crappy book, that I knew he'd done it and was there to bag 'im. Maybe in detective stories it ain't so, but in this *business* 99% of the time a suspect is guilty. Or he wouldn't be a suspect. Follow me?"

I had a time keeping a straight face. "The law states a man is innocent until proven ...?" I began.

"The law my ass," Kolcicki cut in flatly. "I know the law. It's my job to enforce it. Look, if a car is stolen and then I come upon you sitting in it, or even leaning against it—that's enough for me. I bag you. Sure, this big bastard Anthony started giving me the bunko about his wife having an accident, and all that. You know all I said?"

I shook my head.

"Every time he tried giving me the sauce I just said, 'Bull.' That's all, one word. It done the trick."

He waited for me to say anything. I didn't say a word. Kolcicki suddenly didn't seem comical, just as a moron behind a wheel or a gun ceases to be funny. If anything, he somehow seemed evil.

"That works when you're interrogating certain kind of jokers. He got all flustered after I told him that a couple times, kept changing his story. Then he didn't talk and I says, 'Anthony, you're a big writer, why don't you stop handing me this baby shit?' So he looks kind of sick for a second, then he says, 'I suppose you're right. Yes, I'll tell you how it really happened.' So I listened and since he was sitting in front of a typewriter, I told him to say it again and I typed it up. He read it and signed it. Easy, huh?"

"Sounds that way."

"That's from years of knowing my business."

"Then you believe he hit his wife and she fell against the side of the boat ... as he confessed?"

"Of course, I believe it. I just told you how he confessed. What's there not to believe?"

I wanted to ask if he thought Matt was guilty but it would have sounded silly. Perhaps he read my mind, for he sucked on the cigar for a long second, said, "Mister, he was arrested, wasn't he? That means he's guilty. Sure, he's still got to stand trial. But they'll find him guilty. Once a bastard gets himself bagged, he's sure as hell guilty."

I wondered if everybody who was arrested became a bastard in Kolcicki's tiny mind. I stood up. "Thanks for your time."

"Think nothing of it, part of my job. Mister, I can tell my saying he's guilty if he's arrested didn't set with you. Maybe you think I'm a hick cop only out to get a conviction. Part of that is right, I am out to get a conviction. But I don't collar nobody unless I'm sure. Why I say, once he's bagged, he's guilty. I ain't perfect, maybe I make a mistake now and then, but in this business when you find 99% of suspects turn out guilty, you're batting pretty goddamn good. And it ain't only me. Take your big corporations, they think the same way."

My face must have been an absolute blank. He gave me a

thick grin as he added, "That's a fact. You ever see an employment questionnaire for a big company?"

"Not recently."

"Look one over. Know what they ask? *Was you ever arrested?* Get it? They don't ask if you were found guilty or innocent, *just* if you were ever collared. Well, a big company knows all the business rules, of course, and they use the same rule I do—because it is a rule—if you're arrested you're guilty. Any business goes by rules. Like, you can be pretty damn certain the last person to see the victim killed 'im. I'm not kidding, if I threatened to kill you and tonight you was found dead, I'd arrest myself. Get what I mean? If you write me up, don't make me out no friggin' wonder man, but just an investigator who knows his business, goes by the rules. Don't worry, that confession will stand up in court. Must have been fifty photographers taking his picture the same night I brought him in—and not a mark on the smart bastard, either. He just saw I was on to him." He raised his arms to his head and yawned—even his teeth were stubby.

"Is there any chance of my seeing Anthony?"

"How long you been a reporter, bud? Ought to know you can't see no prisoner without a special okay."

I thanked him again and walked out—fast. I headed for New York and it took a long time for the sun to warm me up.

Joel Hunter

I was back in New York before one, feeling absolutely wretched. I still had no idea as to what I should do about Wilma, yet I had the feeling I should be doing *something*. I dropped into the apartment to change my suit and shave. The apartment gave me an acute guilt feeling, and I found myself doing such dopey things as suddenly trying to decide where I'd put the crib.

I made a few calls. Miss Park said she had received my card and how did I like Montauk? There wasn't anything happening at the office. Frank had returned the galley proofs that morning. Marty Kelly asked me to phone. I told Miss Park I'd be in touch and phoned Kelly, who wanted me to okay space in a couple of literary quarterlies for one of our books. Marty looked like a woman chaser, and I was tempted to ask him for the name of a doctor but didn't.

Phoning the school, I talked to this Edith, the teacher who

had the house, and told her I wanted to buy it. "Have you been up to see it?"

"No, but ... you know Michele had to go to Paris, her folks are ill, and I want to give it to her as a surprise when she returns."

"If you want to drive up, I can get the keys over to you and—"

"Michele saw it. And I'm pretty busy."

"As you wish. I think it's a good house. I don't know about deeds and titles and the rest. Suppose I phone my lawyer and have him call you to settle the details?"

"That will be fine. I'll be in the office tomorrow. Let me send you a check as a binder."

"Oh, that won't be necessary, Mr. Connor. It's yours." After I hung up I mixed some tobacco and finally told myself to stop stalling: I phoned Wilma. A deep man's voice answered, said she was out. "This is Joel Hunter. Who's calling?"

"Norman Connor. I merely wanted to—"

"Say now, this is something. I phoned your office less than an hour ago, and they said you were out of town. I'm ready to talk to you, Mr. Connor."

The last person I wanted to talk with was Joel Hunter, but I had to ask, "When are you free?"

"My hours are my own. Name the time."

"Well ... eh ... how about now?"

"Splendid."

"I'll be over in a half hour." I felt lousy: facing the cuckolded husband, or whatever the expression—I had never had cause to use it before. Still, I did want to see what Joel was like. Wilma might be in later and ... what the devil would I say to her?

As I left the house I phoned Jackson Clair. His secretary told me I could see him at four. The whole damn ad campaign seemed so unimportant now.

I don't know what I expected but Joel Hunter didn't fill the picture. He opened the door wearing narrow, black dungarees, brushed-ivory loafers and a deep blue Italian pullover. His white hair was crew-cut so short it seemed etched on his dome. He wore thick, black-framed glasses and his face was a furious pink, but his eyes said he wasn't an albino. Hunter was built like an actor; small, narrow shoulders, his face and head the largest part of him. He reminded me of the young men taking over the midtown bars on Second and Third avenues: it takes one a little time to decide if they are fags or not—if *that* matters.

We shook hands hard and for some reason I felt relieved upon seeing him. Whatever Wilma and I decided to do, well, we wouldn't have to bother consulting Joel.

I followed him down the narrow hall of an old-fashioned apartment with all the small rooms opening on the hallway. The walls had a few colorful travel posters and bullfight signs on them. I passed one room painted an unbelievable deep purple, had a fast glimpse of an old-fashioned stuffed couch and a small hi-fi on a table. The living room had the proper foam rubber, wrought-iron furniture, an interesting wall rug and several masks on the walls. As we sat down he asked if I wanted a shot and I said it was too early, which seemed to amuse Joel. He certainly had a deep voice for such a slight frame. I wanted to get the conversation around to Wilma, not sure what I'd ask, but felt it would be a jerky thing to do.

He smiled, said, "Sorry I missed you the other day. I suppose Wilma has told you about my little journeys out of time."

"I think she mentioned it."

"It makes her furious because it's the sort of thing one has to do alone. Really, it's quite good for me. You'd be astonished at the mood, the heady drunk, one can get into by listening all day to Peggy Lee or Billie. How lost you get in Artie Shaw, the Duke ... the lift it can give you. After a day or two you come out completely refreshed."

"Sounds interesting," I said, thinking I could sure use something like that myself.

"Now, Norman—you don't mind my calling you that? I think last names are ridiculous."

"I don't mind, Joel."

"Of course, Wilma has told me what you want. I'd like to help Matt but I must warn you, I can't get any more involved than I am. You know about such things, will this publicity hurt my books?"

"I don't see how."

"Well, a killing and a radical professor aren't the best notices for a writer of juveniles."

"I imagine your name will be lost in the shuffle. After all, you were only a guest."

"I hope to God you're right. I only write these lousy kid books to get some security and now this has to come along. It upset me frightfully. But you're not here to talk about my troubles. Wilma said you want to get the background of the thing. Fire away."

For some reason Joel, the awful apartment, even hearing

Wilma's name, depressed the hell out of me. I kept wondering how I'd ever got mixed up in all this.

"Well, Norman?"

"Sorry, I've been driving all morning—I was out to Riverside—and I'm a little pooped. Well ... eh ... just tell me anything you want about Matt. How long have you known Matt and Francine?"

"Four or five years. Poor Fran, I still expect to wake up and be happy that it's only a nightmare, that it isn't real."

"Do you think he murdered her?"

Joel gave me a slightly pop-eyed stare. "Lord, man, he's confessed it! Oh, oh, you mean whether it's murder or manslaughter. Wilma said you asked her that, too. I'll tell you this, Matt had a bitch of a temper and often he was very crude. I've seen him blow his nose—into his hand—then rub all that into the hair on his chest. Or urinate in a sink. What I'm trying to say, that type of man is capable of anything."

"Do you think he planned to kill Francine?"

"How could I possibly know that?"

"I want your opinion—off the record."

"I really can't say. There's no doubt he did it—Lord, you should have seen the look on his face when he threatened her. The way he grabbed her arm—why, he could have broken it off. I think it was an accident, I mean, he lost his temper and hit her. But then, why did he trick me with the time bit? I don't know what to say. You put me in a difficult position, they were both my friends. Matt has done a lot for me, a great deal, indeed."

"What sort of help?"

"When I was practically a beginner in this racket—and Lord knows I still am—Matt showed me the ropes. Although you're in the publishing end, I doubt if you realize the insecurity writers face. Frankly, I'm constantly amazed I make a modest living at it. It isn't like any other profession—actually we're gamblers. We live by our wits. It's frightening. Of course, I've been writing for a number of years, but up till five years ago it was an avocation with me—I was the manager of a gift shop. A weekend writer, publishing in the 'little magazines,' working on the novel. Did you ever read my first book, *Little Boy Little?*"

"I'm afraid not." Should I have it out with Wilma, see what she wanted to do? Or would I be jumping the gun—she could hardly know she was pregnant; it was too soon.

He laughed, showing well-kept teeth. "Very few people have. I had this naive idea that when the book was published it would make me. It did—it damn near made me a bum. Sold a big fat 1100 copies. All I got out of it was the $500 advance—for three years' work. Oh, it received a nice press. It was a fragile story of a boy's growing up, fighting the silver cord stuff. But as Matt says, good reviews and a token will get you into the subway." He grinned.

I smiled politely. The tension left me. I was being an ass. If it was too soon for Wilma to know if she was knocked-up, hunch or no hunch, why should I talk about it? Even be so damn sure?

Joel said, "You must be wondering where Matt fits into all this. Wilma said you're after background and I'm trying to show how I fitted into Matt's. Or vice versa. Now there's a good title—vice versa. Excuse my horsing around, Norman, but I'm feeling rather gay this morning. Things are working out, in a personal way, that is. Now, where was I?"

"You had a book out," I said, deciding he wasn't a queer—for no reason—and beginning to be a little bored with his chatter.

"Yes, yes. On the strength of a book being published, I gave up my job, became a full-time writer. I took the full plunge—Wilma and I were married at the same time. I soon found out what a crazy business writing is—as a business. A merchant knows his stock, his worth. A man on a salary can put a little aside each payday, make plans. With a writer, every time he opens his mailbox it's like going to the pari-mutual window—you can't plan on a damn thing."

"What happened, you had to return to the gift shop?"

Joel rubbed his slim hands together, as if he was cold. "Indeed not. I was a flash in the pan. One of the big women's slick mags took a chapter of my book, and I landed two shorts with another slick. In the space of two weeks I'd made nearly $2000. You know how you start thinking, a thousand a week, fifty grand a year. Wilma and I moved into a new apartment—we still have a few of the furnishings around here—and I settled down to write more shorts like mad. I think, even now, they were good, yet I've never sold another story for more than a hundred dollars since. Crazy business, no?"

I nodded politely as I lit my pipe. Joel pulled a corncob from a desk drawer, borrowed some tobacco.

He puffed and nodded. "Nice nut flavor, I like this."

"I'll part with my secret formula someday," I said, glancing at my watch.

"I'd also started a new novel—in fact I started two more new novels. Hell, the two grand seemed to vanish and we were in debt. I got nervous, panicky. I borrowed some money from my mother; Wilma and I decided we needed a change. We went to the Florida Keys—à la Hemingway. Everything was wrong—Wilma is the bossy type without meaning to be. Our marriage was going one-sided. I was losing confidence in myself as a man, as a writer. Doc Matt Anthony straightened all that out."

"How?"

"We met Fran and Matt in Key West. Naturally, I'd heard of him and on seeing him, well, he seemed the very personification of a writer: hearty, confident, easy-going, living well ... a real pro. He did so much for me. For one thing he got me off the 'great' writer kick, showed me you have to be a hack to eat regularly. This bit about waiting for the creative mood is only for the dilettantes. He got me into the habit of writing every day, to stop looking on writing as a talent or gift, but rather as a job where you must keep producing. In desperation I'd been trying everything—pulps, confessions, quality yarns. Matt took the time to read much of my stuff, told me I had a knack for writing children's books. He was right. I've had five published with another two due shortly. I write for the six- to ten-year old group, and since there are always new brats of that age every year, you keep selling. My goal is to have about twenty in print, and if each brings in a few hundred in royalties, why I'll practically have an annuity for life. Then I can afford to try other forms of writing."

"Sounds like a wise idea," I said. "But to return to Matt...."

He held up his hand as if to ward off a punch. "I know I must be boring you, Connor, but you want to get the picture of Matt and Fran. Actually it was really Fran who taught me the financial mechanics of writing. Her first husband had been an artist with a big A. Type of joker who convinces himself he's only living for his art—in his case a rather bad novel. As Fran said, art becomes an escape, the artist can't be bothered with the realities of food and rent. Fran was constantly nagging Matt to keep his expenses down. That's the reason we live in this dump—overhead can strangle a writer. Too often a writer has a good year, say he makes ten grand, starts living up to that, and paying taxes on it, only to find—as I did—that the years to come aren't good, money-wise. Poor Fran didn't have an easy life with Matt. But don't misunderstand me, I admire Matt. If he played the clown he was also a man with insight and wisdom. Off the record, things weren't going too well with Wilma and me. A thing that happens to every marriage at some time ... but then I understand you're going through that now yourself."

Wilma and her big mouth. I said casually, "We all have our little battles."

He looked at me wisely. "Oh, no, I don't mean the little ones. Wilma and I still have those, although we're riding a hell of a big wave at the moment. No, I mean being on the verge of a break. Everything I did was wrong. I wasn't selling or even writing much. Wasn't much of a husband, either. I couldn't do a damn thing right. And Wilma is very capable, does everything efficiently."

"I've heard Fran was the same type."

"She was, but Wilma is also good physically at so many things—a crack swimmer, rows like a man, a good fisherman. She was getting to be the man of the family while all I could raise was a bad inferiority complex. And Matt realized that. This is what he did: The four of us had chartered a boat for a few days of deep-sea fishing. It was embarrassing, everybody caught fish except me. Matt and Fran reeled in amberjacks and a baby tuna, while Wilma landed a sword fish. I was a mess. Not only didn't I catch a darn thing, I lost my tackle over the side, got a sniffling cold and ran a temperature. Catching a fish became symbolic of my whole damn life. I kept a line over all the time, even at night or when the others were eating. I couldn't get a nibble. I was delirious with fever. I felt if I went ashore empty-handed it would also be the end of me, of our marriage. You must know what I mean."

"I suppose so," I said cautiously, wondering why I'd ever talked to Wilma.

"Matt realized how sick I was, in body and mind, kept me jacked up on booze. On the third day, as we were heading in, I was still fishless. I was the only one with a line over, and suddenly the biggest marlin in the world hit my line, almost took the rod from me. It turned out to weigh only 206 pounds, actually a small one. But to me ... well! As I said I was sick, and it seemed as if the monster would jerk my arms off. Wilma and Fran wanted to help me, but Matt, who was up on the flying bridge running the boat, shouted for them to leave me alone. It was a rough sea and he kept maneuvering the cruiser to take some of the strain off my arms. Then the motor began acting up, coughing a lot. I just told myself if I lost this fish I'd try suicide—I meant it. It seemed the last straw, the final kick in the butt. The point is, the fish suddenly gave up the fight and I managed to reel him in. Can you believe landing that marlin made a new man out of me?"

"Since I've never caught anything over two pounds, it sounds like a big deal," I said, wondering why I was sitting there, wasting my time.

"It gave me fresh confidence, new respect from Wilma. Why I almost swung on Matt for clumsily cutting the marlin's head with the hook as he helped bring it aboard. Later he told me the truth: up on the bridge he had deliberately made the motor backfire as he pumped slugs into the monster with a hunting rifle he kept handy. That's the kind of true friend Matt is."

"Did you see him often?"

"They traveled a lot—West Indies, Mexico, Hollywood, but we kept in touch. When he bought the End Harbor place, we went out for a New Year's party, and this summer Matt was kind enough to ask us out when Wilma had her vacation."

"Exactly what happened out there the other day?" I asked, going through the motions again.

Joel noisily sucked on his corncob, lit it again. "Wilma has told you about all I know. Fran nagged Matt a lot. Not only about drinking and his heart, but actually old Matt never followed his own advice. She wanted to save a little but he seems to think he'll go on turning out saleable books forever. In his own way Matt considers himself a genius, a great talent that will never dry up. As to what happened that horrible day, what can I add to what Wilma has told you?"

"You said something about Matt fooling you on the time. What was that?"

"It was a lousy thing, to involve me. Well, after he and Fran had it out, Wilma and I went up to our room. I'm starting a book series about seven-year-old twins as they visit various countries. I usually discuss the plots with Wilma because she has a lot of common sense. We heard Matt drive away with Professor Brown. About a half-hour later Fran called up she was going fishing. Wilma and I came down, had a few belts as we took a sun bath on the lawn. I fooled around with the poodle for a time, had him chasing a ball. Anyway, Wilma and I dozed off. I awoke to find Matt playing with the dog. He said it was a quarter to three. I fell off again and then Wilma shook me awake to say it was half past three and time for a swim. Actually the sonofabitch had tricked us, according to his confession. He'd already killed Fran and was setting up an alibi. Neither Wilma or I had a watch on and it turned out instead of three quarters of an hour passing between the time I awoke again, it only had been five minutes. Soon as I went to sleep again, Matt had got Wilma awake, told her it was three-thirty.

You see, Matt's very smart about such things, has a knowledge of all criminal tricks."

"Then you think he might have murdered her?"

He shook his head. "In the light of his confession, temper, the tenseness between Fran and Matt, I think he hit her in a rage and then tried to set up an alibi to avoid publicity. Of course, I suppose he was capable of murdering her, I mean if you and I wanted to murder, we wouldn't even know how to go about it. Matt would. But then, if he really wanted to kill Fran, I think he would have done it long ago."

"What do you think of this Kolcicki?"

Joel shuddered. "That horrible creature! When the maid found the body, all the police and stuff were happening, at that point—when it was thought Fran had killed herself accidentally—I got rather blotto. But just before supper, when Matt came out of his study with this fat thug and we were told Matt had confessed, I tried to get drunker but I was never so sober in my life. That detective lump—he frightens me. He questioned me later that night and merely talking to him gave me a chill. Look, Norman, I tried to do the best I could for Matt. You have no idea how the thought of telling it all again at the trial upsets me. I talked to Kolcicki and then the D.A.—and there's a cold fish—and I hate to be placed in the position of being a witness for the D.A., but what can I do? It's such a mess. I wish to God we'd never gone out there."

We were both silent for a moment. I glanced at my watch. I still had almost an hour before I saw Jackson Clair.

Joel asked, "Like a drink? Just talking about this makes me jittery."

"I have to be on my way soon. I'm seeing Matt's lawyer this afternoon. But I did want to say hello to your wife."

"She should be home soon. Maybe she went to the doctor. Wilma wasn't feeling well this morning. Cold, I guess."

My insides contracted; morning sickness already! I mumbled, "I'm sorry to hear that."

"It's nothing. Wilma is as healthy as that well-known horse. How about that drink?"

I stood up. "No, thanks. Think I'd better go. It's been good of talking to you, Joel. Tell Wilma we'll all get together one of these days."

Walking me to the door Joel asked, "Do you think there's anything for me at Longson? I don't think my publisher is pushing my books and—" He suddenly giggled. "What writer doesn't think that? Wilma wants me to change publishers but I don't see it. What do you think, Norman?"

"We haven't much of a juvenile list, as I told ... Mrs. Hunter. Juveniles aren't the type book any publisher can push. But I'll be back in the office in a few days, talk it over with our children's editor, if you wish."

"That would be swell. Of course you understand this is all in strict confidence. I'd die if it ever got back to my present publisher."

I said of course and we shook hands. Once I hit the street I stood around in a doorway across the street, like a hammy detective. I wanted to have it out with Wilma, find out what the doctor told her—as if I didn't know.

I kept thinking how odd it would look if Joel came out of the house or saw me from a window. I went to a rundown bar on the corner and had a few beers. I had a tangent view of their house, but if Wilma came from uptown I wouldn't be able to catch her before she went in. The bar was depressing and after a half-hour I was glad I had to leave, if I wanted to see the lawyer. Also, I wasn't certain talking to Wilma was a good idea. Suppose she thought it was Joel, or she *wanted* it to be Joel's, why should I force matters? Why should I make any play until she contacted me? Which would probably be damn soon ... maybe tonight. Or was Wilma trying to call me this second?

I stopped a cab and gave him Clair's address, almost wishing we'd have an accident on the way there—a fatal one.

Jackson Clair

"I'm very happy to see his publisher taking an active interest in Matt's case, my friend, for he needs help," Jackson Clair said, leaning back in his fancy tan leather swivel chair, almost beating out the rhythm of his words with a long finger on the desk top.

Clair was impressive and slick. He was tall and lean, with a homely rugged swarthy face topped by wild gray hair. The hair was obviously carefully uncombed and everything about him from his unironed shirt to his slow, booming voice, was set up to give him a Lincoln-like air. And he had it; the honest, strong, trustworthy face, a voice dripping with sincerity. Even the nervous twisting and tapping of the strong hands implied boundless energy. The only thing spoiling the act were his eyes—shrewd, intelligent eyes ... like a good pitchman's.

"Frankly," the deep voice went on, the restless eyes probing my reaction, "Matt needs money. Not for myself. I'm in this case for two reasons: I want to see justice done, of course, and to be open about it, my pay will be in the publicity. We lawyers cannot advertise, as you must know, so our only ads are good court work. I have an established reputation but—" (He smiled, showing a set of buck teeth, very white and strong, that fitted his face perfectly.) "This is big league. However, there are certain expenses in every case and Matt is busted."

"I was out to End Harbor yesterday. No, the day before. And Miss Fitzgerald, the maid, wants to know about closing the house and her salary."

He nodded. "I'll inform Ed. He's Matt's regular lawyer, handles his personal affairs."

"Can't you raise money on the property?"

"What money?" His voice was projected so it hit me like a slap in the belly. I wanted to tell him to take it easy—I wasn't a juror. "Mr. Anthony hasn't a dime of equity in either the house or the land, everything is mortgaged to the hilt. For Christsakes he owes on his boats, his cars. Ed is trying to get some movie outfit that has an option on one of Matt's books to buy it at half price. But those chicken-hearted bastards are afraid of the publicity. That's why I'm glad to see Harpers take an—"

"Longson," I cut in.

"I'm delighted to see his publishers have the guts to take a stand. Now how much ...?"

"It isn't definite yet, as I told you, Mr. Clair. That's why I'm here."

He got up and started pacing the office. He must have been at least six-three. There was a Phi Beta Kappa key—highly polished—hanging from his belt, a brightly beaded affair. He turned toward me like a pug answering the bell. "Assuming you publish one of his books, how much will he realize?"

"Depends upon the sale. About two or three thousand, if we sell out."

"That's all? Well, as you literary people say, it's better than a poke in the eye with a sharp stick."

"Is that what we say? Mr. Clair, will the D.A. get his murder indictment?"

He went to his desk, held up an afternoon paper. "He already has. But an indictment isn't a verdict; I'll get Matt off."

"If I'm not breaking ethics or state secrets, what sort of defense do you plan?"

"Temporary insanity. My staff is doing research on it now. We already have found a quote from Dreiser about writers shouldn't be limited to one woman. We'll find ... say, maybe you at Longson's can help me get some top authors to testify? Fellows like Hemingway, Faulkner, Ferber, O'Hara, Williams?"

"I doubt that. You're losing me: testify about what? You mentioned temporary insanity, but how do they ...?"

"Listen, Connor," he said and his voice made sure you listened, "our contention will be that men like Matt Anthony are creators, the rare creatures of our banal earth. Matt is a genius. Laws and conventions cannot apply to men like him, they are above such petty mundane barriers. They have a God-given gift that requires them not merely to exist, like you and I, but to really taste of life. They must be allowed to dig into life, experiment with it, if they are to write. In short, they must be allowed to look upon life freely, ordinary standards cannot apply to them. Mrs. Anthony failed to understand that; she nagged him to a point where he broke, and in a blind rage he killed to save his genius!"

I realized my mouth was open. I shut it. Then asked, "Mr. Clair, you believe that?"

"Yes! Leaf through history, every great artist either fought the shackles of convention or was smothered by them. Van Gogh, London, Shakespeare, Gauguin. Remember, even the commandment 'Thou shall not kill' is but a convention."

"You'll never get away with that."

He flashed his strong smile. "If I can get the jury to half-believe it, I'm in. I'm aiming at getting Matt off, and that's a long shot. But it will be a feather in my cap. Even if he gets second degree manslaughter, it will be a feather in my cap. I like feathers." He pointed to his beaded belt. "I'm part Indian, you know."

And I bet you milk it for all it's worth, I thought as I asked, "Then you think he's guilty, I mean, he killed her?"

He was wearing out his rug again and he stopped as abruptly as if he'd walked into a wall. He sat down on the edge of the desk, swinging his long legs. Naturally he was wearing hand-stitched moccasin loafers. His eyes bored into me as he said, "He killed her; it would be ridiculous to think otherwise. He's confessed it."

"Prof. Brown doesn't think so."

Clair slapped his thigh. "That runt, he's the thorn in my case. One thing that worries me, red-baiting. Mr. Connor, what I'm about to tell you mustn't go beyond this room. I mean that. I talked to Matt on Saturday for the first time. He started to babble about Francine falling—on land—and hitting her head, that he was aware of the implications of his threatening her, and so he had dragged her out to the boat to make things look more like an accident. I've defended many people involved in homicide, the scream of innocence is a natural lie. Matt was in bad shape, had a minor heart attack in his cell. I hated to be rough on him, but I told him I wouldn't buy that slop, to get another lawyer. My father, God rest his good soul, was not a material success but he was a very learned man. One of the criterions he drilled into me was—never worry about making mistakes, but be certain you never make a *stupid* mistake. A man would look like a fool if he said Matt Anthony didn't kill his wife. It wouldn't be fair to Matt, the jury would certainly hang him. Our defense is he was nagged to the breaking point, and in an insane fury he hit her, killed her."

"What's the D.A.'s chances of proving it murder?"

He batted the air with his hand. "Crap. A bluff. The hick is trying to make a name. Don't pay any attention to it. Be different if a weapon were used. There's obviously no premeditation or intent here. His asking for murder 'one' is a routine bargaining point. He'll want me to settle for murder 'two.' I won't."

"You mentioned manslaughter in the second degree, what's the sentence for that?"

"Maximum is fifteen years and a fine up to $1000. I doubt if Matt would get more than five years, which means he'll be out in two or three. If I can get a change of venue, and I'm asking for that, he might get a suspended sentence or merely a fine. The big factor right now is money. Research is expensive, and I'll have to engage top psychiatrists. We don't have much time. How soon can Matt get a couple of grand?"

"You'll have to take that up with Mr. Long, himself. If we decide to go ahead with publication, I should think you—Matt—might be able to get an advance. Have you talked with Matt's agent?"

"Yes. Trouble with the world, too many faint-hearted people. I told him to fly out to Hollywood, raise some hell, but he's afraid of the notoriety. I told the sonofabitch he'd only get 10% of it."

His phone rang and he said, "Jackson Clair. Yes, Ollie. Aha. That's what we expected. Of course we have to talk it through. I'll be here to five. Good, I'll expect you."

As he hung up I got to my feet, said I was glad to have talked to him. We shook hands, and he had the firm grasp I expected. I told him to call tomorrow afternoon, we would have reached a decision about the book by then.

Chambers Street was hot with home-rushing people. I didn't have any place to rush to. I didn't want to think and I didn't want to get drunk. I phoned Frank. He was just leaving the office, said he had time for a short workout, and where the hell had I been?

I took a cab to the gym and by six we had played two fast games. He wanted me to have supper with him and Liz, take in a preview of the pilot film of a new TV show, but I said I had some work to do, begged off.

I had played hard, beaten Frank both games. I was suddenly fed up with all the phony people I'd known the last few days—including myself.

Frank said, "Let's take a shower. I haven't much time and you know Liz if she has to wait a second."

"Think I'll hang around, see if I can get a few more games ... I'm restless ... without Michele."

"How's her folks?"

"Coming along. However, she may have to stay there longer than we expected."

"I thought we could talk over the ad campaign for Matt's book, while showering."

"I haven't finalized that in my mind, yet," I lied.

Frank gave me an odd look. "Okay, Norm boy. Let's have lunch in a day or so. I'm interested. Liz will be disappointed you're not coming with us, but I know how you feel. A man gets so used to a woman he feels half-alive when she isn't around."

"That's it, Frank."

He slapped me on the can. "I knew something was bothering you—you were playing like a hot pepper." He headed for the showers.

I told the gym attendant to let me know if there was an open game, went over and punched the bag. Bag punching is very conducive to thinking and I saw myself very clearly—a goddamn kid. I'd had it made and didn't know it. The Madison Avenue golden boy—Christ, I must have been crazy. Michele was right ... my wonderful Michele, and little me running after Wilma like a lousy dog in heat. It wasn't just the mess I was in now, but that I had been stupid enough to even *chance* getting into such a mess. And for what—a fast lay that wasn't worth a damn? Norm, the Golden Boy—the boy part was so damn correct! Hustling after Madison Avenue like a character in a cheap book. Michele was so right, what the devil would more money mean—two refrigerators? Big money hadn't done anything for Matt Anthony. Were Frank and Liz as happy as Michele and I ... had been? Oh, God, if I can ever get out of this, if only Wilma isn't pregnant, I'll never ... what the hell had Clair said, don't make a *stupid* mistake? I'd pulled the biggest boner of my life.

No matter what happened, I was sick of being a phony. And why should the details of Matt Anthony's cockeyed life concern me? I was sick to death of drunken Wilmas, of moronic detectives, of a joker like Joel, probably fighting latent homosexuality, a ghoulish lawyer.... I was even sick of Longson's—they wouldn't give Matt a dime until his other advances were covered. And me, the errand boy, digging in the dirt. Damn, I'd had such a pleasant even life ... Michele and I would have made up. Maybe having a kid would be interesting. I was so careful not to go out on a limb in this damn ad campaign but with my own life I'd rushed out on the longest limb I could find like a real ... a real goddamn jerk. A....

The gym attendant tapped me on the shoulder, and said there was an opening in a doubles game. He was staring at me ... I was drenched with sweat, must have been punching the light bag for about ten minutes straight.

I played three more games and was drunk with tiredness. I showered and had a few sandwiches. The gym was the upper floor of a hotel and I took a room and was asleep before ten, didn't awake until eleven in the morning. I felt pretty good, although still full of that hunch I was in trouble. I knew one thing: I was going to stop fooling around and make things come to a head, then see what I could do with Michele.

I went upstairs and had a rubdown and a shave, ate like it was winter. I reached the office before one. Miss Park was out but the receptionist told me Long wanted to see me at once. I said to tell him I'd be right up, went to my desk and glanced at my mail as I told myself to play it cool ... the one thing I wanted was to stay in the comfortable routine of Longson's.

Bill Long looked as fresh and calm as ever. He said, "Happy I caught you before lunch, Norm. Know where I was this morning? No, of course you couldn't. I was talking to Matt Anthony."

"Where?" I asked, almost amused; I'd been out of the office for a week, could have stayed out for another few days, but Long was happy he "caught me before lunch."

"They brought him in from Riverside for some hospital treatment. He's suffered a minor heart attack. Matt insisted he wanted to talk to me and to his agent. The man is fantastic. He not only has been writing stories while in his cell but he wants to have one of those silent tape recorders attached to his throat—I'm hazy on the technical terms—all during the actual trial! Idea is to get his reactions to the testimony on paper—and publish it! Matt thinks it can be a sensational seller—the first real inside story of a murder trial."

"Lord, how commercial can you get?"

"He wanted an advance on the idea. I'm having the legal department check whether it's possible. But I doubt if we can use it—too sensational. However, I told him we'd be glad to consider it when it's finished."

"How is his heart?"

"Good as can be expected. It was a terrible ordeal for me. Matt would be talking in his usual loud, foul-mouthed manner, then suddenly he'd get hysterical. Unnerves one to see a man that big crying. I mentioned the possibility of reissuing one of his books and it cheered him considerably. Have you reached a decision on that, and the ads?"

I nodded. "Yes, sir. Start the press run soon as you wish. Have you seen the cover of the book we'll print?"

"I don't recall it."

"The jacket is an eye-catching pink with a girl who looks like a fashion model leaning against an adobe hut. The expression on her face can mean anything—even nothing. Of course we'll have to update the style of her clothes, the cover is about ten years old. She'll be dressed in smart slacks and a shirt ... could be a *Vogue* ad, except she's also wearing a neat hip holster and a gun. I plan to run that as the ad—run it all over the country."

"Will that be the first advertisement?" he asked, his face puzzled.

"That will be the *only* ad. Bill, I've been getting a clear picture of Matt Anthony and what happened out at End Harbor these last few days. This murder indictment is so much hot air. Actually her death was an accident, as his confession implies. His lawyer is a sharp character and will either get Matt off scot-free, or with a suspended or light sentence. The point is, it wasn't murder. No matter how we advertise I'm convinced our reputation won't suffer. But I plan to play it doubly safe—the ad will be just a routine advertisement. At the same time, with Kelly's help, we'll plant a few items with the syndicated columnists. One will be about Longson really putting out the book to help Matt raise money ... a publisher aiding one of his writers. Another will be—in a behind the scenes vein—a hint there was a long battle in our offices about reissuing the book; we didn't want to capitalize on the headlines, beneath the dignity of Longson and all that. But at the same time we felt a man is innocent until proven guilty, and we also had a duty to stand by our authors, etc., etc. I think we can build up interest without committing the house to a damn thing. The column plants, actually rumors and gossip without any possible backfire, will carry our real message. Almost consider it institutional advertising."

He fooled with his moustache, stroked it. "Are you certain we can reach the columnists? Seems to me it all hinges on that."

"I'm certain. I haven't discussed it with Marty Kelly yet, but it won't be any problem. Do you like the whole idea, Bill?"

"I do. But this is still your responsibility, Norm, you understand?"

I headed for the door. "I understood that from the jump. I'll start the wheels going, sir."

Back in my office I blended some tobacco, was tossing out the ads in my mail when Miss Park returned. She said, "Mr. Connor, why didn't you tell me you were coming back? I would have bought an extra jelly doughnut for this afternoon—"

"I'll share yours. Bring your book in, I have some memos to get out."

"Yes, sir." She stopped in the doorway. "Mr. Kelly wants you to call him. And ... oh, your wife has been calling all morning."

"From Paris?"

"Paris?" she repeated blankly. "Why, no. She said for you to phone your house—"

I was out of the office before she could finish the sentence.

Michele

It was the most welcome sight of my life to see Michele's clothes strewn around the bedroom, to almost smell her warm odor. But she wasn't home and I sat around impatiently, wondering where she could possibly have gone ... and I also had this good feeling that now we were together again, things would work out. I didn't know how, but just having Michele back was a tremendous shot in the arm. And when she walked into our apartment a few minutes later carrying a bag of groceries, the very normalcy of it all delighted me.

She gave me a faint nervous grin as I rushed over to hug her, groceries and all. She looked tired, pale. We kissed like hungry kids and I ran my tongue over the tiny soft hairs of her "moustache." My hands slid over her green cotton dress and she pushed me away, said, "No, Norm-man. Not for a few days. Sit down, we have to talk." She finally put the grocery bag down.

"Honey, I've been crazy since you've gone. Darling, no matter what happens, we can never part again. Call the school, your friend will tell you I'm buying the house. It was to be a surprise for you and ... oh, Michele, Michele!"

I took her in my arms again. She placed a finger on my lips. "Don't, Norm-man. You sound like a repentant husband. I am the one who has been ... wrong."

"No! It isn't a question of right or wrong, but of our very existence, of our—"

"Norm-man, I've lost our baby."

"Our ... what?" Fear came all over me, clear and so damn strong. Could there be any doubt about it now? Wasn't this the working plot of a stupid novel, the jacket blurb of my future? "His wife lost his baby but another woman was carrying his child."

"You're angry, hurt. I felt you stiffen. Oh, Norm, can you ever forgive me?" Her voice was a high moan.

I kissed her, a numb kiss, my head ready to explode. I heard myself saying, "I can forgive you anything but I don't know what you're talking about." I walked her to the couch, sat down, tried to pull her on my lap. She turned and sat at the end of the couch; seemed to shrink, her face full of misery. "Now tell me in basic English—or basic French—what has happened." How far away and strange-sounding my voice was.

She stared at me, her face almost blank, hysteria mounting. I moved over, held her tightly as I whispered, "Michele, I'm the one who should be asking forgiveness."

"No!"

I damn near told her about Wilma then and there. Instead, I stroked her soft hair, said, "All that matters is you are with me again. Do you understand, nothing else matters!"

"I lost our baby."

"Honey, were you pregnant when we battled ...?" I suddenly laughed, an insane chuckle that brought me back to reality. "And we were always so damn careful!"

"I thought I was pregnant," Michele said, her voice dull and fiat. "I wasn't sure. You know how I am often late. I was trying to tell you ... when things got out of hand."

"But that was only a week ago, less. What makes you think ...?"

"The moment I landed in Paris I went to a doctor—a French rabbit said I was pregnant. My mother convinced me how wrong I was to be apart from you. It was your child, too. I was lucky to get a cancellation ... if one can call it luck. All the rushing and traveling ... flying makes me nervous. Yesterday I ... I came around. And spending all that money for a few days."

I laughed, her French thrift always showed. "Darling, I don't care if—"

"Don't you, my Norman?" she asked, sadness in her voice. "Can't you see I want you to care? And I know you do, your face is tense." She shrugged. "I never even cried when it happened ... nature's way ... unless we both want a child. I have no right to—" She began to cry, tremendous sobbing that frightened me.

I shook her gently. "Honey, nothing matters except you're back. We'll still have a baby, still do everything we wanted." But I knew my voice was hollow.

"I have more to tell you," she said, her voice shaking with her sobs. "When I took off, I was almost hoping all the flying would do ... what it did. Norm-man. I have done such a horrible thing! Not only the baby, but I made conditions for our marriage ... I have no right to dictate your life. I had no right to—to...." Her sobbing began a series of hysterical, tiny screams.

I talked fast into her ear. "Darling, darling, don't. I was the wrong one. You want a child, fine. Truthfully it doesn't matter to me, but I'm not against it. I've learned I'm not against anything where you're concerned. I think I've grown up these last days. I've been inside some people's lives—part of a business deal—and I know now that ambition, real ambition, only means trying for happiness. We had it and I damn near threw it out the window. Michele, what I'm trying to say, we're so much a part of each other that when you left I was a sick man ... sick in mind." Was I trying to prepare an alibi? In the midst of her misery I was setting up my excuse for Wilma. A lousy sick feeling joined the fear in my head.

We sat there, holding each other tightly, Michele sobbing and moaning so I thought she was having a breakdown. I got her to lie on the couch. She kept trembling, her skin terribly pale, her eyes staring but not seeing me. I phoned a doctor, then sat beside her and held her hand.

He said Michele was suffering from fatigue and shock, gave her a sedative. I had explained what it was all about and before she dozed off he told Michele, "Mrs. Connor, while I don't want to low-rate French rabbits there isn't any way you could have been positive you were pregnant. Do you hear that? It's actually impossible to tell—in the first weeks. I want you to forget what's happened, get some rest for the next few days. You look like a very healthy young woman and while one can't give any guarantee in this sort of thing, I think you'll have children."

He took me into the kitchen and gave me a couple of prescriptions to have filled, told me, "Your wife must have absolute rest for a day at least. No company and no arguments. I don't want her upset. This isn't serious, but in her state, another shock could have serious consequences. You ought to rest, Mr. Connor. You seem pretty upset yourself."

"I'm okay. Listen, Doc, I—" But I didn't have the nerve to ask him.

"What is it?"

"I ... eh ... wondered if she needed vitamins," I said stupidly.

"One of the items I prescribed is a tonic. Don't worry and get a smile on your face. It's your reaction that adds to her feeling of guilt about the miscarriage. Don't awaken her, even to give her the medicines. The both of you need a relaxed atmosphere around here. Stop worrying. I'll phone you tomorrow."

"Is it okay to leave her alone now? I mean, can I go to the drugstore?"

"Yes, she should sleep for hours. In a day or two I want you to both get out of the house, take in some shows, go away for a few days, if you can. Above all, stop blaming her for losing the child."

"Blame Michele? I told you I don't care about a—"

"Look at yourself in the mirror, Mr. Connor. Your face is full of anger. Best medicine for your wife is for you to relax."

Soon as he left I went out and got the medicines. I was damn sure about one thing—I *had* to settle things with Wilma. I had to impress upon her Michele couldn't stand another shock, that she would have to work out something. It was only three and I walked up and around the living room, knowing Wilma wouldn't be home for at least another hour. Then I just couldn't take it, I had to see her now. I phoned Joel Hunter, trying to think of what excuse I could give him to ask for the address of Wilma's employer. Wilma answered the phone.

I said, "Look, it's damn important I see you at once. Can I meet you someplace?"

"Come over here, I'm not dressed. What's this about?"

"Joel around?"

"No. He's out getting some data on the Bronx Zoo. Really, Norm, you sound like—"

"I'll be over in a few minutes."

I got the janitor's wife to stay with Michele, told her I had an urgent business appointment. I picked up a cab at the corner and within fifteen minutes Wilma was opening the door for me. She was wearing a crazy colored robe and slippers. As I walked in she said, "I'm as curious as the famous cat. Now what is ...?"

"You alone?"

"My, aren't we being mysterious for ourselves. Yes, I am alone."

We walked down the long hallway and into the living room and I was trying to think how the hell I would ask her. All I could come up with was a blunt, "Wilma, are you pregnant?"

Her face froze in an absolute double-take. She fell into a chair, roared with laughter.

I stood over her. "Damn it, are you?"

"Down, boy. I was going to offer you a shot, but you're loaded."

"Sure, it's all a big pratfall, a stage joke! Listen, Joel said you were feeling sick, morning sick ..."

"Oh, for ... I've had a cold. That's the only thing I got that night on the beach. Really, for a smooth character you wash terribly simple."

I turned away, stared out the window at some dirty roofs. "No, it will turn out that you are, it's practically in the script."

"Aren't you full of happy thoughts! Imagine me being with child, as the saying goes. Norm, when I'm ready, I'll have a kid. Now, let me tell *you* the facts of life. When I found out Joel was going to hide out in that goddamn room, well, it was the first time he'd done that—I mean on a several-day spree—in years. It made me sore to have him out of my reach. I decided—before I ever knew about your wife—that I'd go out and have an affair, sort of get even with Joel. I don't know if I actually would have done it or not. This may shock you, but I'm really not a pushover."

"Who said you were?" I mumbled.

"The point is, I took a pill that afternoon, a little medical wonder that leaves the woman sterile for forty-eight hours. So that's that."

"No, it isn't. Look, we—I didn't take any precautions. It's only been a week, you can't be certain. I've had this hunch about you being—"

"You'd better not try the races with your hunches, Buster Brown, I happen to be home this minute because I've had the curse since shortly after the fights on TV last night—to pin it down for you."

"My God, you do?"

"Norm, are you a well boy? I mean it."

"Maybe. I had this hunch and was so damn certain everything was ruined. Then my wife returned today with ... oh, hell, forget it. I'm terribly sorry I've been such a ... an ass."

"Well, let's forget it. And if I had been caught ... now, wouldn't that have been something." She grinned, gave me that intense stare. "You're deceiving, Norm. Soon as I saw you, I knew we were going to take a roll. I not only liked your hands but you seemed so smooth and sophisticated. Really sophisticated. This may sound nuts to you but I got more of a kick out of the whore aspect, you know, thinking I might further Joel's books at your house. Even on the beach, juiced as I was, I knew I had you marked wrong—you're just a nice ordinary guy."

"Thanks for the head shrinking. Please forget the whole damn thing. My wife isn't feeling well and I have to rush."

"I think in its own little way, this has been quite a charming scene. At least it has spiced up my afternoon. And I want you to call us and bring your wife over. I mean that, Norm."

We walked to the door and she suddenly gave me a kiss, pressing her breasts against me, whispered, "Please don't look like such a hurt little boy, Norm, darling. I suppose I simply couldn't resist being the clever bitch, making with the jokes."

I tapped her on the behind. "It's okay, I put my foot in so far nothing makes it any worse or better. Do me one favor, forget this ever happened?"

"Scouts' honor. And don't you be a fool either ... telling your wife or any of that movie crap. Remember, I want the four off us to get together soon."

I said we would and downstairs I started walking back to the apartment. I'd never felt like such a fool. I kept thinking of Jackson Clair and his line about stupid mistakes. Damn, how stupid can one get?

Then, after I'd walked a block or so, the true reaction set in. What did it matter if I sat in Times Square on high noon wearing a dunce cap? I was free! Everything was fine with my own world again. I wanted to dance in the street, do somersaults—I used to be good at tumbling. I wanted to do something crazy, like smash a window, bust a total stranger on the nose.

I came whistling into the apartment, carrying ginger beer and beer. After tipping the startled janitor's wife-nurse five bucks, I undressed, made a pitcher of shandy-gaff, and drank it slowly as I sat beside Michele's bed, admiring my lovely wife. I carefully stretched out beside her, my fingers gently touching the parts of her body I loved the most as I tumbled off into a wonderful sleep.

Later, at about ten, I awoke and ate like a pig, enjoyed an English movie on TV. I was in such a state of bliss I damn near giggled at myself. When I finally got back to bed it was too hot to sleep. After while Michele awoke. She seemed rested, if still a bit groggy. She kept repeating what the doc had said about it being impossible to tell if she'd actually been pregnant or not. The more she talked about it, the greater comfort it seemed to give her.

I told her I loved her in every way I could. Even found myself saying, "... and if you ever leave me again, run across the ocean to mama, I'll kill you." Of course that started me on Matt, and she was interested in the case. We got up and had a snack. I wanted her to go back to bed but she stayed up to see the late-late show on TV, a "ghoulie" as Michele called the pictures in which most of the actors were now dead. It was as if she'd never left me.

I wanted to take a few days off but didn't have the nerve to ask Bill—having been away a week. Michele saw a doctor in the afternoon and he assured her we could try for a baby anytime we wished. We had supper out that night. The following evening we dined with some of her UN friends, took in a play.

While Michele didn't seem too interested in the house, I insisted we buy it. I think I really wanted it. So we bought it, and spent the rest of the summer working like loons, painting, cleaning, planting, decorating. Even fixing the plumbing. It turned out, to our amazement, that we were both handy with tools. I even enjoyed making like a commuter. All in all, that August was one of the most happy and relaxed months we ever had.

Whether it was having Michele back, the house, or even out trying so hard for a kid—time raced by. If it only seemed a few days later, it was actually the end of September when Matt Anthony's trial started. And I'd almost forgotten about him. Except for a one paragraph item in the papers when Jackson Clair changed Matt's plea to innocent by reason of insanity and asked that Matt be examined by state psychiatrists, the case had dropped out of the news.

Marty Kelly hadn't thought too much of my ad campaign but I was sure of it. We ran our first ads two weeks before the trial was due, and along with a few cases of Scotch and other gifts we not only planted our items in all the major columns but sent out special releases to every small columnist we could find. Marty placed Bill Long on several radio and TV interviews where he piously explained the problems facing a book publisher—of course using Matt's book as an illustration.

The book sale was far from sensational, but it did well. Over half the first printing of 12,000 copies sold before the trial, with reorders mounting every day. The sales department ran off a small second edition.

I didn't have much time for handball, or Frank, although we had the Kuhns out to the house for a weekend. When I did have lunch with him, after the book was out, and he told me of an opening in an agency for $10,000—"as a starter, of course"—he was puzzled when I said I wasn't interested. He thought it was the money—I'd told him Bill had promised me a "substantial" raise after the January stockholders meeting—and Frank kept assuring me I'd double the ten grand in "two years, minimum." I guess I didn't do much of a job explaining why I was turning it down. I could hardly explain without insulting Frank.

The trial opened on a Thursday in Riverside. Bill Long thought somebody from the firm should attend. I said it should be me—I felt a part of the case, wanted to be in at the windup.

Michele was back at school teaching: her suggestion. I hated to spend a few days apart, and although she wanted to spend the weekend at the house, see about a boat we were considering, she finally agreed to come out to Riverside for the weekend.

PART II

The Trial

Never having attended a criminal trial before, much less one involving murder, for me there was a confusing air of unreality in the crowded courtroom. I had the feeling of watching an amateur production of a corny melodrama. Certainly there was nothing in the attitude of the morbid spectators, dressed in their Sunday best, or about Matt himself, to suggest a life was being tried.

By the time I arrived I could find a seat only in the rear of the courtroom. I saw May Fitzgerald and the Hunters sitting up front together. Prof. Brown was in the row behind them. Joel seemed nervous while Wilma was dressed to make an impression in a tight mild blue suit which showed off her good figure and red hair.

Matt Anthony appeared calm and at ease, practically lounging in his chair. He was very much "the author" in a shaggy, tweed sports coat that made his tremendous shoulders stand out, a plaid dress shirt and a matching tie. There was a thick pad of paper in front of him and several pencils. When he wasn't writing furious notes, Matt casually glanced around the courtroom, as though he was the spectator. Although the judge had ruled against Matt having a tape recorder in court, Matt was going ahead with his "book" in long hand. Bill Long told me Maggie had already received the first chapter, along with a sealed envelope and some hocus-pocus instructions from Matt that this wasn't to be opened until he had sent in the complete manuscript. Maggie was waiting for more chapters before reaching any decision, of course. Jackson Clair sat next to Matt, also very much at his ease. He was not only wearing his beaded belt, but his tie clasp was in the form of a tiny silver broken arrow from which the Phi Beta Kappa key hung like a neon light.

The prosecutor, Sidney Wagner, looked about forty, a dried-up man with thin features. He wore a very conservative blue serge, a stiff collar and a plain dark tie. He suggested starch and ironing in the kitchen: small time stuff. His pale face was lacking any show of emotion or imagination.

The judge looked the part: plump, gray hair, and a mixture of dignity and self-importance. The jury had been selected the day before, three women and nine men—very average looking locals, and seemingly quite pleased with their roles.

The trial started promptly at 10:30 A.M. when Wagner addressed the jury. I supposed his speech established a brevity record for trial openings. He had a cold, forceful voice and was stingy with words. The second he opened his mouth you knew you were listening to a capable man. And if he looked old-fashioned—so does a rattlesnake. He said, "Mr. Foreman, ladies and gentlemen of the jury. The State will prove that on July 25th last, in the presence of witnesses, Mr. Matt Anthony threatened to kill his wife, Francine Anthony. Several hours later, with clear premeditation and intent, Matt Anthony murdered his wife. It is the State's contention that after threatening his wife's life, when he later noticed Francine Anthony out fishing, Matt Anthony saw this as an opportunity to carry out his threat; that he planned to swim out and beat his wife to death, which he did. He further planned, with his considerable knowledge of criminal methods, to make the murder appear to be an accident. He was not successful in this, and later that same day confessed to killing Francine Anthony. The State will prove all this by testimony and facts, and with such proof will ask that you find Matt Anthony guilty of murder."

Maybe the opening speech took a minute, perhaps longer, yet it had all the power of a short right to the chin. When Wagner finished, Jackson seemed startled—perhaps at the briefness.

Jackson Clair stood up slowly, opened with a show, a curve as I expected. Flashing a practiced and rugged smile at the jury he said slowly, "Ladies and gentlemen, I realize I face you as a stranger. Certainly most of you, being residents of this splendid and booming county, are acquainted with my worthy colleague in one form or another. Of course I know that will not influence your decision in the slightest. And as a matter of fact I do not feel a complete stranger, for my ancestors once roamed and worked this very land. Perhaps, less than a hundred years ago, one of my Indian forefathers fished in the nearby waters. If proof should be needed that America is a melting pot, I could be that proof. I tell you this not for any personal reasons, although I am justly proud of my ancestors, but only to remind you our country was founded upon what was then a new concept of justice, upon principles our sons and fathers have since fought and died for time and again. I don't have to tell you the main principle is democracy: from the days of the Indian councils to our time, democracy has been the very life-blood of America. I am stressing this because the ideals of liberty and democracy will play an important role in this trial, as they must in every trial held in our country. These ideals are not only for the courts and the government, they also form the bases of our businesses, our home life, all our relationships."

Matt was watching him with a slight smile that grew bigger as Jackson began to pace in front of the jury box; slow, deliberate steps featuring the polished moccasins.

"It is in the framework of democracy you sit here, the judges of Matt Anthony. True, you are called jurors, but in a final sense you alone are the judges. Matt Anthony killed his wife. There is no doubt of that, he has confessed it. However he has not confessed to murder. On the contrary, as the defense will prove, it was far from a premeditated killing. In a moment of blind rage this giant of a man lost control of his temper, of his reasoning, struck his wife. She, in turn, hit her head on the side of the boat and died. This is a shocking thing, but we will prove it was not murder. There wasn't any gun or knife involved. The only weapon, if we can term it as such, was the weapon we all possess—this." Clair held up his hand to the jury. "I am sure you all know our hands very often get us into trouble ... even accidental trouble. If Matt Anthony and his wife had argued on land, if she hadn't taken a bad fall, she probably would be alive this moment. Perhaps by this time, she would have forgiven her husband, forgotten the incident.

"It is the defense's contention—which we will prove—that Matt Anthony was driven by Francine Anthony's goading to a point where he no longer knew what he was doing, where for a moment he could not tell right from wrong. Look at Matt Anthony, a big man, far above the average, a man who stands out. Anyone walking into this courtroom would notice Matt Anthony first. You and I think of ourselves as average persons, in fact, I believe we are proud to be called that. Well, ladies and gentlemen, Matt Anthony is not an average person. As I shall prove, he belongs, figuratively and literally to that tiny tribe of giants we call geniuses. Here is a man who can make people like ourselves come alive on paper, who creates and populates entire cities and countries, who can make weather, homes, airplanes, cars, who can delve into the innermost workings of our brains ... with his mind and typewriter. Before you there sits a man of unique talent. I tell you this not to praise Matt Anthony, the writer, although he has won international acclaim as an author, but because it is the defense's contention, which we will back with proof, that the mores and conventions which hold for the average person cannot be fully applied to those rare humans who are above average. The very definition of convention means a fixed usage sanctioned by general custom. Remember those last two words, *general custom*. In other words, mores are made for the average people.

"Now I am not so foolish as to claim that a genius is above the rules and laws of society, but I do say where the above-average person is concerned, there must be a certain flexibility. This is not an original idea of mine, it is accepted in law. There are laws to cover average cases, and there are also unwritten laws for cases that are not average. I am not lecturing you on the law. We have a most capable judge here to tell you the law. But I repeat, we are judging a man of genius here. A man whose very genius was being ruined by his wife's constant nagging. I will prove that Francine Anthony also had a talent: she knew how to nag her husband until she drove him to the breaking point where he could no longer think rationally. At that moment, when his mind broke, he struck out at his tormentor in a blind rage with all of his great strength ... and when he regained his sanity, he found to his horror and amazement that his beloved wife was dead. Oh, yes, despite her nagging, Matt Anthony loved his wife. Matt Anthony had no more control over Francine Anthony's death than you or I. For a man of his strength to strike a smaller person, a woman, is truly an insane act; something he'd never thought of doing before. The defense shall prove all this and when we do, I know you will bring in a verdict of not guilty by reason of temporary insanity. Thank you."

Jackson walked slowly to his seat. Matt was still writing intently. Two reporters in the press section were whispering. I glanced around the courtroom, wondering if anybody, including Jackson, knew exactly what the devil he'd said. Wagner looked mildly bored. Several times I thought the judge had been on the brink of cutting Jackson off or of telling Matt to stop writing and pay attention. Now Clair sipped a glass of water, smiled at the world.

The State opened its case by calling the End Harbor cop who had been the first official on the scene. He fixed the time and day, told of pulling the boat in, examining the corpse. A Harbor doctor next testified death had been caused by Francine striking her head on the side of the boat with "great force." He went into detail as to the exact position of the body, the approximate time of death "... about 2 P.M...."

Matt would gaze at each witness with his set, small smile—a kind of sardonic, plastic grin—for a moment, then start scribbling away. Jackson had only a few routine questions.

Joel Hunter was the next witness. His face was flushed, giving him a weird appearance, what with his short light hair. He kept licking his lips, and his tongue seemed as long as a frog's. Wagner quickly established that Joel was a writer, a friend of the Anthonys, and had been a house guest at End Harbor. In voice slightly shrill with nerves, Joel told of Prof. Brown coming back with Matt that morning, how upset Francine had been upon learning Brown had been in the papers as a Fifth Amendment witness. Under Wagner's dry questioning Joel told of Matt threatening Francine when she said she would order Brown to leave the house. Joel seemed absolutely wretched as he repeated the threat, and the judge asked him to raise his voice. Joel glanced at Matt, his eyes almost a plea, as he repeated the threat in a louder voice. Matt was still smiling, and it seemed to me he winked at Joel, although from the angle at which I was watching I couldn't be positive. Wagner quickly covered the finding of the body, how Matt had tricked Joel on the time, and Hunter's "shock" when Kolcicki took Matt away a few hours later, saying he had confessed.

Jackson arose to point out that the confession had not as yet been placed in evidence, and Wagner said he was merely asking Joel what Kolcicki had told him. Jackson waved his hands, said he didn't want to delay the trial and would withdraw his objection. If this was meant to rattle Wagner, it had as much effect as a baby slapping the side of a battleship. If anything, it annoyed the judge.

Wagner then asked, "Mr. Hunter, during the recent time you spent in the Anthony home, the various other times you were together with Mr. and Mrs. Anthony, did you hear them quarrel often?"

Joel licked his lips, fondled his thick glasses. One could almost see his brain working, trying to figure what sort of answer would benefit Matt. Wagner said softly, "Come, Mr. Hunter, it's a simple question: did they often quarrel, make cutting remarks at each other?"

"I would say they often teased each other."

"Teased? Before July 25th did you ever hear Mr. Anthony shout at his wife in anger? Or Francine Anthony shout in anger at him?"

"Yes, sir."

"Have you heard either of them shout at the other in anger a few times?"

"Quite a few times."

"Did you ever hear Mr. Anthony quarrel with his wife while under the influence of liquor?"

Matt's smile grew larger as he made a fast note.

"I'm not an expert, cannot say whether he was ever drunk or—"

Wagner broke in impatiently, "Come, now, Mr. Hunter, I didn't ask if he was drunk. Have you ever heard Mr. Anthony argue with his wife after you had seen him take one drink or more?"

"Well ... yes, sir."

"Have you ever heard Francine Anthony argue with her husband after she had one or more drinks?"

"Yes."

Matt whispered something to Jackson who made a motion as if telling him to shut up. Matt grinned happily.

"Am I correct in stating that over a period of time you have witnessed the Anthonys in argument over various matters, sometimes when either or both of them had been drinking?"

"Yes, sir—petty family quarrels."

"I see, family arguments. Now, think carefully, Mr. Hunter. At any time while they were exchanging words, arguing, at any time except on July 25th, did you ever hear Mr. Anthony threaten to kill his wife?"

"Oh, no, sir."

"No matter how angry Mr. Anthony was?"

Joel said, "Indeed not," before Jackson could spring to his feet and object that the degree of anger had never been established. Wagner said something I didn't catch and the judge upheld the objection. Wagner bowed slightly—toward nobody—asked, "Mr. Hunter, at any time except on July 25th did you ever hear Matt Anthony threaten to kill Francine Anthony?"

"No, sir."

Wagner said, "That will be all, Mr. Hunter."

Wagner sat down and as Joel started to leave the stand, Jackson climbed to his feet slowly—a deliberate movement emphasizing his gawky, Lincolnesque height. "One moment, Mr. Hunter, I have a few questions."

For some reason this caused faint laughter in the courtroom, even the jurors grinned. Jackson stood beside the witness chair, but facing the court, as he asked, "Mr. Hunter, do you believe in the United States Constitution?"

"Of course I do."

"Do you believe in all of the Constitution?"

"Yes, sir."

"Do you think Prof. Brown invented the Fifth Amendment?"

Joel's large face was utterly confused. As Wagner got to his feet the judge said sternly, "Mr. Clair, I will not tolerate sarcasm in this court. I trust I shall not have to warn you again about this."

Jackson turned toward the judge, his booming voice actually ringing with sincerity. "Your Honor, being a lawyer, I respect the court and the law. I was not being sarcastic. This witness has stated the late Mrs. Anthony wanted Professor Brown to leave the Anthony house because he had taken the Fifth Amendment, as if it was a criminal act. I am merely trying to show that the Fifth Amendment is a part of the Bill of Rights, put into the Constitution for the purpose of—"

"Are you making a speech, Mr. Clair?" the judge asked.

"Sir," Jackson projected his voice so it filled the courtroom, "I am only establishing that it is neither a criminal act nor a sign of guilt to use the Fifth Amendment. This is of the utmost importance to the defense of my client."

"Proceed with your cross-examination, Mr. Clair, but bear in mind I will not tolerate this court becoming a stage or a soap box."

Jackson dropped his voice. "I certainly apologize, your Honor, if I have done either."

Brown was sitting hunched up in his seat. From the side his broken nose actually made him resemble an old fighter. I knew what he was thinking: If he became the object of trial publicity he would have little chance of keeping a job—if he'd found one.

Jackson turned abruptly to Joel, who was trying to vanish into a crack in the chair. "Now, Mr. Hunter, you have stated you heard Mr. Anthony allegedly threaten his wife. Will you—"

Wagner objected to the word "allegedly," and there was some quibbling between the lawyers as to what constituted a threat. When the judge quieted them, Clair asked, "Mr. Hunter, will you kindly repeat the exact words Mr. Anthony said to his wife?"

Joel stammered, "Well, he—he said, 'Francine, some things I'll take from you because it's a kind of game between us. But Hank Brown is one of the few real things in my life. If you ever say a single out-of-the-way word to Hank, I'll k-kill you. I mean that.' That's what Matt said ... I believe."

"Believe? Did he say it, or not?"

"Yes, sir, he said that. I meant those were the exact words, to the best of my recollection."

"When Matt Anthony said it was a kind of game between them, did you think ... I withdraw the question. Mr. Hunter, after hearing Mr. Anthony say this to his wife, what did you do?"

"Me?" Joel asked, bewildered. "I went upstairs with my wife, to our room. Talked over a book idea with her."

"And after that?"

"We came down and went outside to sun ourselves, play with the dog."

"Didn't you call the police, Mr. Hunter?"

"The police?" Poor Joel wiped some sweat from his upper lip with his tongue. "Why should I call the police?"

"Mr. Hunter, if you heard a person threaten to kill another, wouldn't you call the police, do something about it?"

Joel waved his hands, mixing air. "Oh, I knew it was just talk."

Jackson looked astonished. "Then you didn't consider it a threat?"

"No, sir, I did not."

"That will be all. Thank you, Mr. Hunter."

As Jackson walked away, Wagner got up. "One moment, Mr. Hunter. Did you hear Mr. Anthony say to his wife, 'I'll kill you'?"

"Yes, sir," Joel whispered.

As Joel left the stand, Matt sat tilted back in his chair, studying Joel as if he was a painting. Then he smiled and started writing. Jackson made a few notes, glancing at the jury. He whispered something to Matt, who shrugged and pointed to the pile of papers in front of him, went on writing.

May Fitzgerald was the next witness. Matt stared at her for a long time before he went back to his writing. His hand was tired and several times he dropped his pencil, seemed to shake the fatigue out of his right hand. Wagner established—again—that although May had often heard the Anthonys argue she had never heard Matt threaten to kill Francine, or even to strike her. Jackson gave her a friendly smile as he asked, "Miss Fitzgerald, as far as you know, did Mrs. Anthony ever work?"

"Do you mean did she hold a job?" May asked with her slightly clipped accent.

"Yes, did she hold down a job?"

"Not so far as I know."

Jackson took a few strides in front of the witness stand. "Did the Anthonys entertain often? Did they often have guests for the weekends, for dinner?"

"Very often. On some weekends we had as many as twenty people out."

"You were the only maid?"

"Yes."

"Seems you had quite a lot of work. Did Mrs. Anthony often help you with the cooking or serving?"

"No."

"Did you do the shopping, too?"

"I did."

"Did you see Mr. Anthony drink much?"

"I saw him take a drink only now and then, especially when guests were drinking."

"Miss Fitzgerald, you have stated that you often heard the Anthonys argue. Do you mean Mrs. Anthony nagged him?"

"Yes."

"Over what?"

"Over everything. Money, his drinking and his swimming—not watching his heart. She had a sharp tongue."

Jackson stopped his walking. "Did you say she had a sharp tongue?"

"I did."

Wagner seemed undecided whether to object or not, let it go.

"What does a sharp tongue mean, Miss Fitzgerald?"

"Well, she was not gentle in her comments, she was a blunt woman."

Jackson solemnly nodded, as if in agreement that this was a horror. Then he asked, "Did Mr. Anthony use his house for both a home and an office?"

"He wrote every day."

"In the house?"

"Yes."

"Did he have any other office, any other place where he worked?"

"Not that I know of. Every day he went to his den and worked."

"Would you say Mrs. Anthony nagged him every day, every other day, or every week?"

"Oh, I'd say every day."

Jackson said that would be all. Wagner stood up and asked, "Miss Fitzgerald, did Mr. Anthony nag his wife every day, too?"

"Well ... it takes two to tango," May said to faint laughter in the courtroom.

When May stepped out of the witness box the judge announced the court was recessed for lunch. I waited for the others to come out. I shook hands with Brown and asked how things were. He said, "I have a good job as a mathematician with a manufacturer out West—non-defense production. At least I had it before the trial started."

"Have lunch with me," I said, keeping an eye out for the Hunters.

"No, I think it best I duck reporters and people."

"Where are you staying?"

"I haven't been able to locate a room yet. Most places are filled."

"I'm at the motel up on the hill. Twin beds in the room if you want one."

"Young man, I keep telling you it's risky to be seen with me if—"

"Nonsense, Hank."

"Thank you for the kind offer. I may take it. I'll see you later, Norman."

Joel came out with May and Wilma. Joel said, "Come with us, I need a drink something awful."

I nodded at the women and we headed for a restaurant across the street. A photographer begged us—or rather Joel and May—to pose for a picture but Joel refused, practically ran across the street and into the restaurant. Wilma squeezed my arm, asked, "I thought you were going to call us?"

"I did one Saturday afternoon, but no answer," I lied. "We've been busy—fixing up a house in the country. Soon as it's presentable, I intend to ask you and Joel up."

"Careful, you know what happened the last time we were house guests."

We found a corner table and several people stared at us. We ordered cocktails and lunch. Joel said bitterly, "Oh, that Wagner, that cool sonofabitch, why did he have to make me the star witness?"

"Well, you should have stood up to him instead of acting mealy-mouthed," Wilma said.

"Oh, that would have been dandy, get me reams of publicity, all lousy! 'Joel Hunter, writer of juveniles, balks D.A.' The libraries would love *that!* Oh my God, what will my editor say when she sees me on the front pages tonight."

Wilma reached across the table and patted his hand, a motherly gesture. "Honey, you did fine. Say, isn't that Clair an odd one? What a homely face, and so attractive."

"Norm, you know about these things, will this hurt my sales?"

"I hardly think so. You know the old saw: nothing as old as yesterday's headlines."

"You were only a witness, not involved," May said.

The waiter brought the drinks and Joel took his down in a gulp, ordered a second. "Well, it's almost over. They'll probably be done with Wilma this afternoon. I wish it was Wednesday already and we're on the plane."

"Going away?" I asked, like a polite idiot.

"Barbados. I got a break and—" Joel turned to May. "You know anybody on that island? We want a cheap room, way from all the usual tourist slop."

"No, I don't. But if you look around, after a few days you'll find something."

"They're using the characters in one of his Joe and Eddie, the Bunny Boys books for a kid TV series," Wilma said. "I tried to egg Joel into asking for the scripting job, too, but he was so blinded by the few bucks, his tongue got tied."

Joel winked happily at me. "I want to get away fast. Even the option money should keep us down there for a few months. A hell of a fine break, and so unexpected."

Wilma said, "I liked the simplicity of your ads, and of course the items in the columns. Is the book selling well?"

"About better than we expected."

The food came and we all ate in silence. Then I asked May about the house and she said as far as she knew it was still unsold. A neighbor was taking care of the poodle. May had received most of her back wages and was now going to NYU, working in a phone answering service at nights.

Wilma lit a cigarette, said, "Who else can the State call except me, Brown, and that horrible detective? I don't see how Wagner has a case for murder. Did you dig that hick suit he's sporting?"

"He frightens me," May said. "He's so sure of himself, so cool."

"Matt doesn't seem concerned," Joel said. "I almost think he's enjoying the circus. I hope he understands I did my best for him."

"Is it true he's writing a book while in court?" Wilma asked me.

"Yes. I haven't read the first few chapters, but I understand they're in the house. Novel idea, the suspect's view of his own trial. Matt insists the last chapter will be sensational. What that means, I don't know."

"Damn, you have to hand it to the big boy," Joel said happily, "He's a true pro."

"I bet he'd never pass up a TV scripting job," Wilma put in.

"Oh, stop it. I don't know a damn thing about it, never tried TV. After all, they didn't even ask for me and I hate begging. You're greedy, Wilma."

"Greedy is being a pro, dear. Let me go to the john, I don't want to wet up the witness chair. Coming, May?"

I insisted upon paying the check, told Joel it would go on my expense account. When we reached the courtroom it was pretty well filled up. I suppose most people hadn't left their seats to eat. Joel and Wilma found seats down front, while May and I found singles on opposite sides of the room. Brown was in the second row, reading a book.

It was nearly an hour later before the judge returned and I had a rough time keeping awake in the stuffy courtroom. To my surprise, Wilma was the next witness. Somehow I had expected Wagner to call Brown. Matt still had the tiny smile on his big face, as if enjoying a private joke. He was writing rapidly once more but he seemed to be suffering from indigestion, patting his stomach now and then, throwing pills into his mouth.

Wagner quickly placed Wilma at the Anthony house. Wilma's answers were abrupt, her pop eyes staring boldly at Wagner as he concentrated on the threat. She repeated exactly what Joel had said. The prosecutor asked, "Now, Mrs. Hunter, when Mr. Anthony shouted, 'I'll kill you!' was there anger in his voice?"

"They were both shouting angrily."

"Mrs. Hunter, please answer the question. Was Matt Anthony shouting in anger?"

"He was shouting. I can't say if he was angry or not."

"Mrs. Hunter, a second ago you said they were both shouting angrily. I ask you again: When Matt Anthony shouted at his wife, 'I'll kill you!' was there anger in his voice?"

"All I know is he was shouting!" Wilma snapped.

"Mrs. Hunter, have you ever heard people shout at a baseball game?"

"I think so."

"Was Mr. Anthony's shouting of the same tone and intent as that of a person shouting at a ball game?"

"I am not an expert on shouting!"

Wagner stared at her for a moment, then smiled coolly, said, "No further questions."

Jackson strode up to the witness stand, left hand hooked onto his beaded belt. "Mrs. Hunter, you are a redhead and there is a saying redheaded women have a big temper. Perhaps Mr. Wagner will agree with that. [Jackson actually paused, waiting for the inane giggles from the audience.] Mrs. Hunter, have you a temper?"

"Yes."

"In the heat of an argument have you ever said, 'I'll kill you!' to anybody?"

"Probably."

"I'm afraid I have to have a yes or no answer, Mrs. Hunter," Jackson said, his voice almost a caress.

"Yes."

"Have you ever wanted to actually kill anybody?"

"No."

"Mrs. Hunter, according to your husband's testimony, and your statements to the police, after you heard Mr. Anthony threaten his wife, you went upstairs to do some work. Later you were on the lawn, sunning yourself. In view of the threat, didn't you think of calling the police, or at least being with Mrs. Anthony to protect her?"

"No. I didn't think of it as a threat, but rather as just talk."

"That will be all, Mrs. Hunter."

Wagner stood up, asked, "Mrs. Hunter, on the afternoon of July 25th, did you hear Mr. Anthony tell the deceased, 'I'll kill you!' Answer yes or no."

"Yes."

Wagner called Detective Kolcicki, who looked comical in a new suit far too tight for his pudgy frame. The collar of his white shirt seemed to be cutting the bull neck in half. He went through the routine of establishing his official title and duties, said he became suspicious of the "accident" report when he came across the threat. Matt didn't even glance at Kolcicki, kept writing away and when he stopped, he merely stared down at the table.

In a self-important, clear voice, Kolcicki went on to say he decided to "interrogate" Matt, had told him flatly he didn't believe it was an accident. That at first Matt insisted it was an accident and at this point Kolcicki had said, "'Mr. Anthony, as a mystery writer, would you expect any of your readers to believe this bunch of lies you're handing me, if one of your characters said it?' Mr. Anthony sat there for a while, then he said, 'You're right, it does sound bad. It is a lie. I hit her in the boat and then she was dead. I tried to make it look like an accident. I confess it.' He had this typewriter on his desk and I typed while he dictated the confession. Then he read it and signed it. Whole thing took less than an hour."

The confession was put into evidence and read aloud to the jury. Kolcicki volunteered: "Soon as I knew he was lying, I knew he'd done it. An innocent man don't have to lie. That's been my experience in investigations."

Jackson started his cross-examination with, "Detective Kolcicki, have you ever lied?"

"No, sir."

"Are you telling this court that you have never once in your life told a lie?"

"Not that I know of."

"You're not lying now, under oath?"

"No, sir."

"Did you ever tell your wife a lie?"

"I'm not married."

"Have you ever been married?"

"Yes, sir, but we divorced."

"On what grounds did your wife divorce you, Detective?"

"Why ... we didn't get along."

"Aren't you lying, now? Wasn't the actual grounds for the divorce the fact that you beat her?" Jackson snapped.

Wagner stood up to ask the purpose of the questioning as Kolcicki wiped his sweaty face with his sleeve. Jackson said he wanted to establish, since the witness had stressed Matt had lied, that lying is an everyday occurrence, and it would be natural for a man to attempt to lie his way out of a tight spot. The judge told Jackson he wasn't aware lying was such a commonplace thing and he thought it was all irrelevant to the case. Jackson turned to Kolcicki, asked, "You have read and just heard Mr. Anthony's confession?"

"Yeah."

"That's exactly what Mr. Anthony confessed to you?"

"Sure, it's the confession he signed."

"Detective Kolcicki, I understand you have been a police officer for many years. During that time, have you secured other confessions?"

"I have, lots of them."

"In other words, you are an experienced detective, an old hand at police work?"

"I am."

Jackson said that was all.

As Kolcicki left the stand, walking with surprising grace,

Wagner stood up and told the judge, "Your Honor, the State rests."

There was a rush of small talk in the courtroom. I glanced at Brown: he didn't show any emotion at being off the hook. I was a trifle bewildered, somehow I had expected much more depth to the State's case.

Jackson stood up and said he wanted to make a motion. The judge had the jury sent out and Jackson asked that the case be dismissed for lack of evidence. The judge simply said, "Motion denied," and asked if he was ready to open the defense's case. Jackson looked at the clock; it was a few minutes after three—said he was ready.

The jury trooped back to their box and Jackson took several books out of his attaché case, asked they be entered into evidence as exhibits for the defense. He and the judge had some sort of argument, of which I only caught part. The books were the writings of old Ben Jonson, Maugham, Anderson, Dreiser and others. Jackson claimed he wanted to quote a few lines from each of these famous writers, "... who certainly can qualify as experts on their profession ... " in order to establish the special conditions necessary for "... a creative artist to work ... " Jackson and the judge talked for several minutes. Wagner had not even risen from his chair. Finally the judge asked impatiently, "What has the prosecutor to say?"

"I have no objection, your Honor," Wagner said.

The judge fussed some more, had Jackson mark the passages he wanted to read. The judge glanced through them and all this took a great deal of time. I was restless for a smoke. Matt was writing away at his table as though he was in his den and couldn't care less about the proceedings.

Wilma and Joel were whispering, their red and white heads together like a clumsy nosegay. I stared at her without any feeling and wondered why I didn't feel some damn thing. I'd certainly made the most asinine spectacle of myself possible before her. Also, I hadn't slept with more than a half a dozen women in my life, if that many. Yet seeing Wilma didn't remind me of a thing. All I could think of was—she wasn't wearing those awkward health shoes but regular high heeled ones.

The judge finally gave Jackson the go-ahead signal as the court attendants told people to stop talking. Jackson brought the books back to his table, then addressing the jury, he said, "As I stated in my opening address, it is the defense's contention—which I am about to prove—that a creative person, such as a writer, is a genius and not an ordinary person. Nor can the creative person, the writer, be expected to live by ordinary customs and conventions. I am about to read what several world-famous writers, experts, have said about the living and working habits of authors. Obviously they did not write this for Matt Anthony's trial. In each case I will give you the copyright date, and you will note that most of these observations were written many years ago and cover *all* writers."

I left the court as Jackson began to read in a clear, elocution teacher's voice. In the corridor I lit my pipe, enjoying the taste of the smoke. I could hear Jackson quoting somebody who said a writer should not be tied to one woman since the tool of his trade was curiosity. That sounded like pure bunk. Sinclair Lewis, I think, came in for some statement about writers needing to travel, a constant change. Jackson quoted Ben Jonson's "Who casts to write a living line must sweat," followed by a long bit from Maugham about an author does not write only when at his desk, but all day long as he is thinking and experiencing many things. And a writer cannot give his undivided attention to any other calling.

I waited until four, phoned our apartment. Michele said she was going to take the late afternoon Friday train. Liz Kuhn had asked her to a dress rehearsal of a new musical—Michele was beat but hadn't been able to get out of it. She asked how the trial was going and I said the State hadn't presented much of a case.

Michele went into detail about an idea for decorating the fireplace in our "country home." Court over, I watched people streaming out into the hallway. Brown went by, didn't hear my tapping on the booth door. When I finally hung up, the courthouse already had that deserted feeling.

Heading for the street, I found Joel inside the door, almost hiding. Asking me for tobacco, he got a new corncob going as he said nervously, "All this lousy publicity for nothing. For Christsakes, Wagner couldn't convict a fly on his evidence. The judge should have tossed the case out. For the life of me, I don't know why they couldn't have called it manslaughter, fined Matt and prevented this ridiculous spectacle. Anyway, it's over."

"Over?"

"For us. Wilma is checking with Wagner if we're free to return to town now. My God, I'm a wreck, really need a vacation."

"Going to your musical flying saucer, out of this world?"

"Told you we're heading for the West—" He smiled. "Oh, my,

you're pulling my leg about my den. I may retire there for a few hours' relaxation at that. I rarely spend a night there but ... that time. It wasn't just Matt and the case, things had been rather nasty between Wilma and myself. That's over, we're like rabbits now."

"Good for you two. I'll send you Easter cards."

Joel puffed hard on the pipe. "Odd taste to this tobacco. I got a break with Wilma."

"You did?"

"You see, I understand Wilma, she has a great sexual curiosity. Most of the time I'm grateful for that, but it can also be quite ... demanding. Of course we're both broadminded and ... oh, I'm pretty sure she had an affair a month or two ago."

There wasn't anything for me to say, but my insides coiled.

"Hell, we're sophisticated people—I've strayed myself a few times—but, and this proves it's a healthy thing. She must have gone with a kid. Very immature, I mean, he must have been a lousy lay. Ever since she—we—we've been wonderful in bed."

He wasn't looking at me as he said this. He wasn't smiling. If he'd done either I would have hit him, busted his goddamn queer face. I said, "The silver lining. Look, give me a ring when you get back from the islands. I want you both to meet my wife."

He said he would and I walked out. It was only when I reached the car, drove to the motel that my anger—or was it shame?—left me and I could grin about it. Knowing the Hunters had been something.

I washed up and wondered what the devil to do with myself. Michele and I had been so close these last months, I felt strange being alone. The window looked out upon a bay and I wondered if we could get in some fishing over the weekend. If it would turn just a little warmer we might even do some swimming or—

The phone rang. "Mr. Connor?"

"Yeah." It was a man's voice.

"Norm, this is Henry Brown. I can't find a place to sleep. Is that invitation to share your room still open?"

"Certainly. Look, how about supper together? All goes on the swindle sheet."

He hesitated, then said all right and I drove into town, picked him up in front of a drugstore. It wasn't five yet and we rode out to the canal, sat in the car and watched the fishermen going after tiny snappers. Brown said he had decided to stay for the duration of the trial, that he thought Matt needed his friends in the courtroom. I told him, "Looks like you won't be called at all. Matter of fact, the case may be over tomorrow.

Clair hasn't any witnesses except Matt."

"I imagine he'll put on a psychiatrist, or several of them. He's pleading temporary insanity. Then the State will put their own experts on the stand, and when all the smoke has cleared, nothing will have been proved."

"In any event, Wagner hasn't proved murder."

Brown nodded. "If I was Clair, I'd rest my case without putting Matt on the stand, merely let the psychiatrists say it was possible Matt was insane for the moment. But I think Clair wants to make a show of it."

"What has he got to lose? The D.A. hasn't made it murder."

"That Wagner is shrewd. I have a feeling he's waiting for Matt to take the stand. Wagner has something up his sleeve."

"And you still believe Matt didn't kill Francine, even accidentally?"

"Yes. Aside from the reasons I gave you before, Matt's courtroom behavior convinces me. I don't see him acting so nonchalant if he had anything to do with her death. The way he sits there and grins smugly, keeps writing away—what in God's name is he writing? One would think this is all a big joke to him. Another thing that doesn't make sense: I see Matt for the first time in years, and in an argument over me, he threatens to kill his wife. Does that make sense? Or did I point that out when we first talked?"

"Couldn't that be in keeping with your picture of him as an intellectual phony?" I asked. "Matt might not have the courage to openly help you, but in an argument with his wife he goes all out. To make a horrible pun, he went overboard."

"Perhaps, but I don't believe it. I can hardly believe the trial, most times it seems like a dream, that it can't be real."

"I know, I had the same feeling."

We talked some more, then had a few drinks and a leisurely fish dinner. I liked talking to Brown, although the old guy was so dogmatic he infuriated me at times. Like I said something about "professional" men and he claimed that was a snobbish term; it took as much knowledge and time to be a good bricklayer as to be a lawyer. Still, it was all a way of passing time.

We drove back to the motel, picking up the evening papers on the way. It didn't make most front pages—nothing sensational had come out of the court. One paper had a picture of Jackson in action and another of Matt grinning—and looking positively huge sitting at the defense table—all shoulders. Except for a line in one paper, Brown wasn't mentioned at all. I stretched out on the bed, read the papers, feeling very good—remembering how wretched I'd been the last time I'd spent the night out here, worrying about Wilma and ... that Joel was a snide bastard. A lousy lay, a kid!

Brown undressed and went to sleep by nine-thirty. I was amazed at how hard and lean he looked for a man his age. I was far from sleepy and I took a walk in the darkness, then returned to smoke a pipe in the motel driveway, listen to the sound of the waves. A few cabins away I saw Jackson Clair pacing up and down with long, energetic steps. Maybe it wasn't an act, he couldn't know anybody was watching. I walked over and said hello. We shook hands and his bony face was full of a dozen different shadows as he boomed, "Ah, the publisher!"

"No. Longson's advertising manager."

"Yes, yes, I saw the ads. Simple and pleasing. Is the book selling well?"

"About what we expected."

"I trust you fellows are going to give Matt an advance on the book he's writing in court. I'm gambling my fee on that."

"Depends on the book. We only have a few chapters so far and nobody's read them yet. How is the trial going?"

"Splendid. I was afraid the judge wouldn't allow the books, but when he did that was a major victory. Yes, indeed."

"Do you plan to put Matt on the stand tomorrow?"

"Yes. After all, he's my star witness—and the *only* witness to the actual incident. I feel very confident Matt will walk out a free man."

"Wagner certainly hasn't proved murder. Prof. Brown thinks he's waiting in the bushes for Matt to take the stand."

Jackson sighed. "Care to walk with me? Exercise soothes my nerves, relaxes my mind. One reason for the tension of our times, too many cars." As we walked up and down the driveway, Jackson said, "That Brown—a real thorn in the case. If only he weren't a radical! Make the case much easier if he had been kicked out of college for stealing or murder, but ... you noticed, I'm sure, how I laid the groundwork for a defense if Wagner tried to red-bait. Wagner is a square shooter, kept the case clean of red herrings. He's a very puzzling opponent."

"You think he's competent?" I asked.

"Oh, yes, he's clever. The trouble is, stupidity can often be mistaken for cleverness. I don't mean he's stupid, but after all he's a hick town D.A. For example, I don't understand why he didn't object to my introduction of the books as evidence. Another thing, he hasn't tried to bargain, offer us murder 'two' if Matt pleads guilty. Very odd."

"You think he's getting a Sunday punch ready?"

"He has to. Obviously he hasn't proved the slightest intent or premeditation. However, I am not worried, a wild punch is the easiest to duck, as I believe your Prof. Brown will tell you. However, one thing I admire Wagner for, he's a gentleman through and through. He could have had the Hunters give the entire conversation between Matt and Francine Anthony, brought out Matt was a bit of a radical himself in his teaching days. Did you know he was bounced from Brooks for leading the students in an anti-ROTC demonstration? That one of the things he told Francine in that fateful conversation, was she should be damn glad Brown clammed up ... he could have named Matt? Of course it's all silly, but you realize how easy it would be, or have been, for Wagner to have played up the Professor, then smeared Matt. Yes, Wagner is a fair fighter."

"What reason would Wagner have for not bargaining?"

"Frankly, I don't know. Perhaps he knew I wouldn't even consider anything less than a manslaughter charge. Then again, he may be a gambler, playing the long shot. One thing you can be sure of, I don't underestimate him." Jackson suddenly changed the subject, asking if I knew this area had once been the headquarters for most of the Atlantic Coast Indian tribes? Had I ever visited the reservation nearby? He was full of Indian lore. I was almost trotting to keep up with his long legs. About a half hour later, as he was earnestly explaining how the various tribes regulated the fishing rights, I was getting damn tired. I suspected Jackson was, too—I was far younger and in better shape—but he was trying to outlast me; as if we were a couple of kids. Finally I thought the hell with it and when he paused I said, "We'll have to talk again about the Indians. Right now I need to hit the sack."

"Of course. We may talk sooner than you expect. I plan to do a book on it. I'll be knocking on your office door any month now."

I said I was sure Longson would be glad to consider it and we said good night. I took a shower and dropped off into a good sleep, listening to Brown snoring lightly in the next bed.

Friday was a sunny, mild Fall day. After breakfast Brown insisted it was better we part in the courtroom. The court was really packed and if Brown hadn't been such an early riser we probably wouldn't have found seats. I didn't see the Hunters, but May Fitzgerald was still around. Wearing a worn houndstooth sports jacket, slacks, a plain shirt and tie, Matt was the picture of casual high fashion as he took the stand, his big frame cramped in the witness chair.

After Jackson established Matt had been a professional writer for over twenty years, that he had been a war correspondent and employed by a Hollywood studio as a writer—for a few months—Jackson asked, "Mr. Anthony, as a self-employed writer, will you please tell the court your work schedule?"

"I dictate every day, including Sundays, for at least two hours. This is typed up by a secretary in New York City, returned to me for further revision."

Jackson's eyebrows shot up in hammy surprise. "You mean you only work *two* hours a day?"

"That's actual dictation, answering letters. This is rather difficult to explain," Matt said, his voice low and strong. "But since a writer deals with ideas there isn't any time limit on his work day. He can't put in an eight-hour day and forget his job. For instance, suppose I get an idea for a story: although I may only spend an hour putting the rough on tape, I let the idea cook in my mind for many hours, often for days and months, working out the characters, the plot. In reality I would say I am working every minute—thinking about the story—even though I may be fishing, swimming, talking or watching TV."

"Do you work while you sleep?" Jackson asked lightly.

Matt slipped him that little smile—which was beginning to annoy me. "In a sense I do. I keep a pad and pencil near my bed, to jot down ideas that come to me either before sleeping or even in a dream."

"Would I be correct in saying, Mr. Anthony, that you—or any professional writer—is either using his typewriter, pencil, dictation machine, or his brain, twenty-four hours a day?"

"I'd say he has to be ready to use them twenty-four hours a day. To cite another example, I may hear a bit of conversation during a dinner that would fit in with the story. In other words, I have to constantly keep my work in mind. For that reason I make it a point to keep pencil and paper in all my suits, beach robes, on my boat."

"Have you a pencil and paper handy now?"

Matt pulled a small pad and a pencil from his pocket. "I've been making many notes about this trial. I'm writing a book about it, and my experiences while in jail."

"You're working now?" Jackson asked, as if it was all a complete surprise to him.

"I am. I think it will be the first book showing the inside of a trial, as seen by the defendant. My publishers like the idea. As I told you, I work seven days a week, 365 days a year."

"Even when on trial for your life?"

"Of course," Matt said, and for a moment his face clouded as if realizing he was on trial for his life.

Jackson stood in thought for a second, then he said, "In my quote from Mr. W. Somerset Maugham yesterday, he said something about the writer writing all day long, too, consciously or unconsciously forever sorting and making over his impressions. You said you're actually thinking, or letting an idea 'cook' in the back of your mind, even while fishing, driving your car, etc. How can you concentrate on two things at the same time, Mr. Anthony?"

"After a time I suppose it comes naturally. Foremost, I am constantly concentrating on my work. The other things are merely normal actions and reactions I do without thinking. Just as a person may drive a car and carry on a conversation at the same time."

"Do you mean you can fish, have a swim, talk to people without giving it a second thought?"

"Yes."

"You used the word 'normal' a moment ago. Suppose something that isn't normal happens—let us say your car breaks down, or you have a flat tire, would that disturb your working thoughts, your writing thoughts?"

"Yes."

"Would you say that in your profession you need complete freedom of thought?"

"I would."

"Would an argument upset or spoil such freedom?"

"A true argument would. I mean, arguing over the merits of a baseball team, for example, wouldn't disturb my thinking."

"We have heard testimony that your wife nagged you a great deal. Is that true?"

"Yes."

"Did her nagging ever interfere with your creative thinking?"

"Well, when it was intense I'd say it did."

"Was it often intense?"

"Yes."

"Did you also nag your wife?"

Wagner, who had been toying with a pencil, his face emotionless, started to rise, then sat back.

"I suppose every husband nags at some time or other," Matt was grinning again.

"Mr. Anthony, we are not talking about every husband. Did you ever nag your wife?"

"Yes, at times."

"The State's witnesses have testified that Francine Anthony nagged about your exercising, your drinking, your choice of friends. Why didn't you give in to her demands, end the arguments?"

Matt shrugged his thick shoulders. "I felt I not only had a right to live my own life, but that it also had to be an active life. To spur my thinking, I couldn't live in a mental cage. Also, since we were living pretty high, I had to keep jabbing my mind to turn out enough work to meet our expenses."

"Are you in debt?"

"Yes. We went into debt to buy our house, the boats, other items. I haven't any set income I can count on. Some years I've made over $20,000 ... and there have been years when I didn't average fifty bucks a week."

"Miss Fitzgerald has testified you and your wife entertained often. Was that Mrs. Anthony's idea?"

"No. We both liked to live comfortably, entertain, travel."

"Did you give your wife a weekly allowance for household expenses?"

"We had a joint checking account. She took out about two hundred dollars each week for food, help, whatever household expenses arose."

"Was Mrs. Anthony a wealthy woman before you married her?"

Matt shook his head. "No."

"Was she working then?"

"She was a cashier in a store."

"Do you know if she was supporting her former husband?"

"Yes. She was."

"Do you know who paid the legal expenses for her divorce?"

"I did."

"Did you ever buy Francine Anthony a mink coat?"

"Yes, twice, that I can recall."

"Did you ever buy her a car for her own use?"

"We've had many cars, we both used them."

"Mr. Anthony, do you play golf?"

"No."

"Did Mrs. Anthony?"

"Sometimes. Not very often during the last few years."

"Did she have a set of golf clubs?"

"Yes."

"Do you know what her golf clubs cost?"

"About $300."

"Did you ever buy Francine Anthony any jewelry?"

"Only a wedding ring. She never cared for jewels."

"Did Mrs. Anthony have charge accounts at most New York City department stores?"

"Yes."

"Was she fond of fishing?"

"Very."

"Did she have her own fishing gear?"

"Yes."

"Do you know what her rods and reels cost?"

Matt shrugged again. "About $2000. I know her tuna reel cost $650."

"Mr. Anthony, since your marriage to Francine Anthony, have you traveled often?"

"Almost every year. We've been to Europe three times, to the West Indies, to Canada and various parts of the United States."

"Mrs. Anthony accompanied you on all these trips?"

"Certainly."

"Now, Mr. Anthony, let us come to July 25th. Will you tell the court exactly what happened on that day, starting from the time you arose."

"Fran and I got up at about nine, had a swim. Then the Hunters came down and we all had breakfast. I had secretly ordered a skin-diving outfit sent to the Hampton post office—under one of my pen names. About ten-fifteen I took the car and drove over to see if it had arrived. It had and I hid it in the trunk of the car. I was amazed to see Hank Brown walking towards the Hampton railroad station. We had taught together at Brooks University many years ago. I stopped Hank and we talked for ..."

Jackson held up his hand. "One second, Mr. Anthony. You said you had 'secretly' ordered this skin-diving outfit. Why in secret?"

"Fran was against it. She felt underwater swimming might be a strain on my heart."

"Mr. Anthony, do you carry a large insurance policy?"

"Not at present. At one time I held policies totaling $50,000. However, due to the expense of buying our estate, building the house, I was not able to meet some premiums and a few of the policies have lapsed. At present I only carry about $6000 worth of insurance."

"How much insurance did you carry on July 25th?"

"About $6000."

"Did Mrs. Anthony ever tell you she was afraid you might die before your larger policies could be renewed?"

Matt grinned. "Many times. She claimed I had let the insurance lapse merely to annoy her. I kept reminding her the insurance money went into the house."

I—and everybody else—glanced at Wagner, expecting him to make an objection. Even the judge looked his way. But Wagner sat there calmly, making notes.

"So you had to sneak over to Hampton to get this skin-diving outfit, Mr. Anthony. Did you think skin-diving might be a strain on your heart?"

"Mr. Clair, if I thought I was dying I would have shot myself. I don't believe in being a living corpse. I realized I had to take moderate care of my heart, we all do as we grow older. I cut down on my drinking, on exercise, avoided fatty foods. At the same time I swam, I walked, I fished. Skin-diving requires even less energy than swimming. I felt exploring the bottom of the bay, perhaps finding the remains of old ships, might give me material for a book. I looked forward to it as a new experience."

"Now, Mr. Anthony, let us continue with the day of July 25th. You said you met Professor Brown in Hampton—what happened after that?"

"I'd read a little of Hank's troubles in the papers. Naturally, we talked about that, and other things, for a while. He kept saying he had to make a train. I urged him to come over to the house and either take a later train, or stay the weekend. As I said, we hadn't seen each other in years, had much to talk over. He told me he was out of work and stony. I thought I might be able to help him find something. We arrived at the house before noon. Hank met Fran and the Hunters. Fran kept repeating his name, trying to remember where she had heard or read about him. Finally, while I was getting everybody a drink, Fran asked him pointblank—she was always outspoken—and he told her about losing his job. Although she didn't say a word, everybody could see how furious she was and I knew Hank was uncomfortable. Fran and the Hunters went out on the veranda. When I passed there, Fran bawled me out. I told her Hank and his wife had been very kind to me when I was a young instructor at Brooks, that I was very fond of him, both as a man and as a friend, and might have him out for a weekend. She was afraid I was going to lend him some money. Then Fran said she wanted him to leave at once and if I didn't tell Hank to get out, she would. It was then I told her I'd kill ... her ... if ... if she ever said a rude word ... to him." Matt's voice ended in a nervous whisper. Under his tan I thought he looked pale.

"Would you like a glass of water, Mr. Anthony?" Jackson asked.

Matt shook his head, sat up straight and smiled again—a brave little smile this time. He certainly was acting again. He said, "I am perfectly all right, Mr. Clair, thank you."

Jackson rubbed his chin slowly, asked, "What was your state of mind when you told your wife you would 'kill' her if she was rude to your old friend?"

"I was quite angry, upset. I knew most people were avoiding Hank and ... well, a crisis is the test of any friendship."

"Had Mrs. Anthony ever met Professor Brown before?"

"No."

"Have you any idea as to why she wanted him out of your house? Did she find him loud, obnoxious, or—"

"Of course not. She barely had a chance to talk to him. She made the reason very clear—it was a matter of money. She felt if my name was linked in any way to his, it might hurt some movie sales I had in the works."

"Matt Anthony, when you told your wife you would 'kill' her if she ordered your friend out of your house, did you mean that as a threat?"

"I did not! It was merely words—a phrase—one uses in the heat of anger."

"Have you ever used that same phrase before?"

"Hundreds of times—ever since I could talk. It was said in the same sense as saying, if you don't pass the bread I'll break your arm. Or, get off the phone before I wring your neck. Merely words."

"Then, am I correct in stating that in your own mind, at least, you were not threatening to actually kill your wife?"

"Absolutely correct!" Matt half rose from the witness chair. "I loved Fran."

"Witnesses have testified that your wife nagged you, that the both of you often argued. Were you and Mrs. Anthony happy?"

"Yes. As a writer all people interest me, but few excite me. Fran was an exciting person. We had both been married and divorced before. If we hadn't been hitting it off, we would have separated. We were in love, happy, suited each other."

"Mr. Anthony, have you ever in your life actually wanted to kill a person?"

"I have—once."

Jackson looked startled, even Wagner came to attention.

That smile—as if it was the key to a great secret—formed on Matt's face. "During the war a Nazi officer wounded me and killed several of my GI buddies. I tried to kill him with my bare hands."

Jackson gave the court a big understanding grin. "We all know during the war thousands of Americans were killed. Except for that one war experience, have you ever wanted to kill anyone?"

"No. Or hurt anybody, either."

"Now, Mr. Anthony, let us continue with the events of July 25th. What happened after you talked to your wife on the veranda?"

"I went back to Hank. As I said, he couldn't help but sense Fran's hostility. He said he wanted to take the next train back to New York, that he had to see somebody about a job that afternoon...."

One of Wagner's assistants whispered something and they both turned to search out Brown in the crowd, then Wagner shrugged and shook his head. I wondered if he could still call Brown to the stand.

"... I drove Hank to the railway station, said I'd get in touch with him in a week or two. I saw Hank off and returned to the house—"

"One second, Mr. Anthony," Jackson cut in. "Did your wife see Mr. Brown before he left the house? Did she speak to him?"

"No."

"Now, both you and the Hunters have testified that you told your wife '... *if* you ever say a single-out-of-the-way word to Hank, I'll kill you.' Those are your exact words?"

"Yes."

"You said, '... *if* ... Francine ever said anything to Mr. Brown.' After you ... eh ... talked to your wife on the veranda, said the words, did she ever see or talk to Mr. Brown again?"

"No. I told you, I drove Hank to the station."

"Yes. Now when you returned to the house, what happened?"

"I found the Hunters sleeping on the lawn. Fran wasn't around. It was early afternoon, I thought it would be a good opportunity to try out my Aqua-Lung. I took the package from the car to the boat house, undressed. I saw Fran fishing a few hundred yards out in the bay, her back to me. I thought it would be a great joke to walk on the bottom of the bay, yank at her line. Unfortunately, the joke backfired. Since I had only used the lung once before—at a friend's place—I didn't know how to work it and somehow cut off my air supply. I had to surface."

"Where did you come up?"

"A few feet from the boat. Of course Fran saw me. I swam over and climbed into the boat. She was beside herself with rage that I had purchased the diving outfit. I tried to explain it might give me material for a book. She called me a childish fool, and other names. I—"

"Exactly what other names, Mr. Anthony?"

"I don't see the importance of telling ... She called me a dumb bastard and a stupid ... Mr. Clair, there's no point in repeating the names. It might shock some people. Fran and I, being pretty worldly, used language that ... again, her names were merely words said in anger."

"What did you do after she called you the names?"

"I told her to take it easy, I knew what I was doing. I stood up to dive, swim back to shore and see what was wrong with the air valve. Fran got to her feet and tried to jerk the lung from my back. I pushed her away as I told her she would break the tubes. She came at me; grabbed the lines, cursing me. I said to stop it, said we'd talk it over later. She kept trying to break the lung. I got mad, pushed her away, screamed at her to stop. She came at me again, nearly upsetting the rowboat. I got so mad I ... lost my head and struck out at her." Again his voice sank to a nervous whisper.

"You said you struck out at her. You've done a lot of boxing, Mr. Anthony, did you hit her with your left hand or right? Was it a punch, a jab, a ...?"

"I don't know! All I know is I was fed up with her carping about the damn Aqua-Lung! I know I struck out at her. All I remember is—the next thing I knew I was standing in the boat and Fran was ... Oh, God, I keep seeing this over and over in my mind ... poor Fran was hanging over the side of the boat, bleeding ... her blood so dark on the green water." Matt held a big hand in front of his face, bowed his head. I knew he wasn't acting now, that I was watching sincere sorrow.

In a voice syrupy with understanding, Jackson said, "I realize how painful this must be for you, but this is a court and I must ask you to tell us exactly what you did next."

Matt took his hand away, wiped his lips. "I thought she was hurt. I knelt over her, was stunned to realize she was dead. It seemed impossible."

"You were positive she was dead?"

Matt nodded. "She didn't have a pulse. I took a silver spoon from her tackle box and held it to her mouth; she wasn't breathing. I started to pull her back into the boat, raise the anchor. Then I remembered the police wouldn't want me to touch a thing. I dived over and raced ashore. I dressed quickly, hid the diving outfit, and—"

"Why did you bother dressing, hiding the Aqua-Lung?" Jackson cut in.

Matt spread his hands on the air. "Frankly, I don't know. I was in a state of shock. I imagine I dressed because I thought I'd have to go for the police. I simply didn't remember about the phone. I was dazed. I kept drying my face and it was still wet ... I was crying. As I started running toward the house I kept thinking of the mess, the headlines. My aching head seemed to be in two parts: one dazed, the other full of racing thoughts. When I reached the house I saw the Hunters still dozing on the lawn. It came to me that I could avoid a scandal by calling it an accident. Frankly, I don't know now if I was thinking of myself then, or trying to avoid messy headlines for the sake of Fran's memory. Seeing the Hunters dozing, I knew it would be simple to use a gimmick I had once written into a story. A time gimmick that would establish an alibi for myself. As I said, I was thinking very fast and clearly—and at the same time I was confused, shocked. The dazed part of my mind didn't give a damn what happened." Matt stopped talking, stared at the crowded courtroom without seeing it.

Jackson said, "Exactly what do you mean by a 'time gimmick,' Mr. Anthony?"

Matt shook himself, as if he'd been lost in a day dream. "Joel Hunter was sleeping in his swimming trunks, wasn't wearing a watch. I played with the poodle for a moment, making him bark. The noise awoke Joel, but fortunately not Wilma, who was sleeping several yards away. Joel, mumbling, asked if I wanted to take a swim. I held up my wristwatch—but he was too far away to see it. It was 3:27 P.M. but I told him it was only a quarter to three, why not wait until Fran returned from fishing before we went swimming."

"In other words, Mr. Anthony, you misled him about the time—a mistake of about three quarters of an hour?"

"That's correct. He went back to sleep, as I expected. I waited a moment, then tossed a pebble at Wilma. When she awoke I said, 'It's three-thirty, going to sleep the afternoon away?' She then awoke Joel, and I told him I'd just finished reading an article in a magazine lying on the table, that my eyes hurt. The implication was I'd read it during the supposedly three quarters of an hour Joel had been sleeping. I then sent

May down to the dock to tell Fran to come back and join us in a swim. Naturally, she screamed upon seeing Fran hanging over the side of the boat. I told her to call a doctor and the police as I swam out. Although I was still dazed, still terribly upset, I knew I was putting on a good act, that I could avoid a scandal. As it turned out, luck was with me—at first."

"In what way, Mr. Anthony?"

Matt shook himself again. He was no longer smiling, had a faraway look in his eyes. "What? Oh, the luck—the lousy luck. Fran must have caught a shoelace on the duckboards of the rowboat, broke the lace when she fell. Well, the medical examiner decided, in view of that and the 'fact' we were all on the lawn while she was fishing, that she had stood up to cast, lost her balance or tripped over the lace, and fell. He called her death accidental."

"Were you pleased with your cleverness, Mr. Anthony?"

"No. The full impact of losing Fran had hit me, I was sick. Just before supper, while I was dictating, May brought in—"

"You worked the same day?"

"Yes. Work is not only a habit, but also an escape for me. I had to think of something else, get my mind off Fran. Well, May brought Detective Kolcicki into my study. He told me flatly he didn't believe it was an accident, kept stressing that I'd threatened Fran. I ... I tried to explain it really wasn't a threat. Then ... the cobra struck *up*." Matt was staring at the floor, his voice low but clear.

Jackson asked quickly, "Are you feeling well, Mr. Anthony?"

Matt nodded.

"Did you say something about a cobra?"

Matt stared at Jackson for a moment, as if seeing a stranger. "Did I? It's an expression of mine, meaning the fat's in the fire. You see, the fact is a cobra can't strike up."

"Let us get back to what happened between you and Detective Kolcicki."

Matt rubbed his hands together, then looked at the palms. "Of course. Well, I realized how silly my story sounded, that if I stuck to it, things would only be more involved. So I told him the truth. It was a relief, a great load off my mind. He typed it up and I signed the confession. Yes, I signed it!" Matt rose in the chair and then fell back, a cockeyed grin on his big mouth. He looked very sickly.

An attendant rushed over with a glass of water. Matt thanked him in a small voice, drank some. The judge asked if he wanted a recess. Matt shook his head gamely, whispered, "I want to get this ordeal over with, your Honor."

Clair said, "Matt, perhaps a rest ...?"

"No. I'm able to continue. Let's go."

Jackson played with his beaded belt. "I have only one more question, Mr. Anthony. You have told us in great detail exactly what happened—except for the moment when you struck your wife. You obviously have a mind trained for detail, why are you vague about that all-important moment? Can't you recall if you struck her with your left hand, or your right ...?"

"I don't know!" Matt shouted hoarsely. "She came at me and in a blind rage I struck out. That's all I know! Perhaps I blacked out. The next thing I knew she was hanging over the side of the boat.... That's all I know."

"Did you ever strike your wife before?"

"Never."

Jackson said, "That will be all, Mr. Anthony."

As Wagner stood up the judge recessed the court for fifteen minutes. A guard led Matt away. I noticed Matt's shirt front was wet with sweat.

Leaving my hat on my seat, I took out my pipe and headed for the hall. May Fitzgerald was already there, blowing her smoke rings. She said, "I feel sorry for him. Several times I thought he was about to faint."

I nodded. "At times I thought he was acting but—"

"That's a bloody thing to say."

I grinned at her. "I was about to add but at the end I knew he wasn't."

"Seems strange their final argument should be over something as trivial as a diving toy."

I was about to say something trite, like, "That's life," but didn't. May said it.

I said, "I suppose the case will go to the jury on Monday. Are you staying over?"

"I expect to. Missing a few classes won't hurt me."

"Where are you staying?"

"With a colored family I know. Where else could I stay?"

There wasn't any comment to make and I smoked my pipe.

When Matt was brought back to the stand he seemed his old self, grinning at Wagner like a pug looking across the ring at his opponent.

Wagner stood beside the witness chair for a moment, then asked in his hard, emotionless voice, "Mr. Anthony, you have testified under oath you think about your work—your writing—practically twenty-four hours a day—is that what you said?"

"A part of my mind is thinking about my work all the time."

"You let the plots 'cook' is the exact word you used. In other words, some part of your mind is concerned with your writing twenty-four hours a day."

"That's right."

"And you write seven days a week?"

"I do."

"What part of your writing is fiction?"

Matt smiled. "It's entirely fiction."

"Would I be correct in saying that since your writing is entirely fiction, all the characters, incidents and details in your books are a product of your own mind, Mr. Anthony?"

"You would be correct, Mr. Wagner."

Jackson was leaning forward, his long frame ready to leap to his feet, his rugged face listening intently.

"In brief, the subject matter of your books is part of your mind, your thoughts, day after day?"

Matt nodded and the judge told him to speak up. Matt said, "That's correct."

Wagner returned to his table where an assistant handed him a bulky briefcase. Wagner dumped about a dozen books, mostly paperbacks, and a mimeographed paper out on the table. The striking cover of the book we had recently reissued stood out. Wagner turned toward the judge. "Your Honor, these books represent the writings—the work—of Matt Anthony for the last ten years. I wish to enter them into evidence as the State's exhibits, C, D, E ..."

Jackson made his leap. "I object, your Honor. These books are works of fiction, therefore cannot be considered as evidence!"

The judge held up his hands, called both lawyers to the bench. For a few minutes the three of them talked in low voices, both Jackson and the D.A. arguing vehemently. Finally they returned to their tables and the judge said, "The witness will step down. The jury will retire until I settle a point of law."

When the jury left, Wagner stood up, said, "Your Honor, the witness has said that all day long, seven days a week, he thinks about his work. These books represent Matt Anthony's published writings for the past ten years. In order to prove intent and premeditation, I strongly urge that it is entirely relevant to the State's case to show exactly what the defendant was thinking these last ten years. His own writings will prove he was constantly thinking about physical violence, promiscuous sex, crime, murder and rape."

"This is ridiculous, your Honor," Jackson said. "The very nature of fiction means it is imaginary, therefore cannot be considered on a factual basis, nor as evidence."

"I do not claim the contents of these books are factual, but it is a fact, according to the testimony, that these books constitute the major part of Mr. Anthony's thinking during the last ten years. This is not my statement, but his own."

"Your Honor," Jackson said, "These books are a commodity manufactured by my client for a certain type market. He has to slant these books to the demands of that market, therefore—"

"They still represent his thinking, according to his own testimony," Wagner cut in.

"I submit this is merely a cheap bit for sensationalism on the part of the prosecutor to influence the jury. I object to fiction being—"

"I will be the judge of that, Mr. Clair," the judge told Jackson. He turned to Wagner. "Do you plan to read all these books to the jury, Mr. Wagner?"

"No, sir. I will merely read a few sentences and sum up the contents of each book. These books give us a unique opportunity to look into the mind of the defendant, for in the printed form we have his thoughts before us."

"To put these novels into evidence will make this court the laughing stock of the bar, would be a mockery of justice and—"

"Mr. Clair, I am the judge in this court and perfectly capable of performing my duties."

"I object to these novels as immaterial and irrelevant!" Jackson said, his face flushed with anger.

"Overruled."

"Exception!" Jackson snapped, returning to the defense table, where Matt was busy writing. Jackson sat down and began whispering to Matt, gesturing with his hands—as if Matt were the judge.

The jury was recalled and Matt returned to the stand. Wagner picked up the mimeographed papers, asked, "Mr. Anthony, are you a member of the Mystery Writers of America?"

"Yes, although I doubt if my dues are paid up."

"Do they publish a monthly newsletter called, *The Third Degree?*"

"Yes."

"I now show you a copy of *The Third Degree* for January of last year. I show you an article on page three titled, 'The .45

Typewriter' by Matt Anthony. Did you write this article, Mr. Anthony?"

"I did."

"This is not fiction; this is an article, a piece of non-fiction, is it not, Mr. Anthony?"

"Well, yes. It's a puff, sort of an inside bit."

"What does that mean?"

"It's the sort of piece that would only be understood by other writers, mystery story writers."

Wagner handed it to the court clerk to be marked as an exhibit for the State. The clerk handed it up to the judge. The judge glanced at it—and he must have been a hell of a fast reader—then gave it to Jackson. Clair sat down and read it carefully. Matt watched him with an absolute bored expression and the whole courtroom moved restlessly. It was almost noon. Jackson sure took his time. Finally he got to his feet and boomed—jarring everybody—"I object, your Honor, on the grounds this has no relation to fact. Mr. Anthony has already stated this is inside information, written for a select group. This could easily have been written as a joke, a bit of sarcasm or mere boasting before other professional writers."

The judge asked Matt, "Is this Mystery Writers something like a trade union, Mr. Anthony?"

"I wish it were. Perhaps you might call it that, loosely, in the same sense that one might call the American Medical Association a union."

"Is this ... eh ... paper the official organ of the organization?"

"I believe so."

"Objection overruled."

Jackson barked, "Exception!" and handed the paper to the stenographer for marking. Then Wagner took the mimeographed sheets and told the jury, "Ladies and gentlemen, I will now read from State's Exhibit 'C' an article written by the defendant and titled, 'The .45 Typewriter.' Quote: *'In no other writing medium have I found so much technical background data necessary as in the field of the mystery novel. With or without due modesty I can safely say I know more about poisons, knife wounds and ballistics than the average police official, and know more ways to commit murder than any killer. Indeed, I can qualify as an expert in any criminal endeavor.'* Unquote. Did you write that, Mr. Anthony?"

"I did."

"And do you know more ways to commit murder than easy killer, Mr. Anthony?"

"Probably—and so does any professor of criminology in a college."

Wagner went to his table, picked up a paperback book, glanced at some notes, then asked that *Death in Spades* by Matt Anthony be entered into evidence. Jackson went through the routine of objecting that the book was immaterial and the judge overruled him. Jackson thumbed through the book, said, "Your Honor, it is impossible for me to read this, study it, in a short time."

"Do you wish time to read these books, Mr. Clair?" the judge asked.

"Your Honor, that would delay the trial for a number of days, add to the cost of the defense and my client has very little money. I do not wish to delay this trial." Jackson handed the book back to be marked.

Holding the book up before Matt, Wagner asked, "Did you write this book, Mr. Anthony?"

"I did."

"Do you know that in these 152 pages there are nine brutal beatings, six murders, four fornications and a rape?"

Matt said calmly, "I never counted them, but I will take your word for it."

Wagner picked up another book. "Mr. Anthony, do you write under the pen name of Daisy Action?"

"I have used that name. I use quite a few names."

Wagner had the gaudy-covered paperback titled, *The Corpse in Her Life* by Daisy Action put into evidence over Jackson's objections and said, "I will read from page 97. Quote: *'Please, please,'* she moaned as Ad Hardy staggered toward her, bloody hands out.

"*'You lying little bitch, playing me for a patsy!'* he said, the words tumbling from his mouth like a harsh explosion.

"*'Please, Ad ... please. I know what you want ... take me.'* She backed against the wall, eyes closed, her words almost a moan of pleasure.

"One bloody claw of a hand suddenly ripped her silk blouse down the front: her firm breasts stood out. Cursing, Ad began slapping her breasts until she collapsed, screaming with pain. Did you write that, Mr. Anthony?"

Jackson shouted, "Your Honor, I object to this form of questioning. Mr. Wagner is being deliberately sensational, influencing the jury. The defendant has said he authored the book, to keep asking him over and over if he wrote it serves no purpose."

"I'm merely showing some of Mr. Anthony's thoughts, the things that 'cook' in his mind," Wagner answered.

The judge told Wagner not to drag out the evidence.

Wagner next introduced into evidence five more novels, asked, "Mr. Anthony, do you know that in these five books there are exactly twenty-two killings, including the murder of two children?"

"I've never counted them. I don't write with an adding machine, Mr. Wagner."

"Do you wish me to itemize them, Mr. Anthony?"

"If it gives you any pleasure, go right ahead."

Wagner turned to the judge, who ordered Matt's answer stricken from the record. Jackson half-stood, as if ready to jump into a fight. When the judge warned Matt about being sarcastic, Matt told him, "I'm not being sarcastic, your Honor. Mr. Wagner has cited me as a criminal expert. As a D.A. he is also undoubtedly an expert on crime, or should be. I merely thought, as one expert to another, he wished, to compare notes."

This was also ordered out of the record: Jackson sat down, shaking his head. He started to make a note, then loudly snapped the pencil between his fingers. The judge glanced at him but didn't say anything.

Picking up another book, Wagner went through the routine of placing it in evidence, then read: "*'Well honey, I tried my best to make something out of you, but once a lousy whore always a lousy whore. You could of made us both a pile of folding money, but ... this is goodbye. I'll never again put time in a dumb slut.'*

"*As Martin picked up his hat, she slid off the dirty cot, looking thin and childlike as the sunlight painted her nude body. She stared at him with sad eyes. As he reached the door of the shack, with a motion as fast as a striking snake, she pulled a .38 from under the stained pillow, fired.*

"*Martin tumbled to the floor, holding his left knee. Through his torn and bloody pants, part of a bone stuck out: a gruesome white monument to nothing. She walked over, a delicate sway to her thin hips, took deliberate aim and shot his other kneecap away. Then she drawled in a tiny voice, 'Ya see, Marty, you ain't never going to leave me. Not even crawl away from me. A hill gal only loves one man. Didn't ya know that, darling?'* Unquote. Mr. Anthony, can children buy this book?"

Jackson was on his feet before Matt could answer. "Your Honor, I object to that last line, about children. And I move for a mistrial on the grounds the prosecutor has influenced the jury by this cheap—"

"I didn't write these books, your rare genius did!" Wagner shouted.

The judge banged away with his gavel and in the silence that followed Jackson said, "Your Honor, the defense is willing to concede Mr. Anthony wrote hardboiled crime novels, which by their very nature deal with the seamy side of life, have to be realistic. However, Mr. Anthony did not invent or start this ... eh ... this school of writing: There are hundreds of such books on sale this minute, and over the years thousands of these books have been written. Therefore, I move for a mistrial on the grounds that by taking passages out of context the prosecutor has not only influenced the jury, but also deliberately misled them with the implication Matt Anthony is responsible for the literary tastes of our country. Obviously the defendant, as a self-employed writer, must write for an established market—he does not create that market."

The judge quickly denied the motion but ordered Wagner's question about whether children could buy the book stricken from the record. Glancing at the wall clock he asked Wagner, "How many more books do you plan to offer as evidence?"

Wagner eyed the pile of novels on his table, then turned toward the judge. "I should like to read from two more, your Honor."

"I think you've made your point, Mr. Wagner. You may enter one more book into evidence. Only one. Continue."

Wagner picked over the books, held up *The Last Supper*. While Clair was booming his usual objections and being overruled, all I could think was: Would selecting the book help our sales?

Facing the jury Wagner said, "I will now read from page 19. Quote: '*Walking across the bridge they stopped to stare at the brightly lit skyscraper windows—jeweled lace against the dark night. Placing his hands on her shoulders, Walt said, "How lonely it is here. A perfect place for a murder." Helen moved out from under his hands. He held her shoulders once more. "Must you always avoid me?"*

"'*She stared up at him boldly. "You want me but what have you to offer in return? You know what I want of you, but you are a weakling.*

"'*Walt said gently, "You shouldn't push me so hard."*

"'*She laughed, the very coolness of her voice infuriating him. "Do what you do so well—talk. You don't frighten me."*

"'*Wait said softly, "I never wanted to frighten you. But we all have the will to murder—it is only the opportunity we lack. I* have the desire—and this is the opportunity!" His powerful hands raised her to the bridge railing. Helen made only one movement—she kicked him savagely in the groin. His lean face frozen with horror and surprise, Walt did a drunken dance for a moment, then collapsed, both hands urgently pressing what he had always been so proud of. Her cute face showing no emotion, Helen stooped, carefully removed his hands from the apex of his legs, kicked him in the groin again. Watching him groveling in helpless pain, Helen drew back her shapely leg to kick the bloody spot again, then hurriedly walked away. She knew Walt was right, we all have the will to murder.'"

Wagner shut the book: "Mr. Anthony, in the last ten years have you written any other kind of book except what your counsel has termed 'hardboiled crime books'?"

"No."

"That is all."

As Jackson got to his feet the judge looked at the clock. It was after one; he said the court would recess for lunch. Jackson stepped toward the bench, said loudly, "If your Honor pleases, I have but a few questions. I would then request the court adjourn until Monday. As this is Friday and since I expected the State's cross-examination to last longer, the defense's last two witnesses, doctors, are not in court."

The judge motioned both lawyers to the bench. There was a whispered conference—except once Jackson's deep voice boomed "... to have them travel back and forth to Riverside ... fees are very high and the defendant is broke...." There was more low talk with all of them turning to look at the wall clock—as if doubting it was still there.

Matt sat hunched over in the witness chair, staring out at the courtroom, studying us. Once he stood up and waved his arms around like a pitcher loosening his muscles. He was a frightfully big man.

The lawyers returned to their tables and the judge told the jury, "The court realizes it is well past your lunchtime. However, since Mr. Clair says he has only a few more questions to ask the defendant, we will continue. When Mr. Clair is finished the court will adjourn until ten o'clock, Monday morning." The jury looked rather relieved.

Jackson stepped forward, giving Matt his best man-to-man grin, as he asked. "Mr. Anthony, have you ever written any type story except mysteries?"

"Oh, yes. I have written slick love stories, and what is known as quality yarns. In fact when I first started I had a story on

O'Brien's honor roll. This was an annual anthology of the best short stories of the year."

Jackson nodded. "Then, as a professional writer, do you consider yourself capable of turning out any type of fiction?"

"Yes."

"Then why is it, Mr. Anthony, that in the last ten years you have confined your writing to crime stories?"

"They sell."

"Can you give us a rough idea of how many people read your books?"

"Oh, on the average, taking in both hardcover and paperback sales, I would say about 300,000 people buy a copy of each book, which means the book is probably read by at least a million people."

"How many books have you written during the last decade?"

"I turn out about three a year."

"Roughly, then, some thirty million people have read your novels—almost one-sixth of our entire population."

Matt smiled. "Not quite that many. The same person may keep buying each new book as it's published."

"In your opinion, as a professional writer, would romantic ... eh ... sweet, love stories sell as well as hardboiled action?"

"Indeed, no. There's little, if any, chance of a paperback reprint of the sugary love yarn."

"Then you turned to crime stories solely because they sell well?"

"Yes."

"If next year you found love stories selling better than crime novels, would you then write love novels?"

"Certainly. I write for a living, therefore I must always aim at the best paying market."

"That's all."

The judge glanced at Wagner who said, "No further questions, your Honor." After the usual warning to the jury not to discuss the case, court was dismissed for the day. I waited outside until Brown came by, asked, "Where do you want to eat?"

"At the moment all I want is a drink. Let's drive to some place outside town. Wagner crucified Matt."

"You think it was that bad?" I asked, as we went down the steps.

"The worst part was the fact it was true—Matt did write all that terrible trash. I told you Wagner was a clever fellow."

"Actually, what did he prove, that Matt writes tripe? This is a courtroom, not a critics' group. I still don't see any proof of murder."

"I think he influenced the jury, at least shocked them. But the legal aspect aside, Wagner stripped Matt naked in public, exposed him as a pitiful ... literary pimp. Clair was a fool to place Matt on the stand. And he didn't fight back enough—I thought he was on the right track when he started talking about Matt not inventing the sex and violence books. But he didn't go far enough, he should have shown that so-called literary tastes boil down to the publishers trying for the fast buck."

"Oh, hell, Hank, that's pure bunk. I'm not trying to gild the publishing industry, God knows, but you're putting the cart before the horse. Books go in cycles, fads, and right now the public is demanding the fast-paced story that reflects the tensions of our time. If you see a dirty face in a mirror—don't call the mirror dirty."

"That's more bunk, Norm. Big business under the slogan it's good for business always gives the public an inferior product. And that goes for publishing, of course. Don't you know they can make a nylon stocking that will wear for years? That they could seal the lubrication of an auto so that one would never need a change of oil? But think what that would do to the stocking industry, or the oil business!"

As I opened the car door, Brown was lecturing on what the auto industry supposedly did to a Mr. Tucker who was ready to build a better car. I wasn't in the mood for a lecture, nor did I believe his line. As we started to drive I managed to change the subject with, "After hearing him testify, do you still think Matt never killed Francine?"

"I don't know, it all has an unreal quality. Yes, listening to him, I still can't believe he struck her. How easy it would have been for him to simply dive over the side of the boat when Francine tried to take the diving lung from him. And these diving things are hardly flimsy, I doubt if she could have damaged it much. It's all Alice in Wonderland. Why Wagner had the first of Matt's books marked exhibit C—meaning that State had only introduced two other exhibits thus far—and they had already stated their case. In most murder trials there's dozens of exhibits."

"Proving?"

"Nothing, except I have this feeling it's all a play, not a trial. Jackson's strutting, Wagner the villain. Matt with his crazy smile, as if he already knows what the third act will be."

"Yeah. That grin must be annoying the devil out of the jury. What was that cobra thing?"

Brown shrugged. "Some story idea Matt's had for a long time. He told me something about it. Somehow, I smell a frame-up here."

"Oh, Hank. How can Wagner possibly be framing Matt?"

"I don't know, but I smell it. Perhaps Matt is framing himself. Maybe he's in love with the picture of Matt Anthony, harassed genius, Jackson gave the court. The genius writing all that dung—the poor dope. All very confusing, makes me uneasy."

"You didn't come out too badly."

"I'm going to phone Ruth tonight, after six, to see if I'm still among the employed. And that's part of the shocking lack of reality to the whole thing: actually myself, my job, are such a very minor part of Matt's life ... and suddenly it's been blown up out of all proportion. I feel as though I've stepped through the looking glass."

"It has a never-never land air, all right. I suppose Monday we'll be bored by Jackson's head hunters stating Matt was nuts, while Wagner's lads say Matt passed his tests with colors flying. Think the jury will get the case by Monday afternoon?"

"They've exhausted all possible witnesses except me. This must set a record for speed in a murder case."

We passed an old looking inn and parked. The restaurant was empty and we took a table with a view of the water. After we ordered, I went to phone Michele, to be sure she was taking the afternoon train. Then I called Miss Park. She had a few things I had to okay, messages from Bill and Marty Kelly. Two large Midtown book stores had a big window display of Matt's book and were happily reporting brisk sales.

When I returned to the table the professor had finished his second double rye, which reassured me he was human after all. But the liquor didn't seem to loosen him up any. When I told him about Michele coming out for the weekend and that he could keep the motel, as we wanted to drive around, he took off again, asking, "You said your wife is French. Has she become a U.S. citizen yet?"

"No. We were too late for the war bride deal, but she's taken out her papers."

"Then I shall certainly move out, not even meet her, although I would like to. Knowing me could cause her deportation."

"Hank, relax. Don't worry about the motel. We like to bum

around, perhaps spend the night some place out at the point and ..."

"Norman, if you don't realize the danger, I do. Thank you, but I will find other lodgings. Town shouldn't be crowded for the weekend."

"Do what you wish, but we still aren't going to use the motel room."

We had a light lunch and a few more drinks. It was a lovely day, almost like summer. We drove along the waterfront to the canal, looking at the big yachts, watching people fishing from the canal banks for fluke, or maybe they were flounders. At four I drove back to Riverside and couldn't talk the old man out of moving. He found a room in a small tourist house on the edge of town. At five I was waiting at the railroad station. When Michele stepped off the train she was so chic and feminine, so continental and warm, I felt like I was seeing her for the first time. It gave me a tremendous lift to watch her glancing around anxiously, knowing she was looking only for me.

We drove to the motel to wash up, and I asked what she wanted to do first. Michele asked, "But where is this wonderful professor with the broken nose, Norm?"

I tried to explain why Hank didn't want to see her, but certain aspects of our political climate can hardly be explained to an outsider, a new American—or even to most of us old ones.

Michele placed her arms around my neck, rubbing her nose against my ear lobe as she said, "This is childish talk, Norm. Indeed, we shall drive around and sleep where we wish, perhaps out on a windswept beach. All the way on the dull train ride I have been thinking of but two things: the biggest lobster in the world ... and you."

"I'm glad you had us in that order."

She said something in soft French, nibbled at my ear. I think she was saying she wouldn't mind eating me.

My very possessive hands ran over her dress as I said, "Such talk will only delay eating that lobster. Hungry?"

"For both you and the lobster I am very hungry. But almost famished for food. Norm, let us call on the silly, frightened professor, take him out to supper."

"I don't know, honey. If he wants to be alone, I think we should let him be. After all, he isn't a child," I said, wondering if there was a chance being with him could hurt Michele. Lord, what if she were deported as a result? It could happen, I suppose. Was there an opening for a slow-French-speaking ad manager in the Paris publishing houses?

Michele kissed me, pulled out of my arms. "Perhaps we should respect his request for privacy. Let us go, be moving ... ever since you left me I have felt I am standing still. You must tell me all about Monsieur Matt on the stand today."

"Okay. But I'm afraid the big monsieur had a rough time," I said, packing a few things into her overnight bag.

It was still light by the time we reached Montauk but we were too late for the fishing boats. Michele thought the country quite desolate and dreary looking. She also thought Matt's wife must have been an awful woman and that his books were also awful. But she was very much in favor of the lobster dinner we had. We stopped for the night at a rather fancy motel within the sound of the ocean waves. Although we had only been apart one night, we made love with all the passion of honeymooners and when she finally let go of me I stared up at the darkness and smiled—feeling very certain I wasn't a "lousy lay."

I had done nothing but sit around the courtroom all day and I wasn't tired enough to sleep. I thought again, with the same warm amazement, of the odd crew of characters my life had been tied up with the past months. I'd be glad to be rid of them. Sometimes when watching a TV commercial, I'd have the feeling I was looking through the wrong end of a telescope. I'd think of the thousands of dollars, the talent, and all of it for the sale of a little dime can of cleanser. It was the same way with Matt: his big house, his "literary" life, even Francine's death, Wagner and Jackson's skills, the whole operation at Longson—all went in to producing a book about a girl kicking a guy in the groin or getting beaten on the breasts. Perhaps I was over-simplifying things, but I ran my hand over Michele's shoulders, as if she were the only real thing in the world. Yet, in a sense, our being together in this motel was dependent—to some degree—upon that kick in the groin. Maybe Michele was right about the lack of dignity in life here. But hell, the same thing was true in France; I understood Matt's books sold very well there in translation. It was all quite confusing ... and embarrassing.

Saturday was another mild Fall day, but cloudy. After a walk along the beach searching for shells—and not knowing what to do with them—we had breakfast. Michele kept talking about the various things to be done around "the house," including looking at a boat. So we made our way over several charming and old-fashioned little ferries, and finally we were on an old Navy craft and the three hour trip across the Sound was windy but relaxing. We were "home" an hour after we hit the

Connecticut shore.

In the afternoon we went to see our boat and fell in love with a wide, tubby, twenty-one-foot cat boat. It had a tiny little cabin you had to practically crawl into, with an open "head" at one end that didn't work. But the boatyard owner assured us a fine, safe boat with a decent motor. The boat was already up on land and the owner was asking $1500, but as the yard owner explained, "It ain't a firm $1500. I don't want you to get in over your heads, you understand, so I'll give it to you straight—this boat is worth at least double the money. She may look the devil but the wood is good and she's only six years old, engine overhauled this season—I did the job myself. Buy her now and next season you should expect to put about another few hundred bucks in her. Needs new sail, mattresses, anchor, things like that. Let me call the owner, tell him you'll pay cash, see what gives."

By the end of the day we were minus $850 and the sudden owners of a boat. The yard man advised us that for the winter all we had to do was drain and grease the motor, slap a coat of paint on the hull and decks, then ... "cover her with canvas and she'll be snug all winter. Along about April, you'll take care of the seams, give her a real paint job, re-step the mast ... but don't worry about that now. By the by, I just happened to remember, I got an old canvas cover that will fit your boat and I'll let you steal it for thirty bucks."

We purchased several tremendous cans of white paint, brushes and early Sunday morning we were busy as kids painting our "yacht". You'd think a twenty-one-foot boat could be painted in about twenty-one minutes. By noon we hadn't half-finished the job, although we had used up enough paint to do a house. We were tired, dirty and splattered. Michele went off and came back with two giant hero sandwiches and beer and found a fairly clean patch of beach to eat on, and then we stretched out for a rest.

Staring up at the clean sky I thought, "I'm happy. I have everything I want, really want. And if I have to plug Matt Anthony's *pedestrian novels* in payment, well, so be it. After all, what harm do they do, how much of the violent bit does the reader believe? What difference would it make if I earned my living plugging cigarettes, or turning out cars or shoes? I—"

Michele turned on the sand beside me, asked, "What are you mumbling about?"

I faced her, poked at a speck of paint on her face, took in the trim fit of the dungarees over her hips. "Was I mumbling? Must have been thinking aloud. I just decided I'm a very happy man and I was trying to find out why. I mean, Matt's trial ... well, in a sense they are somehow trying to convict him for the books he wrote. God knows they sounded pretty horrible. But those books aren't just Matt's—I help produce them, so does Bill Long and Marty Kelly and every clerk in the book stores and the newspapers and paperback editors and newsstand dealers and ... hey, do you want to hear any of this?"

"I don't understand it. Perhaps I should try to. Norm-man, if you are happy, be glad, as I am. Why must you worry about the know-how behind your happiness? Or do you think you can manufacture it?"

"Probably wouldn't sell, anyway," I said, thinking how right she was. A second ago I'd sounded like the would-be Madison Avenue personality slob I'd forgotten about. I reached over and tapped her backside. "Okay, matey, back to work. Please note the sudden appearance of nautical words in my speech. We have to be careful not to bore our friends talking about the darn boat."

We finished at four, got the canvas cleaned and ready to go on the following weekend. Michele was pooped and after we cleaned up she slept soundly. It was past ten when she awoke and I said it would be silly to go back to New York tonight: if I missed part of the trial Monday it would only be the dull testimony of the couch doctors.

Michele didn't have a class until eleven, so after a big breakfast we took our time driving to the city. I stopped at the office and took care of a few things, had galley proofs sent to Frank Kuhn, mixed some tobacco, lunched with Marty Kelly. It was 5 P.M. when I reached Riverside and, of course, court was adjourned for the day. I tried to find Hank, without success, finally ate supper alone and took the evening papers back to the motel.

There wasn't much in the papers. Jackson had a well-known psychiatrist testify that certain tests proved Matt unstable during emotional stress. The very fact Matt could plot an alibi and a phony crime immediately after his wife's death proved, according to this doctor, that his thinking was not normal, that he didn't know right from wrong, that he was temporarily insane at the time he struck Francine. I didn't get it, but that's what the eminent doctor claimed.

Wagner had then put a State psychiatrist on the stand, who testified that other tests proved Matt absolutely sane, normal and under stress, he would know the difference between right and wrong, that he was sane enough to form a criminal intent. The fact he set up an alibi proved that far from being insane, his mind was working at normal speed and he was thinking of self-preservation. This doctor also claimed that Matt's books proved he had an "addiction for violence." Under a sharp cross-examination by Jackson the doctor had agreed that a capable writer could write about violence without being of a violent mind. I was very happy I had skipped the day.

After a good night's sleep, I shaved and dressed with nothing more important on my mind than trying to think up a clever name for our boat. I had breakfast and was at court early, smoking my pipe outside. I didn't see May Fitzgerald, nor did there seem to be as many spectators going into the court.

Prof. Brown came along and told me he thought both sides would begin summing up today. When I asked about Monday, he said, "The usual stupid hassle, trying to make an exact science out of one that isn't. Matt's doctor seemed the more intelligent, but then Wagner had the easier task, merely to establish any doubt that Matt had been crazy when he hit his wife. So...."

"Then you finally believe he at least did strike her?" I cut in.

"Norman, you asked me what happened in court. I'm telling you. I still can't believe he did it; what's more, he doesn't even seem to be putting up a real defense. Of course, Jackson is, but yesterday Matt was back to his cat smile and working all day. He kept writing away, barely paying attention to the proceedings, morning and afternoon."

"I suppose they didn't let him write in jail and he had to catch up for Saturday and Sunday. The main thing is, Wagner hasn't proved murder."

Brown nodded. "Nobody has proved anything. Let's go in."

"How are you doing?"

"My wife reports all is still quiet. Of course when I return, I may get the bad news then."

"You're a pessimist," I said, knocking the ashes from my pipe. Brown didn't bother answering as he held the door open for me. The courtroom was filling up rapidly but we had our choice of seats. However, Brown suddenly whispered, "It isn't good for us to be seen together in public so often, Norm," and sat in an empty single seat between two couples.

I felt like kicking the old guy smack in the behind, but then, he was supposedly doing it all for my own good, or something. I found a seat up near the front. Jackson was wearing a change of pace suit—a conservative blue serge, white shirt, blue knitted tie. But he hadn't forgotten his key, beaded belt or moccasins. He sat at his table and looked over some notes, his face very solemn—at one time I almost thought he was praying. Matt, dressed in his casual sports-coat-and-slacks deal, looked very fit and confident. He carefully piled a ream of paper in front of him, spread out a number of pens and pencils. He ran his eyes over the jury faces, making notes after each. Wagner looked his usual cold fish as he whispered to an assistant. Kolcicki was a spectator on the other side of the court, happily chewing gum.

After we stood up for the judge, the court got down to business. When Jackson was asked if he was ready to sum up, he said he was, his great voice sounding very grave. Matt was writing away as Jackson walked slowly to the jury box. Leaning on the rail for a moment he said nothing. He had his man-to-man smile on, but his eyes seemed to burn into each juror, forcing most of them to turn away. "Mr. Foreman, ladies and gentlemen of the jury," he began softly, "you will shortly face a great responsibility—probably the greatest you will ever have to face in your lives: a man's life will be in your hands for judgment. You may recall I said in my opening address that you and you alone are the true judges in this trial. It is a solemn duty and a most important one, for trial by jury is indeed the very spine of our democracy. For my client's sake I am pleased that you are to judge him, for I know you to be honest and decent people."

Jackson stood up, tall and straight, began walking slowly back and forth before the jury box, his voice projecting now. "A case like this is embarrassing to all of us, for we have to look into the very heart of a person's private life, beyond the personal walls of a marriage. It's like the fabled Pandora's box, one never knows what will come out—and some of it is far from pretty. Matt Anthony's wife is dead. That's a fact, and not a pretty one. The Grand Jury indicted Mr. Anthony for first-degree murder. His Honor has denied my motion to dismiss both the first- and second-degree murder counts of the indictment. Now his Honor will give you the law in his charge, but let me point out that a man is innocent until proven guilty. *Proven!* Neither the indictment or his Honor's decision not to dismiss the charges can be taken as proof. The fact is, not once in this trial has Mr. Wagner offered the smallest shred of proof that Matt Anthony ever planned to murder his wife. There has not been a single bit of evidence of intent or premeditation. Mr. Wagner's entire charge of murder is actually based on three words, that Matt Anthony in the heart of argument told his wife, 'I'll kill you!' Mr. Wagner has taken upon himself, although he was not present at the scene, to interpret these words as a real threat. Yet you will recall that Mr. and Mrs. Hunter, who were witnesses to the scene, stated they did not consider the words a threat at all, but merely a figure of speech. Ask yourselves how many times in either jest, or anger, you have told someone, perhaps even your wife or husband, or your child, something like, 'If you don't bring me the paper this minute I'll wring your neck!' It is obvious that to gather the true meaning of words we must recognize the intent behind the words. Certainly when you tell a person to 'go to the devil,' you actually don't mean for them to die and be sent to Hell. Yet that is what the prosecuting attorney would have you believe. If you told somebody, 'Oh, go jump in the lake!' and hours later that person did fall into a lake, on the basis of his logic, Mr. Wagner would claim you must have pushed him, therefore you are guilty of assault."

Jackson smiled. Most of the jury grinned.

"Actually, the State's entire case is based on Matt Anthony's alleged 'threat' to his wife, his saying, 'I'll kill you.' But there really wasn't any such threat. If you recall the exact words he said, they were, '*If* you ever say a single out-of-the-way word to Hank, I'll kill you.' Let us concentrate on that first word, *If*. The fact is that Francine Anthony never saw Prof. Brown again, never had a chance to say a word to him! So no matter what interpretation one gives Matt Anthony's words, the fact remains there was no reason for him to carry out such a threat—and I do not consider it a threat. Two letters, i ... f, wipe out the entire basis of the State's case!

"Let us forget interpretations and come down to the known facts of the case. You have heard the only—I repeat, the only witness to Francine Anthony's death, her husband, state under oath that in the boat they got into an argument about skin-diving, that in a moment of blind, insane rage, he struck her. The subject of their earlier argument, a friend of Matt Anthony's, had left the house, so that family spat was over, finished; probably forgotten. Matt Anthony was out to play a practical joke on his wife, yank at her fishing line. His oxygen tank failed and he surfaced, causing a *new* argument. If the tank hadn't failed Matt would have returned to shore and later Francine Anthony would have returned with stories about the one that got away. Obviously there wasn't, there couldn't have possibly been under those circumstances, any premeditation or intent.

"As to second-degree murder, which—as his Honor will tell you, means killing with design to effect death but without premeditation, Matt Anthony didn't pick up a weapon that would have caused death. He didn't even pick up an oar and strike his wife while he was in a fit of blind rage. No, indeed, he hit her with his hand. Certainly the hand cannot be considered as a 'design to effect death.' Actually, the cause of Mrs. Anthony's death was an accidental fall.

"Let us consider the testimony of Detective Kolcicki, a trained and veteran police officer. Certainly the possibility of first-degree murder must have entered Detective Kolcicki's trained mind. Remember, he has stated that he had secured hundreds of confessions. Yet nowhere in the confession did you hear any mention of planning on Matt Anthony's part, any hint of intent or deliberation. Obviously, if Detective Kolcicki had the slightest suspicion of murder, he would not have accepted the confession, hammered away until he secured one of murder. But to Detective Kolcicki's trained mind, the confession sounded truthful. Premeditation and intent must not only be proven, but *proven beyond any reasonable doubt!*" Jackson's voice hit me with force, it must have stunned the jury. Even Matt looked up from his writing. Clair thundered, "Where has a single iota of such proof been offered during this trial? When? The answer is simple—there has been none!

"Mr. Wagner read some lively sentences from Mr. Anthony's works. We each have our own tastes in literature. Frankly, I don't understand his purpose in reading excerpts from these books to the court. Although I must admit Mr. Wagner reads well, and that's about all he proved. As Mr. Anthony said, he wrote detective books only because they made more money than any other kind of book. I take it Mr. Wagner would have you believe that a man writing about crime must have a practical knowledge of crime. This is nonsense. How many writers of westerns can win a rodeo, as their fictional heroes do? In fact how many writers of cowboy stories have ever ridden anything but a library chair as they did their research? Millions upon millions of Americans read Matt Anthony's books for relaxation and enjoyment. Nobody forces them to, they do it out of free choice. Mr. Wagner would have us believe that America reflects Matt Anthony's books. In reality, it's the other way around, his books merely reflect America. We are a rather violent nation, quick to fight and anger. This is the reason we make such good soldiers in time of war, that our athletes are among the world's best."

Jackson hesitated, as if about to add something and changing his mind abruptly. He hooked his thumbs in his belt, doing it in slow motion, collecting his thoughts. I had the feeling either he had been about to say violence had won the West, but that would bring him in—the Indian bit. Or was he about to give them the old chestnut about the Bible being full of sex and violence, and afraid it might offend a juror?

Matt was resting his chin on his left hand, looking like those horrible author portraits on old fashioned jackets. Kolcicki was chewing away—undoubtedly Jackson had joined his personal list of "bastards." Or did any defense lawyer automatically get that title?

In a normal voice Jackson said, "Now let us open the Pandora's Box that was the private life of Mr. and Mrs. Matt Anthony. They had a sophisticated life, different from ours. For example, few of us have either the time or imagination to play a joke on our wife by swimming underwater and pulling at her fishing line. Nor do we wake up one morning and suddenly decide to go to Europe. They were happy—at least Matt Anthony was. He has not only testified to that, but you have seen photos of Francine Anthony. She was neither a young woman when she married Matt Anthony, nor a beautiful woman. Since ..."

Matt sat up, a scowl on his face. I expected him to jump up and say he didn't want his wife talked about. He began writing.

"... they had both been divorced before, there weren't any religious or ethical grounds on which they were against divorce. Therefore, if they hadn't been happy they would have separated years ago. What sort of a woman was Francine Anthony? The State's witnesses, the Hunters, Miss Fitzgerald, have given us a clear picture—she was a carping woman, constantly nagging her husband. Unfortunately that is not an uncommon practice, at one time or another we have all been nagged by our wives or husbands. But as I have proved, writing is a special kind of occupation. You and I, if we have a little family quarrel at night, or during breakfast, we go to our offices, our jobs, and there is a cooling off period for eight or more hours. But suppose your wife followed you to your job, kept nagging you there? It's a strange picture but the picture you must see—you're a grocery clerk and your wife enters the store a few minutes after you start work and keeps carping about some petty family matter all day long. Obviously you would be unable to work. You would either have to get her out of the store or lose your job. Probably if she did that, you would have her sent to a mental institution for observation.

"A strange picture? *But an everyday one in the Anthony home!* For Matt Anthony's office, his store, was his home. You have heard him testify he thought about his work, his creative work, all day long. And all day long Francine Anthony nagged about his friends, his swimming, an Aqua-Lung. Obviously this put Matt Anthony under a terrible strain, and not merely for a day, but from the evidence of the State witnesses, and from Mr. Anthony, this went on constantly. Why did she do this? Was Matt Anthony a bad husband, stingy and unkind, narrow and demanding? Or didn't Francine Anthony understand the nature of his work, his urgent need for inner peace?

"Let us look at the facts. Francine Anthony has previously been married to a writer—a not successful one. At the time she married Matt Anthony he was already an established and well-known author. In other words—she knew from her own experience exactly what it meant to be a writer's wife. Also, if she had read the papers and magazines she certainly knew of Matt's dynamic way of living—a way of living which several famous writers have said is of vital importance to spur the brain juices from which a writer's creative skill flows. In short, Mrs. Anthony was not a sheltered school girl suddenly thrown into a life too exciting and different for her. On the contrary, she was a mature woman well acquainted with writers and their working methods.

"Then perhaps she was doing this out of spite because she thought her husband was mean, a man squeezing every cent? Let us again consider the *facts*. Before she married Matt Anthony, Francine was supporting herself and her husband by working as a cashier. What could she have been earning then, certainly not much more than $50 a week. Her husband was a failure, their marriage was one of these on and off affairs—is this not a picture of a lonely, bitter and frustrated woman?

"Matt Anthony comes into her life. They fall in love. He pays for her divorce, they marry. Practically overnight this woman—neither pretty or young—is suddenly raised from a dreary life of frustration to a dream of luxury. She traveled about the country, in Europe, the West Indies. She had a fabulous house not far from here, boats, a maid, charge accounts and good clothes, mink coats. Through her husband she met famous people, had expensive fishing and golf equipment, hundreds of dollars a week for household expenses—she was *Mrs.* Matt Anthony. You heard Miss Fitzgerald, the maid, testify that at no time did Francine

Anthony do a bit of work around the house, not even the shopping. She didn't have to, she was the wife of a successful man. She and Mr. Anthony lived big. True, Mr. Anthony was not a millionaire, nor was his income in the upper brackets, but the Anthonys lived better *than most millionaires do!* From the testimony it is obvious Francine Anthony also enjoyed this luxury living. Sometimes, we have been told, she complained that Matt was spending too much money—but wasn't that sheer hypocrisy when she spent thousands of dollars on her fishing equipment? I have yet to hear of a $350 set of golf clubs or a $650 fishing reel being considered a family necessity! And if they were spending too much money—mind you, I said *they*, for they spent it together—what perverse mental quirk made Francine Anthony literally bite the hand that fed her so well? For every cent of their income came from Matt Anthony's brains, from his wits and creative imagination—and these she tried to strangle with her nagging. Was she jealous of his success? Did this neurotic woman envy her husband's ability? Indeed, our Pandora's Box reveals an odd and twisted relationship, twisted by a woman so used to failure she couldn't stand success, thus had to destroy it!" Jackson flung out his hands in appeal. Then he held on to the jury box rail, his rugged face full of tragic sadness; the silence in the courtroom was absolute.

Suddenly he slapped the rail, a hard slapping sound, as he boomed, "What other fact can explain this except that some part of Francine Anthony's mind had cracked? Was Matt Anthony doing anything that would upset his wife? Was he running with other women? Was he drinking to excess? Was he lazy? Did he deny her anything? Did he beat her? No! You have heard the testimony of the Hunters, long-time friends of the Anthonys—they said nothing about women or his being a drunkard. Then, coming to the fateful day of July 25th, let us see why she was nagging her husband on that day. She was annoyed because Matt had brought an old friend to the Anthony home! A friend Matt had not seen in many years, a buddy in trouble, and because Matt Anthony asked this man into his own home for a drink, showed him ordinary hospitality, Francine Anthony threatened to make a scene! In the name of common sense, I ask you, ladies and gentlemen, was Francine Anthony a rational woman? A wife isn't expected to like all of her husband's friends, but she most certainly is expected to have sufficient manners not to insult them! Certainly a man has the right to choose his friends—but not Matt Anthony—his wife set herself up as the supreme judge of who should be Matt's friends and who should not! Mind you, all this despite the fact she had never met the friend in question before, that Matt Anthony's friendship with this man dated back to Matt's days as a college instructor—long before he ever knew of Francine. She didn't even have the decency to upbraid her husband in private but nagged him openly—before their houseguests. If your husband or wife tried to make a fool of you before friends, wouldn't that put your nerves on edge? Was this the act of a loving and considerate wife? Indeed not, it was the work of a shrew, a woman perhaps mentally upset by a change of life process, a mental midget who tried to henpeck a giant of a man—her loving and tolerant husband!"

Jackson slapped the jury rail again, lightly this time, as if in disgust. When he mentioned change of life I saw two of the women jurors actually blush. In fact Matt had looked a bit startled, then started scribbling away like mad.

"Now, let us examine the scene in the rowboat. I want you to keep in mind that there were *only* two people in that boat, therefore the *only* true story of what happened, the only actual facts we can possibly know, is what Matt Anthony has told us under oath. Well then, what exactly did happen? Matt Anthony bought himself a skin-diving outfit. A trivial matter? Normally, yes, but in the eyes of Francine Anthony, Matt had done a monstrous thing—because she didn't approve of the idea. Obviously, she also set herself up as the judge of his hobbies, as well of his friends. Is this not the picture of a tyrant wife? However, as Matt has testified, he purchased the outfit not only for enjoyment but also because he thought it might give him ideas for stories. He tries out the Aqua-Lung and has to surface. His wife sees him. Remember his frame of mind when he entered the water, as he has testified under oath—he was about to play a mild practical *joke* on his wife—play with her fishing line. A joke ... certainly not the frame of mind of a murderer!

"At two in the afternoon when most wives are either finishing their household chores or perhaps thinking about the evening meal, Mrs. Francine Anthony was busy, too—at her favorite sport, fishing. Fishing with her expensive rod in her own boat in her own private bay! She sees her husband surface and when he comes aboard she immediately upbraids him savagely—the second time in almost as many hours. Matt has a heart condition, but was she really worried about that? Did she think of his heart when she upset him by insulting his friend? Did she consider his heart when from the second he got into the boat—before he could rest—she started nagging again? I say in plain language she didn't give a damn about her husband's health! I say the only thing truly worrying her was that Matt's insurance policies were not fully paid up! What more telling picture of a heartless, selfish woman!

"Naturally, Matt resents her bickering, but he agrees to swim to shore and take off the Aqua-Lung. The fact is he stood up, ready to dive in, but that wasn't enough for his dictatorial wife—she must attack him, try to tear the lung from his back. And this woman was allegedly worried about his heart!

"As Dr. Strong, the noted and respected psychiatrist, has told us, we all have a breaking point, a mental loss of control. As Dr. Strong also testified, this breaking point depends upon a number of factors—a person's general health, his emotional stability, and of course all of these are conditioned by the tensions the person is under. I shall not go into a general discussion of psychology. I not only am unqualified to do that, but the very capable doctor testified on the subject and how it related to the defendant. However, I would like to dwell for moment on a few points, namely the tensions Matt Anthony was under.

"First, we have an active man, an athlete, suddenly restricted somewhat by a slight heart trouble, and certainly worried about it. He is a creative man harassed by a carping wife. He is a man under constant pressure—every cent he earns comes from his imagination. He enjoys living and is under great expense. He hasn't a salary or income he can rely upon each week—so he must keep producing original ideas and novel characters. He must put his mind to his work yet his wife's constant nagging cuts into his thoughts, makes his work all the more difficult. These are the tensions he has been under without letup for years. On the day in question, his wife makes a scene over an old friend, makes a fool out of Matt. He is then trying to relax, calm down, by trying out an underwater swimming device. This, too, she tries to spoil. And he reaches his breaking point, this mental loss of control, as Dr. Strong called it. Skin-diving is a petty matter, but is it not the little things which throw us into a rage? Your wife tosses out that old pipe, your husband wisecracks about a hat ... and we have our most bitter quarrels.

"Ladies and gentlemen, you heard Mr. Anthony testify as to his resentment at his wife's constant nagging, how when Francine Anthony came at him as he was about to leave her, attacked him by trying to rip the lung from his back ... how at that precise second Matt Anthony lost control of his mind, blind crazy rage took over. His mind blacked out—Matt Anthony didn't know what he was doing. Yet I want you to note that even in his blind rage he didn't strike her with an oar, with any weapon, but with his fist ... almost in self-defense. If Matt Anthony was a smaller man, the blow would have stunned his wife. She would either have sat down and cried, or perhaps Francine Anthony might have swung at him with an oar and be on trial herself. Matt Anthony is not a little man—look at him. He's a big man, no doubt he packs a punch. The force of the blow sent Francine Anthony against the side of the little boat, crushing her head. This is not murder, this is not manslaughter—Francine Anthony died an accidental death after being punched by her husband in a moment of blind, insane rage! It was a moment of blind revolt against her years of henpecking, her constant interference with his work. Matt Anthony came out to play a joke, he certainly had no thought of harming his wife, much less of killing her, but she forced his mind to break, to a point where he had no control over his hands. Mind you, he didn't attack her, *she came at him*, clawing and cursing, trying to grab the lung on his back.

"When Matt Anthony came to, when his mental blackout lifted, he swam ashore. He realized nothing he did could ever bring Francine back to life, just as nothing this court can do will bring her back to life. His blind rage was over, he could think clearly. He wanted to avoid a scandal, he made up a white lie of a story on the spur of the moment. Mr. Wagner has called Matt Anthony an expert on criminal methods. This doesn't make him a criminal any more than a cancer expert must have cancer. But I say to you, the State has exposed the very lack of logic in its own arguments, for certainly *if* Matt Anthony *had* murder in mind, he would have made up a much *better* story than the feeble yarn he did. And if Francine Anthony had even the slightest doubt her life was in danger, she had plenty of time after their first argument to leave the house, to seek the police. Instead, she went fishing; obviously she knew there wasn't any danger.

"Ladies and gentlemen of the jury, every man is liable for the natural consequences of his acts—when he knows what he is doing, when he knows the difference between right and wrong. At the time he struck his wife, Matt Anthony didn't know right or wrong, he didn't know anything but a blinding insane rage. There was an accidental death and I say he has already been punished enough by the loss of his wife, the ordeal of jail and publicity—a punishment that will forever sear his soul. With all honesty I ask you to look into your own souls, find compassion for Matt Anthony. In the name of justice I ask you to bring in the only verdict possible in the face of the testimony and medical evidence ... I ask you to find Matt Anthony not guilty by reason of temporary insanity. Thank you."

Jackson had finished with his voice in a low key, throbbing like an old-fashioned preacher's. He sat down beside Matt, his face very solemn and full of tired lines—more Lincolnesque than ever. Matt shook his hand, that tiny smile on Matt's face ... and for me there was an air of cheap sarcasm in the handshake.

The judge nodded toward Wagner who started walking towards the jury box. I don't know what I expected, a lull, a recess, but somehow it shocked me ... sort of a belt line production form of justice. Before Wagner addressed the court and jury he did something out of character, something funny: he ran his hand over the part of the jury railing Jackson had been slapping, as if examining it. The jurors grinned, there were enough giggles in the courtroom for the judge to pound once with his gavel.

In his dry, level voice, Wagner said, "I had looked forward to Mr. Clair's summing up. Not only in my position as prosecutor, but also out of a professional and personal curiosity. Mr. Clair is a big city lawyer, a top trial man, and I was anxious to see him work, thinking a country boy like myself could learn something. I was impressed by his dramatics, by his oratory, which I will not attempt to match. But I was puzzled. Judging from Mr. Clair's remarks one would think Francine Anthony was on trial here for killing her husband. Francine Anthony is dead, struck down and killed by this man!" Wagner made a mildly sweeping gesture toward Matt.

For a second the two men stared at each other, then Matt started writing slowly. I noticed that he was sweating a little.

Wagner turned back toward the jury, standing stiffly, and said, "There has been a lot of loose talk in this trial. Justice is determined by facts, not general words. However, since this talk has been a part of the trial, let us go over that before presenting the facts of the case. The defense has read a number of statements attesting that writers are different from shoemakers. We can dismiss all these learned statements by pointing out that although famous writers went off on erratic and erotic tangents, none of them ever claimed a writer had the right to murder his wife! And under the law, which protects us all, a person has not the right to take another person's life—no matter how much they are supposedly 'nagged.' We have heard Mrs. Anthony called a shrew, a mental midget, who didn't appreciate this 'giant,' Matt Anthony. Just remember that picture came from Mr. Clair's nimble brain. Certainly not from the testimony. The fact is, the testimony states that Mr. Anthony often nagged his wife, 'teased' was the word used. Mrs. Anthony has been presented as a terrible wife, yet if we sift all the words, exactly what did she do? Her husband has heart trouble and she wanted him to stop drinking, stop exercising. Does that sound like a shrew or a woman with her husband's best interests at heart? Even assuming she was a nag—and I repeat, *assuming*, she was a nag, that didn't give Matt Anthony the right to kill her. Mr. Clair would have the court believe nagging violates the law, is a crime punishable by death."

Jackson started to rise, but didn't. Instead, he muttered something to Matt, who was watching Wagner as if he were some exciting character he'd never seen before.

"Now let us get to the facts," Wagner went on, "to the testimony of the witnesses. Mr. and Mrs. Hunter stated that although the Anthonys frequently quarreled, and the Hunters had witnessed these quarrels over several years, they had never heard Matt Anthony threaten to kill his wife *except on the day of her death*. Miss Fitzgerald, who was not present at the time of the death threat, but who—as their maid—was with the Anthonys every day for about two months and often heard them fight, also stated under oath she had *never* heard Mr. Anthony threaten to kill his wife. On the morning of July 25th Matt Anthony said to his wife, in the presence of witnesses, *'I'll kill you!'* Now these witnesses, Mr. and Mrs. Hunter, have also said that at the time they did not believe his threat, that they thought it was only a phrase, a manner of speech. It seems fairly obvious to me that when you have heard a man and his wife have numerous arguments over a period of years and never hear him threaten her with physical violence, and that man suddenly says, *'I'll kill you!'* that's a threat, not a manner of speech! But evidently the Hunters did nothing about this threat, they didn't believe it because it was said in a moment of anger. But when is a real threat made except in anger? Certainly a killer doesn't walk up to his victim and make small talk with, *'I'll kill you!'* In this case, whether the Hunters thought or didn't think Matt Anthony was actually threatening his wife, can we doubt it wasn't a threat when a few hours after he said, *'I'll kill you!'* he actually did kill her?

"What sort of man told Francine Anthony, *I'll kill you!*'? Mr. Clair has stressed that Matt Anthony is no ordinary man. I agree. By his own admission Matt Anthony is an expert on ways and means of murder. He has stated he knows more about murder than most police officials. He is a man who, by his own admission, said under oath, plots and thinks about his writing twenty-four hours a day, and for the past ten years he has written only about sex and violence. One only has to look at him to realize he is physically capable of violence. There are various kinds of violence. A war novel might be full of violence, for example, but remember this—for the past ten years Matt Anthony has only written and thought about criminal violence! This was the type of man who told his wife, *I'll kill you!* Can we even doubt that he meant it, that this was not a clear, outspoken threat?

"Ladies and gentlemen of the jury, it is the State's contention that Matt Anthony with his vast knowledge of murder, would not and did not make an idle threat. He was sick and tired of Francine Anthony's objecting to his wild spending and wild living. She had shown him up in front of an old friend by asking him to tell the friend to leave. Why did she do this? It wasn't anything personal, she never knew the college professor; she wasn't trying to pick and choose her husband's friends. No, indeed, she merely felt the man's presence in the Anthony home would jeopardize Matt Anthony's future.

"So it is the State's contention, and one we have proved, that when an expert on ways of murder threatens to kill a person, he means to kill. We believe from the time Matt Anthony shouted at his wife, *I'll kill you!* he was thinking of ways and means to kill her. Mr. Clair has stated that since Mr. Anthony is the only actual witness to the killing, we must take his word. On the contrary, that is all the more reason to doubt his word. A man on trial for murder is not worrying about perjury.

"Then what is the true story of what happened in the boat? The State contends that Matt Anthony, having decided beforehand to murder his wife, deliberately put on the underwater apparatus and swam out to the boat, knowing he was doubly safe—he was swimming underwater so his wife couldn't see him, and since he owned all the land surrounding the bay, there wouldn't be any witnesses to the crime. That he suddenly climbed into the rowboat and deliberately struck this frail woman with all his might, knowing full well his fist had sufficient power to kill her. Francine Anthony may have been dead before her head ever hit the side of the boat—it is medically impossible to pinpoint death time down to a matter of seconds. Then Matt Anthony deliberately tied his dead wife's shoelace around a duck board and broke the lace—to make it all look like an accident. Matt Anthony then swam back to shore, underwater, dressed, and fooled the Hunters, sleeping on the lawn, about a difference of three quarters of an hour in the time—to establish an alibi for himself. All this was child's play for an expert in criminal tactics, a man who as the defense has said, created people and whole cities out of his typewriter—and who also killed and murdered and maimed people with this same typewriter.

"Matt Anthony knows the law, that's part of his business. He felt he was playing it safe. If his wife's death was called an accident, fine. If the police were suspicious of his yarn, as in this case where Detective Kolcicki saw through the lie, why then Matt Anthony would sign a confession full of a cock and bull story that he and his wife argued over an Aqua-Lung and he struck her. He thought the most he would get would be manslaughter—a few years in prison. Since we have been told he works so hard at writing, perhaps Mr. Anthony even considered a few years in prison a wonderful investment, give him material for a dozen or more books.

"Members of the jury, it didn't work! Despite his being an expert, when Matt Anthony went up against Detective Kolcicki, it was the old story of an amateur against a professional. In less than an hour Detective Kolcicki had his confession. The defense has asked why it wasn't a confession of first-degree murder! I'd like to ask, who says it *isn't* a confession of first-degree murder. This wasn't a full confession. Matt Anthony admitted he killed his wife, it was then up to the District Attorney to prove premeditation, and I think we have. Granted that since there were only two people involved and one of them is now dead, there is no way we can take Mr. Anthony's mind apart and give you the actual thoughts. But there are other circumstances involved and these all prove and cry out—*murder!*

"Can anyone believe a man would kill his wife over an Aqua-Lung? Especially a man of Matt Anthony's size—he could have pinned his wife's arm with one hand. Can anyone honestly believe—according to the defense's story—a man would strike his wife merely because she protested skin-diving might strain his heart? Even if we accept the defense's claim that Francine Anthony's death was an accident, why would Matt Anthony have lied about it at first, *immediately* establishing an alibi? An accident—I would insult your intelligence if I asked you to believe that! A man thinks of alibis only when he knows he's guilty. In the course of my job I have come into contact with murderers. No man would kill if he thought he would be caught. But a murderer is arrogant, certain he can outwit the police. I'm talking now of an ordinary murderer—consider the arrogance of an expert, a man who has outwitted the police hundreds of times—on paper. Here was the big-time crime writer about to pull the wool over the eyes of some 'hick' cops, sure he could hoodwink a 'yokel' court and—"

"Your Honor," Jackson roared, springing to his feet, "I have never interrupted a summing up before in my life, but I must object to Mr. Wagner's hitting below the belt. He has made one unfair generalization after another. He has put words into my mouth I've never said or thought of. Now he's off into a dream fantasy of what went on in the defendant's head. At no time in this trial has the words 'hick' or 'yokel' been uttered except by Mr. Wagner."

Wagner still stood with his back to Jackson. He looked annoyed. So did the jury. Matt shook his head slowly, as if he couldn't believe what he was hearing, then Matt started writing.

Wagner slowly turned and faced the judge, who said, "Mr. Clair, in summing up, a lawyer has the right to interpret the evidence. You did that in your summing up. The court is perfectly capable of reprimanding anyone violating courtroom procedures. Continue, Mr. Wagner."

Jackson made a slight bow toward the judge, sat down. Wagner turned back to the jury—I don't think he'd moved a step since he started summing up.

"Let us examine the claim that the defendant was 'temporarily insane' at the second he struck his wife. What a convenient form of insanity! We have not heard any testimony that Matt Anthony was ever mentally unstable before in his life—although he has lived an adventurous life and been in trying situations. You have heard noted doctors state he was insane at the moment of striking his wife, and that he wasn't. The State's psychiatrists have proved he knew the difference between right and wrong. Now the science of the mind is not as exact as the science of mathematics. For one thing, the science of the mind is relatively new. In mathematics we can state positively two and two equal four. We can't be that positive about the mind, and that will be up to you to decide. However, it seems to me any man who can write a book while in court on trial for his life is far from emotionally unstable—under *any* circumstances!

"I say to you that from the moment Matt Anthony shouted, *'I'll kill you!'* at his wife he fully intended to murder her and carefully planned the murder. She was fishing, alone in the bay, as she did almost every day. That Matt Anthony had this underwater outfit she didn't know about. He deliberately and with intent to kill, swam out, killed her, tried to give it the appearance of an accident, returned to his guests and set up a false alibi. Francine Anthony's death wasn't an accident, nor was it manslaughter. It was a cold-blooded planned murder by a man who thought his cheap mysteries put him above the law. Far from being blind with rage, or blacking out, Matt Anthony *knew exactly* what he was doing from the second he threatened his wife until he lied to his guests its order to establish an alibi.

"Francine Anthony is dead, her head crushed, and her killer must be punished. The law must be upheld, we do not live in a jungle. On the basis of the facts brought out in the testimony, I ask you to punish Matt Anthony for the killing of his wife by bringing in a verdict of first-degree murder. Mr. Clair asked that you have compassion for Matt Anthony, I ask you to have compassion for a dead woman. Thank you."

As Wagner sat down an old lady two seats away from me whispered loudly to a young woman sitting next to me, "What did he say? My hearing is poor on the left side and I got a stiff neck."

"He said he thought Mr. Anthony killed his wife."

"Well, I think so, too," the old biddy grunted.

It was a quarter to twelve. The judge told the jury, "I know you have had a tiring morning. You may return to the jury room and rest for fifteen minutes. At noon I shall start explaining the various points of law, the charges involved. It will take about an hour. I want to get this over with before lunch, so you can immediately start your deliberations. Also, once I have finished my charge you will be locked up and the lunch will be on the court." He gave them a yock-yock grin and like faithful citizens about to save two-bits, most of the jurors beamed their gratitude.

I was too restless for a smoke to listen to the finer points of law. I went outside and lit my pipe, waited for the court to recess so I could have lunch with Brown. But when I finished the pipe a half-hour later the judge was still charging the jury, so I had lunch alone, walked down to the inlet and as a *nouveau* yachtsman bulled with an owner of a work boat and found out I might easily have put in another four or five hundred bucks into my boat before I put it 'over' next summer. This character must have been looking for a listener and soon had me dizzy with all the things that can go wrong with a boat. When I finally begged off, saying I had to get back to the trial, he said, "I hope they give that murdering slob the works."

A lot of people were talking and getting the sun in front of the courthouse. I saw Jackson holding up the building and talking to a pot-bellied man. I went over and Jackson introduced us; the man was a reporter. I asked Jackson how things looked and he said, "Shoo-in. Wagner was comical, with that high school dramatic act, repeating 'I'll kill you!' over and over. But he's a clever man—made me lose my head and object while he was summing up."

"What's wrong with that?" I asked.

"Looked bad in the jury's eyes, like I was trying to take over. If they don't bring in a not guilty verdict, I'll appeal the manslaughter verdict. Judge was wrong in allowing Matt's books into evidence—I can even ask for a new trial. Hope the jury comes in by five, I have a supper engagement in town. Excuse me, fellows, there's a man from *Life* I know."

As Jackson walked away the reporter asked me, "Have you read any of this book Anthony is writing?"

"We have some chapters in the office but no one's looked at it."

"This is one book I'd be willing to buy. Time I put on the feedbag. Like a beer?"

I shook my head and walked around the short main street, stopping to buy a dainty shell necklace for Michele. At two I phoned her at school, said there was a good chance I'd be home that night. I walked main street again, bought a paper and leaned against the courthouse as I read. There was a big crowd milling around, afraid to go too far away in case the jury came in. At three-ten there was a whispered roar that the jury had reached a decision and we all started pushing our way in. Brown appeared from out of nowhere and I asked, "Like to drive back to New York with me?"

"Thanks, Norm. I'd like to."

"Looks good for Matt. Jury was out only about two hours."

"I hope so."

We found seats in the rear of the court. Matt was brought in, looking very pale. An attendant told us to rise as the judge entered. The jury's speed must have caught him by surprise, his robe seemed a trifle cockeyed. The foreman was a thin, middle-aged man in tacky clothes. When asked if the jury had reached a decision he stood up and reading from a trembling slip of paper, his voice shrill with self-importance, said, "We have. We find the defendant, Matt Anthony, guilty of murder in the second degree."

There was a terrible hush in the courtroom. I couldn't believe my ears. Jackson looked as if he'd been punched in the stomach. Matt's big frame began shaking, his eyes grew large. The little smile appeared on his lips, grew bigger—and then he threw back his head and *laughed*. It was a horrible laugh, unreal, insane, filling the courtroom. I don't know, it seemed to last forever, but I suppose it only took a brace of seconds. As the judge raised his gavel, Matt collapsed, pitching forward across the table with a great thud-sound. The courtroom was in an uproar as everybody jumped to their feet. I saw Jackson, Wagner, and an attendant bending over Matt. Somehow I heard Brown mumble, "Jesus, that means at least twenty years!"

The judge was pounding his gavel like an idiot and yelling for the court to be cleared. A deep voice, probably Jackson's, called for a doctor.

Several cops appeared and began plowing through the crowd and with everybody shouting and asking what had happened, I had a feeling I was in the midst of a riot. Somebody kept climbing up my back and I dug my elbow into a belly, heard a gasp. Brown was pushing toward the front and I followed. I couldn't see Matt but Jackson suddenly boomed, "Please, step back! Give him air. Air!" I had a brief glimpse of the jury members leaning out of their box, horrified, as if they had struck Matt down. An attendant cupped his hands and bellowed, "Silence!" In the immediate hush, before the talkers could gather steam again, the judge yelled, "I order this court cleared at once!"

The cops started pushing, but now we all turned and headed for the doors, quickly and almost orderly. Outside, everybody milled around, the crowd growing. I kept telling Brown, "I simply can't believe it," over and over, as if it made any difference whether I believed it or not. Brown looked sick and kept shaking his head, fingering his broken nose.

A man with a press card finally pushed out past the cops guarding the door. People rushed at him, knocking the press card from his lapel and I heard him say, "There's a doctor with Anthony. He's suffered a heart attack but the doc says it isn't serious."

While I was trying to get closer to the reporter—and being bounced around on the fringe of the crowd, I saw the newsman

Jackson introduced me to come out. I grabbed his arm as he headed down the steps, probably making for a phone. "Remember me? From Mr. Anthony's publishing house? How serious is his attack?"

"I think he merely fainted. How about that jury! The doctor says he'll be okay. Second degree, I never figured on that ..."

"Are you sure Matt's all right?"

"That's the doctor's statement. They have Anthony on a cot, waiting for an ambulance. They gave him a shot of something. He's able to sit up and talk."

Brown and I hung around for another ten minutes. Finally I said, "We might as well go. I'll pick you up in front of your rooming house."

We left Riverside a half-hour later, and at first we didn't talk at all. Then I said, "How in the hell did the jury ever arrive at that verdict? What is second-degree?"

"Killing without premeditation, but with intent to kill. I suppose it means if there's a gun around, you suddenly pick it up and shoot. Twenty years to life. Poor Matt, he'll never come out alive."

"I don't understand it. I thought they'd let him go. Wagner's summing up didn't impress me. Saying, *'I'll kill you!'* over and over like a stuck record."

"Isn't repetition the secret of advertising?"

"Cut it out, Hank. That was a lot of crap."

"To you, but you weren't on the jury. Wagner's clever, he pulled out all the stops with that stuff about 'hick' cops and 'yokels.' And tying in all that violent trash Matt has written. When you come down to it, a man thinking of violence for any length of time probably would turn violent."

"You think Matt really meant to kill her?"

"I still think he had nothing to do with it. But that's my little opinion."

"Jackson will probably do something on appeal, a new trial."

Brown was silent, staring at the dashboard. Then he said softly, "Seems so damn wasteful. The fruits of ten years of writing summed up by a kick in the nuts and slapping breasts."

"What the devil, it was merely a way of making a living."

"Matt should have done something else for porkchops."

"Why? What difference would it have made if he'd been writing copy? Or if he spent eight hours a day driving a bus, or standing behind a counter? Don't tell me you think he would have written the great American novel in his spare time. That's a crock."

"No, Matt would probably have never written a line then. That isn't the point, he betrayed his talent, prostituted it. It would have been better if he had let it die."

"Look, Hank, as long as we do anything we don't want to do, for money, security, or whatever you wish to call it ... I mean, you're working at a job you don't especially like now. Advertising is just a way of earning a buck for me ... aren't we being whores? I think Matt knew exactly what he was doing: knew he could only be a good hack writer and nothing more."

Brown shrugged. "He told me something like that, the last time we talked. I still think it's a tragic waste of time and ability. He should have—"

"Let's drop it," I cut in, angry. It seemed to me we were kicking Matt when he was down. "Let's get off the pious soapbox."

He slapped me on the leg. "Sure, Norm. We're both a little on edge."

We talked, or rather Brown did, about a number of things on the drive to New York. Brown had a theory about the popularity of wrestling—people liked to see violence but at the same time because they knew the bouts were acts, were secretly relieved and could go on believing there wasn't any violence about them. Somehow, Brown even got around to the life of cats, debunking the idea cats are shrewd and have an easier time surviving than dogs. I wasn't listening. I was still shocked by the verdict. Also I wondered if I had left Riverside too hastily: Bill Long might expect me to see what happened to Matt's manuscript.

As I stopped to pay the toll at the Triborough Bridge the radio in an auto on the next toll line was on. We heard a newscaster saying: "... and out in Riverside, the trial of Matt Anthony took a fateful twist a few minutes ago when the noted author died of a heart attack after being found guilty of murder in the second degree, in connection with the death of his wife. Mr. Anthony collapsed upon hearing the jury's verdict. Although he seemingly recovered under a doctor's care, Mr. Anthony suffered a second and fatal attack while in an ambulance on his way to the prison hospital. When he first heard the verdict, Mr. Anthony actually laughed, as if the verdict were a great joke.

"In foreign news, the...."

I stared at Brown, my mouth dry. The old guy seemed on the verge of tears. It took me a second to say, "Well, perhaps it's for the best. Matt wasn't meant for prison."

Brown fingered his nose and didn't speak.

The cars behind me began blowing their horns. I drove up, handed the attendant a quarter. As I drove on I told Brown, "At least we'll never know, now, if he killed Francine or not."

Brown merely shrugged. When I let him off at a subway station he just waved and disappeared down the steps. I put the car in the garage and decided to phone Bill Long. He would be home by now. But when I called his house I was told he was still at the office. I called him there and he said, "I've been waiting for your call, Norm."

"Shocking news," I said, stupidly.

"Norm, did you by any chance pick up the rest of Matt's manuscript?"

"Why no. I thought in all the confusion ..."

"Maggie and I are driving out to Riverside right now to get it before it's lost. I want...."

"I'm sorry I messed up. I have my car and can head back out there."

"No. I want you to come down to the office and read that sealed last chapter of his book. Along with a letter he wrote before the trial started. You wait in the office ... No, since it will take several hours to make the round trip, will it be all right if we come to your house? There's something we have to settle tonight."

"Of course it will be all right," I said, puzzled.

"Hop right over here, Norm, and when you finish reading this last chapter, put it under lock and key. We'll see you along about midnight or sooner."

I took a cab to the office. Miss Park was still there. She handed me an open large manilla envelope as she said, "My, wasn't it awful about poor Mr. Anthony? Mr. Long asked me to stay and give you this. What's it all about?"

"I don't know," I said, taking the envelope into my office.

"Shall I stay?"

"You can go, Miss Park. Thanks."

I sat at my desk and started to phone Michele that I'd be late. But on opening the envelope I saw a slim pile of scribbled pages and figured it wouldn't take me long to read these. There was a letter from Matt to Maggie and clipped to everything an interoffice memo with Maggie's name printed in one corner. She had drawn a big exclamation mark across the memo. That was all.

Lighting my pipe, I started on the letter.

PART III

The Letter

Dear Maggie:

How's my favorite editor and southern beauty? (Not even prison walls dampen my trite line. Still, you must admit it has a novel ring—I bet you never received a letter before from a guy sitting in the can on a murder rap.)

I'm sure you've been wondering all these months about this sealed letter and large envelope. I hope you haven't peeped. I've sent this directly to you. Not even my agent knows about this chapter. I feel the entire concept would be far too startling for his timid soul. Yes, the chapter in the attached envelope is the last chapter of the book I shall write here in jail, and during the trial. That's correct, my sweet, I'm doing the last chapter first, and doing it with a purpose. So no cracks about my usual backward methods.

Seriously, Maggie, I feel I've stumbled upon something that is going to make for one hell of a snapper ending, probably the greatest twist in commercial literature (whatever that may mean!) for in this chapter I tell exactly what happened out in End Harbor. No matter what will have come out in court, this is the truth. (I damn near said, so help me God! No, I shall say it. This is the truth and I swear it, so help me God!)

The way I plan it, the trial will be over by the time you read this, and I will have completed the rest of the book. Of course I shall be acquitted, or at worst, appealing a light manslaughter sentence. In brief, ye wheels of justice will have made their full turn, the mills of the gods will have finished grinding, etc., etc. (This lousy pen!) And this last chapter, the truth, will work either way—proving how blind or clear-eyed old lady justice really is.

I know you haven't the smallest idea of what I'm talking about, but you'll see the light when you read this final chapter. It may surprise you, it's probably the most honest bit of scribbling I've done in years. I think I've given a frank portrait of Matt Anthony. If it isn't a pretty picture, it is true and it is me. We all know our weaknesses, the trick is to be willing to admit them. So if I come out a kind of coward, well, let's face up to it—that's what I am. You see, I had to be a coward or he would have killed me there and then, busted my heart. No point in being a dead hero, nor do I have to add anything about the terrible strength of self-preservation. You may also ask why I haven't shouted out the truth in court. Honey, I'm trapped. Maggie, if it's bad to be a coward, it's worse to be a fool, and an unbelieved fool is what I would look if I even tried to tell the truth. I think court will be like poker, you have to stay with the hand you decide to play. While I made my original decision because I was afraid of being beaten to death, now I know it's all for the best. Otherwise there wouldn't be our twist, this last chapter. If I can't say it in court, I can write it. And what you have to understand, dear girl, is that nobody is master of their fate nor captain of their soul—Mr. Henley's "Invictus" to the contrary. Perhaps in the old days when he wrote his poem. But in this atomic era far too much happens to us, so we cannot be master of circumstances. Maggie, I'm probably not saying this too clearly, but it's all rather straight in my little mind.

Now, as to the last chapter. Of course as of now I have no idea how the rest of the book will turn out. But I've given a great deal of thought to this final chapter, and am rather mixed up as to whether to be subjective or objective. Or clever. It may very well be that I shall do the first part of the book with my tongue in my fat cheek. At one time I considered writing this last part as a kind of fable and be witty about the names. Call myself Mark Anthony and of course Francine would be named Cleopatra. May Fitzgerald would be called Zelda, while Prof. Henry Brown would be Prof. Patrick Henry. And so on. Only I'm not certain (aside from whether that's being witty or not) if this chapter—as the truth—should be anything but my normal writing.

Of course if I were in my den, I would have experimented and written it several different ways. But I'm not used to scratching away with a pen, and find it very tiring. (How do some guys write a rough in longhand?) So I've written it straight, and in the third person—as I intend (at this moment) to write the balance of the book. That's our gimmick: Matt Anthony writing as a spectator at the trial of Matt Anthony. However, by the time you're reading this I shall be in your office, either free or out on bail, and by then you will have the complete manuscript ... so we can bat around any revisions. (And I know how dear rewriting is to your hard heart.)

As to publication. I think we might consider issuing it with this last chapter sealed. A sort of soft sell on: this-is-what-came-out-at-the-trial.... Now-can-you-guess-the-true-story. Naturally I shall not give the reporters a word of the truth until the book is released. As to time, I suppose the sooner the better. On the rest of the book I suggest you get cracking on it at once. (Why tell you this when you won't read the letter until the trial will be over? Stupid me.) What I'm trying to say is, if I'm found innocent, then publication must be as quickly as possible. However, if they give me manslaughter and a suspended sentence, or a fine, I will most certainly appeal. That will give us time to decide when the book shall be released. (As I will be sitting across your desk when you read this, have a bottle ready.)

Here's a bit we can use for publicity. I had to have permission to send this out of jail. I merely told "them" it was a piece of *fiction* I was finishing up. They let it go after a fast reading of the first page! Of course, could be my handwriting discouraged them. (This entire chapter is worth a ton of shirts in any Chinese laundry! Told you I still have my corny humor.)

Maggie, if you should open this before the trial is over, please *don't* read the last chapter. You'll appreciate it more when things are finished here. Do what I ask, even as you shake your pretty head and mumble, "What is that idiot Matt Anthony up to now?" Be sorry for me, Maggie, jail has a cold loneliness to it, a reflection of man's insanity to man that ...

My arm is numb with fatigue. Ah, if only I was allowed a typewriter in here. And the condemned man wrote a hearty last chapter. Well, my love, let us both hope this turns out to be the big one I've been fishing for all these years, the kind of bombshell seller I know it will be ... if you get behind it.

Love and sleep comfortable,
Matt

The Last Chapter

July 25th was one of those hot summer days and May Fitzgerald was sweating as she dusted the living room. She heard Matt drive up and soon he stood in the doorway with another man, a stranger. He asked May where Francine was.

When May told him, "Mrs. Anthony is out back feeding cantaloupe to the poodle," Matt noticed a faint smile on Henry Brown's thin face. Matt was annoyed.

Little smiles were very important to Matt Anthony. Usually he was the one who smiled, in fact he often set the stage for them. These faint (and meaningless) smiles were his "secrets" and gave him the same false sense of superiority joining a "secret" lodge gives other people. Matt needed to feel superior and his tiny smiles were his mystic rings and pins.

He would smile at the awe on a person's face when they found out Matt was a writer, was *the* Matt Anthony. Matt would grin slightly, eating up their astonishment when he told them he was also Daisy Action, and the rest of his many pen names. Or when he was called "Mad" Matt Anthony. Then Matt might not only show off his muscles, but often wrap a towel around his right fist and split a thin board with one punch. (He kept a supply of such boards on hand.) He would also make his favorite crack, "Only difference between Papa and myself—he's a far more successful hack." And of course smile at the other person's reaction to Matt daring to call Hemingway a hack.

There was a special smile when Matt met a guest at the station and as they stepped into his Jaguar, Matt would say, "Off to the cottage," and his big grin when they saw the large house carefully screened from the bay by a row of immense pines. Again the little smile when he casually said, "Oh, I own all the land around this end of the bay. Might call it my private bay."

Now he turned to Brown and with a grin (of self-pity) said, "Guess that sums up my life, Hank; feeding the poodle cantaloupe. Still, it is a long way from being an English Lit. instructor—only most times I can't figure in which direction it's a long way."

"A comfortable way, at least," Brown said, sitting in a pigskin camp chair, rubbing his broken nose. Matt was terribly envious of that busted nose.

"A 'comfortable' weight around my neck," Matt said. "I need a minimum of twelve grand a year for living expenses. Means three books a year, unless I'm fortunate enough to have a movie or TV sale. And with my lousy luck, those have been few and far between."

"Lord, three books a *year?* How many have you published, Matt?"

"Oh, I've lost count. Around forty. And a few dozen novelettes, and perhaps five hundred stories. Although I haven't done much short fiction in recent years."

"How do you do it?"

Matt smiled. "The secret is to do ten pages a day. Trouble with most writers is they're lazy. Stall themselves with crap about having to be in the mood, all that. No matter how much hell I raise, how crocked I get, I do my ten pages a day, seven days a week. Rain or shine. Okay, Hank, don't look so damn horrified. It really isn't much. I dictate it in about two hours, then mail the tape to my secretary in New York. Hell, I once dictated a complete novel in three days. Listen, I'm a slow writer compared to a fellow like Simenon. I can't complain, where else could I make this sort of money for a fourteen-hour week? You know, Hank, I often think back to the old days when we'd argue for hours over a line, the right word, or—"

Francine Anthony came into the living room followed by a black poodle licking his chops, and the Hunters. The Hunters wore bathing suits. Wilma Hunter had a strong figure with sturdy hips and a great bosom. She had an average face, but intense eyes, and her very red hair was rough and kinky. Joel Hunter was slim and stooped. His face was flushed and in sharp contrast to his white-gray hair which was cropped very short—like a worn brush. He was smoking a corncob pipe and wearing thick black-shell glasses. He dropped into a chair with a decidedly feminine movement, stretching his thin legs. He said, "I've never seen a dog like that before, eating fruit like a pig."

The poodle looked up, ran over and mounted one of Joel's legs. Joel yelled, "Matt, will you get this sexy mutt off me!"

Matt looked at Hank Brown and smiled.

Francine Anthony said sharply to the dog, "Come here, Clichy." She walked over and kicked the poodle's backside, and he whined, then sat down and went back to licking his whiskers. Everything about Francine was small and compact. Her features were sharp and her shorts and striped blouse showed off a slightly scrawny figure. She could have been forty years old, or fifty. Her face was weatherbeaten and her hair stringy and wild. She asked, "Anything in the mail, Matt?" as she ran her eyes over Brown's worn tropical suit.

"No checks; honey, this is Hank Brown. Prof. Hank Brown. We used to teach together at Brooks. Hell of a thing, haven't seen him for years, and I run into Hank in Hampton, of all places. Hank, these two slightly drunk jokers are Wilma and Joel Hunter. Perhaps you've read some of Joel's children's books, Hank. They sell faster than contraceptives."

Joel waved as he said, "Oh, Matt, you always do that to me."

"I wish they did sell that fast," Wilma Hunter said, nodding at Brown.

Francine said, "Glad to meet you, Professor. What were you doing in Hampton, Matt?"

"Out for a ride and there was old Hank waiting at the station. Must be at least sixteen or seventeen years since we last saw each other. Hasn't it, champ?"

"About that. I'm really an ex-professor, Mrs. Anthony," Brown said as the poodle came over and sniffed him. Brown rubbed the dog's wooly head. The professor had big hands for a little man.

Francine lit a cigarette, blew thin clouds of smoke through her nose as she said, "Seems to me I've read something about you, Prof. Brown. A book out recently?"

Hank Brown glanced at Matt, who smiled. "I only published one book. That was quite some time ago."

"A textbook, and a damn good one," Matt added. "Joel, that's the racket we should be in, writing textbooks. The dough pours in, year after year."

"But somehow your name rings a bell," Francine said. "You can have the bedroom in the ..."

"Thank you but I have to be back in New York tonight."

There was a moment of silence which Matt enjoyed, then Francine asked him, "How many drinks did you have in Hampton?"

"I didn't even sniff a cork, my darling. I stopped to look at some new reels, glanced at the magazines," Matt said, fingering the car keys in the pocket of his plaid shorts, certain the "stuff" was safe in the trunk of the roadster.

Brown said, "It's nearly one. I want to catch the 2:05 train."

"Plenty of time, champ. We have a lot of talking to do. Want some lunch?"

"Thanks, Matt, but as I told you, I've already eaten."

"How about a cocktail?"

Francine said, "Matt, the doctor said—"

"Okay, honey, but the doc didn't say my guests couldn't drink. What are you guzzling these days Hank, gin and tonic, Scotch?"

"I could use a beer."

"Splendid, I have some imported brew that's terrific. Wilma?"

Wilma shook her head. Joel said, "Much too early for beer. I'll take a Scotch, please, Matt."

Matt gave his wife a very tender smile, "Are you gassed-up for the day, yet, darling?"

"Don't be so goddamn smart, Matt. I don't want anything."

As Matt started for the kitchen Francine said, "Ring for May."

"I'm not too old to fetch a drink for a buddy. And don't worry, honey, I really don't want a belt." Once inside the kitchen Matt leaned against the door and listened. After a moment he heard

Francine say, "Names stick in my mind—a lousy habit. Haven't you been in the papers recently, Professor Brown?"

"Yes."

"Divorced your wife?" Wilma Hunter asked.

"What? No, no, nothing like that. I ... uh ... refused to sign a loyalty oath and was dismissed from Brooks. I also had the misfortune to do this on a day when there wasn't much news."

Matt grinned at the sudden hush in the living room, broken somewhat when Francine said harshly, "Oh, yes!"

Joel asked, "Why didn't you sign the damn thing? I mean, what the hell, avoid all the ... mess?"

"Well," Hank said slowly, obviously not wanting to discuss it, "I felt it wasn't a question of loyalty at all, but rather an invasion of privacy. Also, it's rather complicated. If I had signed I probably would have been called upon to ... perhaps ... become a kind of informer. I couldn't do that."

There was a long silence and then Joel Hunter suddenly came to life, as if hearing the conversation for the first time. He sat up straight, his red face full of worry. He said, "Oh, my!"

Matt, who was standing in the doorway holding a large glass of dark thick beer and a jigger of Scotch, said, "Don't jump, Joel, Hank isn't a leper."

Francine actually glared at Matt, then calling the dog, she left the room. Matt said sternly, "Fran!" The Hunters remained for a moment, ill at ease, then Wilma said, "Come along, Joel, show me what you want typed."

Joel nodded at Brown and as he passed Matt gave him a sickly grin. "Don't forget your goddamn drink!" Matt said, shoving the glass at him, spilling Scotch on Joel's smooth chest.

Matt handed Brown the beer, sat down opposite him. "The smug sons of bitches. Why didn't you tell them off, champ?"

"Can one explain hysteria in a few sentences? You were wrong, Matt, I am a modem leper. To associate with me can mean blacklist, loss of employment. Really, Matt, I wish you'd drive me to the station. You know I didn't want to come here."

"Don't worry about the damn train, we have time. Hell of a deal when you, of all people, can't feel at ease in my house. But don't mind Francine, she's the world's biggest bitch."

Hank stared at him over the glass of beer.

"We've hated each other from the moment we got married. That's why we're so compatible."

Brown looked puzzled, as Matt knew he would. After the tiny smile, Matt said, "Francine is right for me, she's a pusher and a worrier, and you know what an easy-going slob I am.

Then we have great times in bed. We're a couple of sexual sadists and since we hate each other, well ... we're fantastic between the sheets. Don't look so damn shocked, Hank, I'm only telling you what ..."

"Matt, why tell me?"

"Oh, come now, champ. You know damn well every man is curious—even if only passively—about every woman's sex life. Christ, not you—you just can't have become a hypocritical old bastard. Man, when you see Wilma's big knockers, don't you wonder what she's doing with a fag like Joel? Admit it, Hank—could you take your eyes off that breastwork?"

Brown looked a bit sick as he said, "A man my age loses a great deal of that ... eh ... curiosity and ... Matt, what's happened to you?"

Matt's smile opened into a laugh. "Nothing very much, champ, I'm a success. A big gassy success. I make money. Everything I write sells, my books are translated all over the world. Don't look down your busted nose at me, champ, because I write about sex and violence. In your old age, Hank, you're naïve, real simple."

"Thank you."

"It's a fact, you still put a halo around the word 'writer.' Let a pro tell you about writing. It requires a great deal of research—for example, I know all there is to know about police work, detection. And everything I read or see must be translated into a gimmick for a crime plot. Those floods out West the other day—I may use them in a murder story. A month ago I happened to read that a cobra can only strike down, not up. That's been burning and turning over in my mind ever since. I've read up on it, even. A cobra can only strike *down*. I'll use that ... someday. Oh, my mind is full of many such fascinating thoughts. Just as my relationship with Francine helps put sex in my books and ... skip the vomit look, champ, I know it sounds rough, but I'm safe. I am. I'm safe because objectively and subjectively I'm one of the few writers in America *who knows exactly what he's doing.* Yes, sir!"

"Matt, what are you talking about?"

"Salvation!"

"What's all this mean?"

"That I don't kid myself. That's the secret—not to fool the fooler. It means all writing today is a series of compromises. It has to be or it will never reach print. Things are reduced to the degree you compromise. You can't be honest if you compromise. Yeah, they talk about the mediocrity of TV—as though compromise hasn't leveled all our culture, our lives. Your so-called serious writers, who think they're writing honestly, they're lying in their brains and don't realize it. Don't realize they have compromised, and begin believing the stuff they write is honest. They're lost."

Matt pounded his fist into his other palm. "Of course, it's tougher today. Different in the old days—the good old days! At least then you could write honestly because everything was so new, even the publishers couldn't detect the truth. People are too smart today. 'Greatness' gives me a laugh. One major reason for Shakespeare's 'greatness' was the mass illiteracy, hence the worship of any printed word. London could write about Alaska, Twain about the West, Hemingway about war and the Paris of 1920, Faulkner and Caldwell about the South, Lewis about main street ... and not many people knew if it was real or not. Today, as a result of the travel two wars have brought, radio, TV, paperbacks, greater education in general, people are smarter. There aren't any new frontiers—unless you write about pansies, and that will soon become too well known—to write about. So people know when a writer is compromising, faking. Education has made people tolerant in an unhealthy way: they're actually cynical and indifferent to whatever issues a writer tries to give. But above all, they damn well know when he's lying, or half-lying. Well, by God, I'm no fake, I never lie to my readers!"

"Honest Matt Anthony! By what rationalization do you picture yourself writing the truth?"

"Truth? That's the whole point, champ, I don't pretend to write the truth. I write crap fantasies—the modern fairy tale—two-fisted, gonadal whimsy. But I never fool my readers or myself. Once a writer fools himself he's lost. But not little Matt. Plain and simple, I'm a hack and I'm writing to make a big buck. I haven't any fuzzy notions I'm turning out literature; I don't worry whether my name will live two seconds after I die or not."

Matt was staring at Brown, as if waiting for an answer, an argument. Brown sipped his beer. Matt asked, "Isn't that something? I get it by the case from Austria."

"Very good." Brown glanced at his wristwatch. "Matt, I simply must make that train. I should have taken the early one. I'm looking for a job and I'm to see somebody this afternoon who may be able to arrange for me to ghost several textbooks."

"Relax, champ, I'll get you there. I might even drive you into New York. Don't worry about Francine or the Hunters being uncomfortable around you. I—"

"Matt, I'm the one that's uncomfortable. I must catch that train."

"Okay, okay, Hank. Just don't worry. I can make the station in six minutes flat. Champ, I want you to come out and spend time here. I'll clean house of all jerks, ship Francine to town for a shopping spree. Just the two of us to bull about old times."

"Thanks, Matt, but Ruth is waiting for me in Chicago."

"Relax, champ, you've had a tough time. You need a vacation, I have the house, the beach, the boats. Ruth would agree with me."

"Let me see how my time turns out, Matt. I might have to remain East over the weekend. I'll call you."

"Not this weekend. I'm having Gary Rawn, the screen star, and his current gal, down. What about the following weekend?"

"I'll see how things work out. If this job comes through, I may settle in New York. Matt, let me call you."

Matt stood up, took a boxing stance. "Great seeing you, champ. You're a breath of clean air. So we have a date. Finish your beer. I'll see if Fran needs anything in the village, then drive you to the station."

Francine was sitting on the rear steps, sipping rye and water. The poodle was busy worrying a lemon, which he thought was a ball. Joel Hunter was stretched out on a dull red lounge—two empty glasses on the floor—glancing at an English magazine. Wilma Hunter was sewing a bra strap. Before Matt could open his mouth, Francine sprang to her feet, told him, "I've been waiting for you to step out here. Matt, are you out of your goddamned mind? If the papers, the gossip columnists, ever found out you're entertaining a Fifth Amendment Red or that you even knew him, why Hollywood would drop the option on *Slug In The Gut* and you'd be ruined as a writer!"

"No, my darling, not as a writer. What you mean to say is my sales might dip. Although I even doubt that. Hank is one of the oldest friends I have, and I certainly do not intend to let anybody tell me who my friends are to be."

"I'm telling you, Matt Anthony!" Francine said.

"Keep your gentle voice down, honey. Anybody is a noun that can be both male and female."

"You might have the decency to think of Joel's career," Francine said, stooping to pick up her drink.

"Francine, my sweet, don't tempt me."

"Seriously, Matt," Wilma said, "Fran is right. We're not the martyr type, we—"

"Wilma," Matt said, his eyes staring at her breasts, "will you please explain what sort of movement would make a bra snap? I'm dead serious. They're not like an arm, or even the hips, where there is a certain amount of movement, or muscular contraction. They lay in the bra like eggs waiting ... waiting for what?" (Matt loved to shock people with his clever "hot" talk. But actually he enjoyed it because deep in his mind, Matt himself was the one most shocked by his own bold words.)

"Stop it, Matt," Wilma said. "This isn't a joke."

"Do you think this professor fellow will ever mention meeting me?" Joel asked.

Matt smiled down at Joel, aware of the narrow shoulders—and how huge he must look in comparison to this runt. "Joel, what do you think he's rushing back to New York for? He wants to shout it from the top of the Empire State Building. Listen to me, all of you; maybe you don't agree with what the champ did, but that's no call for this display of goddamn rude manners." He turned to Francine. "You acted with all the taste of a two-bit whore stuck with a lead quarter."

"You know what you can do, Mr. Sonofabitch. If your friend wants to get his rear kicked, fine. But don't bring him here so we all get the boot."

"As usual, you're talking sheer nonsense, honey," Matt said. "You'll be slobbering about witches and bogeymen next." He paused to smile. "Matter of fact you should be grateful for the champ's courage. You see, if he wanted to save his job and name people, he could have very easily named me!"

Wilma stopped sewing. "Really, Matt?"

"You?" Francine blurted the word out. "Now I've heard everything!"

"Indeed, darling, little old me," Matt said, his voice mocking them. "I know my dearest wife thinks of me only as a drunken dumb ox so it may come as a shock to learn I didn't quit college to write—as a jacket blurb once stated. I was thrown out for being the only instructor backing a student anti-ROTC demonstration. I was the only teacher with guts. True, that was over twenty years ago, but mere mention of my name would still make headline reading now."

They were silent for a moment, Matt enjoying things thoroughly. Then Wilma asked, "You were the only teacher? Where was the professor at the time?"

"He was lecturing at—"

Francine stormed over to Matt, her head barely reaching the

bushy grey hair on his chest. "You damn fool! Did you lend him any money? You know how tight—"

"I told you to keep your sweet voice down. Hank refused money. But I am going to see if I can do something about finding the champ a job with Longson."

"They'll love that! Just eat it up! Bill Long is after you to make good the money—" Francine noticed the Hunters straining their ears and stopped. She shouted up at Matt, "You'll have nothing more to do with him!"

"No? I've asked him out for a weekend. If the champ gets a job in New York, I shall certainly see him as often as possible."

"Matt Anthony, that man is not coming into my house again!"

Matt laughed. "While it isn't your house, nor mine, but the bank's, I am still able to ask my friends here."

"Matt, I've taken all I can stand from you. I won't see us broke because of some sentimental whim of yours." Francine started around his big bulk. Matt grabbed her shoulders asked, "Where are you going?"

"To settle this! To tell that ... Red bastard to get the hell out of here!"

Matt squeezed her shoulder and Francine's face screwed up with pain. She tried to get away but Matt shook her hard, his face going paler than his stubble of gray-white whiskers. Matt told her, "Francine, honey, some things I'll take from you because it's a kind of game between us. But Hank Brown is one of the few real things in my life. Do you understand that? He's an isle of reality in this phony world. If you ever say a single out-of-the-way word to Hank, I'll kill you! I mean that." He pushed her away, sending Francine sprawling against the wall, then walked out.

The poodle whined, Wilma sat there pop-eyed and Joel Hunter said, "My, aren't we melodramatic!"

Francine Anthony stepped away from the wall, rubbed her shoulder.

As they walked toward the roadster, Henry Brown asked, "Something wrong, Matt? You look sick."

"Nothing. Another row with Francine—as you probably heard."

"I didn't hear a thing. I'm sorry I caused any—"

"It really isn't about you, champ. She's such a scheming bitch. A silly doc claims my heart does a rumba now and then. Hell, I guess he knows his stuff but ... it isn't anything serious."

Francine keeps harping on it. Every time I take a drink, a swim, for Christsakes she looks ready to step aside so I won't fall on her when I drop dead."

"Don't you think you should take it easy?"

"Look, champ, I carried a large policy but two years ago we were stony and I had to borrow to the hilt on it. I couldn't meet the payments and they had to cut down the insurance. Francine wouldn't mind my dying—if I had the full policy again. She's trying to get me reinstated. I guess I couldn't pass a new physical."

"All those books, how could you be broke?" Brown asked, getting into the Jaguar.

"Don't talk like a hick, champ. Writers never make real money. In the last census the income of the average professional writer was substandard. In a way we're like pugs: a few writers are in the top brackets, a few more make a fair living—and most writers need a working wife to keep above water. Anyway, we were building this house that year." Matt started the car, the motor purring with power. "Hank, we're really equipped for decent living here. When you come out I'll take you tuna fishing—I have a hell of a fine sea boat and ... damn, I never had a chance to show you the boat, the beach. This was some visit. When you come out we'll do nothing but fish and bull about the old gang. I won't do a drop of work, won't think about my damn cobra gimmick. We were all so full of purpose, so sure of life in those days. Sometimes I wonder if it wasn't all a kind of binge. Tell me, do you ever hear of Nick and old Pete? What's become of Hazel; the pretty kid with the haunting eyes?"

They talked about "old times" while waiting for the train, an awkward conversation since neither could recall much about any one person. Brown again refused a check, said he would phone about the weekend the moment he knew about his time. When the train pulled out, Matt drove down a deserted side road and parked. He ran around to the car trunk and eagerly opened a large cardboard carton—the real reason he'd gone to Hampton.

Through the mail, and under a pen name, he had ordered a complete skin-diving outfit: mask, fins, spear gun and two compact air tanks that fastened over the back. A month ago, after he had tried a friend's outfit, there had been a bitter fight with Francine over buying one. "That's all your heart needs!" she had said.

"Nonsense. I won't go down more than fifty feet. We'll buy two and both of us can explore the bay."

"Forget it, Matt. Or better yet, let's call the doctor and have him tell us it's okay?"

Now Matt fingered the gadgets like a happy kid. He thought, It will be a cinch, hide it in the sail locker in the boat house, she never opens that. I'll only use it at night or when Fran is away. I can stay under for nearly an hour. My God, they're always talking about the British ships sunk here in 1776—be something if I find them. Maybe treasure! Has anybody used skin-diving as a plot gimmick yet? Must have been used.

When he reached the house Joel Hunter was sleeping on a beach mat on the front lawn, a shaker of cocktails sweating in the sun beside him. Wilma was dozing in a chair, a yellow scarf flung over her eyes. The dog was curled up in the shade of the chair. For a second Matt grinned down at Wilma, mentally taking off her bathing suit—as he had, in his mind, so many times before. Couple of years, he thought, she'll be a pot. But right now ... mine for the asking. What the hell am I afraid of?

He walked on into the house, walking softly. Upstairs he heard May working. Quietly he walked to the veranda, opened a closet—Fran's tackle box was gone. Matt glanced at the pines which screened the view (and the wind) of the bay. He looked at his wristwatch and nodded to himself. Crossing the rear lawn, he opened the trunk of the Jaguar, and glancing around like a ham actor, took out the cardboard box, and headed through the pines toward the boat house.

He suddenly came up on Francine, walking toward the main house. She was wearing a floppy straw hat that they had bought in Haiti and an old Italian sports shirt over her bathing suit. She was holding her fishing gear. Matt asked with real annoyance, "Where did you come from?"

"I forgot my spinning reel and ... what's in the box?"

"Nothing much. Tools, oarlocks ... a few things I ordered last week," Matt said, walking past her, shielding the box with his body.

"We don't need oarlocks. Come back here, Matt."

He kept walking. She said, "You louse, you have a case of gin in there!" Francine turned to run after him. She fell over a root, and unable to break the fall because her hands were full of tackle, she cracked her head on a large rock imbedded at the side of the rough path. The big hat didn't even touch the rock but her skull and the stone made a dull sound.

Matt dropped the box, raced back to her. He said, "Honey, are ...?" as he started to lift Francine, then let the body fall again. Her head hit the stone once more—hardly any sound this time—and Matt jumped back in horror: he knew she was dead.

Matt was dazed. He stared at the body and couldn't believe what he saw. He knelt beside her and felt the back of her neck. He massaged the pulseless wrists, turned Francine over gently and started to put his hand under her bathing suit to feel for a heartbeat, but the unseeing open eyes stopped him. She wasn't stunned or hurt; she was dead.

Matt was numbed, shocked, grief-stricken: he began to weep—a little. And under all these emotions there was another one pushing its way to the top of his mind—relief. For a second the tears came, and he seemed to be kneeling in prayer and crying. But the more he stared at her body, the stronger an entirely new thought grew—one which filled him with fear and horror. He mumbled half aloud, *"Nobody will ever believe this was an accident!* The Hunters heard me say I'd kill Francine a short time ago ... 'She tripped and hit her head on a rock....' No, no, oh, my God no! I wouldn't believe that myself. I'm in a hell of a jam unless ... unless what? Can I make the Hunters forget they heard me threaten her? Joel would break under any kind of questioning and Wilma—she'd hold it over me the rest of my life. No, there's only one thing to do and I have to do it damn fast—make it look *more* like an accident."

He stood up, studied the body, the ground: he was thinking clearly, the top-flight mystery writer looking for a plot switch. The rods weren't touched. Her canvas shoes hadn't been torn by the root. He pulled back the floppy hat: there was a suggestion of blood on her lips and nose but no blood on either the rock or the ground. Her forehead was discolored and of a queer shape, like a cracked egg. Matt turned the hat down over her eyes.

"Don't understand why there isn't any blood," Matt told himself, "But it's a break. Now ... Fran must have told the Hunters she was going fishing. Okay, she stood up to cast, lost her balance, struck her head on the side of the boat, fell over and drowned? No, that's out, any medical examiner could prove she was dead before she hit the water. Suppose she's found hanging over the side of the boat, just her face resting on the water? That would hold up, hitting the side of the boat would be the cause of death, not drowning. Sure, she stood up to cast, lost her balance, hit her head. Would such a blow cause death? Hell, it had to, it did! What's my alibi? Do I need one? May probably heard me drive up in the car even if the Hunters didn't. But no reason for May to check the time I arrived. As for the Hunters, they're half-bagged, shouldn't be hard to confuse them on a time lapse of a half hour. Can I work that corny bit of changing and rechanging the clocks I used in the old pulps? I'll think of ... damn, wonder if anyone else is fishing in this end of the bay? Although I can swim out and back underwater with my outfit!"

Matt picked up the cardboard box and ran to the boathouse—the bay was empty. He ran back and picked up Francine, carried her down to the little rowboat beached on the sand. He raced back and picked up the fishing gear, carefully studied the ground in the shade of the pine trees. He ran back, his heart pounding. He quickly put an old reel on Francine's rod, hooked and baited the line. Matt thought: Damn, good I posted all the land around here, little chance of anyone seeing me—although always a chance of some dumb kid being in the woods. I don't have to worry about fingerprints, I've often used her tackle. Now—what made her trip? A shoelace caught on the broken duckboards. Poor Fran, always after me to fix them. Then her head would hit about ... here. Would it make a dent in the wooden gunwale? I think so. But have I the guts to bang Fran's head against the boat?

Matt quickly stripped nude, found a large rock on the sandy bottom of the water, a rock almost as large and smooth as a skull. He took careful aim and banged it on the gunwale, slightly crushing the wood. It seemed to make a terrific sound and Matt froze for a second, waiting to see if the noise brought anybody on the run.

For a horrible, fleeting moment, his nerves started to snap, like the rubber bands flying off an open golf ball. He forced himself to be calm as he thought: I *have* to get this over with. If anybody sees me now, this second, I'm cooked. Oh, my God, I have to be careful. I must think clearly ... so very, very clearly. And I must work fast.

Throwing the rock as far out into the bay as he could, Matt then washed the beaten wood to remove any particles of rock or sand. Feeling sick to his quivering stomach he deposited Fran's body on the seat and worked a shoelace under the duckboard. With sudden inspiration he jerked her canvas shoe hard enough to snap the lace, leaving part of it still entwined in the boards. Taking the bailing can, he doused the shoe and lace with water to remove any prints. The sun would soon dry the shoe. Besides, a damp shoe was common in a rowboat.

Racing time, Matt put on the face mask and tested the air tanks. They worked fine. Strapping the big rubber flippers on his feet, Matt next put the anchor in the front of the boat, after first dragging the rope through the water to remove the sand. Then, pushing the boat free of the beach, he was about to pull the outboard down into the water and start it ... but yanked his hand back as if he had touched a flame. "That was close!" he whispered to himself. "Real dumb! Motor makes such a racket it might have been heard at the house. Damn, I have to think, think clearly."

He started swimming, one hand holding the bow of the boat, swimming and drifting out with the tide, carefully checking the bay and the boat. "There's only two holes in this," Matt told himself, "Somebody can be watching me from the lousy woods. And the post office clerk in Hampton might remember my getting the package, even under a phony name. Knowing I have this diving outfit could make the cops suspicious ... nothing I can do about it now but chance it. Oh, God."

Several hundred yards from the shore, Fran's favorite spot for kingfish, Matt pulled the anchor over. He let out some fishing line, and on further thought, released the brake on the reel so the line went out with the tide: Fran would have had the reel free when she started to cast. Next, Matt adjusted the mask on his face and the air intake. Closing his eyes he reached up, nearly tipping the boat, cupped his free hand around the back of her head ... opening his eyes he brought the front of her skull down exactly where the rock had hit the side of the boat.

Her body hung over the side of the boat, the floppy hat resting on the water, one limp hand in the water. The fishing rod stuck out at a crazy angle from under her bent body. Matt swam to the stern and pulled the tilted outboard so that the propeller was in the water. Then, floating on his back, he slowly ran his eyes over the boat, checking every detail—his heart pounding so he wondered if he was about to have an attack. The weight of her body made the rowboat list to that side, but there wasn't any danger of it tipping, nor of the corpse falling overboard. The anchor was holding, and swimming closer he saw traces of blood and hair in the smashed wood.

For a long moment Matt stared at his wife, at the body he had enjoyed and tormented so often. His grief and sorrow twisted his stomach into a knot. He swam over and held on to the anchor rope, pulled off the glass faceplate and gave up. A moment later his strength and calm returned and he submerged and swam toward the shore. His nose was bleeding slightly as he stood up on the beach and his ears ached. He carefully spread the mask and oxygen tanks on the docks to dry. As he walked up and down, letting the sun warm and dry his skin, he thought: Perhaps tomorrow I'll drive back to Hampton, hang around the post office. No way the clerk can place the exact day when the box arrived. Or is there? It was insured. Why am I worrying about the damn package so much?

Dressing, he debated whether it would be best to hide the lung in the boat house, or take it back to the car trunk. He could always say Fran had known all about his ordering the skin-diving outfit. Then why under a pen name? But then he had checking accounts under his several writing names ... Matt decided to hide the box in the sail locker but it worried him. Somehow, he had a feeling the Aqua-Lung was the weak link in things.

Walking back toward the house, he nearly fainted when passing the spot where Fran had fallen; but forced himself to study it for a moment, then walked on—rapidly. Exactly forty-seven minutes had elapsed. And Joel Hunter was still sleeping on the beach mat and Wilma snoozing in the chair. Matt sat (gently) in another chair, noticing with relief that neither of them was wearing a watch. He wanted a drink real badly, looked at the cocktail shaker but didn't touch it. As Matt picked up a magazine from the wrought iron table, the poodle stretched and yawned, came over and sniffed at Matt's legs.

Matt glanced at the house. May? But afternoons were her hardest time. Of course, she *might* have looked out of the window, *might* have even noticed him sitting down just now ... Still, there was little chance of May being certain of the time. Matt thought: Hell with May, let me set up the Hunters. Use the time switch I had in the first Inspector O'Cohen book. Jeez, so damn much hinges on this play.

Matt pushed the poodle so his hind legs touched Joel. Joel blinked. Shielding his sleepy, drunken eyes with a slim hand he said, "Oh, it's you, Matt. Want to take a swim?"

"Where's Fran?"

"Fishing. What a delicious day. The sun is just exquisite."

Matt glanced at his watch—holding up his wrist for Joel to see—knowing he was too far away for Joel to make out the hands. It was 3:27 P.M. as Matt said casually, "It's only a quarter to three. Why not wait until Fran returns?"

Joel nodded and Matt opened the magazine. After staring up at the clean sky for a moment, Joel dozed off. Matt glanced at Wilma—she was still sleeping. He watched the even movements of her chest and smiled into the magazine. He thought: This sure changes things. Poor Fran was right, no sense in having Hank around too much. Risky. I'll try to help him ... whatever way I can and ... I can't even fully realize yet what this does mean. Why, I can get married again! First I'll take a trip to

Europe, fruit around, then settle down with a young babe. Oh, God, I sound like an old roué. I need a drink, but bad.

At exactly 3:30 P.M. he picked up a pebble, tossed it at Wilma's bare stomach, pretended he was reading. Wilma sat up, pushing her breasts out as she stretched. She tasted her tongue, ran a hand over her thighs. She said, "I feel dehydrated—if that's the right word. Anything left in the shaker?"

Matt rubbed his eyes, yawned, then got up and carried the shaker to her. They each took a swig of mostly ice water and he said, forcing himself to sound gay, "I'd love to see you naked now—the dehydrated nude."

"Stop it. What's the time?"

He tried not to show his relief as he held his wrist in front of her face. "Three-thirty. Going to sleep the afternoon away?"

"Be too late for a swim soon," Wilma said. She got up and went over and tickled Joel's ear with her big toe. "Rise and shine, sleepy-head. It's nearly four."

Joel sat up, yawning. "Wish I'd put some oil on myself. Scotch and the sun—best sleep pill ever invented."

Matt said softly but clearly, "You've been snoring for the last three quarters of an hour. I could hardly finish this article for the racket."

"Now, Matt, I really don't snore."

"Yes, you do." Matt reached over and stuck his wrist in Joel's red face. "Remember when you asked me the time before and I showed you the watch and you saw it was only 2:45? Well, now it's 3:30 and man, you should have the appetite of a lumber jack because you've been sawing logs and making a hell of a racket all that time."

"Professor Anthony and his corny lectures on the fine art of snoring," Wilma said. "Frankly, if Joel does snore he does it artistically, like he does everything else."

"Thank you, my good wifey," Joel said. "Fran have any luck?"

"Why, I didn't hear her return," Matt said. "Surprising, too, she usually doesn't have patience for more than an hour's fishing." Matt rubbed his eyes. "I read a lot, listening to Joel snoring. Rather interesting article on Africa. Read it, Joel, you might try a serious kids' book—plight of two half-colored kids in Capetown." Matt shadow-boxed his way over to the house, called for May. When she appeared—an apron over her shorts—he asked, "Has Fran come back yet?"

"No. I haven't seen her."

"Would you mind going down to the beach and if she's within shouting distance, tell her we're ready to go swimming," Matt said, thinking: It should take her about three minutes to reach the dock.

He glanced at his watch as he returned to the Hunters. Exactly three minutes and eight seconds later they all heard May scream.

Matt was dictating in his den when the village cop knocked on the door. He'd had several good hookers and while Matt wasn't high, his nerves were relaxed. To his surprise—and admiration—he had been able to get into the story he was working on and had actually done a dozen pages.

Matt stood in the doorway and nodded at the local cop, said, "Hello, Ted," and glanced at the thickset man standing behind the young policeman. The dumpy-looking man was wearing a cheap and badly fitting summer suit. The coconut straw hat—still on his head—was stained with sweat and other things. The plain sports shirt struggled to circle the bull neck. The man looked like a barrel of lard to most people, but Matt, who had gone in for weight lifting and had studied muscles, knew the man was tremendously strong.

With a mild note of apology in his voice, Ted said, "Sorry to disturb you again, Mr. Anthony. Ah ... this here is Detective Walter Kolcicki, from the D.A.'s office in the county seat."

"Not disturbing me at all. How do you do, Detective Kolcicki," Matt held out his hand. Kolcicki's hand weighed a ton.

"Let's sit down. I got some routine questions." The detective's voice was low, almost bored.

"Of course," Matt said, amused by the round stupid face. He walked to his desk and pulled up two chairs. "I was in the midst of some work. I not only have a deadline to meet, but I find work helps take my mind off the tragedy."

Kolcicki sat down beside the desk, nodded at Ted who had remained in the doorway. As Ted started to close the door, from the outside, Matt called out, "Ask May to give you some imported beer I have."

Matt sat down and tried to smile. Kolcicki stared at Matt, his eyes large and emotionless. Matt asked, "Have you ever read any of my books?"

"Nope."

"Well, I'm anxious to cooperate in every way."

Kolcicki pushed his hat back on his head, said nothing. "You may be interested in knowing I have worked with the New York City Police Department, and with the D.A's office in Los

Angeles. In my work I ..."

"Did you threaten to kill your wife this afternoon?" Kolcicki's voice was hard and blunt.

Matt's heart began to race as he held out his hands, shrugged. "No. Not really."

"These other people, the Hunters, they say you did."

"Oh, I said it, you know, we had a little fuss. Words that have no real ... hell, man, you call somebody a bastard without meaning it."

"I never say it unless I mean it. You bastard, why did you kill her?"

Matt nearly jumped out of his chair. He fought to control his voice as he asked, "Do you realize what you're saying?"

"Yeah."

"Now see here, while I understand you have a job to do, I've been through a great deal today and ... Look, there's nothing to be gained by bluffing. I talked to the police and the medical examiner, and both their reports clearly state my wife's death was an accident. Obviously while fishing she—"

Detective Kolcicki said a common four-letter word, one that Matt had used hundreds of times in his books, yet it never sounded as harsh and brutal as when it came from the detective's fat mouth.

Matt began to sweat and the pounding of his heart shook his whole body. He had read and written a great deal about the third-degree methods of the police, undoubtedly exaggerating it in his mind, and had a deadly fear of such torture. There was a case where the police drilled a suspect's teeth until ... Matt ran a hand over his face, forced himself to say calmly and slowly, "Hadn't we better get a few things straight, officer? I'm not some migratory farmhand who doesn't know his rights. I'm a well-known writer, and not without influence. You're a small-town cop and view this as a chance to make a name. Be careful you don't make a fool of yourself."

"Yeah, I'm a hick cop. But before this I worked Homicide in Chicago for fourteen years. Cut the bull, Anthony. You threaten to kill your wife and two hours later she's dead. For me, that adds. I ain't here asking *if* you did it—I want to know *why* you killed her."

"Don't be an ass! My wife obviously tripped while standing in a boat, struck her head on the—"

Almost in slow motion Detective Kolcicki reached over and punched Matt in the stomach. It was a terrible blow, bent Matt double, paralyzing him with pain and fear. Matt had done a lot of careful boxing, once or twice even sparred with pros, but he had never been hit like this. His heart seemed to be galloping out of his open mouth.

"Bastard! Tell me *why*, then *how* you did it!" The voice was still low and horribly impersonal, except for the word 'bastard' which had the chill of death about it.

A hundred story twists for outwitting the stupid cop, a dozen judo holds he had so well described in his books, ran through Matt's brain like a runaway film. He gasped, "You ... you ... don't you realize I glorify ... guys ... like you?" He took a deep and painful breath. "I ... I ... make you heroic ... Yes ... I make you guys famous ...!"

Kolcicki didn't seem to hear, his eyes watching Matt with a cold calm as if he was studying him under a glass. More air returned to Matt's tortured lungs and scenes of swinging rubber hoses, gouged eyes, blackjacks and their metal cores, broken faces, joined the racing movie in his mind. He said, "See here ... I ... I demand a lawyer!"

"Yeah, when you've signed a confession. Louse, why did you do it?"

Matt frantically thought of yelling into the phone, of screaming for help, even of turning on the recorder switch, getting it all down on tape. Would the swish of a sap make enough sound? He said, "Listen to me; I have proof that I was with Joel Hunter at the time the medical examiner fixed Fran's death. The police know this ..."

As his own hand crept toward the recording switch he saw the detective's wide fist coming at him again. Matt tried to scream, yell, but only a weak hiss came from his open mouth as the fist seemed to ram his jumping heart through his back. The blow knocked Matt over the back of the chair. He hit the floor hard, both hands pressing his agonized belly. Without showing any strain, Kolcicki straightened up the chair, then picked up Matt's big body, actually tossed him into the chair. He hadn't even disturbed his straw hat as he sat down and asked, "Come on, *why?*"

Matt gasped, "I ... have ... a bad ... heart ... you're ... killing me."

Kolcicki said his favorite four-letter word again, almost spit it out.

Through a jumble of thoughts flashing in his mind Matt thought: This dirty sonofabitch is treating me like a punk. If I can only get to my feet, clout him with a good right ... but then he'll take out his blackjack and beat me to death. Lord, is this the end? Am I such a coward? Is this real? Is this stupid cop too smart for me? There *must* be a way out of ...

"I'm waiting, *why* did you kill her?"

"I demand the—" Matt saw Kolcicki draw back his pudgy fist again and Matt cried out, "I'll tell you! Tell you exactly what happened! I lied to the police. But it was an accident! I never touched her. We were in the pines and she wanted to know what I had in a box I was carrying. She tripped and fell against a rock. I'll show you the rock. I realized after what I'd said ... about killing her ... how things would look. I tried to make it look more like an accident. I took the body out into the bay in the boat. I'll show you the skin-diving outfit I used. I'll show you everything. That's the truth! I swear it!"

Kolcicki said the four-letter word again and it hit Matt like a whiplash. The detective punched Matt squarely over the heart. Matt went tumbling over and over into a welcome darkness. He thought he had escaped and it was a maddening shock to come to seconds later, find himself face down on his desk, hearing the dull voice saying, "Keep talking but give me the truth. You clever bastards with your fancy words. So you was skin-diving? What did you do, swim out underwater and take her by surprise?"

Matt's head was spinning so he suddenly wished his pounding heart would explode, take him out of this nightmare. But his heart began to beat normally, although the rest of his stomach and side were afire with pain. "I told you, I didn't—"

"Don't give me this accident jive unless you want another taste of my fist."

"But it was a ... a ..."

Kolcicki punched him on the shoulder this time. Matt mumbled, "I really have a bad heart and—"

"Bastard, who you think you're stalling? Now the truth!"

Matt sat up. "Damn you, I am telling you the truth! It all happened the way I said. You see Fran had the fishing tackle in her hands, couldn't break her fall, so ... her head struck first and—"

As the fist started for him Matt drew back hard against his chair and screamed—although hardly any sound came from his lips. There was a low thud of Kolcicki's fist smacking Matt's stomach. Matt collapsed in his chair, gasping for breath. He was sure of only one thing: he couldn't take another blow.

As Kolcicki stood up, Matt heard himself cry in a distant voice, "Don't! Don't hit me! All right, all right! Please don't hit me again. I'll say what you—you want. Tell me what to say, but don't hit me." His words died in a whisper.

Kolcicki pulled Matt erect in the chair, grunted, "I ain't even started on your kidneys yet. I'll have you pissing blood for weeks."

"Tell me what to say!"

"You know what to say. Just make it good. Good. You understand, bastard? None of your fancy crap. You ready?"

Hands pressed to his aching body, Matt nodded dumbly.

The detective glanced about, saw the typewriter on its little metal table. He carried it over to his chair, took a piece of clean paper from Matt's desk, inserted it in the machine. He said, "Now you start talking. If you talk right, you'll sign this. If you don't, I'll bust every rib in your goddamn body. Now talk—and not too damn fast, either."

Kolcicki began typing. Even in his daze, the opening sentence of a confession suddenly appeared very clearly in Matt's mind: I, Matt Anthony, voluntarily do....

Sitting there with his dirty hat still on, Kolcicki typed with expert ease. The detective's typing efficiency was the last straw for Matt, completed his fright and terror—increased it. And he knew he was trapped, that the confession would stand up in court. Kolcicki was good, he'd make him write a logical confession.

Matt shut his eyes. Shame, reason, everything fled. He was too frightened to care about anything except to be free of Kolcicki's animal eyes and iron fists.

Kolcicki said coldly, his stubby fingers resting on the typewriter keys, "Start talking. And talk right, or I'll really work you over. I ain't even got a sweat up yet, bastard!"

His voice a whine, a lifeless whisper, Matt Anthony began dictating another mystery, another fiction story.

THE END

Shakedown for Murder
Ed Lacy

"... of course I got here as soon as possible, but I was too late—he must have died within seconds after phoning me. I found him over the hall table. You and I, we're more than merely old friends, so believe me when I tell you that in a case like this, there isn't anything a doctor can do. At his age, the heart grows very tired." Doctor Edward Barnes placed a hand on the other's damp, trembling shoulder; a hand both firm and gentle.

"Yes ... I ... I understand, Edward." The voice was dazed, sullen with mounting hysteria.

"What?" the doctor asked, cupping an ear, brushing the rain from his face with his other hand. "What did you say?"

"I said ... I'm okay. It's just ... I'll miss him so. You know how close we were."

The doctor pulled his old felt hat down as he said, "Come now, no weeping. There isn't much one can say about death, especially the death of an old friend. Yet I always find myself groping for the meaningless phrases. Our only consolation is to remember he lived a long and useful life. And he died without pain. Remember the old Indian saying you once told me.... Death is but the opening of a new trail. Do you recall telling me that?"

"Yes. I suppose I knew this would happen—someday. But ... oh God! Ed, it's all so sudden!"

"Let yourself go, weep." Barnes reached into the car for his bag. "Naturally you're in shock. I'll give you something to calm your nerves, make you forget."

"I don't need any drugs."

"Listen to me. It's late, there isn't anything either of us can do till morning. Standing out here in the rain will only give you a chill. If you like, I'll spend the night here."

"No."

"Come now, at a time like this ... I can stay the night with you."

"No, Ed, I'm ... fine."

"Then take this pill and you'll sleep for ..." The doctor's wet and wrinkled face expanded with astonishment for a very brief part of a second as he was viciously kneed in the groin. Gasping, Barnes bent over—arms out like a racing swimmer ready to dive—then he stumbled back against his car, hands now pressed hard to his middle.

The killer clamped a hand over the doctor's open mouth, another over the sharp nose. The old man's watery eyes bulged—pain still mixed with surprise. He started to claw the air, then slumped to the wet ground.

Opening the door of the doctor's heavy Buick, the murderer

dragged the old man across the front seat, yanked a woolen muffler from around Barnes' thin neck, then savagely jammed it over the doctor's pink face. For a moment the doctor's legs jerked and thrashed as the muffler cut off all air.

Certain Barnes was dead, with great effort the body was picked up and slowly lowered to the floor of the rear of the car. Placing the medical bag on the front seat, the killer slid behind the wheel—moving gracefully—and drove off, driving along the dark roads of the village.

Reaching Bay Street the murderer stepped out and listened long and carefully, sweating face almost touching the wet pavement. Certain no cars were coming, the doctor's corpse was quickly pulled to the middle of the road. Then backing the Buick up, the killer shifted gears and pressed the gas pedal to the floor.

The big car jumped as it ran over the dead body.

The murderer stepped out and stared down at the rain striking the crushed face, then picked up a pebble. The Buick was aimed at a large tree off the road, the ignition turned off, and the pebble wedged under the accelerator—forcing it as far down as the pedal could go. Then reaching in and turning on the ignition, the killer awkwardly jumped back as the Buick leaped forward, crossed the road and smashed into the tree. The thick rain slightly muffled the crashing sound.

Standing perfectly still and hidden in the nearby woods, the killer waited to see if the noise brought anybody, then ran over to the wreck. The pebble was removed, the front and rear seats carefully examined. The doctor's woolen scarf was on the floor beneath the crumpled steering wheel. Grabbing the scarf, the murderer pulled a thin, pencil flashlight from Barnes' bag, quickly played it over the tires. Nothing of the doctor's flesh or clothing had stuck to the new tires. The killer rubbed the scarf over a red spot on a tire wall, then realized it was merely red paint.

Dropping the flash back into the bag, the killer went home, walking and running through unlit streets and woods wherever possible. At the gate of the house the killer was still clutching the doctor's scarf, and with a moan of utter dismay and horror, dropped the muffler with a frantic motion, ran sobbing into the house.

Minutes later, the murderer returned, picked up the scarf and went back into the warm house.

Chapter 1

My "vacation" started off as I expected—by giving me a hard time.

The railroad station at Hampton was full of sleek cars and people standing around as nude as they could get, without being arrested. I never saw so many scrimpy shorts and stuffed halters in my life. The young people showed off their trim thighs and bosoms, while even the old duffers walked around without shame, holding their sloppy stomachs in. I stepped off the train with my battered bag in one hand and Matty in his wicker basket in the other. I was sure a standout: I was the only person not sporting a tan. Also, I had on a tie and a shirt, not to mention my old blue serge suit. Everybody looked at me as though I were an escapee from a museum.

I was sweaty and in a bad mood. I didn't want to come out here and a three-hour ride on the Long Island Railroad isn't exactly any laughs for me. Matty was evil too, cooped up in his basket all that time. On the train he'd been wailing and making a small racket. When I poked my finger in to quiet him, he'd showed his feelings by biting it. I'd snapped my finger in his gut and he had hissed like a snake, then shut up.

As I was looking around the station, sorry I hadn't told Danny to meet me, a fat little man in worn slacks, high shoes, an outrageous sport shirt and an ancient sweaty straw hat hustled over to me and made a pass at my bag. As I snatched it to me, he asked, "Hey, mista, you wants the taxi, huh?"

I nodded and followed him to an old Dodge. I sat on the front seat, Matty's basket on my lap. The car was hot as a Turkish bath. The driver went up and down the platform trying to drum up trade, finally got in and started the car with a jerk. "Mista, where you go?"

"End Harbor."

"Gooda summer, now. That my town. Cost you one dolla. You visit some-abody?"

"Know where the Lund cottage is, on Beach Road?" I never found dialect funny, even on TV.

"You bet I know. Vera nice people. You a friend?"

"I hope so. Dan Lund is my son."

A real smile flitted across his weatherbeaten face as he turned into a main highway. The Dodge kept edging toward the road shoulder. "Your Danny is a lucky man, his Bessie is a wonderful wife. The second I first saw her I knew she was a Greek, like me. She has all the warm beauty of the ..."

I didn't have time to wonder what happened to the dialect. I shouted, "You're going off the road!"

He turned the wheel too hard. The car went into a shimmy dance, finally got squared away as Matty growled savagely. This joker stuck a fat hand in my face, told me, "I'm Jerry Sparelous, a true friend of your daughter-in-law. Will you stay in the Harbor long?"

"A week," I said, shaking hands fast so he could put the paw back on the wheel. "Then I visit my daughter in the mountains for a week." Matty seemed to sigh. Or maybe it was me.

I had a month off and Dan insisted I spend the first week with him. The second would be with Signe and her basketball team of noisy kids. Then maybe I could get some real rest in my flat on Washington Heights, sitting in my underwear next to the big window fan, watching TV or doping the nags.

"End Harbor is nice—I've lived here for thirty-five years," this Jerry said, the car starting off on a tangent again. "What you do, Mr. Lund?"

"I'm a cop. Look, Mr. ... Jerry ... side of the road again."

"Don't worry," he said, jerking the car around. "In twenty years I never had an accident—that was my fault. Yes, yes, Bessie has told me about you. They want you to retire. You and me. I sold my store and some land a few years ago. I have enough money. But people ask why I drive a taxi. They think a man of sixty-four is fit for nothing but dying...."

We went around a turn and made directly for some bushes on the side of the road. I tried to put my foot through the floorboard before he headed down the highway again. I said weakly, "Perhaps you need glasses."

"I have two pair—at home. Hot in New York?"

"Yeah."

"Big city is all rush, crazy. I haven't been back to New York in thirty-two years. Who wants to rush?"

I didn't answer. Three hours away and he hadn't been to the Big Apple in a third of a century! They couldn't drag me away from New York.

We drove in silence for a while, except when I told him he was going off the road. It was starting to grow dark and we seemed to be driving through a lonely, wooded section. But on reaching End Harbor we passed a lot of new ranch-type houses. With a scream of tires he turned into a wide road that went by a pond the size of the Central Park skating rink. "Plenty big bass in there, and they bite on a plug. You a fisherman?"

"I can take it or leave it."

"Me, too. Funny, you don't look like a policeman—you're too thin. Me, I wish I was thin. Every day I'm getting more like a squash. Too much beer. Doctor gives me plenty of hell. But I say, what difference does it make if I'm fat, I'm not making a show for the girls. How old are you, Mr. Lund?"

"Fifty-eight."

"Your wife is dead, too. Bessie told me. Jesus, I almost went crazy when my Helen died eight years ago, God rest her soul. I got three boys. Two of them run a garage in Chicago, the other is a tinsmith out in Los Angeles. My boys all leave the Harbor fast." He shrugged, waved both hands. "But everybody has to live their own life."

The Dodge went over the only bump in the road and Matty whined.

He turned to smile at the basket. "You have a cat, I have a dog—when he comes home. Strange, isn't it, how in our old age we turn to the companionship of animals?"

"I always had a ..."

"Now we don't talk, Mr. Lund. I have to cross a busy highway on which people race toward Montauk like they are going to St. Peter's gates."

He brought the car to a complete and jerky stop, screwing up his eyes as he peered up and down the road. Cars were going by doing at least seventy. A motorcycle cop stationed here could keep a town tax-free. Jerry kept looking up and down the road, waiting for a break, and talking all the time. Some junk about the days when End Harbor was a whaling port, the houses that still had shell marks, or something, from the days of 1776 when, according to Jerry, the British Navy bombarded the village.

He suddenly stepped on the gas and I banged my forehead against the windshield as the car leaped across the road. Then he stopped abruptly to ask if I was hurt, shaking me up again. I had a hell of a headache but told him, "I'm okay. How much farther to the house?"

"Just down this street," Jerry said, starting the car before I could get out. He drove past a few houses and I could smell the salt in the air. Then he stopped, said proudly, "Here we are, Mr. Lund."

I wanted to say I wouldn't have given even money we'd get here, but I paid him a dollar as the cottage door opened and Andy yelled, "Grandpa is here!"

It always gives me a start to hear myself called grandpa.

Andy came leaping at me and almost knocked me down with a hug. He's big for his age but still lardy. When my Danny had been ten, he was already muscular, and coming down the porch steps now, in shorts, he still looked in good shape. Maybe Andy got his softness from Bessie—she had an apron around her bathing suit. She wasn't fat but all a kind of sensuous softness that went with her creamy skin, dark hair, and flashing eyes. Sometimes I thought Bessie was too much woman for Danny—or any one man.

They were all over me, pumping my hand, everybody talking at once. Matty was yelling to get out of his basket, and Bessie and Jerry were rattling off Greek. The noise didn't help my headache any. Somehow we finally got into the cottage and I put my bag in the room I was to share with Andy. I wanted to take a hot bath but Andy was trying to show me a spinning reel he'd just bought and Matty was screaming. I opened the basket and the cat immediately made a quick sniffing tour of the cottage. I asked Bessie for an empty box and began filling it with torn newspapers. She said, "Oh, for—can't that beast do its business outside?"

"Matty isn't for any outdoors stuff. Doubt if he'll even leave the house. And he might get ticks. I'll take care of his box. Just leave him alone for a while, he has to get used to the place. Will I have time to take a hot bath?"

Danny burst out laughing. "Bath? All we have is a shower. Bess, have we time for a fast swim?"

"If you make it real quick." She patted my face. "Special for you I'm making *rice pilaf* and that wine pudding you love, *moustalevrai*."

"That settles it, we'll take a swim," Danny said. When I hesitated, he poked me on the arm—and my head rang—and asked, "What the devil kind of a Norseman are you?"

"Yes, Grandpa," the kid chimed in, "We have the blood of Leif Ericson in our veins. That's what you told me."

"Did I say that? And I bet old Leif never took a dip if he could help it. Okay, I'll change."

As I got into my old woolen trunks the room seemed quiet and my headache eased up. I unpacked my suitcase into a drawer, carefully hid my empty service gun. I didn't want to leave it around the flat in Washington Heights, in case the place was robbed or something. I could smell Bessie's cooking and I was real hungry, so I decided to get the damn swim over with. Swimming! I sure missed the peace and quiet of my flat!

Everybody remarked about the whiteness of my skin as I gave Andy a boat kit I'd brought for him. He let out a whoop of joy that split my eardrums. Then Danny rushed us out to his new Ford and we drove the two blocks to the beach. I felt dizzy. As they used to say during the war, was this entire trip necessary?

The water was smooth and the tide low. I splashed around in the damn chilly water, then banged my toe on a rock, while the boy showed off his underwater swimming. He pointed out a rowboat in which we would go fishing tomorrow. Dan had to swim under my legs, come up and throw me over. I spit out a mouthful of salt water and tried to hold my temper.

As we stood on the sandy beach and toweled ourselves dry, Danny started working on me. First he made some crack about my wool trunks with the white belt being the only pair in existence and why didn't I live it up a little and buy a new pair? Then, driving back to the cottage, he told me, "Dad, I'm a sure thing to be made head of the accounting department next month. It means a big raise and ... well, if you want to retire I could easily give you fifty or sixty dollars a month."

"Who wants to retire? I like being a cell block attendant, hanging around the precinct house all day. No walking a post or worrying about the weather, no carrying a belt full of junk."

"But Dad, you're practically a janitor there!"

"He's not a janitor, he's a cop," Andy said quickly.

I stared at Dan with surprise; being a phony had never been one of his faults. "What's wrong, son? Are you getting that snob executive outlook, too, along with your big desk? Sure, I sometimes sweep up and put out the ashes, depending on the tour I'm working, but there's nothing wrong with that. No work is degrading—as long as you always have a choice of work. And you know how simple my wants are—anytime I feel like retiring my pension will do me fine."

"Okay," Dan said, "It was just an idea."

When we reached the cottage Bessie gave me a small hug—and she smelled fine—asked, "Matt, don't you feel invigorated?"

"You bet," I said, slapping her plump behind, and going to my room to dress—and sneak a nip of brandy to ward off a cold. Matty was sitting on my bed, switching his tail nervously, his eyes seemed to be asking me, "What the devil are we doing out here?" Andy came in to put on a sweatshirt and poked at the cat. Matty got up on his hind feet to box and I told the boy, "Take it easy, he's hungry."

"Mama put down a saucer of milk for him but he wouldn't drink it. Gosh, Grandpa, I go for that boat kit you gave me. After we go fishing tomorrow, I'll start on it."

"Do we have to go fishing?" I was thinking of spending tomorrow sleeping.

"Sure, porgies are biting. I want to try out my spinning reel. Pops wanted to give it to me but I insisted on paying for it. Two dollars. Pops is some fisherman, can catch any ..."

Bessie called us in to eat. I added a little beer and sugar to Matty's milk before I sat down and the cat licked it up like a pig. Dan said, "I'll be damned!" While Bessie said, "Really, Matt, you and that fat cat. You need a wife."

"Figure out a way of doing away with Danny and I'm your man," I cornballed. Bessie blushed with pleasure. Her good breasts seemed ready to pop over the top of her skimpy bathing suit. I glanced at Dan. His eyes met mine and they were full of pride—like when he was a kid and Martha would be telling me about some smart thing he'd done. Martha would have liked Bessie.

The *rice pilaf* was a dish of steaming spiced rice packed with livers and other meats served like an upside-down cake. I tried not to stuff myself only I couldn't resist the wine pudding and I was barely able to get up from the table. I gave Matty some scraps which he picked over. Bessie said, "Don't leave the scraps around, they'll bring bugs."

"Don't worry, he'll eat it. But he likes to take his time," I said. I got my pipe working and sat on the couch, knowing I was in for a rough night, my guts drum-tight. Andy and Dan washed the dishes while Matty sat by the screen door, gazing cautiously out at the country night.

Andy went to bed after warning me, "You hit the sack soon, too, Grandpops, we have to be full of pep for fishing tomorrow."

Bessie brought out a bottle of Irish whisky and we sat around, had a few belts, she and Dan going over some local gossip. When Matty curled up on the couch beside me we had a mild argument as to whether cats were cleaner than human animals. My stomach eased up a bit and I asked, "What's with your friend Jerry? One minute he talks like a bad comedian, and then all the dialect vanishes."

"Oh, he's a character," Bessie said. "Waged a one-man war with End Harbor for years. When he first came here he really had an accent and they gave him the cold shoulder. You know the jive: most people in town can trace their ancestors back to 1776, as if that means a thing. Then it seems Jerry wrote a letter to the local paper against the execution of Sacco and Vanzetti, making him the village radical. So he said the hell with them and purposely kept on talking with his horrible accent. Why, he even refused to buy a brick for the Legion building here, but he always marches at the head of the July Fourth parade and they can't leave him out—he won the Distinguished Service Cross in World War I, highest medal anybody in the Harbor has. Whole thing is pretty silly: on both sides."

"Yeah. Still, a man has to have plenty of moxie to thumb his nose all his life at his neighbors," I said.

"And a stubborn capacity for loneliness," Dan added, yawning. "I have to catch the seven A.M. train back to the job, I'd better turn in."

"Me, too. I can't let a weekend husband sleep alone," Bessie said. She rubbed her knee. "My leg aches, bet it will rain."

"Dad, don't you bother getting up early tomorrow," Dan said, coming over to take a mock punch at my head. "I'll see you Friday night—all tanned and rested."

And with a nervous breakdown, I told myself. I feinted a left and jabbed his belly with my right. We used to box a lot, until he reached sixteen and got too big for me.

They washed up and went to their bedroom. I listened to the radio, and the noises in my stomach, read through the local paper. The radio had a lot of static. So did my belly. If I'd been home, I would have soaked in a hot tub, read a book. I could hear Bessie and Dan whispering and laughing behind their door. Finally at ten, as it began to rain hard, I went to bed, Matty following me.

The bed was soft as mush and I kept twisting and turning like a live pretzel. After years of working round-the-clock tours sleep either comes easily, or it's work. It's always a battle for me. I kept sinking in various parts of the mattress, for a time I fanned at a buzzing mosquito, then I listened to the rain and tried to think about Jerry's one-man fight, and if it was all worth it. I got up and took a swig of brandy, sat in the john for a time reading a woman's fashion mag that was all ads. Then I made myself some tea.

As I was puttering around in the kitchen, Bessie came out wearing hip length baby-doll pajamas, and my God, she looked like a walking barbershop calendar. "Anything the matter, Matt? Told you it would rain."

"Be my luck, a rainy week. I couldn't sleep so I'm making some tea. Want a cup?"

"Nope. Heard you padding around." She pointed to my flannel pajamas and shook her head. "You're a goner if an antique shop spots that outfit. Right out of *Esquire*—1910 issue."

"You ought to be more careful how you walk around."

"Why, does it excite you?"

"Okay, okay, it's too late for the super-sophisticated chatter." She reached up and batted a finger against my long nose. "I've thought about you, father-in-law. You worry me. We're going to have a talk during the week. Now go to sleep."

As Bessie walked across the room I couldn't keep my eyes from the sway of her hips. "I worry you? A talk about what?"

"Sex," she called over her shoulder, closing their bedroom door.

For a second I was completely confused. I had my tea and wondered why young folks think it's smart to make conversation about four-letter words. Or was my generation any brighter in keeping them hidden, making them words of fear? When I got to bed Matty fixed himself around my big feet and I closed my eyes, waited for sleep to come. It turned cold and I had to get up to adjust the blanket. Suddenly I hated summers: Things were so simple the rest of the year, weekly suppers with Danny and Signe, then coming back to the comforts of my own place. No soft beds or mosquitoes, no ... or was I getting cranky in my old age?

I fell off into a deep sleep and the next thing I knew Andy was shaking me. I opened my eyes to see a cloudy dawn outside the screened window. The boy said cheerfully, "Six o'clock. We're going fishing today."

"Damn it, can't you let me get some rest!" I snapped.

He backed away. "Dad and Mom are up and I ... I thought you'd want to ride to the station with them. Then we'd go fishing. That's all."

The uncertain look in his eyes made me ashamed. I reached out and rubbed his plump shoulders. "Sure. I always wake up ... eh ... cranky. You got the bone structure, now it's time you started making muscles, young man. Maybe I'll get you a barbell for Christmas. Rowing is good, too."

The boy left and I lay in bed for a moment, wishing I could go back to sleep, knowing I couldn't. I still felt bloated and a little tired. I finally got up; a soak in a hot tub would cure me. Matty gave a sleepy whine in protest as I pulled my feet away from his back.

Dan and Bessie were moving around in the kitchen-living room, Bessie in a robe, Dan wearing shorts. As I waved and headed for the bathroom, Dan asked, "What are you up so early for, Dad? Want to take a quick dip?"

"Keep up that kind of talk and I'll spank you—with a baseball bat," I said, closing the bathroom door. I cursed, forgetting they didn't have a bath. But I took a hot shower, and things came out all right, and I felt better as I dressed, my clothes slightly damp.

Dan was now wearing a tropical suit, coconut straw, shirt and tie, and we had a big breakfast. Andy talked about fishing and Bessie kept reminding Dan of things she wanted brought out the following weekend. The milkman drove up and Bessie said, "I'd better pay him for last week's milk."

She left the screen door open and I was surprised to see Matty up and stretching. The cat went outside and sniffed around with disdain, then followed Bessie back into the cottage, shaking the dew from his paws. Bessie sat down to finish her coffee, said, "The milkman told me Dr. Barnes was killed last night in an auto accident."

"It's six-twenty, we haven't much time," Dan said. "Who's Barnes?"

"You know, that old doctor who has the big house just past the shopping district on Main Street. A fat man with a ring of gray hair around his head like a monk. Only doctor in End Harbor. Seems he ran his car into a tree, not far from here, was thrown out on the road, and run over by another car."

"Can we see where it happened?" Andy asked.

"You certainly can't," Dan told him. "Everybody drives too sloppy-fast around here."

"They can't take much of a driving test," I put in, enjoying my first cup of coffee for the day. "Take your friend Jerry, he can barely see the road."

"Imagine, the poor man out on the road, dead all night in the rain," Bessie said, crossing herself.

"You mean he was *killed* by a hit-and-run driver?" I asked.

"I don't know. A post office truck found the body two hours ago. Perhaps whoever ran over the doctor thought he'd hit an animal or something."

"Nuts. When you hit 'something' weighing one hundred fifty or two hundred pounds, you certainly know it isn't a squirrel," I said.

Dan got up and locked his briefcase. "Lots of dogs killed by cars. Sometimes even a deer."

"Sounds odd. If I hit a dog or a deer, I'd damn well get out to see what I hit."

"Well," Bessie said, stacking the dishes in the sink, "now you understand, Andy, why I wouldn't bring your bike out here.

This means we'll have to go to Hampton if we need a doc."

I wanted to stay home, sit on the porch for a while, but Bessie insisted I drive to the station with them. Andy argued all the way about how careful he'd be if they let him have his bike. There was a small crowd at the station, mostly wives giving their husbands last minute advice, or vice versa.

It was cold and damp, the coffee had worn off, and I sat in the car, feeling irritated, wishing I was home in my own bed. Jerry drove two young girls to the station, stood around chattering with Bessie in Greek. The old man looked like I felt—as if he'd been up all night. We saw Dan off and Bessie said I had to see the countryside. She and Andy got into a long argument over whether he could go fishing if it was cloudy. I wanted to tell them both to shut up.

Bessie had to make like a guide, stopping at every goddamn landmark, even making me walk through a cemetery full of jokers who had been killed while whaling long ago. I couldn't have cared less.

Andy was making a pest of himself, impatiently asking the time every few minutes and Bessie told him if he didn't stop it there wouldn't be any fishing even if the sun came out. We finally parked in front of the End Harbor supermarket at a little after eight. The sun was dodging behind rain clouds and it was a muggy day. End Harbor was sure a hick town: a small movie house, a dozen or so stores including the big supermarket. There was an ancient building, a three-story brick job, that I later learned was a combination hotel, city hall, police and fire department headquarters, post office, and telephone company. There was a small crowd in front of this building.

Andy wanted to see what was up and Bessie said, "You go down there with Grandpa while I shop. Yes, yes, I won't forget to get clams for bait. Don't you forget to buy a paper."

We stopped at the one stationery-tobacco-newspaper store, where I bought the *Times* and the moon-faced woman behind the counter gave me a silly grin as she said, "You're new to End Harbor. Now I know the summer has really started."

"Has it? Do you carry the *Morning Telegraph?*"

"Oh, my, I never even heard of it. A new paper?"

"It's a racing sheet."

"We wouldn't carry *that*," she said, clamping her fat lips together.

The week was growing worse every minute. I couldn't even dope the nags.

Outside, Andy headed for the crowd and I said, "You go along, I'll sit in the car and read the paper."

"Come on, Grandpa, don't be such an old crab," he said, pulling on my arm. I was too mad to even swat his rear.

The crowd was around an old Buick, the front battered in, all doors open. The entire motor was shoved back, the steering wheel almost touching the seat. Andy asked if this was the doctor's car and somebody whispered, "Yes. It hit a tree and he was thrown out."

A young cop in a fancy light blue uniform, red bow tie and red shoulder patch, black leather belt and puttees, was leaning against the fender of the car, obviously enjoying his self-importance. He looked like a store cop. His cap was carefully crushed down the center, as if he was a plane jockey.

Andy met some kid he knew and when they took a few steps forward to get a better look at the wreck, the cop actually screamed, "Hey! Get back there!"

The kids jumped with fright. Andy said, "My Grandpop is a cop, too, a *New York City* policeman!"

People turned to glance at me. I felt like a fool. The boy-cop, feeling he had to prove his authority, walked over to the kids, barked, "I told you to keep back." He pushed them—Andy nearly fell.

I said, "Take it slow, buster, the kids aren't doing anything."

"Okay, old-timer, you keep out of this."

Andy looked up at me, to see what I would do ... *and that's how the whole mess really started.*

I couldn't let this badge-happy jerk talk me down in front of Andy. I strolled over to the wreck, casually examined the front doors. Buster yelled, "What the hell you doing?" and grabbed my arm.

Pulling my arm away so hard he stumbled, I said, "Keep your mitts off me." As I took out my wallet, flashed my tin, I heard the crowd whispering.

"You haven't any authority here," junior said, his voice not sure.

"Haven't I? You don't know your law—I'm a peace officer *anywheres* in the state of New York." I only intended going through the motions of looking at the wreck and let it go at that, but the boy-cop spoiled things by pointing to the building, telling me, "You'd best go in and see Chief Roberts."

Everybody was watching me and I *had* to follow through. It still would have been a snap to get out of, if Andy had remained outside, like I told him. Instead, the dumb kid followed me into the building, which was older than the NYC precinct houses—which are older than God. In the lobby there was another bronze marker, something about the British shelling the spot in 1777. I was ready to turn and walk out, when Andy suddenly opened a door marked POLICE CHIEF, yelled, "Here it is, Grandpa!"

It was a small office and the man behind the desk was sporting the same musical comedy uniform, and a big gold badge. End Harbor had the youngest police force in the world: Chief Roberts looked like a heavyweight boxer, with a collar-ad face. He was doing some paperwork, snapped, "I'm busy."

With the kid in the room with me, I couldn't back out, so I flashed my badge, said in a small voice, "Matt Lund, New York City Police. Thought I ... eh ... might give you a hand."

"Chief Art Roberts," he said, holding up a big paw for me to shake. "A hand with what?"

"With the Doctor Barnes case," Andy cut in. I put hand on the boy's shoulder; to keep him still.

For a second Roberts looked as if he were being kidded then he said, "We're used to accidents here and can ..."

I couldn't just stand there like a dummy. I asked "Accident? Is that for true, or just for public gossip?"

He tried to hold himself in, but he jumped a little. He waved a big hand at me, said, "Plain as the nose on your face: The doctor skidded into a tree, was thrown clear of the car. Medical Examiner isn't sure if death was a result of the fall or came from being run over."

"Chief, my nose is plainer that that. I don't like sticking it in anybody else's business, I'm here on vacation ..." I nodded down at Andy, hoping Roberts would understand why I had to make the play.

He merely growled, "What are you trying to say, pop?"

Maybe it was the "pop" that did it. "That it couldn't have been an accident. Look at the steering wheel, it would have pinned the driver against the seat."

"Maybe yes and maybe no. No witnesses. Also possible he was thrown out of the car on impact, before the wheel was pushed back. I think it was an accident."

I should have let it go at that, but Andy said, "My grandpa is a peace officer, too," although I squeezed his shoulder hard.

"You don't say," Roberts said, his voice loaded with sarcasm. "I'm busy, so if you'll ..."

"Look, I'm not trying to tell you your business, but if you'll come outside I'll show you something that says it *couldn't* have been an accident."

He stood up, and Lord, the tight uniform showed off his fine build; like Maxie Baer in his prime. "Now, listen, Mr. ..."

"Lund."

"Lund, ain't you pushing your badge kind of far? One of our best citizens is killed in a routine accident and you start calling it something else."

"Aren't you interested in how your best citizen was killed?"

He stuck his cap on—at a practiced cocky angle, said—as if talking to an idiot, "Okay, I'll look to make you happy."

"I merely want to have you explain one thing, then it's all yours. I'm going fishing."

We went out and the boy-cop whined, "Chief, I tried to tell him ..."

The Chief waved him silent, then the son-of-a-bitch tried to showboat me. He said, loudly, "Pay attention, Wally, a big-time cop from the big city is about to show us yokels how to operate."

"I didn't say that, or that I ..."

"You got me out of my office, Lund, now either put up or shut up."

He was so childish I wanted to take a chance and hang one on his square jaw: he was built so perfectly there had to be something wrong, like a weak chin. The crowd was watching us with mild curiosity and that made me sore, too—I must have looked pitiful next to Mr. America in the fancy uniform.

"Well, come on, what have you got to show me?" Roberts asked.

I went over to the door by the driver's seat, shut and opened it; did it again. "Notice it isn't loose nor in poor working condition. Look at the lock, it isn't sprung, not even scratched."

"What you trying to prove, that they made better cars in the old days?" Roberts wisecracked.

"It proves that unless the doc drove with his door open, he wasn't in the car when it crashed into the tree. If his body had hit the door with enough of a wallop to force the door open, or if the impact of the car hitting the tree had been great enough to fling the door open—the lock would have been sprung."

Roberts glanced around at the crowd like a ham actor, whispered, "What the devil are you trying to say, Lund?"

"Just that with the steering wheel pushed to the back of the seat, and the door lock in good shape, it seems clear to me that Doctor Barnes wasn't in any accident—he was murdered." I wasn't talking loudly but a gasp went up from the crowd and I heard the word *"murdered"* repeated in a shocked chorus.

"We haven't had a murder in End Harbor in seventy-six years. As for the steering wheel, like I told you, the doc might have been thrown out before the steering wheel could pin him."

"That's possible, but not probable. But tell me how a man can be thrown through a closed door without springing the lock?"

Roberts' handsome face flushed. "It was a muggy night, maybe he was driving with the door partly open."

"The car must have been doing at least seventy when it hit the tree, judging by the battered motor. What man drives that fast on a rainy night with the door open?"

The boy-cop who had been staring at the door with puzzled eyes, now said, "Chief, everybody knows Doc Barnes was a bug about safe driving. He was always preaching ..."

"Aw, shut up, Wally!"

I gave Roberts a small smile, I suppose I was really enjoying myself. "I hope I haven't given you more work. I didn't mean to butt in, it's your case, but my grandson here ... well, you know how it is. I had to play cop for him."

There wasn't anything more to say and I walked Andy through the crowd. Glancing at Roberts, I saw him glaring at me. Murder would sure upset the quiet routine of his job.

As we headed for the supermarket Andy looked up at me with big eyes, said, "Gee, Grandpa! Gee!"

Chapter 2

Bessie was waiting with a pile of packages outside the cashier's counter. "I've been standing here so long the butter and frozen foods have probably melted. Let's take these out to the car. Imagine what they're saying—that Doctor Barnes was murdered. If that isn't the most fantastic thing I ever ..."

"Grandpa told them so, Mom!" Andy cut in, his voice high with excitement. "Oh, Mama, you should have seen the way Grandpa told the Police Chief why it *had* to be murder. Grandpa is a *peace officer*, too! I bet like Wyatt Earp in the cowboy ..."

"Keep still, Andy. Matt, you didn't start this horrid rumor?"

"Isn't a rumor, but murder. I told you this morning that hit-and-run business didn't rest right with me. Newspapers to the contrary, most people aren't hit-and-run drivers. At least the guy would have stopped and ..."

"Guy?" Bessie asked, opening the car door for us. "We women drive, too, remember?"

"... slowed down, even if he didn't stop. Once he saw the wrecked car, knew he wouldn't be blamed for hitting the doc, he certainly would have reported it."

Driving away Bessie said, "A murder in End Harbor, in this quiet little village ... Matt, are you positive?"

"Let's put it this way: Certain factors point to murder, and until they're investigated and explained, the case should be handled as a homicide."

"Tell Mom about the door locks," Andy called out from the back seat. "Grandpa, how many killings you been on?"

"None."

His "Oh" oozed with disappointment.

Bessie's knee nudged mine and she made a waving motion with her little finger. Andy must have been watching her in the windshield mirror, for he asked, "Who you telling to shut up, Mom?"

"Nobody, mister big eyes and ears. I don't like all this murder talk. I don't want to hear another word about it—especially from you."

"Can I ask Grandpa one last question?"

"Go ahead. Lord, you should have heard the way the gossip spread through the supermarket. An absolute stranger, a woman, came up and whispered it to me as if ..."

"You said I could ask the question," Andy cut in. "Grandpa, when are you going to catch the killer?"

"Andy, all I plan to catch is some sleep. I'm on vacation." I tried to change the subject. "Clouds seem to be lifting; don't you want to try your spinning reel?"

"Sure, but I thought ..."

"Andy, police work is exactly that—work. I merely put my two cents in because I didn't like the way that young cop was pushing you around. We'll let the End Harbor police do their own work. You and I are going to pack a few sandwiches, take our lines and see what's in the bay."

Bessie groaned. "Don't know where my head is, I forgot bread. We'll stop at Tony's."

She drew up before a small store and I said, "I'll get the bread." A beefy young man was leaning across the counter, looking bored. He straightened up slowly when he saw me, said, "Now that you're here, I know it's summer."

"What? Let me have a loaf of whole wheat."

"Yes, sir. And what else?"

"That's all. Give me a couple cans of beer, any brand."

He looked bored again as he got the beer. "Tell you, mister, business ain't worth getting out of bed for these days. It's after nine and I just broke the ice with you. That goddamn supermarket is squeezing out every merchant. My folks made a good living from this store as far back as I can recall but now ... big chains put the whole town on its back. Oh, they give jobs to a few people, but they drain all the money out, spend it elsewhere and.... Sorry, didn't mean to cry on your shoulder. Suppose you heard about Doc Barnes' accident? Now I hear some state trooper says it's a murder. Gives you the creeps."

"Murder always does," I said, paying and taking my bag.

Reaching the cottage, Bessie found Matty sleeping on the couch. When she pushed him off, the cat arched his back and spat at her. "Give me any back talk, you fat tom, and you'll be crab bait. Andy, go down to the Johnsons and borrow their oars."

"You bet," the boy said, dashing out.

As I helped Bessie put things away she told me, "Matt, I don't like all this murder talk around Andy. He sees enough violence on TV. Thank God he's getting a summer off from that."

"Don't shield him too much, this is a pretty violent world."

"Matt, you're not taking part in this ... murder, are you?"

"Hell, no. It's none of my business. Technically I am a peace officer but I only opened my yap to show off for Andy, I suppose. The local cop was a young snot."

"Let's not talk about it in front of Andy. And don't let him horse you into rowing way out—the weather can change fast here. And take it easy rowing, you've done enough grandstanding for one day."

I patted her cheek. "Since when did you become such a worry bug? Matter of fact, I don't intend to touch the oars; about time Andy got rid of his baby fat. He's growing up fine, Bessie."

"Of course. It's been fourteen months since my miscarriage. We're trying hard for another child."

"Don't worry about it. If it happens, it happens. And if it doesn't—you have Andy. Martha and I had two kids within three years and after that, nothing."

"It isn't a fixation with me, or anything. But I do so want a girl. Would you like to play bridge tonight? I can ask John Preston over."

"I don't care. Better make it tomorrow night, I didn't sleep much last night. Guess I'll get into my trunks."

"Take pants along, in case the sun comes out and cooks that pale skin of yours."

I changed while she made lunch. Then I fed Matty and cleaned out his box, stretched out for a snooze just as Andy returned with the oars. He got his fishing tackle together, including a pair of old metal binoculars. I picked them up, hung them around my neck.

Andy said, "Dad's letting me use them this summer. They're powerful."

"I know." They were good glasses, cost five dollars—back in 1929 when Martha gave them to me for Christmas. I gave them to Danny on his sixteenth birthday. Now Andy had 'em. It gave me a happy warm feeling—and made me feel old.

I carried the oars and the lunch while Andy took the fishing gear. As we walked to the beach he asked, "Grandpa, why do people kill each other?"

"Because we haven't learned to control our anger, I suppose. We're all under tensions which ..."

"What's tensions mean, Grandpa?"

"I thought I told you to call me Matt?"

"Mama says not to. What's tensions?"

"Oh ... people worry too much," I said, wondering what I'd started. "They worry about a job, money, even clams. Then maybe they start fighting and one party gets so angry he doesn't realize what he's doing, swings the clam rake ... and the other man is dead. Or two countries start shouting over a boat or something, and then there's war. Remember, never let your anger master you. These glass rods any good?" I asked, changing the subject with a clumsy hand.

He was a true fishing nut, talked rods and reels all the way to the beach. I hoped he would outgrow that soon. I've always found guys who go in for a lot of fishing gear to be bull artists—and not just about fish, either.

In the light of morning, even a dull one, the bay seemed far prettier than last night. It was a large rough circle of water opening on the Sound, or maybe the ocean. Andy started swimming out to get the rowboat. While I didn't want to get wet, I couldn't let him swim alone. The damn water was still ice cold. When we got the boat ashore, Andy wanted to empty some of the water and I almost broke my back tipping the heavy tub. We finally pushed off, and to my surprise the boy rowed well. As I lit my pipe the sun came out for a spell. I examined some of the anchored yachts through the glasses, and if it wasn't for my damp trunks, I would have enjoyed things.

Dropping anchor outside the breakwater, we got our hooks over. Fishing wasn't exactly a success. Not only didn't we catch anything but Andy's spinning reel wouldn't work. The fish kept eating my bait without my feeling a bite. I realized I was getting a burn and put on my pants and shirt. I didn't have to worry about the kid, he was brown as coffee. He was upset over the reel. I tried to monkey with it but mechanical gadgets are always over my noggin. I gave it up, asked if he wanted a sandwich. He pointed at the remains of a rotting dock, told me, "Pops usually fishes there. The reel was working for him yesterday. You should have seen him cast with it—sent it out a mile."

I put the glasses on the dock. "Nobody there."

"Pops may be fishing from the beach, on the other side. He can fix the reel, I bet."

I motioned for him to pull up anchor as I took the oars. I couldn't remember when I last rowed. Although I once had a post that included the lake at 110th Street and I did a lot of rowing then. I was still pretty good at it.

The dock and the beach were empty. Andy said, "Damn. I mean darn—Pops is always here."

I rowed back out into the bay and tossed out the anchor. The kid fished with my rod while I had a sandwich and some chocolate milk Bessie had fixed. My backside ached from sitting on the hard boat seat and I felt sleepy. I sat there, holding my head in my hands, feeling the stubble on my chin, almost dozing, when Andy caught a small blowfish and startled me with his shouting. He tickled its white belly to show me how it blew itself up into a ball, then said it was too small to eat and tossed it back. Funny, when I was coming up we never ate them—now they were a delicacy. The kid wanted to row some more. He didn't head out into the bay but followed the shoreline. "There's Pops," he said.

Andy was pointing a chubby finger at an old-fashioned but well kept-up house that stood above a cluster of trees. It was a large square house, painted white with red trim and in the center of the roof there was a small glass-enclosed room with a railing running around it. A man was lying on a cot, taking what little sun there was. He seemed to have a blanket over most of him and a large floppy straw hat covered his head and face. Sneakers and old army suntans stuck out of the bottom of the cot. I put the glasses on him; couldn't see any better. There was a paper on the floor, he was probably sleeping.

"Grandpa, you know what that is? That kind of ... of house up on the roof?" Andy asked with the self-importance of the newly learned.

"No," I lied. "What is it?"

"In the days when End Harbor was a big whaling port, the wife of the captain of the ship would walk on the roof every day, looking out on the bay, see if her husband's ship was coming in. I bet from up there she could see for about fifty miles, maybe a hundred. Anyway, they call it the widow's walk because she never knew whether she was a widow or not. I mean, if the boat never came back." He was making for the shore and now he stood up and called, "Pops!" and waved his hands.

"Sit down, you'll turn the boat over. You're too far away for him to hear. Besides, he looks like he's sleeping. What's the man's real name?"

"I don't know, everybody calls him Pops. He knows lots of things about fishing and ... heck, I thought I'd ask him to fix my reel. He sold it to me."

There was a faint line of narrow beach, then a steep bank that rose ten or fifteen feet and disappeared into a layer of trees. The house sure had privacy. Maybe he was just resting. I asked, "Do you think we'd be bothering him if we took the reel to his house?" I had enough of the boat and water.

"No. Mom says he's a very spry man for his age. What does spry mean?"

"That he has pep. We'll go to the house, but if he's asleep we'll let the reel go till tomorrow."

"Okay, we have to row back to that old dock. The road runs by ..."

"We'll go ashore here and walk up. I'll row and you watch out for rocks. Has he any dogs?"

"I don't know," the kid said, moving forward as I took over the oars. "He lives with Mr. Anderson. He's the mailman here. He also has a big vegetable truck."

We beached the boat and with obvious delight Andy scolded me for not burying the anchor in the sand. I helped him up the bank, getting myself dirty. After the trees we came to a large field that ran up to the house. It was a nice hunk of land. Behind the house there was an open garage with a large new truck. A station wagon stood in the driveway which circled through a well-kept lawn. Everything about the place showed a lot of care, and except for the truck it looked like a rich man's estate.

We were about halfway across the field when one of the side windows of the house flew up and a shotgun barrel covered us as a man's voice yelled, "Hold it! Don't you read signs? You're trespassing on private property!"

I grabbed Andy, said, "Don't move." Then I called out, "Put that damn gun away. The boy merely wants to see Mr. ... Pops. I didn't see any NO TRESPASSING signs."

"Should have come around by the road. Well, don't stand there, come along. Be careful where you walk, stay on the path." He stood in the window, the gun still on as. He was a stocky joker. I kept the kid behind me and I was puffing as we reached the house. It was quite a slope.

The man and gun left the window and a moment later appeared on the screened porch that ran around the house. He was holding the gun by the barrel now. It was an expensive pump shotgun. He had on a thin polo shirt that showed off his bulky shoulders, and work pants. He looked about forty-five, a strong man with a thick neck, heavy iron-gray hair, and wide, homely face. He wasn't tall, in fact looked smaller than he was—like Marciano did in the ring. "What do you want to see Pops about? He's not feeling well."

"I wanted to ask him about this reel he sold me," Andy said, "It don't—doesn't work."

The guy smiled and it completely changed his face, gave it some life. "You must be the kid who wouldn't take the reel for a gift, wanted to buy it. He told me about you. What's wrong with it?" he asked, coming down the porch steps.

"Stuck."

He rested the gun between his knees as Andy handed him the reel. I said, "If you're so fond of guns, learn how to handle them. If you should happen to kick the shotgun now, it would blow your head off."

"I know about guns, but thanks for the advice," he said, resting the shotgun against the steps.

"And you ought to think twice or three times about pointing it at people—even trespassers."

He looked up from the reel, eyes staring right into mine. He had honest eyes. "You must be this city policeman causing all the fuss." He held out a large hand. "I'm Larry Anderson."

"Matt Lund," I said, shaking his mitt.

"Sorry I shouted at you. This used to be farm land and it's full of ruts and holes. I'm always afraid somebody will break a leg. As for the gun, I've been jumpy as a cat all morning. Pops had a mild heart attack right after breakfast and—you know about Doc Barnes. I couldn't even get a Hampton doctor to come over, those society snobs. Anyway, Pops' condition isn't serious and one of the docs gave me instructions over the phone. Pops will have to rest for a week or so, absolute rest. Meantime, just to play it safe, I've contacted a specialist in New York." He took out a penknife and loosened a screw in the reel. It spun smoothly. "It's okay, son, you had it down too tight."

Andy thanked him and as we turned to walk back to the boat, Anderson said, "I'd better show you the path."

"I don't want to put you out ..."

"That's okay." As we followed him across the field he said over his thick shoulder, "Of course the doc's death upset me too. As a member of the town council, I—and Art, Chief Roberts—have called a meeting for noon. Murder makes it a terrible mess. But you were right, Mr. Lund. At least the Chief agrees it's murder. But it sure don't make sense, anybody killing a sweet guy like Ed Barnes who always.... Careful, step around these wooden boards. Old well here and the weather may have rotted the cover. I know Doc would have been the first to agree with us about the publicity."

"What publicity?" I asked.

"The summer season hasn't been too good, as it is. Now this murder talk—it won't help business or the good name of the Harbor."

When we reached the beach he said something about wind taking the POSTED signs he'd tacked to the trees. He showed Andy how to oil the reel, and pointing to a red buoy out in the water, said, "Tide should be in strong soon, brings in the fish. I've always found Buoy 9 out there a good spot for kings." He turned to me. "On behalf of the Harbor Council I want to thank you for helping out the police department."

"Guess in time Roberts would have noticed the door lock. He was excited. Young bunch of policemen you have."

"Chief Edwards died of kidney trouble last year, just after Jim Harris resigned to live with his girl in Brooklyn; she married a big dress man there. Art was new to the force, but that left him chief. Maybe you can give him a hand on this case?"

"Nope, I'm on vacation here, for a week."

"Well, thank you again for your interest. Don't think we'll have much more sun, I'll take Pops back to his room. I'm trying to get a woman to help out around the house, but help is difficult to find during the summer." He touched the binoculars around my neck. "Getting a lazy man's view of the harbor?"

"Yeah."

"Well, I have to tend to Pops. Treat that reel with care and it will work fine, sonny."

Andy said he would and we rowed out to the buoy. The kid

got off some long casts while I pulled in a fair-sized porgy and the bastard cut my hands with his fins. Andy gave me a lecture on how to land a fish and I gave up fishing for the day. I saw Anderson up on the widow's walk, talking to Pops. Then he lifted the old man in his arms, stopped for second as if to point us out to Pops, then easily carried him into the house.

The sun came out again and we hung around the buoy for a long time, Andy catching a couple more porgies. I was getting stiff and when it started to cloud up again, over Andy's protests, I said it was time to head for home.

Neither Bessie nor the car were at the beach. Andy asked some women where she was but they said she hadn't been down as yet. We went to the cottage and Bessie wasn't there either. While the boy took the oars back, I showered and shaved, and then climbed into the mushy bed for a nap. It started to rain lightly and I lay there, listening to the rain hit the roof—an interesting sound for anybody accustomed to working in the damn rain. I was too pooped to sleep.

I was only wearing shorts and my knees were lobster red; in fact my skin was so hot I couldn't cover myself with a sheet and had to shove Matty off the bed. He tried to jump back on and I got up and pushed him into the living room, closed the door. I took a belt of brandy and stretched out again. If I was in the city now, just coming off at four o'clock, I'd go back to my old beat and play cards with some of the storekeepers after they closed. Or sit around the house and watch an early cowboy movie on TV.

Pain in my legs awoke me. Bessie was sitting on the bed, shaking me, her slacks pressing against my sunburnt knees. Her dark eyes were large and frightened. I asked, "What's the matter?" and moved away from her. It was still raining and at first I thought the shades were down, then I glanced at my watch—it was after eight.

"Matt, Andy and I have been riding all over town looking for you, and here you are, pounding your ear!"

I sat up and groaned; my skin felt as if it was cracking. "Damn, but I've got a burn. Got anything for that?"

"I saw Matty on the couch outside so I thought you had gone to town or ... I'm all mixed up. Matt, Matt, they've arrested Jerry for Dr. Barnes' murder!"

I stood up and shook with a small chill; my red skin seemed to change from hot to ice every second. I was afraid to put on a robe. "Jerry, the dialectician? Where did you learn that?"

"It's all over the village. And every one of these bigoted souls is pleased as punch now that the village 'foreigner' is labelled a murderer! I tried to see him but that dumb-ox police chief wouldn't even let me talk to him. Matt, there's nobody to help him. You saw Jerry, I know him—he couldn't possibly kill anybody."

Stiffly, I headed for the door.

"Matt are you sleepwalking? Didn't you hear what I told you?"

"I'm not deaf, but when I get up the first thing I *have* to do is take in the john. I'll be back in a second."

Washing was torture and I couldn't find a thing in the medicine chest for sunburn. When I came out, Bessie had tea bags in a pan of hot water, cotton, and a bottle of baby oil. She told me to stand still and began dabbing my red skin with the tea bags. It embarrassed me to have her touch me all over so I cornballed, "Thinking of serving me with sugar?"

"No, with an apple in your mouth. Tannic acid is the best thing for a burn. Now I'll put on the oil, and dress you warmly before you catch a cold. Matt, we simply ..."

"Where's the kid?"

"Visiting down the street. Matt, we must help Jerry. I'm certain they're making him the whipping boy, the goat."

"Do you know why they think Jerry did it?"

"Oh, something about his having an argument with the doctor last night. Jerry is a diabetic, or on the verge of becoming one. He felt ill last night and called the doctor, who bawled him out for drinking beer. A neighbor heard them shouting at each other. Mrs. Barnes claims Jerry's was the only call the doctor had last night. There, that's enough oil, now get dressed. I have supper working."

"I'm not hungry, stuffed myself on sandwiches in the boat," I said, going to my room and dressing. Matty was wailing for his supper.

Bessie had hamburgers, potatoes, and a cup of strong spicy tea waiting. She sat down opposite me and lit a cigarette. When I asked when she started smoking, she said, "Only when I'm nervous. Matt, you have to *prove* Jerry is innocent."

"Me?"

"You're a policeman and the only one who can—and will—help him. You know he's being framed."

"Bessie, honey, because he's your *landsman* doesn't make him innocent. They must have something else on him beside what you've told me."

"They don't! You can almost feel the sigh of relief in the

village now that he's arrested—they all hate him."

"You sure he's arrested or merely held for questioning?"

"Oh—I don't know the legalities ... Matt, what are you going to do?"

"Go back to sleep. I'm on ..."

"Matt, I'm serious!"

"So am I. Bessie, no matter what you may think, people are rarely framed for murder. At least not in New York State. I'm on vacation, not to mention that I have no business here as a cop."

"Matt, I'm counting on you. You're the one who started this murder business, you just *have* to help!"

"Bessie, be sensible. I acted like a horse's ass this morning, playing the big cop. It's ... well ... like a matter of professional ethics. Suppose Roberts was in New York and tried playing cop—they'd laugh him out of town, if they didn't actually boot him out of the station house. Actually, as a peace officer, I have no more authority over Roberts than ... well, than any citizen. I mean ..."

"Matt, you're spouting about ethics like this was a debate, a bull session. A man's life is at stake!"

I nibbled at the hamburger. "Easy, Bessie. You say go out and solve a murder like it was the same as going to the store. I mean, exactly what do you think I *can* do? This isn't a movie. I'm not a detective; all my life I've been a plain old beat-cop. The truth is that except for couple of busted store windows and petty house robberies, I've never taken part in a real crime. Jerry will get a lawyer, a chance to prove his innocence. Damn it, Bessie, what I'm trying to say is: I'm not sure I can help him or ..." I let the rest of the sentence die, turned away to give Matty a piece of hamburger.

I saw disgust and shame in Bessie's eyes. "I hate to say this, Matt, but you're an old maid. All you want is your bed and to fool around with a dumb cat. Jerry is a good man, doesn't that matter to you? I suppose if he was a lousy cat with a broken leg, you'd run to ..." She held her face in her hands and began to weep.

I'm a sucker for tears—any kind. I went around the table and put my hands on her shoulders. She hugged my waist. "Okay, Bessie, I'll see what I can do. But don't expect me to work miracles, be a super-sleuth."

She wiped her face on my shirt. "Matt, I'm sorry ... about calling you an old maid. You're like Jerry—a good man. I know you'll solve this. I just know!"

"Yeah." It sounded like nothing. "Let me have the keys to the car. I'll see what I can get from this alleged Chief of Police." My fingers were stroking her hair, it was very soft.

Bessie insisted I wear one of Danny's windbreakers, which was too big for me and I knew I looked comical as I parked in front of the Harbor's main building. I was hoping Robert's would be out. He wasn't. He was behind his desk sucking on a big cigar, and from the sneering expression on his face I had the feeling Roberts had been waiting for me. I was all set to explain about Bessie nagging me and how I was on vacation, and hardly wanted a fight with my daughter-in-law on any occasion. But the sight of him got my dander up, making it harder for me to apologize for sticking my nose into his business. I fully realized I was being a prize pain in his rear.

Roberts boomed, "If it isn't Peace Officer Lund. I suppose you heard the news?" The sarcastic "Peace Officer" bit didn't help my mood.

I relit my pipe and sat in the chair beside his desk "Yeah, I heard. I know this sounds kind of dumb—I mean, this morning I was talking up because of the boy and now, well, my daughter-in-law is after me. You see, she's Greek, like Jerry, and she wants me to ..."

"How come you let your son marry a Greek?"

That ended any explanations I had in mind. I puffed on my pipe and stared at this big young handsome dressmaker's dummy. He puffed, too—puffed out his chest, said, "Not bad for a hick cop: murder in the morning, an arrest in the afternoon."

"I never called you a hick cop, Roberts. Yeah, it was fast work. How did you do it?"

"Common sense. We checked with Pris ... Mrs. Barnes, on the doc's night calls. His last one was at Jerry's house. Mrs. Ida Bond—she lives across the road from Jerry—she heard the doc bawling Jerry out for drinking beer and Jerry telling him to leave him alone. She is ready to swear she heard Edward, Doc Barnes, shouting, 'Then I won't be responsible for your life,' and Jerry answering, '*And I won't be responsible for yours.*' That's the exact words. Naturally when we questioned Jerry he denied the killing, but did admit he had some words with Doc. Claims he was home all night, but living alone... that ain't much of an alibi."

"You arrested him on that evidence?"

Roberts waved a long hand at the smoke in the air. "Sounds good to me: two men have an argument and later one of them is found murdered."

"Find any fingerprints?"

"Didn't look," he said calmly. "First off, being out in that rain all night, hardly be any prints or tire tracks. Then, we were so sure it was an accident ... I mean, the undertaker was already working on the body when you convinced me it had to be murder. But I got all the evidence I need."

"Come off it, Roberts," I said, not blaming him for holding out on me. "Your evidence won't stand up in court."

He blew a cloud of lazy smoke, watched it drift up to the ceiling. "If it doesn't, Jerry's acquitted." He leaned across the desk, lowered his voice. "Between you and me, being a diabetic, old Jerry could plead he was in a state of shock, sort of nuts, get off with that."

This was the screwiest cop ever! "Anything missing? Wallet or money gone, any signs of robbery?" I asked.

"Nope. Made a careful check with Mrs. Barnes. Everything's there. This wasn't any robbery."

"What time was the doctor at Jerry's house?"

"Around nine-thirty. Jerry phoned him just before nine. Mrs. Barnes says the doc was peeved at having to make a night call. And before you ask what time the doc died—I'll tell you. Medical Examiner puts it around eleven P.M., but he can't be positive, give or take an hour or two. So that fits."

I was fed up with this hot air. I got to my feet. "Jerry has a lawyer?"

A shrug of the heavy shoulders—and it wasn't padding either. "He must have plenty of dough, been living like a miser all his life. He can get himself a good one. He's over at the Riverside jail—that's the county seat."

"Think I can see him?"

The handsome face tightened. "Look, it's an open and shut case ..."

"Can I see him?"

Roberts stared at me, his eyes narrowing. There was a silent pause while he made a fist with his big right hand, balanced it on his left palm for a second, examining it. Finally, convinced he still had all his fingers, or something, he looked at me again, asked, "What you making a production of this for, Lund?"

"No production. He's a kind of friend of the family. I merely want to see that he has a lawyer, cigarettes, understands his rights."

Roberts opened his fist, slapped the desk—lightly. "You should know it isn't up to me. Go down to the jail in the morning, if it will make you feel any better. Only if you're still on this peace officer kick, remember I'm in charge here and you'll do what I say or ..."

"You're the one making a thing of it. I told you why I'm here: Jerry is a friend of my daughter-in-law and ... uh ... I'm only doing this as a friend."

"Suit yourself, friend. But don't let me trip over you."

"Thanks." I zipped up the floppy windbreaker on the way out.

I didn't feel like rushing back to more of Bessie's needling. There was a dreary-looking bar across the street. I went in and ordered a beer. The bartender was a tall man with the kind of shoulder and arm development that came from doing something a damn sight harder than mixing drinks. He had weak eyes and his thick glasses gave his fleshy face an unreal look. There were a couple of young kids, about eighteen or nineteen, hanging around a pinball machine. They were drinking straight gin, or maybe it was vodka.

I bought a bag of potato chips and sipped my brew slowly. Bessie said Jerry used his mumbling dialect on everybody in town—did that include the doc? If so, how could a woman across the road understand what he was yelling? And Barnes—now, why would a doctor be shouting at a patient? The whole dumb village was acting screwy: first they didn't want to call it murder, pass it off as an accident. Then they tagged Jerry and from the way Roberts acted, he couldn't care less if it held up in court. He seemed to *want* an acquittal.

" ... I hear he's a big-time private eye." This was followed by a nervous giggle from the pinball crowd. I looked into the dirty mirror behind the bar; the three punks were leaning against the machine, staring at me with crocked eyes. One of them said, loudly, "I heard he's FBI. Sent down here to root up trouble. I ain't hit an FBI yet, but there's always a first time."

I felt a chill, which had nothing to do with my sunburn. These were tall husky young fellows, with SOP crewcuts and loud sport shirts. But they were wearing work shoes and looked accustomed to hard work—and in shape. There was more mumbling and I finished my beer as quickly as I could—without making it look fast, nodded at the barkeep and headed for the door.

I'd reached the sidewalk when they came out, all of them swinging. I blocked a wild right and punched one of them in the eye. A smack on the chin dropped me. I sat on the walk, dizzy, and trying to think of a lot of things—like curling up to protect myself from kicks. And if the bastards had busted my bridgework.

My head was spinning but I saw the bartender come out and give one of the kids a swift kick in the can, tell him, "I warned you about starting any roughhouse in my place, Tommy. Try this again and I'll dropkick you through the wall. And I ain't kidding."

A pair of long legs in black puttees passed me. Roberts moved nicely. He grabbed the nearest kid and slapped him across the face. A hell of a slap, the mouth went out of shape for a moment and his hair shook. When he let go, the punk went reeling down the street. The others started to run but Roberts took two steps and backhanded another across the nose, making it bleed. He was damn good, always had his right fist cocked for real trouble.

He reached down and lifted me to my feet. "You okay, Lund?"

I put a finger in my numb mouth; my bridgework was still in one piece. I said, "Yeah."

The bartender said, "Sorry, mister. I thought they were only fooling. Come in and get a shot on the house, fix you up."

"I'm okay." I started toward Bessie's car. Roberts walked along with me. "They thought you were here to look into a hot-rod accident. A kid was killed in a race, in a car stolen out of state from New Jersey. Was some talk about the Feds coming into the case. They were just scared."

"They weren't scared enough." Feeling returned to my jaw.

"Kids used to do a lot of cop-fighting down here, their form of juvenile delinquency, I guess. Matter of fact, that's why I was first taken on, as a special, to handle the kids. Sure you're okay, Mr. Lund?"

I got in the car and said I was fine. Hell of it was, Roberts really sounded sincere.

"It won't happen again, Lund. You understand, one of those things. I'll drop in on the kids, at their homes, in an hour or so, put the fear of the law in them. I don't stand for cops being slugged here."

"Sure, they were liquored up. Thanks."

"Anyway, I'm glad you socked one of the clowns. Handle yourself good for a guy your age."

I waved and drove off, wondering if he was kidding me; not sure. I couldn't make this hick burg, couldn't figure it even a little.

Chapter 3

If there's one thing I can't take, it's to be awakened suddenly. Bessie shook me awake and said, "It's seven o'clock, Matt."

I sat up in bed and thought maybe I was lucky: she could have started at five A.M. She began talking about Jerry and I told her to hold it—she didn't want to mention murder in front of the kid. Maybe she knew I was sore; when I came out of the bathroom she had some of this thick Turkish coffee waiting and a few cups of that put me back in a normal mood. Andy took the boat kit I'd brought him to a friend's house and by eight, Bessie was driving me to Riverside. Her pretty face looked tired. I asked, "Didn't you sleep last night?"

"How could I, worrying about Jerry?"

"Honey, don't carry this *landsman* stuff too far. Frankly, I don't get the play here, but even Roberts doesn't seem to think a court will find the old boy guilty so ..."

"No, Matt, that won't be good enough."

"What won't?"

"He's an old man, we can't even have him stand trial. Don't you see, it would kill him, be the final victory for End Harbor. We have to prove he's innocent before trial. Another thing, nobody can be positive of an acquittal."

"Bessie, come back to earth. You say we 'can't let him stand trial'; like it was up to us. There's only so much we can do."

"Matt, I got to know Jerry because he is of Greek descent, like I am, but I'd go to bat for him anyway. I mean, his being Greek has nothing to do with it. You know how damn biased the Harbor is toward him."

"Aren't you just as biased, in his favor? At this point we don't know he didn't kill the doc—we merely think so. Now let's get some facts, find out exactly where we stand, before we do any more gum-beating."

"Of course. And I'm very proud of you, father-in-law, for helping poor Jerry."

"What the hell, looks like a rainy day anyway," I said, not entirely kidding.

"You louse!" she cried, hitting me with her knee. "For that I won't buy Matty any liver for supper. What enjoyment do you get from that fat-assed cat? All he does is sleep."

"At least he doesn't talk much."

"Very funny! Matt, ever think of getting married again?"

"As the joke goes, marriage is nice to think about—if you

only think and don't ..."

She cut me off with a four-letter word and drove the rest of the way in silence.

At the Riverside Police Headquarters they flatly refused to let us see Jerry, since we weren't relatives. I got the sergeant-in-charge aside and showed him my badge. He said, "You must be the joker who started all this. I worked out of the 130th Precinct in New York for a couple years myself—harness bull. Then I moved out here for the summer and got on this force. Slower life, and better for the heart. This is a screwy case, they got nothing against this Greek that will wash in court."

"Think he'll be indicted?"

"Are you kidding? You know these grand juries, do anything the D.A. asks. We told Roberts he had a watery case but he seems happy."

"I know, but why?"

"Tell ya, in these villages, what the hell, the 'chief' is lucky to be taking home fifty bucks a week, and no civil service standing or pension. Not much cushion money around, either. Roberts is a glamor boy and beside showing off that fancy uniform all he does is chase a speeder now and then, maybe lock up a drunk. So he's puffed up about 'solving' this murder. Hey, how come you're interested in all this?"

"He's a friend of my daughter-in-law. You know how it is, she expects me to act like Dick Tracy because I have a badge. I just wanted to be sure Jerry has a lawyer, cigarettes."

"Well, I don't see no harm in your seeing him. We can't even understand what he says—when he talks. I hear he won't have either of the two lawyers in End Harbor. Guess the court will have to appoint somebody. I'll give you fifteen minutes with him. As for the babe, your daughter-in-law, that's out."

Bessie was sore as a boil when I told her she couldn't go in, but finally agreed to do her shopping and meet me outside the station house in a half hour.

The cells were pretty good, modern and heated, with a sink and toilet in each one. The cell block attendant was a sleepy-looking fat character. When he started to recite the rules, I told him I had the same job in New York, and he said in a bored voice, "Then you know the score. Don't cause me no trouble, pops."

"Pops" yet, and the fat slob looked less than a dozen years younger than me.

Jerry seemed to have doubled his age overnight, his body was shrunken, face more wrinkled, his color splotchy. He didn't get up and I sat on the clean bunk beside him, explained about Bessie wanting to see him.

He muttered, "Mista, whata you want with me?" We were back to the dialect.

"Jerry, we only have a few minutes, so cut the crap and talk straight. Have you money to hire a lawyer?"

"Money? What gooda is money? Whatta good any lawyerman do me? This all one frame."

I shook him. "Damn it, talk straight! What do you mean, a frame?"

He stared at the floor a moment, started to cry. I shook him again, whispered fiercely, "What's the matter with you? Bessie and I are your friends. Look, you can still lick the bastards. You fought them all these years, why give up the last round?" As usual tears had me spooked.

Rubbing his hand across his face he asked quietly, "What do you want to know, Mr. Lund?"

"Did you do it? Now, wait; understand, I have to know that for sure."

He shook his head slowly, as if it took a great effort. "The doc and me, we never rubbed together well, especially when I first came to the Harbor, but I always admired him. Town never had much use for him either. No, of course I didn't do it. Do you believe that?"

"I wouldn't be sitting here if I didn't believe you. Exactly what happened the night before last? What were you fighting with Barnes about?"

He straightened up. "What fight?"

"A Mrs. Bond, who lives across the street from you, claims you shouted at the doc, something about you wouldn't be responsible for his life. And the doc was yelling at you. Did you say that to Barnes?"

"Well, yes. Because my garden has always been better than hers, all the time this Bond woman must spy on me. I said that to the doc, but only as a joke."

"If it was such a joke, why were you shouting it at the top of your lungs?"

"Ed—Doc Barnes—used a hearing aid but it wasn't working so good. Maybe the batteries were weak. So we were talking loud. Now you talk as if you don't believe me, Mr. Lund."

"Look, I have to ask questions because I need the complete picture if I'm going to be of any help to you. Now what happened that night?"

Jerry shrugged. "Nothing happened. I keep telling you that."

"Damn it, Jerry, wake up! Can't you understand this isn't a game or a ... look, tell me everything you did from the time you dropped me off at Bessie's cottage."

"That was the last train for the night, so I went home for my supper. I had a couple bottles of beer. After I eat I'm listening to the radio—music—and I begin to feel sick, real dizzy. I know an attack is coming on so I phoned the doc. I'm feeling miserable until he comes over and he raises sand because I'm off my diet. The doc was sore at me. I told him, like I always do, to fix me up, that I'm too old to worry about a diet, eating is one of the few joys left in life for me. He said that if I didn't stick to the diet he wouldn't be responsible for my life. So making a wisecrack, I tell him nobody but God is responsible for life. He didn't hear and I yelled I wouldn't be responsible for his life either. He gave me an insulin shot, and a pill to make me sleep. Edward said he had to see the old goat, then he could get some sleep himself. Then he left."

"What's this 'old goat' mean?"

Jerry shrugged. "That he had another call to make. I didn't ask him."

"What time did he leave?"

"Maybe nine-thirty, maybe ten. The pill made me sleepy and I went to bed at once. In the morning I took some ladies to the train, you saw me at the station, and there I hear about Edward being killed in an accident. It upset me, like I said, I admired him. In the afternoon they come and arrest me. You see it's a frame. They kept asking can anyone prove I was at home all night. That's silly—they right well know I live alone."

"Did you tell Roberts about the 'old goat'?"

"Sure. I told him exactly what I told you."

"Where's the medicine bottle the doc gave you, the stuff that put you to sleep?"

"What bottle? He gave me one pill."

I tried to think of something else to ask but my mind was going in circles. "I don't believe they have anything on you that will stand up in court, a jury will find you not guilty and ..."

"But in the eyes of the Harbor I will always be a murderer! Bad enough for me in town up to now.... Even if I'm free, I will have to leave the Harbor."

"Jerry, you either have to fight this or give up. First step is to get a lawyer, a young kid just starting out, if you can. A Riverside lawyer. A kid will act like a legal-eagle because an acquittal means good publicity for him. You want Bessie to find a lawyer for you?"

"All right, I'll get one."

"Okay, but do it at once. Did anybody in End Harbor, or in any of the other burgs around here, have any reason for killing the doc? Did he have any enemies, any at all?"

"No, no. Edward is—was—the only doctor in the Harbor, a big man in the town."

"But you just told me the Harbor didn't have much use for him either."

"I don't like to repeat ... gossip. They keep this quiet because Barnes was the mayor at one time, an important man in the church ... but he told them all to go plum to hell, even his wife."

"Told them to go to hell about what?"

"You know how the town got its name, End Harbor?"

"I suppose because it's at the end of the bay."

He shook his head. "A long, long time ago a tribe of Indians lived there, part of the Shinnecock Nation, called Endins—sounds like Indians. That was a couple hundred years ago. When I first came to the Harbor there were still several Indian families, but they moved away. Only one family left, Joe Endins and his daughter Jane. Jane grew up to be a fine girl but there was nothing for her in the Harbor, no job, no man to marry—because she's Indian. All she can do is work as a maid. Her papa died and she still hung around, maybe she's twenty-three, twenty-five, a very lonely young woman. Then the story starts she is going with Doc Barnes. That was about ten years ago. This is all gossip, you understand, but this I do know, Edward trained her to be a nurse and took her on all his calls. His wife is mad as the devil and the town is buzzing with whispers. After a year or so, Jane stops working for the doctor. She still lives in the Harbor but works in a Hampton factory. But the doctor, he keeps seeing her, you can usually find his car parked boldly in front of the Endin house a few times a week. Gossip is the devil's tongue in a small town. Because Priscilla Barnes helped Art Roberts, sort of kept an eye on him when his mother died, why some dirty people hinted ..."

"Wait up, Mrs. Barnes and Chief Roberts are an item?"

"No, no! She's old enough to be his mother. I merely show you the evil power of gossip ... and how well I've known that power!"

"But this other bit, Doc and an Indian gal, jeez! Changes everything, gives the doc's wife a motive for the killing."

Jerry patted my knee, as if he was talking to a kid. "Indeed not. You shock me, Mr. Lund. But of course you don't know Priscilla Barnes. A very quiet and meek woman. If she stood the cross of gossip all these years, when Jane was working in the Barnes home—Edward had his office in the house—why should she get angry now, when the affair, if it was that, seemed to be dying out?"

"Some people carry a long fuse and you never know when ..."

The attendant rapped on the bars. "Time's up."

"Think hard: the doc didn't give you any hint as to who the 'old goat' might be? Didn't say in which direction he was driving to see the goat, for example?"

"Nope. He said it in passing; you know."

"Let's go, break it off." The cell block attendant opened the door.

"Whatsa the bigga rush with you?" Jerry mumbled.

"When you get that lawyer, I want to see him. And don't talk to anybody but the lawyer," I told him.

"What is there to talk about?"

I stood up. "Maybe I'll be back to see you tomorrow, or the next day. Need any cigarettes, cigars—anything?"

Jerry shook his head. "I am glad you came, Mr. Lund," he said, getting up and shaking my hand. "You made me feel better—a little."

Bessie was sitting in the car, puffing on a cigarette, bags of groceries on the rear seat. She started pumping me with questions and I said, "Relax, Jerry is fine. Bessie, the whole Harbor is lying in their carefully brushed teeth."

"But it's such a peaceful community—I know they dislike Jerry, but to frame him for murder—that I can't understand."

"Let's get going, I have a lot of work to do. The why is the usual old one: your pillar of the community, Doc Barnes, was carrying on for years with an Indian woman, a descendant of the tribe that founded End Harbor. Name is Jane Endin. You know her?"

"No. We tourists rarely get to know anybody but the storekeepers. You think this Indian woman killed him?"

"She had more reason than Jerry. Not to mention the doc's wife, who's been having the affair flung in her face all these years. But this explains Chief Roberts' attitude—from the go he knew darn well it was murder but all he can think of is the Harbor doesn't want a scandal. In a small town everybody is close friends—especially Mrs. Barnes and Roberts. He's even willing to call it an accident and let it go at that. Then enter the clown—me—who has to shoot off his big mouth. Now the Harbor has to call it murder but they find a custom-made patsy—the doc was known to have visited Jerry, the village bogeyman."

"But to put Jerry on trial for his life, Lord, how can they be so heartless!"

"Honey, that's the angle, the reasons Roberts doesn't give a fat damn his evidence is weak and circumstantial—he knows Jerry won't be found guilty. So what? The mess is over, hushed without any scandal. I told you I was the joker in the deck, well, honey, I'm going to knock over their can of peas, bust this wide open!"

"Matt, I knew you would!"

"You didn't know a mumbling thing, and neither did I. Frankly, I only went to Riverside this morning to go through the motions. But that's all changed now—I *know* he's being railroaded. Being an ordinary patrolman, a harness bull, I've never looked upon 'police work' as anything but a job. But like everybody else I sometimes thought, had daydreams, about being a real detective. So in my old age I'm frankly going to give it a try."

The odd thing was I said this rah-rah pitch cold sober, actually meant every word. Listening to Jerry I'd decided to goose End Harbor wide open, expose all the petty scheming and hatreds, a kind of concentrated form of big city vice. If I was doing it for Jerry, I was also doing it for my own ego. And all the time I knew I was showboating; a four-flusher—for the case was a setup and I would knock it over with the speed of a fiction private eye.

Bessie wanted to know what I had in mind but I merely puffed on my pipe with great self-importance, told her I couldn't discuss it at the moment, but I would need the car.

She said I could have it and even managed not to talk all the way back to the cottage. I gave Matty his lunch in three seconds flat and with Bessie watching with admiring eyes I dashed off—the great detective about to run himself ragged.

Roberts was out but the boy-cop was holding down the desk. He told me Roberts was working. I asked, "Did you know the doc was deaf?"

"Yeah. Everybody knew that, he had one of them transparent hearing buttons stuck in his ear."

"You know why Jerry was loud-talking him, why the doc was shouting back? The hearing device wasn't working that night."

"That so? There wasn't enough left to say if it was working or not. Who told you all this?"

"Jerry. Didn't you fellows question him at all? He claims Barnes had another call to make—which means Jerry wasn't the last person to see the doc alive."

Junior fooled with his red tie, almost yawned in my face. "Guess that would change things—if you can prove it. We grilled old Jerry, but who can understand the way he talks? After a couple questions he wouldn't say a damn word. To my way of thinking, this proves Jerry guilty—for he'd sure as hell make up a story about the doc having another call. Mrs. Barnes says he only had to see Jerry."

"She might say anything. Jerry says the doc told him he was on his way to see the 'old goat.' Any idea who that would be?"

He showed a mouthful of teeth in a big grin. "Offhand that could be anybody over the age of thirty. There's a summer population of around 2800, not to mention the 1468 actual residents of the Harbor, and at least half of them are over thirty—you plan to question about 3000 people, mister?"

"I might, to save a man's life," I snapped, knowing I was wasting time: the End Harbor police weren't interested in finding the killer. "Where does Jane Endin live?"

"Out on Bay Street, couple houses past the entrance to Tide Beach. So you know about her?"

"I sure do," I said, starting for the door.

"All this rushing about will tire you out, man your age."

I spun around. "Don't let that pansy uniform go to your head, sonny. I've put in more years as a cop than you have weeks!"

"Take it easy, mister. I'm only trying to save you work. She ain't home. We been trying to locate her since yesterday."

I almost swallowed my tongue: a possible suspect leaves town and they sit on their butts! "Know where she works in Hampton?"

"Sure, at the watch factory. We phoned there, she wasn't to work yesterday or today. What you want to see her for?"

"To ask who she thinks will win the pennant!" I said, walking out.

He called after me, "Hell, I can tell you that—the Giants."

Outside I sat in the car and got my pipe going—watching the people on the main drag—trying to figure my next step. I knew what I had to do but I didn't want to rush it, act like a jerk—the way I'd just done with the uniformed happy boy. One thing was for sure; I couldn't shake this village loose by myself.

I made a list of all the names I'd heard since coming to the Harbor—Jerry's, Doc and Mrs. Barnes, Chief Roberts, Jane Endin, Mrs. Bond, Larry Anderson, Pops (but what was his name?), even copied the names from the store windows on Main Street—obviously the big apples in the village. Getting a handful of change I put in a long-distance call, which would also take it away from the ears of the local operators, to Nat Reed in New York. Nat and I shared a post for a brace of years before he quit to go into private work, ended up in a cushy spot with a credit agency. Credit outfits have become the largest snoop agencies in the country outside the government. They have complete files on millions of people. I gave Nat a fast rundown on what I was doing, the list of names. As I expected, he said, "Matt, you know I can't give out info like that. It's only for our subscribers."

"I know—that's why I'm wasting dough on a long-distance call."

Nat sputtered a little before he said, "Okay, I'll send you whatever we have, get it out today."

"Put it in a plain envelope. Seal it good."

"Things that bad?"

"I'm playing it safe—wind blows a lot of ways out here."

"I'll mail it special delivery." He laughed. "Going in for police work as a hobby in your old age?"

"Isn't it about time? And if I'm in my old age, where does that put you, you old belch? Thanks, Nat. Say hello to the wife for me."

I drove along Main Street until I reached the picture-window white house set back on a neat lawn with Doc Barnes' shingle hanging from a post made to look like an old whaling ship's mast. I rang the doorbell and a stout woman with a healthy face and heavy gray hair in a big bun topping her head opened the door. A plain worn short red dress showed off arms and legs that belonged on a football team.

"Mrs. Barnes?"

"No, no, I'm only staying with Priscilla in her hour of need. I'm Mrs. Jenks."

"Can Mrs. Barnes see people? It's important."

The bright eyes in the large face turned suspicious. "You're new in the Harbor, ain'tcha?"

"Yes. My name is Matt Lund. I'd like to speak to Mrs. Barnes."

"Well, you certainly don't look like a reporter. They've been ringing our phone like.... Well, I keep telling them all this excitement is bad for shock. My son is a doctor, too, you know. Practicing in Brooklyn. Edward urged him to come home and share his practice but Don thought there wouldn't be enough for two doctors to ... Say! You're that city police inspector!"

Gossip was promoting me fast. "Your son going to take over

Doctor Barnes' practice now?"

"I should hope so. After all, Edward would have wanted it that way—he practically insisted Don go to med school. This is what I've been dreaming about—Don back in the Harbor, where he belongs and ... But this is no time to talk about such things."

"Maybe not. Will you ask Mrs. Barnes if she'll see me for a few minutes?"

"Priscilla is piddling around in the kitchen. This morning she was busy with the funeral arrangements. You'll only upset her and she needs her rest."

There was a moment of silence while we stared at each other. I suppose I should have gone away but I stood there, waiting. Finally she snorted, "Hmmm! I'll ask Priscilla," and shut the door in my face.

A frail little woman with an unhealthy waxen skin and thin white hair opened the door a moment later. Her delicate features and mild eyes added up to a washed-out look, and the mouth was merely a faint pink line. She was wearing a white apron over a black dress. The apron was even starched. But the more I looked at her I realized she wasn't exactly frail—more on the wiry side. She had been a pretty woman at one time, in fact still had a kind of beauty—if you go for the fragile type of looks—which I don't. Her voice was a shock; it was far from delicate—it was hard, almost brittle, as she said, "I'm Mrs. Barnes. What do you wish to speak to me about?"

"May I come in?"

She seemed to wince and shake, as if I'd hit her. She closed her eyes for a moment and I had this feeling the very last thing she wanted was to talk to me—or even see me. Then she opened her eyes, stared at me boldly, and that strong, harsh voice said, "Of course. Excuse my manners."

I followed her into a spotlessly neat living room: a mixture of old-fashioned heavy furniture, a big new TV, and two modern plywood chairs. Everything was neat-as-a-pin-so. She was a real Dutch housewife, as they used to say in my day. She pointed toward a stuffed leather chair and I sat down while she perched on the edge of a plain maple stool. Maybe she wasn't as old as I figured—her legs were pretty good, hardly a vein showing. I fooled with my cap as I said, "I realize the strain you're under, Mrs. Barnes, and I wouldn't be here ... if a man's life wasn't at stake."

"I understand, it's your job."

"Yes, it is, if you believe it's every citizen's job to uphold the law."

"I respect the law, I always have. But you might as well know this: I do not—I cannot—believe Edward was murdered."

"Then all the more reason to aid a man under arrest for his murder. I'll be blunt, Mrs. Barnes, do you really want to find the murderer of your husband? The rest of End Harbor doesn't seem ..."

"I can't stand the sound of that word—murder!" Her hard voice rose in a wail; brought the picture of an icicle to my mind. I noticed the swinging door that led to the kitchen move slightly—where Mrs. Jenks was at her listening post. "Ed—Doctor Barnes—devoted his life to the health and welfare of people. Who would want to kill a saint? Why, why?"

"Do you think Jerry killed your husband?"

"No. I refuse to believe he was killed by ... anybody! It was an accident."

"Mrs. Barnes, did you act as a secretary for your husband, keep track of his calls?"

"Naturally, if the phone rang and Edward was out, or busy, I took it."

"I understand Jerry phoned the doctor at nine P.M. Did you take the call?"

"Yes. That is, we both answered. Edward had this stranger in his office, but as I picked up the extension, Edward answered, so I hung up. But I knew it was Jerry."

"What stranger?"

"Why, some elderly man, a Mr. Nelson, drove up to ask if Edward knew about a man he was looking for, an old army friend, a Mr. Hudon ... or some name like that."

"Why did he think your husband would know him?"

"I don't know exactly, I didn't pay much attention to it. Mr. Nelson was driving along the Island and his friend was supposed to be living in the Harbor, at least he sent Mr. Nelson a card from here a few years ago. Since Mr. Hudon suffered from gallstones, Mr. Nelson thought Edward might have treated his friend. It's all rather complicated and of no importance."

"It may be of great importance. Did you say Mr. Nelson was an elderly man?"

"Oh, yes. But very tall and well preserved for his age. Edward had never heard of the other man, so Mr. Nelson left."

"Does Chief Roberts know about Mr. Nelson?"

"Yes, I mentioned it to Artie."

"Did Nelson say where he was staying in the Harbor?"

"No."

"Are you certain Doctor Barnes had never seen Nelson before? Did he act excited, or upset after Nelson left?"

"Edward never put eyes on the man before. I gathered that Mr. Nelson was merely passing through the Harbor. Really, Mr. Lund, I don't see the point of all this."

"Jerry claims the doctor told him he was on his way to make another call, that he had to see the 'old goat.' That might have been this Nelson."

"That's ridiculous, Nelson wasn't a patient."

"Have you any idea as to who the 'old goat' might be?"

"No." She suddenly batted her ear nervously with a finger. "And Edward had no other calls except Jerry's."

"How do you know, Mrs. Barnes?"

"Sir, are you doubting my word?"

"No, ma'am, merely checking. I don't have to tell you that if I can prove Doctor Barnes had another stop to make after he left Jerry, it might set Jerry free. Are you positive there wasn't another phone call after Jerry's?"

"Edward never said a word about it and he always told me where he was going, in case of an emergency. I was sitting here watching TV and after Mr. Nelson took his leave, as the programs were changing, Edward came out of his office and was rather angry. He hated night calls. He said there was nothing wrong with Jerry if he'd watch his diet."

"How do you know he wasn't angry over something this Nelson said?"

"I know. I mean he wasn't really angry. Lands, Mr. Lund, this Mr. Nelson merely dropped in to ask some information. Only reason Edward took him into his office was to check his files for the other man's name. As Edward left, a few minutes later, Mrs. Jenks came over to watch TV. She stayed when I became nervous, that is, when it neared midnight and Edward didn't return."

"What did you do, when he didn't return?" It was neat, the way she set up an alibi without my even asking.

"What could I do? I thought he'd been detained but I was surprised he hadn't phoned me. Around midnight I took a sedative and went to my bed."

"And Mrs. Jenks went home?"

"Of course, where else would she go at that hour?"

"Let me get this straight; while Nelson was with your husband, Jerry phoned. Then Nelson left, and Doctor Barnes left, cursing Jerry."

"Indeed not! Edward never uttered a harsh word in his life."

"Excuse me. Did Nelson and Doctor Barnes leave together?"

"No, no. Really, Mr. Lund, I find this very tiring, going over and over the same thing. Some minutes after Mr. Nelson left Edward put on his hat and coat, then went back to his office—for his bag, I imagine. A few minutes later he walked through this room, looked at the TV show for a moment, kissed me, said he wouldn't be late."

"You were listening to TV—suppose the phone had rung in those few minutes, are you certain you would have heard it? Was the TV on loudly?"

She poked her ear again, hesitated. "I did have the set on fairly loud. I'm a trifle deaf in one ear."

"Then you can't be certain the phone didn't ring again?" I said, feeling excited.

"Well ... no."

"You haven't even the smallest idea who the doctor meant by the 'old goat'?"

"Indeed not. Edward would never refer to a patient like that!"

I stood up. "Thank you for your time, Mrs. Barnes, you've been most helpful. One more thing—was your husband's hearing aid working that night?"

"Of course. He had several and would have worn another if anything had been wrong." She got to her feet. "Mr. Lund, you're new to the Harbor, never knew Edward. He was a tender and loving man. I've been sickly all my life, couldn't give him children. Yet he was always considerate of me, never complained, although he dearly wanted a child. Everybody spoke well of him, he was a man in a million, without an enemy in the world. He gave unceasingly of his time and money. Why, he even loaned Mrs. Jenks the money for her son's schooling, for example. I'm telling you this because there's absolutely no reason for a man like that to have been murdered, it's ... it's ... just impossible!" She worked her ear over for a moment. "I'll do everything in my power to help poor Jerry."

"That's most commendable, Mrs. Barnes. Did you tell that to Chief Roberts?"

"I did. Landsakes, everybody knows Jerry Sparelous is a bit touched, but he barks, doesn't bite. I've never known him to harm a soul."

I thanked her again and at the door I asked, "Do you think Jane Endin would have harmed Doctor Barnes?"

The pale lips formed a tight slit after she said, "Get out!" The words came with bullet force.

It was raining again and I sat in the car, slowly cleaned out my pipe and lit it. Mrs. Jenks came running out of the house, a shawl half over her big head. When she saw me, she opened the car door, pushed in. "Drive me to the drugstore! I could break your neck, upsetting Priscilla like that!"

I wanted to remark that I hadn't the slightest doubt but that those arms could break my neck. I drove off without saying a word, then I asked, "Where is the drugstore?"

"Straight ahead on Main Street. Where did you think it would be? You made her sick."

"Sorry. But I have to ask certain questions and ..."

"Why?" she shouted. "Why do you have to ask *any* questions? This isn't your town!"

"Unfortunately murder isn't the property of any one town. Do you want to see Jerry sent to jail?"

"If he killed Ed Barnes he ought to be hung!"

"The 'if' is why I must ask questions. Like, where were you that night, Mrs. Jenks?"

"Me?" It was a mild explosion.

"Like I said, I have to ask certain questions."

With a movement amazingly fast for a woman her size she suddenly put an immense sandaled foot on top of mine, banging it down on the brake, causing the car to screech to a stop. "You dirty old skunk, stop this car this second!"

She opened the door and jumped out. I wiggled my toes. She shook a fat fist at me. "If I tell my son what you just said—I hate to think what he'd do to you! And for your information, I was home all night after I left Priscilla's. Why I even sat up until three in the morning, watching out the window to see if Edward came home. Then my younger boy, Mike, got up and made me go to bed. There, you dirty-minded ferret!"

I watched her walk away in the rain, the jelly-flesh on her wide backside shaking. I drove to Hampton, letting the talk with Mrs. Barnes cook in my mind. The "evidence" against Jerry was getting downright silly, and there were at least five leads that made a damn sight more sense than Jerry's alleged motive. Nelson, whoever he was, could be the 'old goat.' Mrs. Barnes had reason enough to kill her husband, so had Jane Endin—if what Jerry said was true. Nor could I even rule out burly Mrs. Jenks—she might have wanted her son to practice in the Harbor awfully bad.

Any lawyer could prove Mrs. Barnes was far from positive the doc didn't make *two* calls that night. Why, I could take the stand and disprove Roberts' "evidence" on the basis of my conversation with Mrs. Barnes. I considered Roberts a hot lead, too. As the guy in Riverside said, not much in the way of a salary or pension for a small-town cop. Not impossible Artie decided to get something going for himself, and Priscilla must certainly be the Harbor's richest widow right now. That fitted, he needed other reasons beside hushing up a town scandal for making such a sloppy case. But—it takes a certain kind of sharpie to make a realistic job of playing an older woman, and Roberts was all lardhead. Of course, you can never tell about motives—he could be framing Jerry merely to spite me. That was fantastic, but then what was my motive for being an eager-beaver in my old age?

However, I felt quite pleased with myself. Detective work was only using horse sense—shame I hadn't been more ambitious when I first got on the force. This job was far from over, though. Tracking down Nelson would be hard, I didn't even know his first name. Probably mean a lot of digging into Doc's past—I had the hunch they'd known each other years ago—and that would require spade work. The thing to do was take a crack at what I had on hand—Jane Endin.

You'd never guess Hampton was only seventeen miles from End Harbor, everything about the town cried money: solid, father-to-son folding dough. The large houses and great estates looking like something you see in the movies, the swank shops—branches of famous Fifth Avenue stores—the expensive cars, even teenagers zipping around in foreign jobs. I had to ask a couple times before I found the watch factory—a new brick building covered with vines and flowers, the windows large and clean, bright neon lights inside. I would have taken it for a small ritzy school.

People rarely question a police badge, the gal at the reception desk didn't when I flashed my tin and said, "Peace Officer. I'd like Miss Endin's home address."

"This is something, the police phoned yesterday and this morning asking for her. She lives in End Harbor."

"I know that, but she hasn't been home," I said, thinking I was wrong not to have tried her house instead of taking the boy-cop's word for it. "Did she have any address here in Hampton? You know, some place to call in an emergency?"

"No sir, we only have the Harbor address for her."

"I see. Can I speak to whoever worked next to her, any close pal she has among the girls here?"

"I suppose it's about that murder in the Harbor. Gee whiz, we never have nothing here but hot-rod jerks wrecking themselves." She phoned in to somebody, then told me, "Girl be out in a second. This Jane in trouble?"

"No."

A young girl in a tight red turtleneck sweater, and tighter jeans showing off her round basketball rear, walked up to me. When she walked the basketball was far from still. "You the detective? See, I work next to Jane. Is she in a jam? When I saw her this morning she didn't act like ..."

"Where did you see her?"

"On the Dunes Road. I can't sleep much when it's muggy and my old man is too cheap to get air conditioning, so I was up early this morning. I drove around and she passed in her old struggle-buggy. She didn't stop, just waved at me. Jane looked bad, like she'd been up all night." The girl had a jerky way of talking—and thinking, for she reached up to brush her close-cut dark hair with her fingertips ... and to make sure I saw her tiny pointed breasts.

"Did Miss Endin ever mention any friends in Hampton? Say, some place where she might go on her lunch hour, or after work?"

"Naw. She didn't talk much. Even though I've worked beside her for over a year now, Jane ain't the buddy-buddy type. You see, she's old, and an Indian. Last ..."

"Old?"

"For crying out tears, I bet she's thirty if she's a day. Last summer I suggested we might take in the pow-wow at the reservation. I figured her being Indian and all. Man, she near flipped, told me off. You can't figure a woman like ..."

"What reservation?"

She brushed her hair again, with both hands this time, to give me the full view. It wasn't much of a view. "Mister, you don't know a *little* about this end of the Island. Guess you must be a big-time dick brought in special for the murder. I know that's what it's about." She gave me a cute wink.

"Where is the reservation?"

"Outside Qotaque there's this Indian reservation. Every summer all the Indians living in Brooklyn and the other cities, they're supposed to return and hold dances, and all this old square stuff. I went once. It was from hunger, strictly tourist bait jive." She glanced at the wall clock. "You know, I'm losing time, this is a piece-work deal. Anything else?"

"That's all. Thank you."

"What they want Jane for, witness against this old Greek?"

"No, I'm merely checking."

She winked again. "You wouldn't tell me anyway. You know, you ain't what I pictured a dick looking like."

"Sorry, I left my muscles home," I said, heading for the door.

The rain was coming down harder and my back started to ache. Twenty minutes later I was in Qotaque, which was even smaller than the Harbor. A stiff wind was driving the rain and it was almost dark enough to be night. I stopped for coffee and a hamburger, got directions on finding the reservation. I followed the directions and when I reached the Shinnecock Canal I knew I'd passed the turnoff.

I drove back slowly, the windshield wiper fighting a losing battle, and found it—not a road but a country lane with a faded wooden sign. The rain had made the dirt road into a mud rut. I inched along, not seeing any houses.

If I'd been going faster I might have made it: the car slid into a hole, or some damn thing, and stuck. My right rear wheel raced like a runaway prop, sending up a shower of mud. The car skidded a few inches from side to side, sank back into the hole. I tried backing out; it was a waste of time.

I sloshed over to the bushes on the side of the "road" to pull out a handful of branches; nothing gave except my skin. I took out my penknife and hacked away like a cub scout. By the time I was thoroughly soaked, the rain chilling the remains of yesterday's sunburn, I had an armful of small branches. I packed these in front of the rear wheels and the car went a big fat two feet, then slid back into the mud. Locking the ignition, I started walking in the rain, cursing myself for not having the sense to stay in my comfortable New York flat.

After I walked a few hundred yards there was a turn in the mud and I came upon a couple of shacks and a store. I felt as if I'd stumbled on some forgotten Tobacco Road. There was a light in the store. I tracked in mud. The guy behind the counter looked more like a Negro than an Indian, although he had long white brushed hair reaching his shoulders. He was wearing a worn beaded vest over a faded shrimp-colored sport shirt. He was short and wide.

"Come for souvenirs? Fall in the mud, mister?" His voice was a rough croak and his wide mouth toothless.

"My car is stuck. Can you ...?"

"Ah, you need gas. I have a pump behind the store."

"I'm stuck in the mud. Can you help me?" The light was one small bulb and the few cans and boxes on the shadowy shelves seemed terribly stale-looking. In a separate showcase he had some dusty toy tom-toms, beaded belts and feathered hats, left over from the last tourist invasion.

"Ah, the mud. Washington still robs the Indian, for us we have asked for a paved road. I'm Chief Tom. I have a truck if you want a tow. Ten bucks."

"Ten bucks! That mud ambush out there your work?"

"You want tow or not?" There was an evil gleam in his bloodshot eyes. "You're blocking the road so I'll have to tow your car out of the way. Still cost you ten bucks." He pulled back his vest with a proud movement to show me a large, highly polished gold badge. "I'm a deputy, in charge of traffic here."

"Thanks for going through the motions of asking if I *wanted* a tow." I felt tired, no longer the super-detective. I dried my face with my handkerchief, pulled out my pipe. It was wet. "This the reservation?"

He nodded. "Indians dumb. Government give them land and a house here for free, but the young bucks, they leave. Maybe go into army, never come back here. Live in lousy tenements in Brooklyn."

"Sure, they're crazy to leave this paradise. You know Miss Jane Endin?"

His eyes became cagey. "I know her. That's what I mean. She has house and land in End Harbor, but if she was smart she would sell it and come live here for nothing. She's not smart."

"I know, she isn't a customer of yours. Where can I find her?"

"What you want to see her for?"

I flashed my buzzer but he grabbed my hand and pulled back his vest—held my badge against his. He gave me a grin full of purple gums; his badge was bigger. "What she done?"

I jerked my hand away, put my badge in my pocket. "Nothing. I want to ask about a friend of hers."

Chief Tom gave me a wise look. "You're a Federal man. Income tax trouble?"

"No. When did you see Miss Endin last?"

"Let me see ... five, six years ago. Ain't she in the Harbor no more?"

I suppose I should have asked more questions, visited the other shacks. But my back was aching, I had a chill, and was so damn tired all I could think of was soaking in a hot tub—if I could find one. I was too weary to even haggle with him about the price. I said, "Get your truck."

He pulled a fancy white trench coat from under the counter that made him look ridiculous, carefully brushed his long hair before putting on a battered fishing cap. Locking the door, he told me to wait. A moment later he came roaring around in an old six-wheeled army truck so high I had to pull myself up to the running board.

Reaching my car, Tom said he would push me out. I asked if there was any way he could circle around, come up behind the car and pull me out. He told me there was another road but it meant driving miles out of the way, and he pushed cars out after every rain. I got behind the wheel and he inched the big truck forward. His bumper seemed to be on my headlights. When I shouted it was all wrong he yelled back, "Just keep her in neutral and don't worry. I push you to the main road."

I told him to be careful. He had the truck in low and I kept the door open, leaning out to see where I was backing. My car moved backwards as if it was a toy, the glare of his lights in my eyes. When the main road was in sight I signaled he could stop pushing me. At that second I went into another damn hole and his bumper came down on my lights with a sickening crash of metal.

We both jumped out. Tom croaked, "What's the matter with you, you crazy!" and examined his bumper—which a tank couldn't have dented. Both my headlights were smashed, the fenders dented, and my bumper was hanging.

He said, "What did you put her in gear for?"

"Who put her in gear? Didn't you see me waving for you to stop?"

"I thought you were waving me on. I said I'd push you out to the road."

"You dumb bastard!" I kicked the bumper. It fell off and I picked it up, tried to shake off the mud, then put it in the back of the car.

Tom put his hand under my fenders. "They're not touching the tires, you can drive." He held out his hand. "Ten bucks."

"I ought to sue you for ..."

"Mister, ten bucks. That's the rate."

"I'll give you the back of my hand ten times! I'll ..."

He suddenly grabbed my windbreaker and before I knew what the devil was happening, he actually picked me up and threw me into the mud. "Don't get yourself hurt, Mister. You don't know how to drive, ain't money out of my pocket. Ten bucks, please." He glanced down at his trench coat—it wasn't even muddy.

I sat up in the mud. I had to tangle with a muscle man, and this long-haired son-of-a-bitch probably was older than me, too! My behind was soaking wet. I stood up, wanted to slug him but decided he'd flatten me. Without a word I gave him two five-dollar bills, got in the car and backed out. I headed for End Harbor, expecting to be collared any second for driving without lights.

I'd never been this angry before in my life. The great Sherlock Lund—a mass of mud! One thing, I couldn't have Bessie and Andy see me like this.

I cooled off as I drove, paying full attention to the rainy road. I could see fairly well, there were enough cars going the other way to light up the road. I didn't stop at Hampton but pulled into a garage on the outskirts of End Harbor. A young fellow eating his supper in the office came out wiping his mouth with the back of his hand. "What happened to you? New car, too."

"I ran into Sitting Bull. Tell me how bad it is. Got a rest room?"

He nodded toward a small white door. Inside I washed most of the mud off, using a lot of paper towels. I looked pretty good, considering the damn oversize windbreaker, but I was still wet all over. When I came out the mechanic was back in the office, finishing his supper. I went in, tried drying out my pipe bowl with matches as he said, "Nothing wrong with your lights, just need new glass and bulbs. Where you heading for?"

"I'm staying in the Harbor."

He finished his container of coffee, said, "Brooklyn license plates. Well, I know the summer has really started with you ..."

"Aw, cut it off. Can you fix the lights now? I want to get back to my cottage."

"Can't put the glass in, but I can give you bulbs. Look, suppose you bring the car around in the morning and leave it. I'll straighten out the fenders, paint 'em, take care of the lights and the bumper. Do it in a day if I ain't busy. Cost you thirty-five dollars."

"Okay."

He went out to the car and put in bulbs, carried the bumper back into the shop. The lights weren't much good, but at least I wouldn't get a ticket. As I lit my pipe and started the car, he said, "That's seventy-five cents for the bulbs. Deductible from the thirty-five dollars but payable now."

"It's touching to see your faith in your fellow men," I said, giving him three quarters.

He smiled. "I'm a union man—*E. Pluribus Unum*. See you in the morning, Mac."

He was so pleased with his corny wisecrack I didn't say a word, puffed harder on the pipe. I still had to kill time until Andy went to bed. There was one thing I'd overlooked—the scene of the crime. Not that I expected to find anything there *now*. I should have gone there yesterday. As a detective I was a good cell block attendant. I rolled down the window, asked, "Know where the killing of the doctor happened?"

He came to the office door, a sugar doughnut in his dirty hand. "Crazy the way people are on the morbid kick. I went out there myself to have a look this morning. Instead of turning into Main Street, take the other fork—that's Montauk Road. Follow that for about a mile and you'll see another road crossing it, a wide road. That's Bay Street. Make a right turn on Bay, away from the water. Couple hundred yards down you'll see a busted tree—that's the spot."

"Bay Street?" I repeated. Jane Endin lived on Bay Street—Roberts was trying hard to overlook the obvious clues.

"Can't miss it, jack. There's a new brick house on one corner, boarded up—some rich cat who's been in Europe for last two years. On the opposite corner, toward the bay, you'll see a picket fence and a house. Not much of a house but nice piece of land. Belongs to an Indian gal. Don't forget, make a right turn on Bay."

Ten minutes later I was on Bay Street, looking at the big tree with the splintered gash in the thick trunk. The tree was at an angle, its roots torn up. It would probably die soon. Keeping my faint lights on the scene I walked around in the rain, not knowing what I expected to find ... and finding nothing.

Turning around I drove back to the highway. I stared at the boarded-up bright ranch house. The way Roberts operated, it could have belonged to Mr. Nelson. Then I looked at the Endin house. It was a weatherbeaten two story affair with at least an acre of land behind the low picket fence. There was an old car in the driveway; no lights in the house. I pulled off the road, decided to snoop around the house.

Of course there wasn't anything to see. A grape arbor in the back of the house, an unused chicken coop, a locked shed. On the door there was a knocker shaped like an arrowhead, or maybe it was an arrowhead. I looked into one of the dark windows. As I turned away a porch light came on and the door opened.

A woman stood there who made me forget all about Indians, being a detective, even about feeling tired. She wasn't any beauty. She was tall and straight, black hair with streaks of gray pulled severely away from her angular face. Her eyes were bright and tired, and her face came down to an overlong jaw. Her skin was creamy and she was wearing a man's gray shirt and dungarees. Perhaps she was far from a beauty, but there was such a bitter, sullen look about her—she looked sexy. In fact, she looked like she was ready to explode with sex. I mean, she seemed about thirty-five and ... well, as if she'd been storing it up all those years.

Her eyes took in my wet and dirty clothes before she asked, "What do you want?" It was a cold voice, proud and clear.

I took off my cap. "Excuse me, I was looking for a Miss Endin."

"I'm Jane Endin. Why are you snooping around my property?"

Chapter 4

Being an amateur detective, I hadn't given much thought as to the type of man Doc Barnes had been. If anything, I'd pictured him a prissy sort, a bluenose. My respect for the doc soared—this was indeed a *woman*. Then I told myself to act my age, stop the schoolboy crap—Jane Endin looked capable of anything: passion and/or murder.

"Why must you stare at me—so rudely? What do you want?"

"Sorry, I don't mean to be rude. I expected a ..."

"A tommyhawk in my hand?" Her voice was sharper than one.

"My name is Matt Lund. Perhaps you've heard of me, the New York City policeman interested in Doc Barnes' death." I went through the motion of flashing my badge.

"I haven't heard of you." Her voice became a talking-to-herself whisper. Her eyes looked through me, as if I weren't there. She seemed dazed and when her face slackened the high cheekbones stood out.

"I've been looking for you, Miss Endin. Can we talk?"

"What have we to talk about?" She turned and started to close the door. Her hair was a thick juicy braid that went to her waist—an exciting braid.

"Aren't you interested in finding Doc's killer?"

"Killer?" she repeated, back still to me, everything about her straight and tense. "Who would kill Edward? I can't associate killing with Edward, he was only interested in healing, the living."

"Do you think Jerry murdered him?"

"Murder?" She spun around, her eyes coming alive again. "Jerry, the taxi man? But ... I thought it was an accident? Who says Jerry killed Edward?"

"The Harbor police. Jerry's in the Riverside jail this second, charged with murder." I wondered where she could have possibly been not to have heard. Or was it all an act? "I'm trying to help Jerry. I don't think he did it. That's what I wanted to talk about."

"Wipe your feet on the mat as you come in."

She had an odd walk, sort of threw her legs out—and all the stiffness left her. I followed her into a living room which looked too neat to have been lived in much. The furniture was old but the walls were covered with various size abstract paintings, violent splashes of color that didn't make sense yet were strangely exciting. There was also a large photo of a brown-skinned man in a gold frame who had to be her father—almost the same features. She pointed toward a maple chair with red cushions but I said I'd rather stand, didn't want to dirty the chair. She shrugged, lit a cigarette, and sat on an ancient leather chair, curling her legs under her. With that one movement, despite the shirt and dungarees, the stern face, a touch of feminine warmth came over her.

I nodded at the paintings, I guess they were oils. "Very unusual."

"Do you understand them?"

"I don't know, but they give me a feeling of excitement."

She studied me over a puff of smoke.

I got under way. "Miss Endin, I'm a stranger here, a tourist. I'm also a cop. I'm going to ask you some questions. I don't mean to be rude, but I can't be subtle. I'm very tired, especially tired of the runaround I've been getting. End Harbor acts like it's outside the law. I wouldn't care, but a man is being framed—I think. Doc Barnes is murdered and the Harbor acts as if ..."

"You never knew Edward," she cut in, voice clear and sharp once more. "He was a good man, considerate. Perhaps he has now found greater happiness. We Indians have a saying, that death is but the opening of a new trail. We all must die, including Edward, but no one would kill him."

"But someone did. They've arrested Jerry on evidence so thin it doesn't make sense. I think they collared him because he's talked with an accent for most of his life, told the Harbor to leave him alone. Everybody here is trying to hush the murder, pretend it didn't happen—even you. Why?"

"Who can believe a man like Edward could be murdered?"

"Nuts. They're putting the lid on it because you and Doc Barnes have been the village scandal for years!"

She jumped to her feet, a graceful fast movement. "Leave my

house!"

"I said I was going to be blunt. Your personal affairs are your own business. But remember Jerry in the Riverside Jail with not a single End Harbor person caring a cold damn!"

"What do you want of me? I wouldn't hurt Jerry. He's one of the few men who bothered to tip his hat to me. I have nothing to do with his being in jail."

"Miss Endin, all I want you to do is answer a couple of questions."

She sat down again, the braid coming over her shoulder like a snake. "What questions? What can I tell you?"

"The doctor was killed not far from here: did he visit you Sunday night?"

She shook her head. "I last saw Edward on Friday. He came over to have a cup of tea and watch television. He did that every Friday evening."

"Where were you Sunday night?"

"I was here all day Sunday—painting."

"Alone?"

"Of course."

I took my time lighting my pipe, full of mixed feelings: I didn't believe her ... and I wished to God I was twenty years younger.

"If you're hinting I killed Edward, you're so wrong. I worshipped him."

"Excuse the bluntness but were you his girlfriend?"

"I was his friend."

I'd heard somewhere that silence can break a person down. I wandered around the room slowly. The TV set was the only new thing in the room, everything else looked very old. Even the bookcase full of book club novels seemed unused. Through a doorway I saw a spotless old-fashioned kitchen, a polished coal stove. I'd lay odds it hadn't seen a fire in years. I stared at the paintings for a moment, then faced her. She wasn't even watching me, her eyes studying the floor. "Have you any boyfriends?"

"Certainly not."

"Now, Miss Endin, you're an attractive woman, you must have ...."

"I'm an Indian!" She sounded as fierce as her paintings. "Do you know what that means in a town like the Harbor, Mr. ...?"

"Matt Lund."

"Mr. Lund, have you any idea what it means to grow up happy with a loving father, even proud that this is the land of your ancestors? Then it all changes when you're twelve or thirteen, the doors start slamming? The kids you played with and went to school with suddenly become painfully polite. I'm not invited to anyone's house, they never come to mine. Have you any ...? No, how could you know what it means to be the only 'colored' person in a white town!"

"You're not ..."

"I'm proud I am an Indian! And if it was a bitter pill I could take it as long as my father was alive. I never knew my mother, but Dad was a wonderful man, full of living, like Edward. I could forget the rest of the Harbor over Dad's laughter and little jokes at night as we took care of the house, the garden, went fishing and swimming. Best of all were the hunting trips and the stories he remembered from his grandfather—alone in the woods we were living in Indian country again. But it got bad—he died when I was twenty."

Her voice died, too. I kept pacing the room slowly, telling myself not to be a sucker, taken in by a sob story. She crushed her cigarette in a clam shell ashtray, a loud noise in the silent house. Even the rain on the roof seemed muffled. After a long wait I asked, "What about Doc, Miss Endin?"

"I nearly went out of my head when Dad died, I was so lonely. I didn't know what to do with myself. Sometimes I'd read day and night until my head hurt. I turned to painting and that helped a little, more as I gained confidence. You know, for nearly two years I never spoke to a soul, except the storekeeper down the street."

"You mean nobody in the Harbor spoke to you? Why?"

"No occasion to talk. They might nod or wave to me on the street. It was more a case of the Harbor ignoring me. Oh, for a time Larry Anderson was friendly but the kind of relationship he wanted ... seems like most white men think that's all we've been placed on this earth for. I went out to the reservation but there wasn't anybody there I really knew."

"Ever leave the Harbor? New York's only a few hours away."

She laughed, a short, harsh sound. "Who would I know in New York? You forget, this town is named after my family, I belong here!"

"A person belongs where they're happy. How did Doc come into the picture?"

She stroked the heavy braid coming down her side. I suddenly wondered how she'd look with all that hair undone, perhaps falling to her hips.

"About two years after Dad died I needed money. Only job I

could get was as a domestic. I had headaches all the time, felt sick. One day the woman I worked for sent me to see Edward. He remembered me as a kid, was very kind. When he said I was on the verge of a nervous breakdown, I became hysterical, spilled all my thoughts out to him. He was shocked, and that was the start of our friendship. He taught me practical nursing, hired me to help in his office. He was interested in my painting, encouraged me. And the Harbor misunderstood, thought we were having an affair. Even Priscilla! Nobody said it openly, they respected Edward too much for that. But I could feel the snickers, the whispered laughter whenever I passed a group of men. Edward was furious, sickened. But how can you combat gossip, an unseen enemy?"

She was staring at the floor again, didn't expect me to answer—and what is the answer?

"Edward insisted I get active in the church, even held an exhibition of my paintings there. Everybody laughed at them—except a few artists over from East Hampton and Sag Harbor. I worked in Edward's office for over a year and a half, loved it. But I knew he was having difficulties with Priscilla over me, and she's sickly. Against his wishes—our only fight—I left, took various jobs in Hampton and Southampton as a domestic, in a factory. Of course I didn't mind the Harbor rejecting me, I was used to it. But Edward never stopped being my friend, fighting the town. He made a point of taking me for rides, visiting me several times a week. We read the same books, watched TV. He took me to an art school in East Hampton but I couldn't take it; they were friendly, only they treated me like a pet, a freak. He wanted to send me to a nurses' school, but I was afraid; I hadn't finished high school. He told me to join the WACs during the war, but I didn't want to be with all those white women." She looked up, stared right into my eyes. "I'll be blunt too. If Edward had wanted me to be his girlfriend, I would have—gladly! I think he desired me but felt it would be giving in to the gossip."

I leaned against the kitchen doorway, trying to believe what she was telling me. Or had the doc been trying to break off and she killed him? I said, "The police think Jerry was the last patient Barnes saw that night. Jerry insists the doc said he was going to see somebody else, Somebody he called an 'old goat.' Have you any idea who that might be?"

She shrugged and I realized she had good breasts. "I don't know. It could be a real goat. Edward once raced a small boy and his dog to Riverside to save the dog's life. You see, he was a dedicated man, kindness was his religion. That's why I can't think of him being murdered."

Barnes' wife and mistress sure thought alike, at least about the doc. "Did the doc ever mention a man named Nelson, or anybody named Hudon?"

She shook her head.

"Anybody in the Harbor by those names?"

"I never heard them before."

"Where were you yesterday, today?"

Again that interesting shrug. "I heard about his death on my way to work. I felt like the time I'd lost Dad. I drove around, trying to think. I sat on the beach for hours. Then I kept driving about, all the quiet back roads. I couldn't bear seeing anybody. Finally I came back here late this afternoon, tried to sleep."

"You worked for him, which of his patients would be call an 'old goat'?"

"I have no idea. Hardly like Edward to call anybody that. I suppose they'll bury him tomorrow. I know he'll understand if I don't go to the funeral."

"You're in a bad spot, Miss Endin. If the jury fails to indict Jerry, if they need another patsy, they'll tag you."

"*Me?*" She jumped.

"Circumstantial evidence is a darn sight stronger against you than Jerry. You haven't an alibi, Barnes was killed near your house. They could easily cook up a motive—jealousy. Your lover was about to leave you ..."

"Edward wasn't my lover! Let any doctor examine me!"

I was sold. Perhaps I admired the fierce way she said she was a virgin, the almost terrible way she said it. She could have so easily used a smug tone. This was a wail of protest.

But that didn't make her innocent of murder. Could she have insisted on bed and the doc refused? Only how could a man refuse something like Jane? Still—all the old saws about a woman spurned banged around in my head.

She lit another cigarette. "They wouldn't dare accuse me."

She was right about that, they'd be afraid it would blow the village apart. But actually, why would it? According to her, Barnes had only tried to help her, felt sorry for her. This required a little mental cooking on my part. "Miss Endin, is it true Priscilla Barnes is fond of Art Roberts?"

"That nonsense! She helped him, as she would a son. Why, she's ..."

"I know, old enough to be his mother." I zipped up my windbreaker. "Well, thank you, Miss Endin."

"You understand, I want to help Jerry. But I don't know how I can."

She walked me to the door. I asked, "Was Mrs. Barnes still upset over the doc's seeing you every Friday?"

"It was something they never talked about. I don't believe she really knew Edward."

"Would she be so upset as to murder him?"

She stopped, stock-still. "Never! Not Priscilla, she could never do ... that."

"I was only asking." As she opened the door and the rain hit us, I said, "You have a nice piece of land, probably get ten thousand for it."

"Are you telling me to leave the Harbor?"

I grinned. "I'm not the one to tell you anything. But there's a lot to do and see in New York, Frisco, Paris. It's a big world; you'd be surprised how tiny a speck End Harbor is on it. Well, if I think of anything else to ask, I'll call again." I held out my hand. Her hand was firm and cool.

I drove down Bay Street. It was nearly nine-thirty and I was bushed. A police car passed me, stopped. Chief Roberts stuck his over-handsome puss out as I slowed down. "Busy—busy, Mr. Peace Officer? Find any big clues, Mr. City Cop?" Satisfaction dripped from his voice.

"Only that it's raining."

He turned a flash on my battered fenders. "What happened to your car?"

"I've been running into a lot of blank walls today. Why didn't you tell me a Mr. Nelson visited the doc the night he was killed?"

He showed all his white teeth in a grin. "I don't have to tell you a damn thing. Matter of fact, I sent Nelson to see Edward. He asked me about this old guy he was looking for, I suggested the doc might know about him, or maybe the post office. Any other questions, big shot?"

I was too tired to think of anything. I told him, "Why don't you arrest yourself, Roberts, for obstructing justice?" and I drove off.

He laughed at me.

When I reached our cottage Bessie came running out and hugged me. I told her, "Watch it, you'll get dirty."

"Matt, where have you been all afternoon and evening? I've been worried sick. What happened? Did you find anything new?" Then she saw the car and: "Oh, my God, you were in an accident!"

"Relax and let me get out of these wet clothes. Andy sleeping, I hope?"

"Of course. He waited up to show you this." On the dining room table there was a fine model of a cabin cruiser built from the kit I'd brought him. Matty, curled up on a chair, yawned and studied me with an arrogant cat-look. But when I poked his nose he licked my finger.

"Tell me all about it," Bessie said impatiently. "Are you hungry?"

"I could use some food. Above all I need a good hot tub but I'll settle for a shower." Going into my room I undressed quietly and even the mushy bed looked welcome. I put on a robe, watching Andy, the solid way he slept. When I came out Bessie said, "I'm making something special for you, fried chicken simmered in yogurt."

"I'm hungry enough to try anything," I said, closing the bathroom door. I stood under the warm shower for a long time and felt human again. Wearing a sweater over my robe, I got a pipe going and sat at the table, examined the boat while Bessie cooked. "Andy do this himself? Fine job."

"Kids down the street helped him. Matt, do you want me to explode? What happened today?"

I told her about seeing Mrs. Barnes, about the stranger named Nelson, about Mrs. Jenks, and about locating Jane Endin. I found myself talking a great deal about Jane, ended by saying, "A woman like that shouldn't ever be lonely, she looks so passionate."

Placing some food in front of me Bessie asked, "Can you tell if a woman is passionate by her looks?"

"You can *think* she is," I said, tearing into the chicken, which was out of this world. Bessie sat across the table, drinking tea and beaming at me, telling me what a great detective I was. I didn't contradict her; I was too busy eating.

When I finished eating I insisted upon helping her with the dishes, although I was pooped. Bessie asked if I got the number of Chief Tom's truck. I told her, "I'll take care of fixing the car."

"Nonsense, I'm sure Danny's insurance covers it. Send him the bill and the license number of the truck."

"I was too mad to think straight. I didn't get the number. But I suppose I can get it tomorrow."

"Want me to ask this Jane over for supper tomorrow?"

"Oh, for—cut it out. She may be a murderer."

"But from the way you talk ...?"

"Honey, what she said or what I think isn't proof. Now lay off about her."

"I like what you said about thinking a woman can look passionate. Do I look hot?"

"Will you stop it? I'm tired." Sometimes Bessie embarrassed me with her talk about sex. When I was coming up girls didn't talk like that.

"I think it's a high compliment. Do I look hot, Matt?"

"Like a firecracker—as you very well know."

She gave me a fast hug; the nice warm living odor of her body. "Want to know something, you've always looked the same way to me. For true."

"Stop it," I said, afraid I was blushing.

"I mean it. I often wonder, what do you do for a woman, Matt?"

"What's that supposed to be, clever, sophisticated talk? Well, it isn't! And it's none of your business." I felt as uneasy as a kid listening to his father trying to explain the facts of life.

"Don't be prissy, and I'm certainly not trying to be clever. Why, if you looked thin I'd ask you what you were eating. A person needs sex the same way they need food and shelter."

"When I get in need for a woman, I find one!" I snapped, lying.

"This Miss Endin sounds like something you ought to get next to."

"What's the matter with you? I'm an old man."

"Only in your mind. Dan and I worry about you. He wants you to marry again. Matt, you're hard and lean, homely in a way that appeals to women. You could easily find plenty of women. You're not sixty yet, most men your age start chasing chippies. But you, if you'd stop being an old maid, forget that silly fat-assed cat and ..."

"I've had enough of this damn talk. I have no complaints about my sex life, never had!" I didn't realize I was talking so harshly until Bessie backed away. Changing the subject I asked, "Did you feed Matty?"

"The pig ate two helpings of liver. What do you plan to do tomorrow, about Jerry?"

"Oh, there's a lot to do," I said, patting her cheek as we both grinned at each other. "I have to see what I can find out about this Mr. Nelson, maybe talk to him. And I want to learn more about Mrs. Jenks' sons, maybe snoop into Priscilla Barnes' background. I'm going to examine Jerry's car—if I can. Probably have a long talk with the lawyer Jerry hires. I'll be busy—busy all day doing ..."

A car pulled up in front of the cottage. We both looked out at the rain sparkling in the headlights. Bessie groaned. "I hope this isn't the summer plague—unexpected guests. They come barging in and expect you to put them up for the night like it was ..."

There were slow, tired steps on the porch until the door opened. Jerry stood there, blinking at the light. He looked haggard, sickly.

For a long moment we didn't speak, then I whispered, "Lord help us—how did you break out?"

"I came by to thank you both," Jerry mumbled. "Now I go to my house and sleep. I sleep a long time. Yes, I need sleep."

Bessie raced over and kissed him, said something in Greek. He nodded and touched her face with his fingers, his eyes began to water.

"How did you get out?" I asked, trying to keep my voice down.

"Out?" He blinked stupidly, wiped his eyes with the back of a dirty hand. "It's over, they set me free. The District Attorney, the judge, the policemen, they told me to go. They found the real killer. Didn't you hear? They found the body of a man in a car out at Hampton Point. They told me he killed the doctor. Some man named Nelson."

Chapter 5

I was as stunned as if I'd stopped a haymaker with my chin. "Nelson is dead? Who killed him?"

Jerry shrugged. "I do not know. Art Roberts and the police at Riverside were very excited. I'm not feeling well, so when they said they were sorry and I was free, I ask no questions and let them take me home. Now I come over to thank you, then I will go to my bed."

Bessie asked if he wanted something to eat, was he really sick, and Jerry said a good sleep would fix him up. I questioned him about Nelson but he didn't know a thing. I'd been tired before, now I felt exhausted, beat and old.

Bessie said she would drive him home but Jerry said it wasn't necessary and pulled his glasses from his shirt pocket, as if proving something.

When he left Bessie danced over to me. "Matt, you did it! You're the best policeman ever!"

"I did what?" I felt like a terrible fool. That son-of-a-bitch Roberts must have known about the Nelson business when he stopped me before. Matt, the big detective—the first-grade horse's end!

"Why, *you* freed Jerry!"

"All I did was race around in circles, chasing my tail."

"Nonsense. If you hadn't stirred things up, they never would have looked farther, Jerry would still be in jail. You're wonderful!"

I shook myself. "I suppose that's one way of looking at it. Honey, I'm going to turn in ... I'm tired."

"Get a good night's sleep. I'll see to it Andy is quiet in the morning."

"Okay."

Bessie blew a kiss at me. "Don't act so blasé, you're tremendous. In a few hours you've solved everything. Say—I have to phone the news to Dan. I'll drive down to the store."

"Well, be careful, the lights aren't much good. Better wait until morning."

"Oh, no. I'll go to the Johnsons down the road, use their phone. You get your sleep."

I went to bed and started tossing and turning. I kept telling myself I *had* done a good day's work. What the hell, it was rough working *against* the police, even against hick cops. But I couldn't buy that; still felt like a fool. I'd been so tightly smug, bragged and shot off my big mouth ... and all the time this comic-cop Roberts had found the killer. Or was this another cover-up? It did seem too convenient—no scandal, not even a phony trial for Jerry, a dead stranger did it! And who killed Nelson? Had Roberts gunned him to make the collar? That was far-fetched but the way they worked things around here ... Lord, the D.A., and the magistrate sure let people in and out of jail easily here. Well, it wasn't my business any longer—it never had been.

I had a headache. All Bessie's fine chicken stuck in my gut like a dead weight. For a time I lay in bed and listened to the rain, then I knew I couldn't sleep, got up and took a couple soda pills to settle my stomach, went back to the sack. Bessie came in, humming; I heard her wash up, go to bed. About a half hour went by and I was no nearer sleep. Without knowing exactly why, I felt defeated.

Andy was breathing heavily in the next bed. I tried to think about my grandson, but think what? So I said the hell with it and took a long swig of brandy, damn near threw it up. But a few moments later I went off into a good sleep.

I had a number of small dreams. In the last one I was out in a storm, the rowboat rocking like mad. I seemed about to capsize when I opened my eyes. Andy, in a bathing suit, was shaking me. The sun was starting to come through the bedroom window.

I sat up, rubbed my face. I still felt lousy. "What time is it? Finally got us a nice day."

"Yes, Grandpa. Think we can get in some more fishing? It's almost seven-thirty."

"Seven-thirty? Bessie said she'd let me—damn it, Andy, did you wake me up to tell me about fishing?" I asked, angry.

"No, sir. There's a policeman outside. He has something for you."

I put on a robe and nodded to Bessie, washing up in the bathroom. She should have closed the door, the sun silhouetted her figure against her short nightgown.

End Harbor's one police car was parked outside and a cop I'd never seen before, a stocky joker about thirty, waved a letter at me. "Special delivery."

"A special?" Then I remembered, Nat and his credit report. "You fellows deliver mail, too?"

He was looking me over; I guess I didn't look like much. "I heard a lot about you—big city cop. Yeah, when we're cruising around we deliver specials and telegrams."

"They nab whoever killed Nelson?"

"It was a suicide. Found the gun right in his lap, I hear. He had a gun permit, too."

"What makes him the doc's killer?"

"Found the doc's scarf in the glove compartment. Doc was wearing the scarf the night he was killed."

"Roberts said nothing was missing."

"Mrs. Barnes didn't remember he was wearing a scarf until we—I mean the Hampton Point police—found it."

"What's the tie-up between Nelson and the doctor?"

He shrugged. "We don't know—yet. But having the dead man's scarf in his car proves he saw the doc last. That's why he probably killed himself, sense of guilt."

I wanted to ask more questions but told myself to mind my own business. I thanked him for the letter, wondered if he expected a tip, went back inside.

"What's the special about?" Bessie asked. She'd changed to a bathing suit.

"Nothing. Just some info I asked for. You done in the john?"

"Sure."

I went in and washed up. When I came out she said, "Well,

at least open it."

"The case is over."

"It's special delivery, open it!"

I opened it, showed her Nat's report. Bessie said, "That's all? I'll make breakfast, then we'll spend the day on the beach. Andy, take out the milk and juice, set the table."

I dressed and glanced at Nat's report. He didn't have a thing on Jerry, or about Jane Endin. Doc Barnes was rated as a highly respected citizen. A former mayor, his income was over $15,000 a year. Nat had plenty of information about the doc's background, college, war record—but none of it interesting. Larry Anderson also had a good credit rating, although his income averaged under $5000. Art Roberts only made $2800 a year but somehow owned his house and car. The few other names I'd picked at random were either not listed, or mostly considered poor credit risks.

Nat wrote:

"In general, End Harbor is a two-bit town, business-wise. There's a few retired people with dough, and of course the doctor. He's always been comfortable, in fact he married into money. His wife inherited a neat bundle from her folks, shortly before Barnes married her. However, since her older brother had disappeared years before, there was some difficulty settling the estate and Priscilla Barnes (maiden name—Wiston) spent many thousands of bucks hunting for the missing brother—Jack Wiston. He was never found, thought to have vanished in a Canadian gold rush.

"This Anderson seems to be the only merchant making a go of things. He owns his house and land, free and clear, never asks for credit, pays all bills promptly. Of course most of the people there own their homes. Handed down from father-to-son stuff, but everybody is money-poor. Barnes probably has stocks and bonds. By the way, if you're thinking of buying property, real estate in End Harbor is considered a very sound investment. People are pushing out all along the Island, and the summer tourist trade has been growing steadily. There's been a small real estate boom in End Harbor and considerable building—mostly of summer cottages—as a result. However, the contractors are all from Hampton and other towns. Odd there isn't a building contractor in the Harbor. That should be a sweet business if you're thinking of investing. So is real estate. And where did you get your pile from? I always thought you were an honest slob. Or did you finally bring in a horse?"

Matty got up, stalked into the room, stretching and yawning. I cleaned his box, washed my hands, and fed him. I had to coax him to eat. He took a few sips of his milk, started to walk away. I ran my fingers through his fur for ticks. He must have been as irritable as I was—he swung on me.

Bessie put breakfast on the table, told me, "At least wash your hands after touching that filthy beast."

"He's cleaner than you or I," I said, making for the kitchen sink.

She steered me toward the bathroom, as if I were a child. Maybe I felt kind of childish. Or would senile be the correct word?

During breakfast Andy had to tell me—in detail—how he'd built the model boat. Then he started asking when we'd go fishing. I was far too restless to sit in a damn rowboat. I made the mistake of saying I had to see about fixing the car and that started another flood of questions. I finally snapped, "Andy, it's too early in the morning for so much talk. I've had a hard night."

"Doing what, Grandpops?"

"Oh, Andy ... leave me alone."

The kid sulked until Bessie told him to cut it out before he got walloped. No sooner did the kid quiet down than Bessie started to run her mouth. Danny had assured her his insurance covered the damage. If I wanted to wait until he came down on Friday, he would take care of things.

Andy cut in with, "Anybody knows you should be towed out of mud, not pushed."

"Nonsense. How about the time I was pushed out of the sand with the old car?" Bessie asked.

I finished my coffee quickly as they argued, all the petty talk increasing my nervousness. I finally got in a word, told Andy I'd meet him on the beach, to take the rods and stuff there and wait. Then I told Bessie I was merely going to get the Indian's license number, leave the car at the garage.

I undressed and put on my bathing trunks, then dressed again. Matty was back on my bed and I poked him and he hissed at me. I don't know what it was, but driving toward

Hampton I felt depressed as hell.

I found the reservation without any trouble, didn't bother going into the shack they called a store. Chief Tom's truck was parked outside and I got down the license number, and his full name from the fly-specked beer license in the dirty store window. His name was Tom Claude Faro.

Danny's car looked bad in the daylight and I was glad to drop it off at the garage. The mechanic I'd talked to yesterday was there and I got quite a shock when I saw Art Roberts changing from coveralls into his snappy uniform. He called out, "Wait a minute, Lund, I'll give you a lift back to the Harbor."

"What are you doing here?"

"Working. This is my cousin Hank," he said, nodding at the other mechanic. "When will Lund's car be ready?"

"Not for a day, maybe two. Phone me in the morning, Mr. Lund," this Hank said.

Roberts carefully dressed, paying a lot of attention to his hair. A mirror was his best friend. When he saw me watching him he winked, said, "I have to look my best—going to Edward's funeral in an hour. Come on."

He had a snappy white MG and as I sat in the bucket seat, I said, "Some car."

"Keeps me broke. Bought it two months ago from a society kid I pinched for drunk driving. Got a good buy."

We drove for a moment before he said, "Suppose you know about Nelson. We have everything but the motive. Hampton Point police are having the L.A. cops look into Nelson's life."

"How come he had a gun permit?"

"Don't know. He was a retired bank guard, maybe they let them keep their rods. Pretty good work for hick cops, isn't it?"

"Stop that 'hick' routine. I never called you one."

"Sure, but you're thinking it: I'm a hick cop in a gaudy uniform. Okay, I am. And I like it. I have to take another job to keep going, everybody in the Harbor works at a couple jobs. See, plenty of work around here but not any good jobs. Anyway, the case is settled. Jerry is off the hook so I think you're happy. Now stop getting into everybody's hair. Heard you visited Mrs. Barnes and Jane Endin yesterday. I guess *now* you'll stick to fishing and stop throwing your badge around."

"Sure. I only did it because of my daughter-in-law, had to showboat a little."

He gave me a patronizing grin; with his looks, the uniform, and the MG, Roberts must have been God's gift to the women—in the Harbor. He said, "You won't believe this, but I'm damn glad you were so nosey. Matter of fact, I learned something, working with you."

I laughed. "Working *with* me!"

"I was a little steamed at first when you showed me up, my saying it was an accident." We turned into Main Street, stopped in front of the Municipal Building. "Want me to run you up to your cottage?"

"No, thanks, I could use a walk. You know, I was thinking it could have been an accident. Suppose Barnes saw a drunk driver coming at him, had to swerve to escape hitting him, went off the road and was killed when the car hit the tree? The drunk could have stopped, dragged the body out of the car, then panicked when he saw he had a stiff, taken off. Perhaps later the body was run over by a hit-and-run driver. Too much of a coincidence, two lousy drivers, but it's possible. I mean, was possible."

Roberts had real dismay on his big face. "Jeez, you ain't starting to open this all over again, Lund?"

I crawled out of the MG, straightened up. "Nope. Merely talking. From now on I'm just another tourist."

Roberts sort of jumped out of the car, brushed his uniform. "Great. I've had all the action I want for one summer. Let the Hampton Point police dig up the fine details." He held out a heavy hand. "Good knowing you, Lund."

I shook his hand. "Sure. Whenever you're in town, drop into the precinct house. Boys be jealous of your uniform."

He smiled. "I might do that."

"I work out of the ..."

"I know where you work. Checked on you. You're a cell block attendant. Guess you'll be retiring soon."

I didn't know if he was sarcastic or not when he said cell block attendant. "In a year or two."

He sighed. "Wish I had a pension to look forward to. Guess I'll have to die in harness. I plan to take the next state trooper exam. Well, have to get back to the office. Hope you have decent weather for the rest of your stay."

We shook hands again and as I walked toward the cottage I wondered whether Roberts was a ham or sincere. In either case he still was a jerk. But with his looks and setup, be odd if he didn't take himself seriously. It was getting hot and I was sweating by the time I reached the beach.

Bessie was sitting under a striped umbrella with some other young women, all of them in brief bathing suits. She introduced me with a big build-up, great detective line, gave me a sandwich and a cold drink. The women made a small fuss over me, asked a lot of dumb questions. All the talk made me jittery again.

Andy came out of the water, said he was ready to go fishing. He had the model of the cabin cruiser under the umbrella, wanted to try it in the water. Bessie said it wasn't meant for that, he should know better. She seemed to be picking on the boy, or maybe it was my nerves. They argued about the boat. I finally cut in and told him he could take the model along but to keep it in the rowboat.

Bessie told him to dig clams for bait but he pulled a paper bag from out under the towels, said he still had clams from the other day and a hunk of squid somebody had given him. She asked him where he kept it all the time and he said in the freezer. She bawled him out, again, for keeping the stinking squid in the refrigerator. He whined that he wouldn't do it again. Then she started on me, warning me to be careful of the sun. I said okay and that I was going into the swamp grass to take off my pants. The women all laughed as Bessie said, "Oh, for, Matt drop your pants here. My God!"

All this chatter didn't help my nerves or blue mood and I was happy when Andy and I finally got into the boat. He rowed and gave me the glasses to wear around my neck. The tide was starting to come in and when we reached the breakwater we drifted. I had a few small bites, then didn't bother baiting up. Andy caught a large humpback sea-porgy that damn near snapped his rod. He was so excited he didn't nag me to fish. The sun felt good, took the last of yesterday's chill from my bones. I was content to glance around the harbor through the glasses: they almost put me aboard the big yachts. Andy kept up a line of chatter, looking into the pail with pride at *my* fish.

For no reason, before we drifted out of view, I put the glasses on Jane Endin's house. Of course I didn't see a damn thing, except her car was still in the driveway. I examined a few more boats, the shore at Haven Island across the bay. We were drifting in front of Anderson's house and up on the widow's walk. Pops was laying on the cot, Larry Anderson sitting beside him, reading the paper. I turned the field glasses on the Endin house for a last look. Jane was out in the backyard, wearing a loose-fitting loud purple robe, hair hanging down her back like a thick black brush stroke. She was putting small towels on the line. The towels were full of bright red splotches—undoubtedly the rags she used to wipe her paint brushes. But why only red paint?

Andy yelled, "Grandpa!" He was standing, his rod forming a

rigid U as the line jerked.

"Reel it in!"

"It's too heavy! Gee, I must have a whale!"

I moved over to help him and out of the corner of my eye I saw two quick flashes of light from the walk atop Anderson's house. For a second I thought they were shots, waited for the shotgun sounds. No sound came.

It was just a big ugly skate on the line and I held the rod while Andy cut the hook out of the wing, his face full of disgust. Was Anderson signaling somebody? As I gave Andy back the rod, I turned and put my binoculars on the widow's walk. Anderson was standing up, talking to Pops. Larry was holding something in his right hand that at first I thought was an automatic: then I realized what the light flashes were—he'd been watching us through binoculars and the flashes had been the sun striking the lens.

Anderson seemed to shrug, as if having an argument, then got his left hand under Pops and lifted him up. He got his right hand, still holding the glasses, under the old man's ankles, carried him downstairs.

There was something phony about the scene, exactly what I didn't know. Andy said he wanted to row out into the bay. I took the oars: exercise might quiet my restlessness. I told him to troll. As I rowed I faced the top of Anderson's house. Why was he watching us through the glasses? But that wasn't what struck me wrong.

I told myself to stop it, I was no longer playing movie dick. What the devil, with a view like that, he'd certainly spend a lot of time looking through binoculars. Why assume he was watching us—could have been looking at the yachts going past the lighthouse way out in the bay? I put muscle to the oars, we were going against the tide ... and suddenly I knew what was wrong—the way Anderson had lifted the old man—he'd done it with *one* hand! His right hand, holding the glasses, had been used merely for balance.

Strong as Anderson seemed, he'd hardly lift a man with one arm. It sure was a careless way to carry a sick man, even if he could do it. And Pops—the floppy straw hat over his face, arms under the blanket ... maybe that wasn't a man up there but a straw dummy!

I told myself that was plain silly, but couldn't get the idea out of my mind. What would be the point of carrying a dummy up to the widow's walk, the reading act? After all, suppose Pops only weighed ninety to a hundred pounds, a guy built like

Anderson could carry a hundred-pound sack of potatoes in one arm—maybe. Still, to lift a man recovering from a heart attack you'd think he would have put the glasses down, used both hands to carry Pops?

Nuts, I thought, stop acting like a jerk. You're not on the case. You're not on anything but supposedly enjoying fishing. Keep it at that or you'll make a fool of yourself—again.

I rowed out near some red and black buoys and we tossed out the anchor. We were in real deep water and I baited up but we didn't catch a damn thing. I picked up the boat model, it was even a better job than I thought—the kid had fashioned tiny furniture out of cardboard and matches. When I told him he was right smart Andy said, "Heck, I didn't do that part. Jenny Johnson did it. Bob—that's her brother—and I put the hull and deck together, but she fixed up the inside, even painted the name on the back. You'll see her on the beach today. She's pretty and smart."

"Your girlfriend?"

"What? I should say not. Jenny is going on fifteen—she's old."

"That's not ..." I began, and stopped. How old was Nelson? How old was Doc Barnes? Judging from Priscilla who *looked* about fifty-eight, the Doc must have been sixty-five, or so. Hell, of course he could have married an older woman.... But suppose he was sixty-five, anybody he called an "old goat" would have to be at least seventy, seventy-five or even eighty. That could be Nelson, if he was that old ... and it could also be Pops! "Andy, how old was Pops?"

"Not was, Grandpa, but *is*. My teacher told me to always be sure about the proper tense of a ..."

"Too hot for lessons. How old would you say Pops is?"

"Gee, I don't know. He looks awful old."

"As old as I am?"

"No, way older. Heck, I betcha Pops is at least—forty."

I stared at the kid, then grinned—at myself. He'd started me on the idea, what more could I expect? "Andy, how old do you think I am?"

"I don't know," he said, his voice uncomfortable. "Thirty-seven?"

"Come on, now. Your daddy is going on thirty-five, I think, so I have to be at least twenty years older than he is."

"Why?"

"I just have to," I said, not wanting to explain the birds and the bees to the kid. Pops was the man I had to talk to, and right away. I tried to think of a way of going in now, without the kid asking a million questions.

"You could only be fifteen years older than Dad."

"Okay, let's forget it. This is sure a swell model. Next time we go shopping, I'll buy you another kit. In fact, if we row in ..."

"Great, Grans! Make it a helicopter kit this ..."

A siren went off back in the Harbor. "What's that—a fire?"

Andy shook his head. "No. That was only one.... Do you say ring or blast or blow?"

"Blast, I guess."

"One blast means it's noontime."

"I've had enough sun and I'm starved. Think we can make for the beach?"

To my surprise the boy said, "Any time you wish." He poked at the pail with his toe. "I wanted to go in before, show Mom my big porgy. Can I row?"

I gave him the oars, slipped on a shirt and got my pipe working. When we came within sight of Anderson's house I put the glasses on the widow's walk. Pops was on the cot again, blanket and all. The hat was covering most of his face and he was still wearing the tan shirt. But he seemed to be holding a newspaper up on his stomach. Then *I saw him turn a page, adjust his hat.*

Matt Lund and his great deductions! The old straw dummy was me. The hell with playing detective—I'd had it.

Back on the beach I had a sandwich and some warm soda. After showing off his fish, Andy and another kid took it way down the beach to clean. I curled up in the shade of the beach umbrella, listened to Bessie's small talk with the other young women, watched some tots busy making sand pies. I completely forgot the "case." I felt so relaxed I even dozed off for a few minutes.

Then Bessie shook me awake and soon had me digging clams with my fingers, squatting in the shallow water with the women. I managed to find a few. Bessie had a couple dozen small ones down her bosom, in fact all the girls had "clam bras" as they called it.

When the tide came in high enough to make any more digging impossible, Bessie sat on the beach and smashed clams together and ate them. I skipped that—the fresh clams looked too gritty and snotty. I curled up for another nap but didn't complain when Andy said it was high enough for swimming. I fooled in the water with the kids. When Bessie stood up and shouted it was five, time to go home as she had a special meat pudding to make ... I was completely pooped, glad to drag my tired rear toward the cottage.

Walking along the road Bessie kept bawling me out for getting too much sun, but I told her I felt fine. And I did. I was honestly tired without a worry or a thought on my mind. All I wanted was to eat and swim—get some sleep, and the hell with being a jerk detective. When Bessie said something about asking Jane Endin over I was so bushed I only put up a mild argument.

Reaching the cottage I went around to the back, with Andy, to hang out the beach towels. He asked how soon we'd buy the helicopter kit and ...

Bessie screamed. A hell of a scream.

I dropped the towels, damn near fell over Andy as we rushed around front, into the house. Bessie was standing in the doorway, pointing, her face full of horror.

Matty was on his back, his four feet sticking stiffly up in the air. He was laying on the tabletop, next to a dish of food. One glance told me he was dead.

Chapter 6

Andy asked, "Is poor Matty sick?"

I finally took my eyes off the cat, looked coldly around the room. I was frightened, but most of all I was too angry and upset to speak. Before I'd been grandstanding for the boy, maybe for myself, doing Bessie a favor, or perhaps having a little something going for the sake of "justice." But that was all over. Now I was just plain goddamn burning mad!

Andy asked, "What's the matter with Matty? If we give him some warm milk ...?"

Bessie put an arm around the boy's fat shoulders, told him softly, "He's dead, Andy. He took sick and died and he's ..."

"Gone to Heaven? Mom, do cats and dogs go to Hell, too?"

"Keep still, Andy." She turned to me, her eyes troubled. "He is dead, isn't he, Matt?"

Sure, I knew he was dead at first glance. But I stepped over and poked his stiff legs with my fingers, stared into the glassy little eyes. I was putting on an act for Bessie. My eyes kept working the room, waiting for any movement or sound behind the doors, in the other rooms. But the killer wouldn't be dumb enough to hang around. If he'd been down for real action, he wouldn't have bothered with my cat. The room looked okay, not a thing disturbed.

Andy was asking, "But, Mom, how did he die? Did he eat some of the stuff in that plate? Looks like there's some of it on his mouth."

"I don't know," Bessie said, starting for the table.

I grabbed her shoulder, told her, "Don't move. Did you touch anything when you came in?"

"No. Soon as I opened the door and saw Matty, I yelled. I don't understand how I could have been so careless as to leave those vegetables out of the refrigerator. It isn't like me to ..."

"What's in the bowl?" I asked, my eyes still covering the room.

"I was going to make *keftethes* for supper, so I ..."

"What's that?"

I must have been snapping the questions at her, for Bessie sort of blinked and backed away from me as she said, "It's a ... uh ... fried meatball. But there isn't any meat in the dish—just some vegetables I intended to sauté first—tomato paste, peppers, mushrooms, olives, herbs and ... Obviously the heat must have turned the food and Matty ate some and got ptomaine and ... oh, Matt, I know how fond you were of the beast ... I'm sorry I was so careless, really!" She was on the verge of tears.

"Stop it, Bessie." My voice was hard and curt; I knew I had to simmer down, cool off and use my head. "It wasn't your fault, you didn't do anything to Matty."

Andy said, "Gee, think what would have happened if we had eaten the food. I bet ..."

Bessie nodded, her face a sudden sickly white. "Marty saved our lives. But—even if it has been a hot afternoon, why should vegetables spoil *that* fast?"

There was a moment of silence. I was trying to think a few steps ahead. Then Bessie said, "Matt, will you take ... him ... away? I'll clean up and...."

I told her, "Bessie, I want you to stay out of the house, for a while. You and Andy eat out."

"Why?"

"I have some things to do here."

She shrugged. "Well, if you wish. We'll change and eat in the village." She started for the bedroom.

"No! I want you both out right now!"

"In our bathing suits? Please, Matt, while I realize how deeply you felt about the cat, I said I was sorry about the accident but ..."

"Will you stay the hell out of here! I don't care where you

eat—just leave me alone!" I heard the roar of my own voice and Andy's shrill, "Grandpops!"

I suddenly relaxed, got my nerves somewhat under control. Even tried to smile at Bessie as I took her trembling hand, told her, "Honey, don't you see, I'm not only thinking about Matty—he's dead and gone. This wasn't any accident. This is a warning."

"A warning? About what?"

"An attempt to frighten me off the Doc Barnes murder."

Bessie tried to hide the anxious look that slipped across her soft face. "But, Matt, that's over, solved."

"The killer thinks I'm still on the case, didn't fall for that Nelson suicide thing."

"Matty ate some bad food, that's too bad, but aren't you going overboard trying to connect a simple accident with ...?"

"Bessie, Bessie, are you blind? You know what a fussy eater Matty is—was. You commented upon it several times. He wouldn't have eaten that food—I've never seen him jump on the table to steal food in his life! Don't you see, this is a plant, and a clumsy one at that, to scare ..." I saw Andy staring up at me with big eyes—and bigger ears. "Andy, without saying a single word to anybody about what's happened, run over to the Johnsons, or whoever has a phone, and call the police. Just tell Roberts want him up here pronto."

"Yes, sir!" the boy said, taking off like a sprinter.

I waited until I heard him running down the road. "Bessie, honey, this isn't any joke—it's damn serious. The killer came around to put the fear of God in me. He found Matty. Suppose he'd found you or Andy?"

Her face said she still didn't believe me. "Matt, doesn't that sound rather—fantastic? The heat spoiled some food and Matty ate it."

"That's exactly what he wants us to buy—well, no sale! The killer has been riding his luck high, but with Matty he made his first mistake. He couldn't know Matty's eating habits, that Matty would never leap on the table for food."

"Who knows how hungry the cat was?"

"Look, I certainly know all about his dainty appetite—it's impossible!"

"Now, Matt, be reasonable. I mean Matty could have ... *He?* You know who the killer is? Why Barnes was killed?"

"I don't know the *why*, but I have a hell of a strong idea as to *who* did it. Bessie, what are we wasting time and arguing about? Whether you think I'm crazy or not, let's not take any chances. Take Andy over to the Johnsons and stay there for the night. Or until I call for you. I have a lot of work to do here: fingerprints and other clues. Okay?"

"Oh, Matt, you're not making much sense. I think you're ..."

"Damn it, honey, what do you know about murder? Listen, at least humor me, even if you think I'm an old fool!"

"Matt, you know I don't think that. I mean, it's simply that.... All right, I'll wait for you at the Johnsons. Can I at least take some meat out of the refrigerator to cook over there?"

"No. After I have it analyzed, I'm throwing out every bit of food here. Forget food, you ate enough clams to last you a week. Honey, just turn right about and get. And don't worry."

She giggled nervously. "Now you tell me—don't worry! I'll be waiting for you at the Johnsons. Matt, please take care—don't do anything foolish."

I nodded, watched her cross the porch, go down the steps. It suddenly came to me how right she was: the chips were down and I'd damn well better be a good detective—no more second guessing.

I walked through the house slowly. Things seemed okay. But then he hadn't been hunting for anything—except me. I returned to the table and Matty. There didn't seem to be any skin or blood sticking to his claws. Yet I couldn't see him being manhandled without a fight. His mouth was wide open in a sort of gasp and some of the tomato-red food stuck in his throat. I sniffed at the bowl, the food smelled spicy and good. I took another sniff, bending so low the tip of my nose touched the mess. I jerked my head back, laughing aloud like a goon—the food was cold! I stuck a finger in: it was all cool—proving Bessie *hadn't* left it out on the table. There wasn't any doubt, it had been deliberate.

There wasn't anything to do until Roberts showed. I brushed away a fly buzzing Matty, washed up at the sink. I went outside, "locking" the screen door. It wasn't a lock, merely a catch.

I dropped in on the three cottages nearest ours. No one had been home in the afternoon—they'd all been at the beach. But he could have easily checked that first ... seen me on the sand, too, or out digging those damn clams.

The entire End Harbor police motor pool was parked in front of the cottage—Roberts leaning out of the radio car. He waved a lazy hand at me. "Nobody home. What's all the excitement about now?"

My old distrust of him returned—hard and fast. Not that I

thought he did it, but the motive behind everything had to be this small-town scandal—and Roberts' main job was to keep a lid on it.

"Come inside," I said, "unlocking" the screen door. He got out of the car, straightened his shirt, followed me in. When he saw Matty on the table Roberts whistled, pushed his hat back on his head, asked, "Ate some ant poison?"

"No, he was killed."

"Got to be careful leaving these insecticides around. Too bad. What you want to see me about, Lund?"

"What kind of fingerprint equipment do you have here?"

"Not much—actually nothing to speak of. They've got a complete outfit at Riverside, of course, and Hampton Point. Guess if we ever had any need for taking prints, we could call on them. Why?"

"Why? To see if the killer left any prints!"

Roberts pulled at one of Matty's stiff legs. "What killer left what prints?"

"The guy who killed my cat. I think he also killed Doc Barnes and maybe Nelson. It's obvious."

Roberts gave me a queer look, as if I was nuts. He sat down on a chair, fanning his face with his fancy cap. I asked, "What's the matter with you? If there were prints on the chair, your big ass has smeared them."

"I'm far from getting the message, Lund," he corned. "Send it to me slower. Now what about the cat?"

I told him about coming home from the beach, finding Matty dead, added, "But it's all a clumsy job. First off, the food was cool, meaning it hadn't been spoiled—that it was taken out of the icebox recently and poison added. Secondly, it must have been forced down Matty's throat, he never in his life ate off the table. It was done to scare me off."

"Scare you off what?" Roberts asked, his voice sarcastically polite.

"Come on, Roberts! Off the Barnes killing."

"Lund, you can't be starting that again? *The case is over.*"

"The killer doesn't know that! Listen to me, Roberts, before I was sticking my nose in for no real reason, but from now on I'm in with both feet. That's *my* cat!" He still was looking at me as if waiting for the punchline of a gag. The hell with you, I thought. You won't get off those glamor-pants, you're too much of a jerk. And the devil with trying for prints. Killer would be too smart for that. And there wasn't time, anyway.

"Lund, I got a dog I'd flip over if he died. So I can understand why the death of your cat has upset your better judgement, but ..."

"Stop it."

He got up. "Yeah, I can stop it. I can get back to some paperwork I was doing when your boy phoned. Talk sense, man, you're basing a lot of wild talk on what? That you *think* the cat would never jump on the table! You know how curious cats are, and he might have been very hungry, so he ups and eats some of this spoiled food and ..."

"Damn it, it isn't spoiled! Stick your finger in the stuff now, see if it feels like it's been out all afternoon."

Roberts touched the mess with a thick finger, said, "Yeah, does feel cool." He cleaned his fingertip on the tablecloth. "Let's start again; maybe he choked on a bone or ...?"

"And maybe somebody is being murdered while we're gassing!"

"You're not sure how the cat died—why don't you ask a vet before shooting off your mouth about murder?"

I was too mad to even get riled. "Where can we find an animal doc?"

"Nearest one is in Hampton. You see what he says and then we'll see. Your car is still in the shop. I'll drive you there."

"Thanks!" I got Matty's basket, gently placed him in it. I couldn't bend his legs, so I left the top open. I put the bowl in a big saucepan, held that in my left hand and took the basket under my right arm, said, "Let's go."

Roberts nodded at my trunks. "Your legs aren't that good. Ordinance against walking around in swim trunks—even old ones. Get dressed."

I slipped on my clothes, wondering how much more of this patronizing "humoring" I could take. Even a hick cop should take murder seriously. Roberts carried the pot out to the car as he said, "I'll have to stop at the station, tell 'em where I'm going. Kind of late—best we phone the vet and see if he's around."

I didn't say a word. When we pulled up in front of the "police station" I had cooled off enough to admit Roberts was at least trying to work intelligently. I should have thought of seeing a veterinarian. I should have used my head instead of my temper. I had to play it careful, not risk Andy or Bessie—or myself. I stared out of the car window, Matty heavy and silent in his basket on my lap, watching the people pass by on the street, wondering if I were being watched, too.

About ten minutes later Roberts came out, waved to a couple of passing girls before he told me, "It's after six—the vet shut at four. Wife says he's on his boat fishing, won't be back until late."

"Another vet around?"

"In Riverside. I phoned him, too—no answer. Tomorrow morning we'll ..."

"Tomorrow will be too late. Where can I get this food analyzed?"

"At this hour?"

"Right now!"

"We haven't a lab and the county lab at Riverside will be shut. Doc Barnes would have been our man. Guess Jessie—the druggist—might help us."

"Think he's out fishing, too!"

Roberts gave me a stupid grin. "Let's walk across the street and see."

The druggist turned out to be a serious-faced kid of about twenty-six or so, wearing a loud yellow sport shirt and Bermuda shorts. We went to the back of the store, waited while he made a soda for an old lady. Then I told him we wanted to know what had killed Matty, showed him the dish of food. He sniffed at it, rubbed some between his slender fingers. He ran water over a spoonful of the stuff, washing away the red tomato paste. He held up a small white sliver. "I don't have to be a research chemist to spot this—piece of toadstool. There's a quantity of mushrooms here and at least one of them is toadstool."

He handed it to Roberts who said, "Yeah, it is a toadstool. That makes for a simple answer, Lund, your daughter-in-law picked wild mushrooms and ..."

"She buys her mushrooms."

"Lucky you—got a good lawsuit. Hope she got 'em at the supermarket."

"I doubt that, Artie," Jessie the druggist said. "Store mushrooms are cultivated and there's little chance of a toadstool mixing in. Besides, this type is a cinch to spot. Of course, remember there could be something else in the food and if you give me a few days to ..."

I cut in with, "What would have happened if we—I—had eaten some of this? Would it have caused death?"

"You understand, I'm not a toxicologist, so this is far from an expert opinion. There are various species of poisonous mushrooms, or toadstools, as they are commonly called, and I imagine some are quite deadly. However, judging by the structure of this sample, it's a local variety. I used them for doll umbrellas when I was a kid. I believe you'd have to eat a far larger quantity than could be found in this plate to possibly cause death. But there's enough here to have made you miserably ill for several days."

I nodded. "One thing more, doc, wouldn't ...?"

Jessie gave me a solemn grin. "I'm not a doctor."

"But you're a country lad and maybe you know about animals. Wouldn't an animal by instinct leave a toadstool alone?"

"I couldn't say. I suppose an animal might know food was poisonous by the smell, but mushrooms are odorless. And it seems to me I recall pictures of cows dying out West when they were driven by thirst to drink at alkaline wells. Notice how the cat's neck is swollen and the large, almost abnormal amount of food in the throat, as if the food were forced down his throat." He gave me a suspicious glance.

"But, Jess, couldn't the swelling be caused by the toadstool making the cat sick?" Roberts asked.

Somebody called out from the front of the store, "Jessie?"

"Yes."

"Leaving a dime for the paper on the counter."

"Thanks." The druggist turned to Roberts. "That's possible. I really don't know. Say, Artie, what's this all about?"

"Nothing," I said quickly. "Thanks for your time, Mr. ... Jessie." I picked up Matty's basket and the pot of food. Roberts followed me out to the police car, opening the door for me. I told him, "I'd appreciate it if you'd drive me back to the cottage."

"Why, sure, I always give door-to-door service," he said, starting the car. "Well, guess you're convinced now it was an accident."

"Accident? How often have you had a case of toadstool poisoning in the Harbor?"

"Never heard of any, but they do happen," he said, glancing at a car making a brake-screeching turn off Main Street, muttering, "Dumb kid drivers."

"I'll tell you what happened. The killer came to our cottage with a toadstool while we were at the beach, found the food in the icebox, cut in the toadstool. He figured after eating the food we'd get sick enough to pack up for New York. I'd be off his back. Then he saw my cat, thought he had a better way of making sure his plan worked fast—forced food down Matty's mouth and left the bowl beside him on the table."

"You're going off half-cocked, Lund. All that is only what you *think*."

I patted Matty's basket. "I didn't think up this!"

"But you can't be positive that ...?"

"I'm positive!"

"Look, Lund, all we know is your cat ate a toadstool and died. That doesn't prove a thing. You heard Jessie, he wasn't even certain how the cat died. And don't keep saying 'he'—if you think the cat was deliberately killed—I recall hearing your daughter-in-law wasn't keen on the cat. And her boy—some kids get kicks out of hanging dogs and ..."

"Oh cut it. I've had enough talk."

"What the hell do you expect me to do? *If* the cat was killed deliberately, so what? I'm not the SPCA. Killing a cat isn't any crime. As for this being part of the Barnes business, old man, you're way off your rocker."

We finished the ride in silence. Roberts helped me into the cottage with the stuff, planted his rear on a chair again—his favorite hobby. I wondered what he was hanging around for. I knew I was wasting valuable time talking to the big dope. The toadstool told me all I wanted to know ... except for one other thing I had to clear. I asked, "How old would Jack Wiston be now?"

"Who?" His face looked blank and I doubted if he was that good an actor.

"Priscilla Barnes' missing brother," I said.

"You really get around, Lund. I don't know. That was long before my time. I never saw or knew any of her family, not even when I was a kid."

"How old was Barnes?"

"Around sixty-three. I have his exact age in my files. Had a nice funeral for Ed today. Worked out fine."

"You mean Jane Endin didn't show. How old was Nelson?"

"Seventy-one."

"And Pops?"

Roberts looked startled. "What's Pops got to do with this?"

"How old is he?"

Roberts shrugged. "Never could count that high. This a quiz program?"

"It was, up till now. Roberts, do me one favor, give—or sell—me a handful of .38 shells." I touched his polished belt lined with bullets. I knew there was little chance the hardware store carried them.

Roberts couldn't have jumped to his feet faster if a shell had goosed him. His eyes actually narrowed—again—as he asked, "What for?"

"For my empty gun."

"That tears it, Lund. You've been a wild-hair from the moment you came to the Harbor. Pack a gun and I'll jail you!"

"The law says I can carry a gun anywhere in the state."

"Then I'll lock you up for disorderly conduct, for being a loony! You sore because your Greek buddy is free and you haven't anything to do now? Who the devil do you think you are? Dick Tracy? I'm warning you, Lund, and only this once, annoy anybody else in the Harbor and I'll throw your ass in jail so fast it will make your badge smoke!" He started for the porch, his big frame filling the doorway.

"Maybe the Hampton Point police will be interested."

Roberts spun around so quickly I thought he was going to swing on me. "Sure, go tell them about your cat—they'll toss you in a cell, a padded one! Maybe you don't believe this, but I'm doing you a favor—although you sure act like you're cracked. Well, here's the favor, some free advice: don't make a fool of yourself in Hampton Point. They have a big force, a rough one. It's a rich town and they got plenty of cops because they're afraid the migratory potato pickers might get out of hand in the summer. You go there and they'll laugh you out of town!"

He ran down the porch steps, and into the radio car. I leaned against the wall, watched the lights of the car disappear—wondered what to do next. For a second I was full of doubts ... But it *had* to be Pops. He was the "old goat," and for some reason he'd killed Barnes, then taken off. That accounted for the dummy up on the widow's walk. I'd seen the hands move this afternoon, but whose hands? On a hot day why would anybody, even a supposedly sick man, keep a hat over his face, a blanket on? Somehow Larry Anderson was in this, probably protecting Pops, maybe being blackmailed. It all fitted. Larry had seen me out on the bay this afternoon with the glasses, thought I was spying on Pops again, that I hadn't been taken in by the Nelson "suicide." So Larry told the "old goat." Or he and Pops could be in this together.

Hell, everybody in the Harbor might be in on this. Jane Endin hadn't been at the funeral, she only lived a few blocks from here, must know about mushrooms and herbs. She could be working with Pops, trying to scare me off. But off what? What possibly could be going on in this peaceful lousy hick burg that called for murder? I didn't know who did the other killings, but Matty had to be the work of Pops, whoever he was and wherever he was. That was why Larry had put his glasses on me this afternoon.

I either had to pack up Andy and Bessie, get away from here at once, or if I stayed, I had to solve it before anything happened to them. And I had to do it alone—me, the do-it-yourself detective. Maybe I was being an old fool, but I just couldn't run.

I went inside and dumped every bit of food I could find—the stuff in the icebox along with sugar, salt, cereals—in the garbage can. Even the toothpaste. Some flies were on Matty. I rummaged around until I found an empty hatbox and put Matty in it. I carefully wrapped the box in aluminum foil, tied it securely with fishline, then put the package in his wicker basket. I scrubbed the tabletop, threw out the cleanser and a box of soap powder.

There was a clam rake in the back of the house. I took it down the road to an empty field, buried Matty. It took me a long time to dig the grave and it was very dark when I finished. There couldn't be a doubt in my mind now, I was sweating drops of pure anger.

I dropped into the Johnsons where everybody stared at me as if seeing the village idiot—maybe because I was still carrying the clam rake. Bessie asked if I wanted supper. I said no and took her aside, whispered about the toadstool and that I had thrown out all the food in the house.

"I can't understand how one possibly got in. I can easily recognize a toadstool when I ..."

"Never mind that now; you didn't do a thing. Just keep quiet about it and spend the night here."

Mr. Johnson, a character with a big belly and lard shoulders, boldly assured me he would most certainly ... "look after Bessie and the child ..." meaning Bessie had let her big mouth go.

Everybody talked in hushed tones, as if not to excite me. I told Bessie I had buried Matty, not to worry if I didn't return that night. I asked for Jerry's address.

"What do you want his address ... for?" she started to ask. But something in my face stopped her and she said in a loud whisper, "He lives on Belmont Lane. Not far away. Matt, be careful."

"Don't worry about me. And remember, don't leave this house."

I stopped at our cottage for my gun, feeling the silence of the house, before starting for Jerry's place. I suppose it wasn't far at that, the whole Harbor wasn't much, but I kept walking in circles until I asked a couple of people and finally found this one-block side street with the ritzy name. In the dark all I could see was a small house set in a large garden. I lit a match to read a crude TAXI sign nailed to a small fence. He wasn't home. The garage was empty, too. I wondered where he was.

But it didn't matter much, I'd wanted to ask what he knew about Pops. And borrow his car—see if I could get any help and ammo from the Hampton Point police. But Roberts was probably right. If I walked in and told them I was gunning for a killer, that the Nelson thing was a setup ... all because my cat was dead ... they'd laugh me into a straitjacket. These village cops, washing each other's hands. I had to play it alone.

I headed for the bay, walking across the harbor. Through the open doors and windows I saw everybody in their houses, silently watching TV, and maybe nibbling at a bottle. Crazy yokels who never went to a big city, maybe never to another village unless they had to.

Cutting across Main Street, I walked toward the water down a narrow street I'd never been on before. To my surprise next to a boat and bait place I found a small store still open. It was a tiny shop, the downstairs of a house, and seemed to stock a little bit of everything. I wanted a flash and also I was very hungry. A fat woman with wispy gray hair and wearing a bag of a dress waddled out of a back room, asking, "Yes, sir, what can I do for you?"

I bought an expensive light, the only kind she had, glad she hadn't cracked about my being a sure sign of summer. I ate a candy bar as I went over to a basket of fresh vegetables, felt of the string beans and cabbages—like I knew what I was doing, asked if they were local produce.

"Only the potatoes and tomatoes. Be more truck vegetables in a week or two. Long Island potatoes ain't much this year."

Over a bottle of soda I listened to a speech about what the local potato growers did wrong, how expensive the California and North Carolina crops were. I had a hunk of over-sweet cake before she mentioned Anderson, said he went into Patchogue for vegetables three times a week. I said, "I've seen his truck around. New one. He must be making out pretty well."

"He's always cheerful. Joy to have that man around. And once you're straight with him, he's easy on credit. Frankly, I don't know how Larry does it; he can't meet the supermarket's prices. I used to sell four or five baskets of fruits and vegetables a day during the summer. Now I'm lucky to sell that much a week. Had anything else to do, at my age, I'd give up the store. I order less and less from Larry, but I suppose he does better in the other towns."

"This Anderson lives with his father, doesn't he? Old man

they call Pops?"

"That's not his daddy," the fat lady said, getting up steam. For ten minutes she told me what a wonderful man Larry was, how Pops wasn't "even a relation," merely an old friend, but Larry couldn't have treated him any better "if the old man had been his father." It also seemed that Pops was a wonderful man, always full of jokes and willing to help out; sometimes he brought her fish.

End Harbor was simply full of "wonderful" men and women—when they weren't killing or getting killed. The storekeeper went on to tell me how active Larry was in the city council, had organized a Scout troop—only there weren't enough kids interested. Pops was busy in the various cake sales and used to sell chances for the annual Legion car raffle—up till last year when his arthritis got real bad. I paid her and left in the middle of a speech about the younger generation.

I walked down to the beach, along the shore toward the spot where Andy and I had landed a couple days ago.

I had company, a big Irish setter tagged along behind me. I threw some stones for him to chase and when I reached Larry's property I shooed the dog away. Climbing the bank I saw a light in the kitchen of Anderson's house. I walked carefully through the rough grass until I reached the garage. The doors were open, the truck standing inside, and the concrete floor was wet. Stepping inside I covered the flash with my hand and turned on the light. All I saw were stacks of empty wooden crates and bushel baskets. On the truck there were crates of lettuce and fruit, all recently watered down. Everything was neat and businesslike. I don't know what I expected to find but I didn't find a damn thing. There was an outboard in one corner, on a rack, a ...

I heard a sound outside the garage and froze, my hand sneaking toward the gun inside my belt—until I remembered it was empty. Somebody was walking around the outside of the garage, walking softly. I heard them come to the door as I strained to see in the darkness. The padding sound came directly toward me, despite the fact I was hidden behind a pile of peach crates. A moment later there was a small whine and the cold muzzle of my buddy, the dog, touched my hand. I was so relieved I nearly giggled as I whispered, "Beat it, boy."

It must have seemed a caressing sound to him for the big son-of-a-bitch put his paws on my chest and tried to lick my face. I pushed him away and he hit one of the stacks of empty crates—which came down with all the thunder in the world. I ran out of the garage, knocking over more boxes, headed for the beach. I heard a door slam and then heavy steps as a flashlight sliced the darkness. I kept running as fast as I could, bent low and zigzagging, my breathing harsh. I hit a rut, or some damn thing, and went sliding on my face and chest in the heavy grass. The air was knocked out of me, the lousy gun in my waist felt like it had gone through my stomach. I lay there, sobbing for breath, wondering if I'd busted my store teeth. The heavy footsteps came closer and I clamped a hand over my open mouth to muffle my breathing.

The night was split with the roar of a shotgun blast, followed by a tiny, unreal scream.

The footsteps approached slow, cautiously. I pulled my gun from out of my stomach—a bluff was better than nothing. Then some fifteen feet to my right a flash snapped on and I saw Anderson, shotgun in work-gloved hands, bending over. He raised the bloody remains of the Irish setter by one leg, the head resting on the ground. Anderson remained bent over like that for a few minutes, an odd smile on his thick face. It could have been a smile of relief or of sorrow. I wondered what he was doing ... he seemed to be listening to the night. Then I knew he was waiting to see if the sound of the shot brought anybody on the run.

I was as flattened to the ground as I could get. I was scared outright silly—he hadn't known it was a dog he was shooting at. And I was impressed by the gloves touch—Anderson believed in being prepared—fingerprints must have been uppermost in his mind at all times.

Satisfied no one was coming, he dropped the dog and walked back to the garage, the light bouncing ahead of him. The fall had knocked my own flash from my hand and I didn't try to find it, but crawled toward the beach like a frightened snake, thankful I hadn't broken any real bones or false teeth. When I heard Larry returning I played dead in the grass again, grateful I could still play at it. He held the gun in his right hand, a shovel in his left. Dragging the dog farther away from me, he sent the light dancing around—trying to decide where to dig, then finally dug a deep grave and buried the mutt. It was a rough night in the Harbor for animals.

It took him almost an hour and all that time I was flat in the damp grass, fighting gnats and watching his powerful movements. He was sure a strong clown. One thing was for certain: my theory about Pops being out of the house, that dummy on the widow's walk, was right. If the old man was sick in the house with a bad ticker Anderson sure wouldn't be blasting a shotgun on the grounds. And if Pops had been hiding in the house, the gun blast would have brought him out. He was probably on the run for killing Barnes and Nelson. But theory wasn't worth its salt unless I found the motive. If I went to Roberts he would stall me with his Anderson-is-a-big-citizen kick. I might try the Riverside or Hampton Point police, but I'd have to come up with more than I had. Suppose Pops wasn't home—what did that *prove?* Pops and this Anderson were doing something shady and the only way I could get a lead on them would be to find out everything about Anderson and his too prosperous business.

When Anderson returned to his house I got up and walked stiffly along the beach, then over to Jerry's house. He was still out and I stood on his porch, wondered again where he could be. There was a light in the house across the way and I saw a shadow behind the curtain. That would be nosey Mrs. Bond.

I crossed the street and the shadow disappeared. I rang her bell and a moment later this little old lady opened the door. I said, "Mrs. Bond, I'm ..."

"I know," she squeaked, her beady eyes bright and a faint whiff of port clinging to her words, "You're that secret service man."

"You know where Jerry went?"

"Oh, my, what's he done now?"

"He hasn't done a damn thing, I ..."

"See here, young man, don't raise your voice to me."

"I ... uh ... wanted to hire his car, taxi me to the station," I said, almost floored by that "young man."

"I haven't the slightest idea where he is. He drove away in the middle of the afternoon and hasn't been back since. You were here before, weren't you?"

"Yeah. If he returns soon, tell him I'd like to see him."

"If you think I have nothing better to do than watch for that—that foreign devil to come home ..."

"You've been watching him for years, what's a few more hours?" I said, walking away. I walked across the Harbor till I reached our cottage; suddenly kept walking. Jane Endin's car was in the driveway and two of her windows were lit. I worked the arrowhead knocker. When she opened the door she looked different—much younger. Some of the tenseness was gone from her face, her eyes rested. She was wearing a mannish sport shirt and jeans, the pants full of paint stains. I said, "Hello," and she nodded, asked, "Mr. Lund, what has happened to you now, or do you always dress this sloppy?"

I looked down—hadn't realized my pants and shirt were streaked with grass and dirt stains. "Seems I had another accident."

"Be careful, you may be accident-prone. Come in. Like to wash up? Your face is dirty."

She took me to the bathroom, and as we passed through the living room I saw her latest work standing on an easel. It seemed to be a picture of a rough sea but the water was a violent red, the wave-caps a terrible purple, and the sky a dead, sickly green. At least it wasn't a picture you forget quickly.

The bathroom fixtures were bulky and ancient. I washed, drying my face and hands on toilet paper—the towels looked like they'd never been used. For a second I glanced at the big bathtub with envy, then went back to the living room.

I stared at the new painting and she asked, "Do you like it? Don't touch it, please, it's still wet."

"That's okay, I'm wearing gloves."

For a fast second her eyes seemed to harden, then she giggled—and for a moment she seemed about eighteen. "That's a wonderful joke."

"And very old. Yeah, I think I like it. It's the nightmare terror a rough sea can give you."

"Thank you, that's exactly what I had in mind. The other day, when I was staring at the sea all day ... it seemed so terribly ruthless. Since I decided not to go to Edward's funeral today, I worked hard on the painting to pass time. I'm glad Jerry is out. I knew he couldn't have done such a thing. Who is this Nelson, the man they say did it?"

"I never saw him. Did you?"

She shook her head as we sat down opposite each other. She lit a cigarette, started to hand me the pack, said, "But you smoke a pipe. I'm sorry about what happened to your cat."

"Who told you?" I patted my pockets; my pipe was some place in Anderson's field. It was a damn good piece of briar, too. I reached over and took one of her cigarettes.

"I have *Newsday* delivered here every afternoon, and the boy told me. First time I ever heard of anybody making a mistake about toadstools. Lucky it was only the cat."

"Yeah, *only* a cat. And it was a mistake all right, a big one," I said slowly, wondering if I'd be booting things by taking her into my confidence. I had a hunch Jane was completely straight, still these Harbor people were all hard to make. Any horse player knows a hunch addict is a fool, but I couldn't waste any more time. And I couldn't go it alone. I took the plunge. "You see, now I'm sure I know the real killer."

"Killer? You think somebody killed your cat?"

"I *know* the louse who killed my cat also murdered Doc Barnes and this Nelson."

She jumped a little, went pale. "But I thought ...? That is, they are so sure; they said they found Edward's scarf on the dead man?"

"Forget Nelson for now. I think I know who killed the doc. But I don't know the motive, the reasons why, all the little things that will round out the full picture. I need your help for that."

"My help? I'll do anything to get Edward's killer, but ... but I hardly see how I can be of any help. What can I do?"

"You ..." I wiped tobacco crumbs from my lips. I never could smoke cigarettes, not even when I was sneaking a smoke on my post. "You can be a big help. I need background information about Pops. I want to know all about him. And about Larry Anderson."

"Not Larry. He's ..."

"Skip telling me what a community pillar he is. I'll give it to you from the shoulder—I think he and Pops are in some kind of racket. I've checked, and he's making too much dough from his vegetable business. Wait—let me talk for a second. Pops is supposed to be very sick—Anderson takes him up on the roof, that widow's walk, every day for the sun. I'm sure that's an act, with a dummy. I think Pops killed Barnes—but I don't know the motive, yet—and is in hiding. I was out on the bay this morning, with my field glasses. I believe Larry thought I was watching the house, that he told Pops, and my cat was killed to scare me off the case."

"Mr. Lund, do you realize what you're saying? It's ridiculous. Strong as he is, Larry has never struck anybody, not even in anger. As for Pops, why, he's a jolly, gentle old man. They're like father and son."

"Maybe. But Pops has to be the 'old goat' the doc was going to see after he left Jerry. And if Pops didn't kill the doc, he knows who did—that's why he's hiding. The point is, Larry isn't acting like he has a sick 'father' in the house, he's firing a shotgun like he's in a battle. Nor was my cat an accident—and it couldn't have been Nelson, he's dead. There's a lot of whys I have to answer, and maybe I'm all wet. But if I'm not, there's a killer loose. I need your help to see if I'm wrong."

"But Larry and Pops—they're the last two people in the

world I'd think of as ... killers."

"Will you help me, Miss Endin?"

"I simply can't believe they are crooks or ... even bad."

I crushed the damn cigarette in a clam shell ashtray. "Okay, you answer a few questions and convince me I'm wrong. Who is Pops? What's his full name?"

"I don't know his first name but his surname is Brown. Long as I can recall he was just called Pops, Pops Brown."

"Know where he came from?" Maybe Pops knew Nelson in California and they both had something on Barnes.

"No. Seems to me he was always around the Harbor, always an old man. When Mrs. Anderson was alive she needed a farm hand. Of course it really wasn't a farm, more of a truck vegetable patch. But it was plenty of work and she needed a part-time helper, or she'd have to take Larry out of school. Pops was working around: clam digging, potato picker, fixed up the roads—he helped Mrs. Anderson out in return for room and board. He's lived there ever since. When Larry started his wholesale business Pops helped him for a time, mostly on the raising end. But it became too much work for him. For the last couple of years, even though he was too old to work, Larry has taken care of him, treated him fine. Pops always has spending money."

"I bet," I said, wondering if maybe Larry was working for Pops. "Did Pops ever leave here, say for a few days or weeks at a time?"

"No."

"Doesn't anybody know where he came from? Has he any relations?"

"Pops is about the oldest person in town, all his pals have passed on. Guess there isn't anyone who knows much about him. I do know he sometimes has a friend or two, also old men, visiting him for a month or so."

"Any of Priscilla's family live around here?"

Jane shook her head.

"Did you ever see or hear of Jack Wiston?"

"No I think that's Priscilla's maiden name but her folks were all dead before I was born. Who is Jack Wiston?"

"Forget him, I'm crossing him off. Let's get back to Pops."

"Mr. Lund, you're terribly wrong about all this."

"I don't think so, there's too many phony angles about Pops, and Anderson. Larry's mother leave him any money?"

"Oh, no, they were always very poor."

"And from what you've told me Pops was a bum, so he didn't

have any. Anderson's post office job isn't much, he gets around $1500 a year. Yet he pays his bills promptly and with cash, his business is the only one in the Harbor that's able to buck the supermarket—why only Larry's?"

"I don't know, but if he was so rich, why would he keep the mailman job? Also, Larry doesn't deal only in the Harbor. He serves a number of stores from Patchogue out to Montauk. Most of these other towns haven't any supermarkets."

"Is Anderson the only wholesale produce man in these parts?"

"In End Harbor, but I'm pretty sure there are others around. Of course there are, the Henderson boy works for one in Hampton, come to think of it."

"So we have a lot of two-bit stores and competition for their trade, but for some reason Anderson is rolling in dough—the new truck, station wagon, top credit rating, well-kept house. I think he has too much money, more than his business can account for. In both his jobs, mailman and trucker, he gets around. Could he and Pops be in some kind of racket, like the numbers, or making a book?"

She smiled. "You don't know Larry."

"That's why I need your help, I want to know all about him. I don't seem to know anybody in the Harbor. Yesterday you told me he'd made some ... passes at you. Yet now you're defending him."

"Not defending him but trying to have you understand how wrong you are about him. Larry was always a mama's boy. His father died when he was about eleven or twelve and Larry ..."

"How did he die?"

"Heart attack while clamming in the winter. They found his frozen body in the boat. I was just a kid then, but I think Edward was starting his practice and Larry's father was his first real case. I remember he had him stretched out on the dock, trying everything to revive him. You see, up until before the war, when factories started springing up in Hampton, and even in the Harbor, this was a very poor town. Everybody was on short rations. They clammed, fished, rented rooms, picked potatoes—in addition to whatever regular jobs they might have. My dad used to go out in his old leaky boat over the weekends at low tide and bring in a dozen bushels of clams. It's hard work and in those days brought in about ten dollars a weekend, more in the winter. Of course now they get as much as five dollars and six dollars a bushel, but the bay is pretty well cleaned out. It takes over fifteen years for a clam to grow and...." She shook her head, as if scolding herself. "I'm talking all around what you want to know—about Larry. He just lived to make money for his mother. Always was a hard worker; delivered papers, peddled berries in the summer, any odd job he could get. And of course he worked hard on their farm. He never had time for girls. Although he's about eight years older than I am, since there's only one school here, we knew each other—a little. Larry never had time for school games either. He was even deferred from the army on account of his mother being sickly and he was her sole support, but he was drafted when she died in '43. It was just before he went into the army he began seeing me."

"What does 'seeing me' mean exactly?"

"Not what you think," she said quickly. "We saw each other for a few weeks. He would take me driving—at night, to a movie—in some other town ... always careful we weren't seen together in the Harbor. One night he tried to paw me and that was the end of it. He even apologized afterwards, but I never saw him again, except on the street, of course. I imagine he was very lonesome. It was hard for the single men who weren't in the army, what with fathers being taken. I never cared for him and I resented his thinking he could ... you know ... just because I'm an Indian."

"Why hasn't Anderson married since his mother died? Has he any girlfriends?"

"None that I know of. I suppose he's married to his business, he works very hard at it. If you really think Pops and Larry are mixed up in this, that Pops is gone, why not ask Chief Roberts to look into it?"

"I don't trust him. Frankly, I don't trust anybody in the Harbor—except you. Everybody seems to be working hand in hand to cover up this mess."

"Why do you trust me, Mr. Lund?"

"I don't know why. I just do. When are you going back to work?"

"In a day or two. I'm still pretty jittery, even though I had a restful day, today."

"The main thing I'm lacking is the motive, the *why*, to all this. Anderson was around the house today, which means he should be out on his vegetable route tomorrow. I have this ... hunch, I guess, that his traveling around the countryside is the key to everything. It's the only thing he does different from anybody else in the Harbor. Maybe he has a couple of wives or gal friends stashed away, maybe he's peddling dope—that would tie him in with the doc. Most likely he has Pops hiding out someplace around here. I'd like to tail him tomorrow and I need a car. I busted up my son's. Can I borrow yours?"

"If he had anything to do with Edward's death, I'll not only let you have the car, I'll go along with you."

"I don't want to put you out," I said, full of suspicion again.

"I haven't anything else to do, and I know the countryside. But there's one condition: if you don't find anything to definitely prove that Pops is gone, what I mean is, if you're not absolutely sure, one way or the other, I want you to go to Chief Roberts, have him ask to see Pops."

"I'll buy that," I said, my suspicions melting—a little. "What time do we start?"

"Larry is usually at Patchogue by five A.M. Sometimes when I'm too nervous to sleep I take long rides during the early morning hours, before going to work. I enjoy driving in the dawn fogs. I often see him leave his house at four A.M. That's when we should start, too."

"Good," I said, getting up, thinking of the dizzy young thing in the Hampton watch factory. Driving seemed to be a psychiatrist's couch out here. "I'll call for you at three- thirty."

Jane got up slowly, seemed to stretch. "It will save time if I pick you up in front of your cottage."

"Okay. I live at ..."

"I know where you live, Mr. Lund."

I said that would be fine and stopped to look at her painting again. Standing beside me, she asked, "Would you like to have it?"

"Well ... I'd like to buy it," I said as if I bought paintings every day. "How much?"

"That's being silly. If you want it, I'll give it to you."

"I do want it. Thank you."

"It should be dry in a day or two. I'll have it framed and ready before you leave the Harbor. I'm glad you want one of my works."

Walking back to the cottage I was confused. For no reason except my instinct, which I didn't trust, I was taking Jane into my confidence. But I didn't like the business of her going with me, began to doubt who was actually tailing who. And it was odd she knew where I lived. Still, it was a small village, she would know ... maybe.

It was after eleven and I stopped at the Johnsons to tell Bessie I'd spend the night in her cottage. Mr. Johnson was playing solitaire on the kitchen table, said, "Bessie and Andy went home about an hour ago. It's all right, their ..."

I ran out of the house and sprinted for the cottage as if I were a kid. I came busting into the place, puffing like a whale and there was Danny grinning nervously at me. I fell into a chair as I tried to ask, "What are you doing here?"

"Take it slow, Matt. Man your age shouldn't be racing down the street. Anybody chasing you?" I noticed he had the kid's baseball bat leaning against a chair.

I shook my head. "Where's Bessie and Andy?"

"Sleeping. They've had a big day. I happened to get some time off, thought I'd make it a long weekend, be with you."

"Cut the slop, Danny, Bessie phoned you to come."

He came over and sat on the arm of my chair. "Yes. She's worried about you, Matt. Dad, I've always looked up to you as a man with plenty of good old common sense—so tell me one thing and I'll be quiet—are you sure you're not going off the deep end on Matty's death?"

"Matty's death got me angry but it didn't make me hysterical, if that's what you mean. I'm not going off half-cocked. Before I was kind of playing at solving this murder, now I'm serious. I think I know what I'm doing."

He slapped me on the back lightly. "Okay, Dad. What can I do to help you?"

"Stay with Bessie and Andy every minute of the day tomorrow. Don't frighten them, go to the beach and all the other things you usually do, but don't let them out of your sight. Having that bat around isn't a bad idea, either. I'm going to set the alarm and sleep on the porch because I have to be up in a few hours. I'll be gone most of tomorrow."

He wanted to ask where I was going, but didn't. He pointed at my clothes. "Been in a fight?"

"Nope, merely crawling on the grass. Now stop worrying. Tomorrow I'm only going riding, to see some of the other towns. With a woman. No danger."

"This Indian sex-boat Bessie told me about?"

"Sex-boat? I ought to fan Bessie's.... Go to sleep, Dan, and let me work things out in my own way."

"Hungry? I have tea on and ..."

"Where did you find food here?" I shouted.

"Easy, Dad. Bessie told me over the phone that you'd thrown out everything, so I brought some down with me. Hungry?"

I nodded.

I washed up, had a cup of tea and a few sandwiches, made up the porch cot, set the alarm. I didn't need a clock to wake me—I never went to sleep. I listened to the country noises, and thought of nothing and everything. I was bushed but my mind kept spinning like a top. Mostly I lay there waiting—waiting for something to happen. I had this feeling I was in way over my head, had dragged Dan and his family in, too. I wanted bullets for my gun, I wanted Roberts at least working with me ... and most of all, I wished I was back in the precinct, had the platoon with me.

In the quiet I couldn't kid myself any longer—as a cop I didn't have much confidence in me. I was goddamn frightened.

Chapter 7

I got up at three and turned off the alarm. I must have slept a few winks, I felt rested, although my mind was still down in the dumps. I washed and shaved, careful not to make any noise. When I came out of the bathroom I found Bessie at the stove. She had a robe over her baby dolls, but the robe was open and gave her a very *deshabille* effect. "Coffee, Matt?" she whispered.

"What are you doing up?"

"I've always been a light sleeper. Danny and Andy—take a bomb to wake them."

"What did you have to send for Dan for?"

"You have me worried, Matt. Danny says you're going out with this Jane Endin today. Any danger?"

I laughed. "That's what you've wanted, me to take her out. No danger, we're merely going around and asking a few questions."

"So early in the morning?"

"Okay, take me off the witness stand. Can you make some of that thick Turkish coffee? It will stay with me awhile."

"Certainly. How about toast, eggs?"

"Just coffee."

I went into my room and watching the sleeping boy, I hid my empty gun. The kid had a big knife in his fishing box, but I didn't know much about using a knife.

I was sipping a tiny cup of the thick, soupy coffee when a car pulled up outside. I went out and asked Jane if she wanted coffee. The dim light from the dashboard hit the planes of her face at an odd angle, making it look like a long soft mask. She was wearing slacks, a tight white blouse with a big jade pin at the neck, and a short suede jacket. The tightness of the blouse said she was a bigger woman than I'd imagined. She hesitated, then said she would take a cup. We walked to the house and I introduced her to Bessie—for a second they looked each other over like pugs listening to the ref's instructions. Jane drank her coffee in silence, and drank it fast. Then she stood up, told Bessie, "I never had anything like that before. It's very good. Thank you." She turned to me. "It's getting late." She walked toward the door, the odd, stiff-legged walk, her thick braid doing a saucy dance on her back.

I put on Danny's too-big windbreaker, told Bessie I'd probably be back in the afternoon but not to worry if it was later. Bessie put her lips to my ear and whispered a single word:

"Wow!"

As we drove toward Riverside and Patchogue the sky was bright with pale stars and the road spotted with fog pockets. Jane was a good driver, real good. After a while she said, "Your daughter-in-law is a very attractive woman. It must be a joy to have children, visit with them."

"I don't know. After kids grow up they should stay out of their parents' way, and vice versa. I don't think they want to be bothered with an old man. And I didn't want to come out here. I have a better time alone in the city."

"That's a strange thing to say."

"Why? I'm old, set in my ways, and I know it. Next week I have to go up to the mountains to see my daughter Signe and her kids. It's a routine. Another crowded, noisy cottage. I won't get any rest there and neither will Signe."

"The fortunate are not always aware of their fortune."

I didn't know if that was supposed to be an old Indian saying or not, and didn't ask. "Shouldn't we see if Anderson has pulled out with his truck?"

"He's left. We'll pick him up at Patchogue. He never makes any stops until he starts back. He'll return to the Harbor by nine, then take out his station wagon to deliver the mail. About ten-thirty he'll pick up his truck, head out toward Montauk."

My mind began to wrinkle with doubts as I wondered how often Jane had tailed Anderson before—or driven with him?

"That was an odd coffee Mrs. Lund served. I hear she makes an interesting wine pudding."

I turned and stared at her. "How did you know that?"

"Just heard it."

"Hasn't anybody in the Harbor anything to do but snoop on ...?" I saw her face tighten up and added. "What I mean, exactly how does this village gossip work?"

"Very simple. Mrs. Lund asked Charley, who has the store as you turn into Main Street, for grapes, said she was going to mash them. Naturally he asked why and she told him about the wine pudding. I happened to be in the store later in the afternoon when he was repeating the recipe to some other woman. Don't people talk to each other in New York?"

"I suppose so, but there's so many people it's hard to tell."

The roads were empty and she kept the car at fifty, only slowing down as we went through Riverside, and as we neared Patchogue an hour later, in a lot of truck traffic.

It was starting to turn light as she pulled up before some old buildings, nodding down the street. There were lights on in a warehouse beside a railroad siding, and several trucks were backed up to a loading platform. Anderson was watching two colored men loading his neat truck.

"What do we do now?"

"Wait," I said, reaching into a pocket for my lost pipe and a notebook. I borrowed one of her cigarettes as I wrote down the name of the wholesaler and the time. Jane sat there, staring at nothing; she made me uneasy. I couldn't entirely lose the feeling I was walking into a trap.

At six forty-eight, the day starting bright and sunny, Anderson headed back toward the Harbor. I nudged her knee, told her not to stay too close. If I'd had my wits about me, I would have brought the glasses along. But there were more cars on the road and it wasn't any trick tailing the big green truck. Anderson drove some twenty miles before he stopped at a village of two stores; a hardware shop and a general store. The owner of the general store helped Larry unload a few crates of stuff. Although we were parked behind a bend down the road, I could make out a kind of mild argument—the storekeeper evidently wanted Anderson to take back a small basket of tomatoes. Finally Anderson was paid and drove off.

I made a note of the store and time, told Jane to drive on. She asked, "I thought you were going to talk to the man in the store?"

"We'll return later. You know Anderson's route, don't you?"

"No. From here on he'll make a lot of stops. Suppose you get out and talk to this man, while I follow Larry? Takes him five or ten minutes at each stop, and when I find where he's stopping, I'll come back and get you."

"We can return here later in the day...."

"I'd like to get this over quickly. I don't like spying on people."

"But suppose we lose him?"

"Island's so narrow here if we cruised about for ten minutes, we'd run into him," Jane said, opening the door for me.

There wasn't anything for me to do but get out. I told her, "If you don't see me when you come back, honk your horn twice. And park a ways down from the store." She nodded and drove off. I knew I was making a rock play. Why had she practically put me out of the car? Was she warning Larry? But she could have done that last night, or refused to come with me, or give me her car.

The storekeeper was a pudgy Italian, or maybe a Syrian, with a very straight large nose and dark eyes. He was opening a crate of melons, feeling each one, as I walked in. I bought a corncob pipe and some tobacco. He gave me the, "Now I know summer is really here, seeing you. Stopping at the Fan Tail Hotel, sir?"

"No, I'm staying at End Harbor, merely riding around this morning."

Giving the last melon a feel he took the bait, told me, "My vegetable man comes from there. You know Larry Anderson?"

"I've seen his truck. Hard worker."

"Kills himself three times a week, and of course he's the mailman, too. But in the winter he only makes a trip here once a week. Me, I stand on my feet all day long, winter and summer."

"I bet," I said, trying to turn the conversation around to something—and not knowing what "something" was. "Guess you know Pops is sick? Larry must have his hands full."

"I know. Larry takes good care of old man Watson. Tell you, you won't find many people these days giving a hoot about anybody else or.... Up early, Mrs. Kane."

A young woman customer was at the door. "I have the baby in the car, Joe. Give me a bottle of milk, package of bacon, two packs of cigarettes. Put it on my tab."

I waited until he had taken care of her, feeling excited. Then I asked, "Did you say Pops' name was Watson?"

"Sure."

"Of course I'm only down for a week, but my son knows him and I thought his name was Pops Brown?"

He shook his fat head. "Naw, not the old man living with Larry. Used to help him out. His name is John Watson, I know."

"I suppose you do, but I'd have sworn it was Brown."

"Well, you have him mixed up with somebody else."

I considered flashing my badge to get more dope, but tried talk. "I don't want to contradict you, mister, but I never forget a name. I'm sure it's Brown."

The storekeeper sighed. "Look, *I know*, every month I cash his Social Security check. John Watson—no middle name. For seven years I been cashing them every month. Mister, if I was on Social Security I'd sit for the rest of my life."

A horn honked twice outside. "None of my business, but why does ... eh ... Watson come all the way over here to cash his check?"

He shrugged. "Maybe he don't want the End Harbor bank to know his business. Maybe it's a habit—I started cashing the checks when old man Watson was helping Larry on the truck. Now—every month Larry brings me the check. It's for ... I don't even know why I'm telling you this, Larry always says he don't want people knowing his business. But like I said, that's how I'm sure his name is Watson."

The horn sounded again. "Guess you have me," I said, making for the door. "First time I've been wrong on a name in years."

"Always a first time for everything," the storekeeper said, opening another crate.

Jane's car was down the road. When she saw me she turned around and as I slid in beside her she said, "Larry's about seven miles from here, making a delivery to a roadside diner, having breakfast there. Learn anything?"

"I don't know. What did you say Pops' name was?"

"Brown."

"Are you positive?"

"Certainly. Why?"

"Nothing, I couldn't remember it. We'll wait until Larry leaves the diner then do the same thing—you go on to the next stop, come back for me."

The diner was a fancy chrome job at a road intersection, and seemed too imposing for the orange juice I ordered. I said I noticed Anderson's truck leaving, were these his oranges? The place wasn't busy and the counterman bent my ear explaining how all juices come canned these days and what a great timesaver it was. I had to order another juice before I could turn the talk around to Pops. But he only knew Pops as Pops.

Jane returned to tell me Anderson was at a store a dozen miles away. At this store and the next one, as I stocked up on tobacco, and cigarettes for Jane, I found out nothing. One storekeeper was a newcomer, the other knew Pops, but had no idea of his last name. I was beginning to think the first storekeeper had been batty, when at a few minutes before eight we stopped at a small store outside Riverside, several minutes after Larry pulled out. The store was run by a skinny Jewish woman who insisted Pops' name was Robert Berger. When I started my polite argument about having a memory for names, she cut me off with: "Mister, I don't like to contradict a customer, especially you, for now I know the summer has started well, but on this I'm sure. Berger himself wanted it."

"Wanted what?"

"When he was driving around with Larry, years ago, he personally asked me to cash his Social Security check. I remember, it was the first time I'd known the old man's name and I asked if he was Jewish—a name like Berger. He told me he was part Jewish on his mother's side. Tell you the truth, I admire Larry for being nice to the old man, all this time, even though they're of different religions. And every month Berger insists Larry bring his check here for me to cash," she said, proudly—I thought.

"Doesn't he trust the End Harbor banks?" I cornballed.

"Berger doesn't want his business mixed up with Larry's. That's smart, I say."

"I suppose so. Do you go into the Harbor to visit Berger often?"

"Me? Mister, I'm lucky to have time to read a book. My husband takes care of the chickens, I run the store, and any free time we have isn't for visiting—we rest."

"This Anderson certainly sounds like a good soul. Does he have many old men living with him?"

"Look, he isn't running a hotel. Just Pops Berger, and believe me if others looked after their old workers the way Larry does, this would be a better world."

I said it would; wanted to add it would be a world full of cemeteries.

Anderson made a fast stop in Riverside and Jane told me, "Now he'll go home, leave his truck, and take out the mail for an hour. Shall we follow his mail route?"

"No, that would be too obvious, a store is a public place, a home isn't. Let me talk to the guy in this Riverside store."

I bought some bacon and eggs and learned nothing—the storekeeper vaguely remembered Pops—but as Pops.

Back in the car I asked Jane. "How often do you go to these little villages we've stopped at?"

"Never. I don't know anybody there."

"Do the people in these villages, the storekeepers, do they come to End Harbor much?"

"Of course not. They might go into Riverside or Patchogue at times, to the bigger stores, once in a while. Like on Christmas. What's the bacon and eggs for?"

"I had to buy something. Thought we might have breakfast at your place, then pick up Anderson when he starts on his route again."

"Worried about taking me into a restaurant?"

I heaved the package of eggs and bacon out the open window. She stopped the car, got out and pulled the drippy package of bacon from the mess, wrapped it in the remains of the paper bag, slid back in the car. As we drove on she said, "Waste is stupid."

"So was that crack of yours. Stop at any diner or restaurant you wish."

"I'd rather make us breakfast," she said. And I didn't make any remarks about understanding women—even to myself.

We put away a healthy snack of blueberry pancakes and coffee, although I'd eaten so much junk at the stores I had to force myself. When we finished she said, "You look tired, lay down while I do the dishes."

I said I was okay, helped dry the few dishes. She didn't talk for a time, then she asked, "Well, do you think we're getting anyplace?"

"Yeah. I'm not absolutely sure yet, but I think we've stumbled on the key to the whole mess."

"You still believe Pops has run away? Do you know where he is?"

"I think Pops is dead."

She spun away from the sink, her hands falling to her side. Even her braid jumped. "Dead?"

"Maybe murdered."

"What did we see today that could possibly make you think that? I mean, I can't believe it. Pops murdered, why it's ..."

I said, "I don't actually know how he died. Could be Barnes killed him. Or ..."

"That's crazy!"

"Miss Endin, I said I wasn't sure yet. Until I am, let's not argue about it. I don't want to blow holes into a half-formed idea."

"All right." The surprising thing was she didn't talk about it again. At ten o'clock we started shadowing Anderson once more. His route took him all the way out to Montauk. After a time I didn't bother to stop at all the stores Larry serviced—the pattern was easy to follow: Social Security checks under various names, eight that I'd been able to find, were cashed each month but always at a store twenty or thirty miles away from the other. Although Hudon hadn't been among the names.

At a few minutes after three we were back in Jane's home, and Anderson's truck was in his garage. Jane insisted upon fixing lunch and I told her, "I'm sure of the motive now. Anderson and Pops had a Social Security racket going for them. Pops was getting checks under eight different names, besides his own, and maybe more that we haven't found out. Anderson has the perfect setup for cashing them, the storekeepers, miles apart, who know Pops under his various names. In fact, Pops himself cashed the checks when he was working, then Larry took it from there when the old guy retired. As you said, there's little chance of the store owners meeting each other, checking on Pops' names."

"Where did Edward fit into this?"

"Here's what I think: Larry was away that Sunday night. The doc got a call from Jerry and then Nelson dropped in to find out about his old buddy, who'd sent him a card from End Harbor. Now, as Barnes was about to leave he got another call—from the 'old goat.' That had to be Pops, who must have felt sick—or maybe Larry was threatening him, over what I don't know, but you can never tell when the crooks will fall out. The point is, I think, the doc found Pops dead and Larry then killed Barnes."

"But why? I can't believe he'd kill Edward."

"If I'm right, he not only killed him but did it up the street, so you'd be blamed."

"Me?"

"Of course, you should have been the number one suspect. But Larry didn't know about Jerry yelling at the doc. Jerry was picked up instead and of course it didn't matter to Anderson."

"But suppose Pops is—did—die? He was an old man, why kill Edward?"

"Way I see it, Larry wanted to continue this Social Security racket and for that he had to have a *live old man*. Once the word went around Pops was dead, he couldn't cash any more checks, no matter what names he used. Let's say Pops had a heart attack and Barnes got there before Larry—Anderson had to think fast, if he killed Barnes and kept up the line that Pops was sick, *but still alive*, his racket could continue for another few months, or years. Even if he supposedly sent Pops to a sanatorium out of the Harbor, he could have Pops lingering for another year or so, keep on cashing the checks. My idea is Anderson had to think fast, so he switched the devil for the witch, as the old saying goes, killed Barnes."

Jane sat on a kitchen chair hard, seemed to fall down on it. She lit a cigarette. "I still can't believe it. This sixty dollars a month, or whatever you get on Social Security, is that worth killing for?"

"I think you can get from thirty dollars to about one hundred and sixty dollars a month, depending on how high your salary was. Let's take an average, say each man was getting ninety dollars a month, and keep to the eight cases we know about—that's seven hundred and twenty dollars a month, over eight grand a year. If they've been doing it for, well, ten years, that adds up to over $80,000. So it wasn't any penny ante scheme. And you see how it all fits—explains Anderson's ready money—not enough dough to shout about, but to quietly repair the house, buy a new truck, pay bills quickly. He undoubtedly has a bundle hidden some place."

"I don't know, Mr. Lund, I simply can't believe it. For one thing, how would Pops be eligible for all these checks under different names? He couldn't have held jobs under those names for any length of time. I mean, he's always worked in and around the Harbor."

"Wait up, Jane, you still don't get it. Remember, if Larry did kill Barnes, then it had to be a hell of a cold-blooded killing, for Barnes was his good friend and Anderson was murdering merely to continue his racket for another few months, or a year. But then it would take a cool killer to strangle my cat, to shoot a dog, and certainly to gun Nelson. Know what makes a cold-blooded killer? Only one thing: practice!"

"I still don't.... What are you getting at?"

"The perfect deal he and Pops had. Larry's place is on the edge of town, surrounded by high trees. You told me Pops sometimes had friends, other old men, out at the house. Did you, or anybody else, ever see any of them leave?"

"But I'd hardly know when they came or went. His house is out of the way and ..." She suddenly froze, her mouth wide open with horror.

"I walked across his ground on Monday, came in unexpectedly from the bay, and he threw a gun at me and Andy. Know why? We were walking on his private cemetery!"

"*Eight murders?*"

"At least. Ever read about the Bluebeard killings—the French guy who married a score of widows and killed them for their money? This is the same idea, but using men."

I felt so excited I got up and started walking around the

kitchen. Jane kept following me with her eyes, her long face sickly. Finally she said, "But to ... to ... kill so many ...?"

"After they knocked off one man ... you know the line: they could only get the chair once. I don't know how they lured the old men to the farm, but I can make a damn good guess," I said, talking aloud to myself, to get things straight in my own mind. "Here's Larry, a single man in a small town. He can't marry—a wife would get on to his racket. Okay, he's young and healthy, must see a woman some place. Has plenty of time on his hands, especially after the summer months. Suppose he drives into Jamaica, New York, Long Beach, hangs around bars to pick up babes. Okay, during the years he also has met a lot of lonely old men hanging around the bars. Be a snap to strike up a beer conversation, find eight who are not only getting Social Security, but who are *alone* in the world. Larry sells them on his big house in the country, maybe Pops goes along on these recruiting jobs, asks the other old guy to come out and keep him company, all for free. When did Larry's mother die?"

"In 1943." Jane whispered.

"They've had well over a dozen years to take their time, pick at least eight victims. They lure an old-timer out and once he starts getting his checks, a matter of weeks, they knock him off. Who would know? No relatives, and the guy probably sticks to the grounds for the first few weeks. So a Social Security check for a ... Robert Berger keeps coming promptly every month. Pops has already set up the storekeeper, in this case the one near Riverside, to cash it for him—and keep cashing them. Except for Pops dying this racket could have gone on for years, in almost perfect safety."

"Somehow I still can't believe it. Doesn't the Social Security board ever check to see if a person is still living?"

"Frankly I don't know. I think a person has to file a yearly report if they continue working. Seems to me the earnings can't be above a certain figure. I'll find out. But in this case the men weren't working, so the only way Washington would know they had died would be when the checks were returned, the envelopes marked DECEASED, and ... Lord, Lord!"

"What is it?" Jane asked, sitting up.

"Merely thinking what a really perfect deal Larry has—he's the postman! I'm sure on the first of every month, or whenever the checks are due, little Larry is in the post office early, boxing up the mail like mad—making sure nobody notices the checks, taking them out when he starts delivering the mail. Of course, that explains Nelson's death."

"I'm bewildered. What does it explain?"

"Now listen: Nelson's story—according to Roberts—was that an old buddy of his had sent him a card from the Harbor. This guy named Hudon. Nelson assumes he's living here, perhaps he'd said so on the card. I'll bet folding money this Hudon was one of the old men killed on Anderson's place, only he got the card off without their knowing it. Okay, Nelson happens to come East, decides to look up his friend. No Hudon. He went to Barnes because his pal Hudon was sickly and Barnes is the only doc. Barnes can't help him, he never heard of Hudon. Nelson asks Roberts, the police chief, who also isn't any help. But who would Roberts send Nelson to, who of all people in the Harbor would know if a man named Hudon had ever lived here? *Anderson the mailman!*" I pounded the table like a debater, delighted with myself.

"Nelson must have given Larry a bad turn, but by this time Anderson has already killed Doc, and somehow still has his scarf. Maybe Nelson doesn't take a fast 'no,' maybe he's asking around too much. Or, because I'm sticking my big nose into the thing, Larry feels Jerry won't even come up for trial and by now the 'accident' is no longer an accident. Larry's in a small sweat. All right. Probably Nelson left a forwarding address in case Anderson should hear about Hudon. Nelson's in Hampton Point. Our boy Larry has to get out from under fast—he remembers the scarf, finds Nelson and kills him with his own gun, the suicide touch. How lucky our Larry seemed, Nelson packing a rod! He leaves the doc's scarf in Nelson's car and Roberts—he swallows the hook, again!"

Jane shook her head. "Edward only wore one scarf, a worn one I gave...." Her voice died to a painful whisper, then came alive as she said, "This is all a nightmare, a murder factory here in the Harbor."

"What better place than a sleepy village? Actually, the only bad mistake Anderson made was killing my cat. Yeah, hadn't been for that, I would have forgot things."

"Mr. Lund, this just can't be true. I can't picture Larry doing all these ... murders."

"Why not? As I told you, you can only burn once."

Jane said slowly, "It's so hard to think of somebody you once knew as a killer. It's an insult to your memory. Well, what do we do now?"

"We could call in Roberts, or the Federal men," I said, not quite certain what I wanted to do. I suppose deep in my mind I had the idea of taking Larry solo—but I was too old for that.

Truth is, I'd probably never been that young. I told myself to stop being a fool, not let my anger over Roberts refusing to do anything about Marty blind my better judgment.

She said, "If Larry is such a monster, we have to put an end to this at once. I think we should get Art Roberts, demand to see Pops."

"Yeah, that's what we should do. But he'll kick like a mule on reopening his nice little neat case, arresting a pillar of the community."

"No, murder is a serious thing, even in the Harbor. Want to phone him from here or shall we go downtown?"

That "downtown" forced me to grin. I said we could phone. When I got Roberts on the phone I told him, "Come out to Miss Endin's house at once—I have something for you."

"Again? What is it this time, a dead clam? I'm busy with ..." The light sarcasm in his voice changed abruptly as he asked, "Jeez, not Jane Endin?"

I didn't want to talk much on the phone, maybe the operator was Anderson's cousin or something. "Look, Roberts, I'm waiting exactly five minutes. If you're not out by then I'm making another call and there will be a flock of tourists in the Harbor, all of them with Federal badges!" I hung up and winked at Jane, thinking what a ham I was. She stared back with solemn eyes, as usual.

I suddenly wondered what her life would have been like if she'd had a sense of humor. Or would she have ended up the village whore?

Roberts and his musical comedy uniform were planted in Jane's living room chair less than four minutes after I phoned. I briefed him on what I'd found and he rubbed his big hands together as he said flatly, "I don't believe that Larry Anderson would ..."

"I know, he's the salt of the earth. Roberts, it's a bit late for the chamber of commerce spiel. End Harbor is in for some messy publicity but that can't be helped. I want you to demand to see Pops Brown. You won't see him because he's buried in Larry's yard—I think."

"But for ... all those murders," he muttered, shaking his big head. "I can't bust into his house without a warrant, and if Pops is alive, I'll look...."

I know what he was thinking and for a second I felt sorry for the handsome slob: Larry was the village big shot and if Roberts crossed him and the case turned out to be a dud, Roberts wouldn't have the pretty uniform for long.

I said, "What have you got to worry about? If for nothing else, we have him dead to rights as a Social Security fraud. Don't stall me or I'll go over your head. Hell, Roberts, I'm giving you a break, letting you make the collar."

"Actually, all we know is he cashed some checks. Maybe people on his mail route gave them to him?" Roberts turned to Jane. "Did you hear these storekeepers say they cashed checks under different names?"

"No, I was in the car all the time, following Larry."

Roberts sprang to his feet—really *sprang*—and turned to me in triumph. "Then I've only your word for this whole ..."

The way the jerk towered over me made me angry.

"You want to question the storekeepers? Go ahead, I'll even you the addresses. But I'm phoning Washington in a minute and I'll give you odds they have somebody at Anderson's house before dark!"

Roberts shrugged his beefy shoulders and sighed like a guy about to ask the boss for a raise. "Okay, okay. I'll see Pops. But, Lund, if he's alive, if this turns out to be a rhubarb, I'll not only collar you as a public nuisance, but I'll work you over!"

"Cut the big talk, you're not a public hero yet. I'm going with you. Another thing, Anderson is shotgun happy, can you get a couple more of your men?" I nearly added, "If there are a couple more."

He sort of pulled himself erect and threw out his wide shoulders—all in one motion. "I can handle Larry."

He looked as if he could handle Floyd Patterson but looks don't stop bullets. "How about giving me some ammo, and I'll pack my gun?"

"No need, there won't be any gun play," he said sharply. "I know Larry ... why, I was trolling for blues with him only last week. And for all I know, you might be trigger-happy over that dumb cat of yours. You want to go, let's do it."

I didn't say another word, he was working up his courage and a push might have spooked him. We all walked out to the polished squad car and he told Jane, "This won't be any place for you."

"Yes, it is. Edward Barnes was my friend."

She said it with such quiet dignity Roberts glanced at her to tell her something; I motioned for her to get in.

Larry's truck and station wagon were parked in the driveway but he wasn't in sight. We walked up onto the porch and Roberts rang the bell. Roberts was sweating a bit, but only over fear of losing his job—the jerk hadn't loosened his gun in its holster. After a moment Anderson opened the door. He had his shirt off, the thick muscles under this thin T-shirt, and a towel in his hand. He said, "Hello, Jane, Artie, Lund. I'm just washing up. What's this, a delegation? Something up for the Harbor Council?"

"Larry," Roberts said, "I want to see Pops."

Anderson was good, nothing changed on his face—but I saw the great muscles of his arms stiffen. "You know Pops is very sick, he can't see anybody or be disturbed. Doctor's orders."

"What doctor?" I asked.

"The specialist in New York. Pops is sleeping right now. Everybody knows a person suffering from heart trouble needs absolute rest. What's this about?"

"I won't do a thing to harm Pops," Roberts said. "Let me see him, I won't awaken him."

"Pops couldn't have done anything, he's been in bed since ... Legally you have no right to bust into my house."

"Larry, don't put this on a legal basis," Roberts said softly. "I'm asking to see Pops, as a friend. You want me to ask as a police officer—I'll have to place you under arrest if you don't let me see Pops."

"Arrest? Artie, are you crazy?"

"Let me see Pops and I'll explain all this."

I smiled—Anderson hadn't bothered to even ask what the arrest would be for—he damn well knew! But he suddenly stepped back from the door, told us, "Come in, but don't make any noise."

Roberts went pale, hesitated. I walked past Anderson followed by Jane ... and then Roberts. We were in an old-type large living room, nicely furnished, everything neat and spotless, and impersonal. Larry started up the carpeted steps to the floor above. As we followed he turned, asked, "Is it necessary for all of you to come up? Any shock can mean Pops' life."

"We'll be very quiet, won't make as much noise as a shotgun killing an Irish setter. Only Roberts will take a look into Pops' room. All he wants to see is his face." I stressed the word "face." Roberts was so jittery he might be satisfied seeing a couple of pillows under a blanket.

Anderson stared at me without showing any emotion. "Then keep your voices down," he said, turning to walk up the steps again. "I'll let you see Pops and then I'll want a goddamn good—excuse me, Jane—a good explanation for this foolishness!"

I saw the back of Roberts' neck become a sickly pink. He stopped climbing the stairs until I goosed him with my knee. Although I was certain Anderson was bluffing, a very tiny clammy feeling was working in the pit of my guts. If I was wrong about things....

The upstairs hall was wide, several potted plants on small tables lining the flower-papered walls. There was another staircase, smaller and steeper, at the end of the hall, that probably went up to the widow's walk. We walked past several open bedrooms, stopped in front of a closed door. Anderson whispered, "This is Pops' room. Artie, the more I think of it, I can't risk his life by letting you see him. I don't know what this city snoop has filled you with but ..."

"Open the door a crack," Roberts said; almost pleaded.

"Suppose he's awake? The shock might ..."

"Cut the production number, Anderson," I said, trying to keep my voice both a whisper and tough. "Suppose he is awake? Roberts isn't a stranger, he's a friend of Pops."

Anderson shrugged, turned toward the door. He dropped the towel as he spun back around and clipped Roberts on the chin with a wild right. As Roberts folded and I leaped at Larry, I thought with a sort of stupid satisfaction I'd always known Roberts looked too good, had some glass in his square jaw. I was diving for Anderson's waist and I stopped thinking as he straight-armed me.

I was sailing through the air and then I hit a wall as if going through it, slid down to the floor, shaken and dizzy. Vaguely I knew Anderson was heading for the stairs going down to the living room ... and that I was crawling toward Roberts to get his gun. My eyes wouldn't focus and I wasn't sure if I was alive or dead.

I heard Larry yell, "Stay away, Jane, I don't want to hurt you!" and the picture turned real and clear. Jane was backed against a wall, letting him run past. Then she calmly picked up a potted plant and threw it like a bowling ball.

She was smart, didn't aim for his head but for his legs. The pot seemed to bounce once behind him, then break into a hundred pieces as it hit the back of his knees, sending him crashing down the stairs.

I yanked Roberts' Police Special from his shiny holster and staggered toward the steps. I expected to see Anderson out cold, but he was a rugged joker—he was standing on the landing below, blood on one side of his face. He shook himself like a floored pug. As he started down the stairs, I grabbed the railing

to keep from falling, fired a shot into the ceiling. The staircase seemed full of thunder and over it—to my surprise—I heard a firm voice saying, "Don't move, Anderson, or I'll plug you! You've had it!" I wished
I felt half as strong as my voice.

He stood stock-still for a split second, then turned and faced me, an open-mouthed, stunned look on his wide face. With the blood, the dumb look, his big muscles under the torn shirt, he looked like a brute, a human ape. I said, "Put your hands behind your head, keep 'em up there!"

My voice was like a whip and as he put his hands up, his bigness seemed to shrink. The great muscles began to tremble and his big face took on a puzzled expression for a second—until it went to pieces.

Anderson was standing with his hands behind his head, body shaking, crying softly. For a split second he reminded me of an overgrown kid being punished ... but only for a very very short split second.

Chapter 8

Dan and I were on the Sunday night train to New York. He wanted to go back Monday morning but I insisted I needed a decent night's sleep in my own bed before taking off to visit Signe and her kids. I even considered postponing seeing her for a week, to rest up in my flat, or maybe recover would be a better word. But I figured it was best to get it over with, then hang around the flat for a straight two weeks' rest before returning to the old grind.

As the train pulled out of Hampton we waved at Jerry, Bessie and Andy. Jerry was talking out of the side of his mouth, probably retelling Bessie how he had come to our cottage the night I was looking for him—before he drove to see the doc in Hampton, but found the cottage empty. Jerry had insisted upon driving us to the station, for free, despite Sunday being his busiest night; and had only gone off the road a few times as Bessie yelled at him in Greek that he was a road menace. He'd felt bad when I told him I'd come to his place to use his car, had to get Jane and her struggle-buggy instead. The old guy seemed to worship me—a new feeling for me; and it wasn't a bad one, either.

I gave them a final wave and tried to make myself comfortable in the seat. I was loaded down: Bessie's gifts for Signe's brood, Jane's framed picture carefully wrapped in an old table cloth—which was just as well, it would have caused a sensation in the crowded train otherwise.

I was also carrying a new batch of mosquito bites, an aching back, a lot of peeling sunburnt skin—and was togged out in one hundred forty-one dollars worth of fancy clothes which Bessie had horsed me into buying. I was wearing a natty coconut straw, tropical blue suit, nylon sport shirt, Italian loafers, and a thin bow tie almost as red and loud as Roberts'. Bessie insisted. I had to look "the part" when the reporters interviewed me. God knows I'd been cornered by enough newsmen and photographers. One magazine writer even rented a speedboat to talk to me while I was fishing with Andy. Of course I'd spent a lot of time with the D.A. in Riverside. The last couple of days had been a marathon—even the hot-rod set had bought me a round of beers in a Harbor gin mill. I should have been exhausted but I felt just fine.

Dan nudged me, whispered, "Your public," and nodded toward the front of the car. A couple of suntanned jokers in their correct summer "gray flannel" outfits were in a huddle, pointing toward me. For once I was glad I'd bought the new duds, looked like I belonged on the train, although my inner man scornfully told me that was a snobbish damn fool sentiment. One of the characters left the huddle and then walked down the aisle toward me with his confident-salesman approach, stopped at our seat and said, "Excuse me, sir, but aren't you Mr. Lund, *the* famous detective in the End Harbor murder cases?"

"You mean the cop in the case," I said. "Yeah, my name is Lund."

He gave me a practiced junior-executive smile, a firm handshake, said his name was Benson, or something like that. I introduced Dan and then Benson-shemson said, "Told my friends I recognized you from the news pictures. Wonderful work, Mr. Lund. I hope you don't mind this intrusion, sir, but there's one aspect of the case that puzzles me—how did Anderson ever think up such an ingenious scheme?"

Of course he had to talk in a crisp board-of-directors voice and more people turned around. I had quite an audience as I said, "He didn't think it up, merely fell into it. As stated in his confession, an old friend of Pops came to live with them in the winter of '47. About a month later the man took sick, died in his sleep. The following morning his Social Security check arrived. They were hard up and had planned to borrow some dough from him when he got his check. Anderson claims Pops said they should take a chance and cash it, as he was certain the dead man had no relatives to ask questions. They shoved the body under the ice at the edge of the bay—to make it look like a drowning—and kept cashing his checks all during the winter. In the spring they quietly buried him on the farm. According to Anderson it was Pops who got the idea of killing more men, doing it wholesale."

"I see," this character said, as if it mattered whether he saw things or not. "One more point, for my wife: you know women and their sense of the morbid. How did they kill the others—shoot them?"

"Your wife should read the papers, if she's that curious. No, they killed them 'painlessly,'" I said, wishing he would leave me alone. I'd gone over the story so damn many times. "After the victim had put in a change of address with the Social Security board, and Anderson was certain it was in the mail, they got the man roaring drunk. Soon as he passed out, they poured a shot of carbon tetrachloride down his throat, or had him drink it as straight gin. Carbon tet is a cleaning fluid and easy to buy. This was Larry's brain storm. Carbon tet and alcohol causes uremia, so in case anything went 'wrong,' they could claim the man died of natural causes. There, that's the details, now you can go into business for yourself."

My new found buddy flung back his head and laughed. "Not me, I know you can't get away with murder." He gave me a flash of his strong teeth, grinning in appreciation of his own cleverness. "Ironic, though—Anderson had no possible way of foreseeing his partner, this Pops, would call in Doctor Barnes and the doctor would find him dead. I suppose if he hadn't murdered the doctor he never would have been caught. Greed is the basis of most crimes, isn't it, Mr. Lund?"

"That's what I hear," I said and we shook hands again and he left to rejoin his pals. Danny said, "My, my, makes me proud to be the son of a famous superman."

"Yeah—I'm a goddamn hero in my old age. Boys at the precinct house will rib me for months," I said, thinking how surprised I'd been that Art Roberts hadn't hogged the publicity. In fact when you got to know him he wasn't a bad slob. My luck sure had been riding the rail, lucky as hell on the case, lucky on the glory angle, too.

I shifted Jane's painting on my lap. It was too big to risk putting up on the luggage rack. And my lap had gotten big, too, with Bessie's cooking. Dan said, "Here, rest the picture on my knees."

"It's okay. I'll hold it. Certainly brighten up the old flat."

"Going to see her again?"

"Stop it. I took enough of that from Bessie."

Danny shrugged. "You'll still have two weeks' vacation after Signe's kids work you over. Be nice, for you both, if you showed Jane New York. Dad, you might as well be prepared to do it—all this coming week my dear Bessie will be working on Miss Endin. If I know my good wife, you might even find Jane waiting on your doorstep when you return from the mountains."

"If Bessie tries to ...!" I stopped, my voice full of alarm—at myself. Of course I had a whole week to think it out up at Signe's place ... but what scared me was I had to admit the idea gave me a kind of happy glow ... the kind a guy my age isn't supposed to have—they say.

THE END

www.ingramcontent.com/pod-product-compliance
Lightning Source LLC
LaVergne TN
LVHW021800060526
838201LV00058B/3169